DAMNED IN PARADISE

The Memoirs of Nathan Heller:

Damned in Paradise
Blood and Thunder
Carnal Hours
Dying in the Post-War World
Stolen Away
Neon Mirage
The Million-Dollar Wound
True Crime
True Detective

DAMNED IN PARADISE

A NATHAN HELLER NOVEL

Max Allan Collins

A DUTTON BOOK

DUTTON
Published by the Penguin Group
Penguin Books USA Inc., 375 Hudson Street, New York, New York 10014, U.S.A.
Penguin Books Ltd, 27 Wrights Lane, London W8 5TZ, England
Penguin Books Australia Ltd, Ringwood, Victoria, Australia
Penguin Books Canada Ltd, 10 Alcorn Avenue, Toronto, Ontario, Canada M4V 3B2
Penguin Books (N.Z.) Ltd, 182–190 Wairau Road, Auckland 10, New Zealand

Penguin Books Ltd, Registered Offices:
Harmondsworth, Middlesex, England

First published by Dutton, an imprint of Dutton Signet,
a division of Penguin Books USA Inc.
Distributed in Canada by McClelland & Stewart Inc.

First Printing, October, 1996
10   9   8   7   6   5   4   3   2   1

 REGISTERED TRADEMARK — MARCA REGISTRADA

LIBRARY OF CONGRESS CATALOGING-IN-PUBLICATION DATA:
Collins, Max Allan.
   Damned in paradise : a Nathan Heller novel / Max Allan Collins.
      p.   cm.
   ISBN 0-525-94225-4
   1. Heller, Nathan (Fictitious character)—Fiction. I. Title.
PS3553.04753D36 1996   96-17110
813'.54—dc20   CIP

Printed in the United States of America
Set in Palatino
Designed by Eve L. Kirch

PUBLISHER'S NOTE
This is a work of fiction. Names, characters, places, and incidents either are the product of the author's imagination or are used fictitiously.

This book is printed on acid-free paper. ∞

To Michael Cornelison—
whose friendship isn't just an act

Although the historical incidents in this novel are portrayed more or less accurately (as much as the passage of time, and contradictory source material, will allow), fact, speculation, and fiction are freely mixed here; historical personages exist side by side with composite characters and wholly fictional ones—all of whom act and speak at the author's whim.

"What the public wants in the way of books on crime is detective stories that appeal to the passions. The public has so long been taught to hate and judge that it seems hopeless to try to teach them any sane and humane ideas of conduct and reasoning."
—Clarence Darrow, The Story of My Life

"Tongue often hang man quicker than rope."
—Charlie Chan

ONE

Poised at the rail of the steamship *Malolo* like an Arrow shirt ad come to life, the handsome devil in black tie and white dinner jacket gazed contentedly at the endless shimmer of silver ocean under an *art moderne* slice of moon.

Occasionally a mist of spray would kiss the rugged planes of his face; occasionally he'd receive an even better kiss from the stunning young society deb snuggled at his arm. She had Harlow's hair and a bathing beauty's body, nicely evident under the deep blue skin of her evening gown; the cool trade winds on this warm night perked the buds of her breasts under the sheen of satin. Stars winking above were echoed by diamonds at the supple curve of her throat and on one slender wrist.

She was Isabel Bell, a name that rang twice, a niece of Alexander Graham Bell—meaning she had the kind of money that could travel long distance.

He might have been a wealthy young man from the East Coast; one of the four hundred, maybe—old family, old money. With those cruel good looks he might have belonged to some other element of Cafe Society—a stage or screen actor, perhaps, or a debonair sportsman.

Or a playwright, a man's man who had chopped down trees and fought bulls and ridden tramp steamers and come back worldly wise beyond his years, penning a Pulitzer prize–winning effort about man's inhumanity to man, and he would be damned if he would allow those Hollywood infidels to destroy his masterpiece. Not him, an American grass-roots genius who had earned the right to hobnob with the elite—even to snuggle and, rumor has it, sneak into the stateroom of a certain Isabel Bell after hours, for some high-society intermingling.

Or perhaps he was a suave detective on his way to a distant tropical isle, having been engaged to solve a dastardly crime perpetrated against some lovely innocent white woman by evil dark men.

Of the hooey you've just endured, the closest thing to the truth is, believe it or not (to quote an American grass-roots genius named Ripley), the last.

The "handsome devil" at the rail with the frail was only me—Nathan Heller, scion of Maxwell Street, on leave from the Chicago Police Department, on the most unusual assignment a member of that city's pickpocket detail had ever stumbled into. The crisp white jacket—like the steamship ticket that had cost just a little bit less than my yearly salary—had been provided me by an unlikely patron saint who also resided in Chicago.

The shapely Miss Bell I'd managed to pick up on my own devices. She was under no illusions as to my social standing, but seemed to have a certain fascination for my tawdry line of work. And I was, after all, twenty-seven years old and a handsome devil.

So the real lowdown is . . . Isabel was slumming—and me?

Damned if I wasn't on my way to paradise.

Several weeks before, an unexpected phone call from an old family friend had taken me away from a job that already had me way the hell off my Chicago beat. In the early stages of the investigation into the kidnapping of the twenty-month-old son of aviator hero Charles Lindbergh, the involvement of Chicago gangsters was strongly suspected; Al Capone, recently incarcerated for income tax evasion, was making suspicious noises about the snatch from his Cook County jail cell.

So for most of March 1932, I acted as liaison between the Chicago PD and the New Jersey State Police (and Colonel Lindbergh himself), working various aspects of the case in New Jersey, New York, and Washington, D.C.

But by early April, my initial involvement in that frustrating episode (about which I have written at length in a previous memoir) had started to wind down. When a phone call to the Lindbergh estate summoned me for luncheon at Sardi's, a restaurant in the heart of midtown Manhattan's theatrical district, I was relieved to be taking a break from a frustrating, heartbreaking dead end of a case.

I left my fedora with the redheaded doll at the hat check stand, and was led by a red-jacketed waiter through a high-ceilinged, open-beamed room that was lent a surprising intimacy by its soft lighting, warmly masculine paneling, and walls arrayed with vivid, full-color celebrity caricatures.

Some of the caricatures were alive. Over to one side, George Jessel—in the company of a blonde chorine—was pronouncing a eulogy over the remains of a lamb chop. Walter Winchell was holding court in one of the reddish-orange booths, his mouth machine-gunning remarks to a packed table of rapt listeners, mostly attractive young women. Barbara Stanwyck, her light brown hair boyishly bobbed, delicately pretty yet projecting the same strength in private as on the screen, was in a tête-à-tête over drinks with a balding older gent who was probably an agent or producer or something. Jack Dempsey—didn't he have his *own* restaurant?—was wooing a cutie over cutlets.

But the most vivid living caricature in the room came not from Broadway or Hollywood, or the worlds of press or sport, rather from a distant prairie way station called Chicago. His back to the wall, he sat on the inside of a half-circle booth whose white linen tablecloth was set not just for him, but for two expected guests.

Even seated, he was an impressive figure, a big bucket-skulled broad-shouldered train wreck of a man in an unmade bed of a gray suit, his loose excuse of a bow tie dangling like an absurd noose; his hair was gray, too—what there was of it, combed in transparent disguise over his baldpate, a thick forelock straying like a comma down over his right eye, punctuating a craggy, deeply grooved face characterized by razor-keen gray eyes and Apache cheekbones.

Clarence Darrow was buttering a roll. There was nothing methodical about it; strictly slapdash. The seventy-four-year-old household word of an attorney glanced up at me with an impish smile and, though we had not spoken since my father's funeral over a year ago, said as casually as if I'd seen him this morning, "You'll forgive my not rising. My legs aren't what they once were, and I'm preparing this exhibit for my esophagus."

"If Ruby saw that," I said, referring to his doting wife and self-proclaimed manager, "she'd object."

"Overruled," he smiled, and he chomped down the roll.

The room was a din of clattering china and silverware and raging egos. The perfect place for an intimate conversation.

Sliding in next to him, I nodded toward the place setting opposite me. "We expecting a third?"

Darrow nodded his shaggy head. "Fella named George S. Leisure. Wall Street attorney, Harvard grad. He's a law partner of Wild Bill Donovan's."

"Ah," I said. "So that's how you knew where to find me."

Donovan, a Congressional Medal of Honor–winning war hero, was a pal of Lindbergh's and had been involved on the fringes of our efforts to locate the stolen child.

"Donovan's firm was recommended to me," Darrow said, talking with his mouthful of roll open, "when Dudley Malone had to bow out."

As slick as Darrow was rumpled, Malone was almost as famous a trial attorney as Clarence himself, and had worked at his side on a number of cases, including the Scopes evolution trial in Tennessee, in which Darrow had made a monkey of William Jennings Bryan, further cementing the national fame he'd gained by defending the teenage "Thrill Killers" Loeb and Leopold back home in Chicago.

"Bow out of what?" I asked.

"Little case I'm considering."

"Don't tell me you're getting back into harness, C.D. Didn't you retire? Again?"

"I know you confine your reading material to dime novels and Sherlock Holmes," Darrow said, slyly wry, "so I would imagine you missed it, when it made the newspapers . . . but there was a little incident on Wall Street, a while back."

I grunted. "I heard you got hit pretty hard in the Crash. But I thought you were writing now. . . . And aren't you a hot ticket on the lecture circuit?"

He grunted back at me; his was more eloquent than mine. "This so-called depression has dwindled even those meager avenues of revenue. Absurd, publishing an autobiography in an age when only a mystery story has a chance to be a bestseller."

"You've been involved in more than your share of real-life mystery stories, C.D."

"I have no interest in distorting the facts of my life and my work into any such popular fiction." He began buttering another roll; he looked at it, not me, but the half-smile that began digging a deeper groove in his left cheek was all mine. "Anyway, son, there's more to life than money. I would have hoped you'd have learned that by now."

"I learned a long time ago," I said, reaching for a roll myself, "that for a man who despises capitalism, you have a more than grudging admiration for a dollar."

"True," he acknowledged, and chomped off another bite of buttered roll. "I'm like all humans—weak. Flawed."

"You're a true victim of your environment, C.D.," I said, "not to mention heredity."

He laughed, once. "You know what I like about you, son? You've got wit. And nerve. And brains. Not that those items will ease your suffering to any noticeable degree, in this sorry state of existence that burdens us so."

C.D. had the most cheerfully bleak outlook on life I'd ever encountered.

"This isn't about money at all," he insisted. He squinted one eye, conspiratorially. "But don't tell Ruby I said so—I have her convinced that our financial plight is the sole stimulus behind my stirring from self-imposed hibernation."

"What's *really* behind it?"

His shrug was grandiose. "Boredom. Loafing as an ideal is one thing; as a practice it's quite something else. Four years of freedom from work may *sound* attractive. But think of four years of monotony. Four years of stagnation." And now a grandiose sigh. "I'm tired, son—tired of resting."

I studied him as if he were a key exhibit in a trial that could go either way.

"If you're talking to lawyers the likes of Malone and Donovan," I said, "this 'little case' must be pretty big."

The gray eyes twinkled; he was like an immense wrinkled elf. "Big enough to shoulder that little Lindbergh matter you've been looking into off to the side of page one."

I felt a chill, and it wasn't from the ceiling fans.

Leaning forward, I said, "You're kidding, right? . . . Not the *Massie* case?"

The half-smile blossomed into full bloom; he looked different than I remembered him from my childhood: that upper plate was a lot more perfect than his real teeth had been.

"I've never been to Honolulu," he said, as if we were discussing the merits of a travel brochure and not a notorious criminal case. "Never been to that part of the Pacific. I hear it has unusual charm."

From what I'd read, there was nothing charming about the Massie case: Thalia Massie, the wife of a naval lieutenant stationed at Pearl Harbor, had been abducted and raped; she had identified five "natives" as the assailants, and the men were arrested—but the trial resulted in a hung jury.

Thalia Massie's mother—a Mrs. Fortescue, something of a society matron—had, with her son-in-law Thomas Massie's assistance, engineered the kidnapping of one of the alleged assailants, hoping to make him confess; but he had been killed while in their "custody," shot to death, and now Mrs. Fortescue, Lt. Thomas Massie, and two sailors they'd recruited to help them on their misadventure were to stand trial on a murder charge.

The Lindbergh kidnapping had indeed been edged out of the tabloid limelight by the cocktail of sex, violence, and racial turmoil that was the Massie case. The Hearst papers were reporting a rate of forty rapes against white women per year in Hawaii, and painted a picture of a "deplorable" situation in America's "Garden of the Pacific." Good citizens all around the nation were abuzz about the stories of bands of native degenerates who waited in the bushes to leap out and ravage white women. Editorials were calling for stern official measures to curb these sex crimes; headlines cried out of MELTING POT PERIL and labeled Hawaii a SEETHING CRATER OF RACIAL HATE. News stories out of Washington reported talk of martial law coming from Congress and the White House.

In short, the perfect case for Clarence Darrow's comeback.

Shaking my head, I said, "Defending the rich again, C.D.? Shame on you."

A chuckle shook his sunken chest. "Your father would be disappointed in me."

"He didn't mind when you represented Loeb and Leopold."

"Of course not. He was an anti–capital punishment man himself."

With one exception, I thought.

His smile was gone now. He was gazing into a sweating water glass as if it were a window on the past. "Your father never forgave me for supplementing my efforts on behalf of coal miners, anarchists, Negroes, and unionists with clients of . . . dubious distinction."

"Gangsters and grafters, you mean."

He raised an eyebrow, sighed. "A hard man, your father. Moral to a fault. No one could live up his exacting standards. Not even himself."

"But the Massie case . . . If what I've read is even close to true, you'd be a natural for the *other* side."

A frown creased the craggy face. "Don't insult me, son. The case does not exist in which Clarence Darrow would stand for the prosecution."

But if one did, it would be the Massie case.

I asked, "How are your friends at the NAACP going to—"

"I have friends in organizations," he said curtly, glibly, "but no organization is my friend."

"Swell. But isn't this Mrs. Fortescue . . . is that her name?"

Darrow nodded.

"Isn't this Mrs. Fortescue from Kentucky or Virginia or something?"

"Kentucky."

"And she orchestrates a kidnapping that results in the fatal shooting of a colored man who raped her daughter? Doesn't that put the Great Friend of the Colored Man square on the side of lynch law . . . ?"

"That's uncalled for," he rasped. The gray eyes were flaring. "I have given more of my time, and money, to the Negro cause than any other white man you, or anyone, could name. Don't question my convictions on the race issue."

Darrow was getting touchy in his old age; he'd always been testy.

"Aren't you raising the question yourself, C.D., just by taking this defense?"

He sighed, shook his big bucket head, the gray comma over his eye quivering. "What you fail to grasp, Nathan, is that I don't blame those who have been embittered by race prejudice. Bigotry is something that's bred into a man."

"I know, I remember. I heard you lecture often enough, when I was a kid. And back then it sounded pretty good to me—'No one deserves blame, no one deserves credit.' But me, I like to pretend I have *some* control over my life."

"Nothing wrong with pretending, son. It's healthy for a child's imagination." He waved a red-jacketed waiter over. "Would you tell Mother Sardi that Mr. Darrow would like two cups of her special coffee?"

"Yes sir," the waiter nodded, with a knowing smile.

Then Darrow turned his attention back to me. "When I was first approached with this matter . . . frankly . . . I did turn it down because of the racial issue—but not out of moral indignation."

"What, then?"

He shrugged; not so grandiosely, this time. "I was afraid that if my clients expected me to argue on their behalf by invoking the supposed inferiority of the colored races, they would be . . . disappointed. I let my prospective clients know that I would not allow myself to argue a position in court that was at variance with what I felt, and what I had *stood* for, over all these years."

"What was their response?"

Another little shrug. "They wrote me that they thought I was right in my position on the race question, and that they wanted me to maintain that attitude in court. And that, furthermore, complete control over their defense would be mine; I would call all the shots." And yet another little shrug. "What could I do? I took the case."

The waiter brought over two cups of steaming black coffee. Darrow smacked his lips and snatched his cup right off the waiter's tray. I sipped mine; it had something in it, and I don't mean cream or sugar.

"Brother," I whispered, and tried not to cough. "What did they spike that with?"

"Something brewed up last night in a bathtub in Hell's Kitchen, no doubt."

Funny thing about Darrow: I didn't remember ever seeing him take a drink, before Prohibition. Back in the days of the Biology Club, the "study group" Darrow and my father belonged to, jugs of wine would be passed around and Darrow always waved them off. Liked keeping a clear head, he said.

Once the government told him he couldn't have a drink, he couldn't get enough of the stuff.

I took another sip, a more delicate one this time. "So—where does a Chicago cop fit in with your Hawaiian case?"

"You're on leave of absence, aren't you?"

"Not really. On assignment is more like it."

His eyes narrowed shrewdly. "I can *get* you on leave of absence. I still have a few friends at City Hall. . . ."

That was an understatement. He'd defended crooked politicos in both Mayor Thompson's and current Mayor Cermak's administrations, and plenty of administrations before that.

"I thought you hated detectives," I said. "You've done your own legwork, ever since . . ."

I let it hang. Back in 1912, Darrow had nearly been convicted of bribery on the evidence of a private dick he'd hired to (if the dick's testimony could be believed) buy off jury members. Many of Darrow's leftist pals had dumped him, thinking he might have plea-bargained his anarchist defendants out to soften the blow of the inevitable bribery trial.

My father was one of the few friends who had stuck by him.

Ever since that time, Darrow was widely known to do most, if not all, of his own investigative work. He liked talking to witnesses and suspects himself, gathering evidence, gathering facts. He had a near-photographic memory and could interrogate casually, conversationally, without taking notes, before or after the fact.

"I told you," Darrow said gently, "my legs aren't what they used to be. Neither is this, I'm afraid. . . ." And he tapped his noggin with a forefinger. "I'm afraid that, out on the street, my mind might not click with the old vigor."

"You're looking for a leg man."

"More. A detective." He leaned forward. "You deserve better than a life on the . . ." And he spoke the words like bitter obscenities. ". . . *police department*. You deserve a better destiny than that shabby circle can give you. . . . When you were a boy you wanted to be a 'Private Consulting Detective,' like Nick Carter or your precious Sherlock."

"I make out all right on the force," I said, trying not to sound as defensive as I felt. "I'm the youngest guy who ever made plainclothes. . . ."

And I let *that* hang.

We both knew how I'd managed my quick promotion: I'd lied on the witness stand to let a Capone-selected patsy take the rap for the Jake Lingle shooting.

"I'm not a judge," Darrow said gently. "I defend. Let me be *your* defender. Let me parole *you* from a life sentence of empty corruption."

I swallowed. That eloquent son of a bitch. I said, "How?"

"Walk away from that graft-ridden pesthole of a department. Your father hated that you took that job."

"He hated *me* for it."

He shook his head, no, no, no. "No, I don't believe that, not for a second. He loved his son, but hated this bad choice his son made."

I gave him a nasty smirk. "Oh, but C.D.—I didn't make that choice, it chose me, remember? Environment and heredity ganged up on me and made me do it."

The smile he bestowed on me in return was plainly patronizing. "Ridicule me, if you like, son . . . but what you say has truth in it. Outside forces do shape our 'destiny.' So, all right, then—prove me wrong—make a choice." He leaned forward and there was fire and urgency in the gray eyes. "This case, this Massie matter, it's no isolated instance. My lovely Ruby doesn't know it yet, but her husband is getting back in the game."

I blinked. "You're going back into full-time practice?"

He nodded slowly.

"Criminal and radical law?"

He continued to nod.

"You're saying you would take me on as your full-time investigator?"

And still nodding.

"But C.D.—you're going to be seventy-five before the month is out."

"Thanks for remembering, son."

"No offense, but even Clarence Darrow can't live forever . . ."

"Perhaps not. But two or three years of working as Clarence Darrow's ace investigator would be a splendid foundation for either a private practice, or a similar relationship with another top attorney . . . wouldn't you say, son?"

I had thought about leaving the department and putting out a private shingle; I had thought about it more than I dared tell Darrow. The stigma of how I'd got my detective's shield was like a mark of Cain, even in a corrupt cesspool like the Chicago PD; *especially*, there. . . . Every time I turned around some dirty cop assumed I was like him, and could be trusted to cover some shit up, or would jump at a chance to go in on some lousy scam or another. . . .

"I still have an obligation to Colonel Lindbergh," I said.

"And I'm a week away from leaving for Honolulu. You have time to think it over."

"What does it pay?"

"A fair question." He gestured with an open hand. "For this

initial assignment, what I had in mind was making sure the PD kept you on salary during your leave of absence. Look at it as a vacation with pay."

"As opposed to looking at it as you getting my services for free."

"I thought we'd agreed that money wasn't everything."

Then Darrow settled back, and his eyes shifted. I turned to look at what he was looking at, and saw that the same waiter who had led me over was now guiding our awaited guest to Mr. Darrow's booth: a tall, slender gent in a dark blue suit that would have cost me a month's pay, and a lighter blue about-a-week's-salary tie. His eyes were like cuts in an oblong face dominated by a strong nose and a wide thin mouth that exploded into a winning smile upon seeing Darrow.

Who half-rose to meet our distinguished, enthusiastic guest and his eagerly extended hand; the old boy seemed vaguely amused as the younger man worked his arm like a water pump.

"Glad you could make it, Mr. Leisure," Darrow said quietly.

"You know," Leisure said, grinning, shaking his head, "I thought this might be a practical joke."

"What? Sit down, please, sit down."

Leisure, who had not yet acknowledged my presence, or my existence for that matter, slid into the booth opposite me.

"Well, when you called this morning," Leisure said, "saying you were Clarence Darrow, and wanting to meet me at Sardi's for lunch, I . . . frankly, my friends know what an admirer of yours I am. They've heard me say how 'one of these days' I'm going to get back to Chicago—I attended the University of Chicago as an undergrad, you know—and how I was going to look you up and talk with you, the greatest man in my chosen profession, one on one."

"I'm flattered," Darrow said. "This is Nathan Heller. His late father ran a radical bookshop on the West Side, near where I used to live. I'm sort of an eccentric uncle to Nate, I'm afraid."

"He used to be an eccentric rich uncle," I said, "till the Crash."

Leisure, clearly embarrassed, half-stood and reached his hand across the booth to shake my hand. "I'm sorry. I didn't mean to be rude, Mr. Heller. I'm . . . it's just . . . well, frankly, I'm a huge fan of Mr. Darrow's."

"Careful," I said. "C.D.'ll hit you up for the check—even if he did invite you."

"I'd be glad to pay," Leisure said.

"Nonsense," Darrow said. "Let's order, and then we can talk. . . ."

He waved the waiter back over. It was amusing to see how flustered this urbane Wall Street attorney was around his idol. And somehow I had a hunch, even if Darrow was picking up the check, this was one lunch Leisure was going to pay for. . . .

"I'm about to try a case in Honolulu," Darrow said, picking at his plate of broiled kidneys, Irish bacon, and boiled Brussels sprouts. The Sardi's menu was an unlikely combination of English dishes and Italian; I was having the spaghetti and so was Leisure, though he was barely touching it.

"As a matter of fact," Darrow continued, "I'm trying to convince Nate to come along as my investigator. . . . He's out here working on the Lindbergh case, you know."

"Really," Leisure said, suddenly impressed. "Tragic goddamn affair. Are you a private operative, then?"

"Chicago PD," I explained. "Liaison with Colonel Lindbergh. Because of the Capone linkup."

"Ah," Leisure said, nodding. The Chicago gangland aspect of the case had been widely publicized.

"I'm hoping Nate will take a leave of absence for a month and work with us," Darrow said.

Leisure's narrow eyes narrowed further; but what little could be seen of them gleamed at the possible meanings of the word "us."

"At any rate," Darrow continued, "I'm about to try this case in Honolulu, and I understand you successfully handled the Castle family's litigation there last year."

"That's right." Leisure was clearly pleased, and a little amazed, by Darrow's knowledge of his work.

Chewing a bite of kidney, Darrow said, "Well, I've never tried a case there, and I thought perhaps you'd be willing to talk to me, tell me something of the nature of the procedure in that jurisdiction."

"Why, I'd be more than happy to . . ."

"*Clarence!*"

The eyes of this jaded, celebrity-strewn eatery were turned upon the jaunty little figure, sharply attired in gray pinstripes with gray and red tie and matching gray spats, who was striding through the room like he owned the place.

He didn't, but did—for the time being, anyway—own the town: he was Jimmy Walker, a sharp-featured Damon Runyon character who happened to be mayor.

"What a nice surprise!" Darrow again half-stood, and shook Walker's hand. "Can you join us, Jim?"

"Maybe just dessert," Walker said.

Big-shot Wall Street lawyer or not, Leisure was looking at this casual encounter between the mayor of New York and the country's most celebrated criminal lawyer with wide-eyed awe. I was impressed by how cocky and cool Walker was when everybody knew he was currently under investigation for incompetence and graft.

A waiter had already brought a chair over for Hizzoner, and Darrow made introductions. Mentioning my connection with the Lindbergh matter caught Walker's attention and the mayor was full of questions about the case, and about Colonel Lindbergh. When it came to Lindy, the mayor seemed as starstruck as Leisure over Darrow.

All talk of Hawaii and lawyering got sidetracked, while we talked Lindbergh and ate cheesecake.

"This graveyard ransom drop," Walker was saying. "It was a complete hoax?"

"I'm not at liberty to divulge certain aspects of the case, Your Honor," I said, "but, frankly—between us boys—it doesn't look good."

Walker shook his head, gravely. "I feel for Slim," he said, meaning Lindbergh. "Celebrity ain't all it's cracked up to be, kids, lemme tell ya."

"Short of getting a table without a reservation," Darrow said, "I can't think of a single advantage."

"There's one helluvan idea," Walker chimed. "Why don't we catch the matinee over at the Music Box? *Of Thee I Sing*—hottest ticket in town—but I'll betcha a buncha celebrities can wangle seats!"

Darrow turned solicitously to Leisure. "Could you get away for the afternoon, George?"

"Certainly," Leisure said.

So in the company of the dapper little mayor—who left his limo and driver at the curb on West 44th, proceeding with no retinue other than Darrow, Leisure, and myself—we cut down Shubert Alley over to the Music Box on West 45th.

This was my first Broadway show, but I'd seen snazzier productions on Randolph Street. It was a silly musical comedy about a presidential race; there were some nice-looking girls, and Victor Moore was funny as a dippy Vice President. Nonetheless, mediocre as it was, it remains one of the most memorable shows I ever attended—though that had nothing to do with what went on, onstage.

The mayor, like a glorified usher, had led us to our seats in the front of the orchestra, and a ripple had gone through the audience that turned into a near roar. Walker grinned and waved at the crowd, but it wasn't him the audience was reacting to, even though the orchestra was graciously playing the theme song Walker had penned himself ("Will You Love Me in December as You Do in May?").

The fuss was over Darrow—he'd been recognized.

Soon the old boy was swamped with autograph-seeking admirers (Walker seemed mildly miffed by the lack of attention), and this went on till the lights dimmed and the overture began.

I was sitting next to Darrow who was sitting next to Leisure who was sitting next to the mayor. Throughout the entire play—which I understand was a Pulitzer prize–winner by George Gershwin, though I couldn't hum you a song from it if you put a gun to my head—Darrow sat whispering to Leisure. Their sotto voce dialogue continued through intermission to the finale, as Darrow filled the young lawyer in on the facts of the Massie case, as well as his theories and plans concerning same. . . .

Mayor Walker ducked out before the final curtain call, and as we were walking out onto West 45th Street, where a cool spring breeze nipped at us, Darrow was saying, "You know, George, I've been retired from practice some time now, and haven't been regularly engaged in courtroom work for several years . . ."

"There's no better man for this job."

"Well, thank you, George, but I'm afraid I'm getting on in years . . ." Darrow stopped, flat-footedly, as if he had suddenly run out of gas. "Frankly, I would be very pleased to have a younger man accompany me on this trip. I wonder . . . would it be possible for you to go to Honolulu with me?"

"I would be honored and thrilled," Leisure blurted.

"Of course, I have to warn you that the fee involved will not be great. In fact, I can promise you little more than your expenses . . . and the experience of a lifetime."

"I see . . ."

"Will you be my associate counsel, sir?"

Leisure thrust his hand out. "With pleasure!"

The two men shook hands. Leisure said he would need to inform his partners, and Darrow requested that Leisure—and his wife, if he so desired—join him in Chicago within a week, to make final preparations; they would talk on the phone in a day or so, so that Darrow could book passage.

Back in Sardi's, at another booth, with Leisure on his way home, Darrow and I had coffee again—unspiked, this time.

"I'm impressed," I said.

"It was a good show," Darrow said.

"It was a good show, all right, and I'm not talking about *Of Thee I Sing*, baby. Not a moment of which you witnessed, by the way."

Darrow just sipped his coffee, smiling.

"How much was Dudley Malone going to soak you as cocounsel?" I asked him.

"Ten grand," Darrow admitted.

"And you got one of the top lawyers on Wall Street to do the job for you, free."

"Not free. Expenses, and probably a modest fee. And price-less experience."

"He's not exactly a damn law clerk, C.D." I shook my head, laughed. "And how'd you manage getting the mayor to drop by?"

"Are you suggesting that was prearranged?"

"Playin' Walker for a sucker, aren't you, C.D.? I bet that poor bastard thinks if he gets on your good side, you'll defend His Honor at the inquiry into his administration."

Darrow shrugged. Definitely not a grandiose shrug.

"Does Gentleman Jimmy know you're going to be in Hawaii when he comes under the gun?"

"The mayor of New York stops by for cheesecake and a pleasant social afternoon of theater," Darrow said, "and you make a conspiracy out of it."

"How much are you getting?"

"For what?"

"For what do you think—the Massie defense."

He thought about ducking the question, but he knew enough not to lie to me. I was a detective; I would find out, anyway.

The piercing gray eyes had turned placid as he said, casu-ally, "Thirty thousand—but I have to pay my own expenses."

I laughed for a while. Then I slid out of the booth. "Tell you what, C.D. See if you can swing that leave of absence for me, and I'll think about it. But I want a hundred bucks a week, on top of my copper's pay."

"Fifty," he said.

"Seventy-five and full expenses."

"Fifty and full expenses."

"I thought you were the friend of the working man!"

"I am, and we are both trapped in a bad, unfair system, stranded on this speck of mud, floating in an endless sky. Fifty and full expenses is as high as I'll go."

"Okay, okay," I said. "After all, you can't help yourself—heredity and environment have conspired to turn you into a stingy, greedy old bastard."

He tried to look hurt. "I picked up the check, didn't I?"

And then he winked at me.

Two

On the train, as our four-thousand-mile journey got under way, I did my best to sleep through the two and a half days from Chicago to San Francisco. My tour of duty on the Lindbergh case had left me wrung out like a rag, and some of the reporters tagging along after Darrow (they were aboard for the duration, steamship tickets and all) had got wind of what I'd been working on, which made me more popular with the press than I cared to be.

"This is like a damn campaign special," I told Leisure in the club car of the Golden Gate, where I sneaked rum from a flask into both our empty coffee cups.

Leisure's wife, Anne—an attractive brunette in her thirties—sat with Ruby Darrow, playing canasta at a table nearby. Ruby, auburn-haired, vivacious, was full-figured but not matronly, a young-looking fifty-some years of age.

"I know," Leisure said, nodding his thanks for my contribution to his cup, "and at every whistle-stop there's another horde of reporters waiting."

I smiled a little. "But you notice C.D. hasn't given them a thing on the Massie case."

Omaha was a case in point. Changing trains there, out on the platform, the old boy had been swarmed by reporters hurling questions about the Massie affair; hot words and phrases—

"rape," "murder," "lynch law," "honor slaying"—peppered the air like buckshot.

Darrow had turned his piercing gray-eyed gaze loose on the crowd, hooked his thumbs in his suspenders, and said with a gash of a smile, "Imagine that—a notorious 'wet' like me, stranded temporarily in the heart of 'dry' country. Nobody to talk to but upstanding moral folk."

Several of the newshounds took the bait, and goading questions about Darrow's anti-Prohibition stance overlapped each other till he stilled them with a raised palm.

"Is there a man here who's never taken a drink?"

The gaggle of reporters grinned at him and each other, but not a man would admit to it.

"Well, then, what's your problem?" Darrow growled. "Don't you want anybody *else* to have any damn fun?"

And he'd got on the train.

As I sipped my rum from the coffee cup, Leisure was frowning; this was our second day of rail travel and he seemed uneasy.

"Trouble is," Leisure said, "Mr. Darrow hasn't said anything to *me* about the Massie case, either. I get the feeling everything he knows about our clients, and their situation, he whispered to me back at the Music Box theater."

"You probably hit that dead center."

"I mean, he clearly has his wits about him—look at the way he finesses these reporters—but he *is* an old man, and . . ."

"You wish he were more concerned about preparation."

"Frankly, Nate—yes."

"George, get used to it."

"What do you mean?"

"C.D. flies by the seat of his pants. You know him by his reputation. I've seen him in action, lots of times in debate situations, a few times in court."

"He's brilliant in court—I've read his summations . . ."

"His summations *are* brilliant—and mostly pitched right off the top of his head."

"That's ridiculous . . . how could anyone . . ."

"Search me. The words just come tumbling out of the old

boy. But you might as well brace yourself: he won't develop his defense strategy until he's seen the prosecution in action. He waits for them to make mistakes, and goes from there."

"That's goddamn dangerous."

"That's goddamn Clarence Darrow."

I had never seen San Francisco before, and once I'd arrived, I still hadn't: the city's legendary fog was in full sway that afternoon, as the train pulled into the Ferry Building station where the foot of Market Street met the Embarcadero.

Despite the fog, or perhaps aided by its mystery, the looming luxury liners docked at the pier were a breathtaking sight, even for a jaded Chicago boy. Against an aural backdrop of clanking massive chains, groaning pulleys, gruffly shouting stevedores, and a bellowing mournful foghorn came the towering apparitions of a steamship city. Emerging from the mist were the red-and-white regalia of a French liner, the billowing flags of an Italian ship, and most of all the pebbled white hull of the *Malolo,* only one of its twin funnels, bearing the Matson Line "M," vaguely visible.

Nearly six hundred feet long, eighty-some feet wide, the *Malolo* was a hungry whale welcoming wealthy Mr. and Mrs. Jonahs up into its innards. Trooping up its gangway they came, the best-dressed damn tourists you ever saw, tuxes and top hats, gowns and furs, often followed by entourages of servants and companions. Mostly older than a kid like me, but a few of them were in my age range if not my social circle; some were honeymooners, though not necessarily married. The Smart Set. Smart enough to still be rich, post-'29, anyway.

At the dock, just before we boarded, a pasty-faced navy lieutenant in crisp dress blues came up to Darrow and saluted; it amused the old boy. In fact, it amused all of us, the Leisures, Ruby and Clarence, and me, clustered together in defense from the fog.

"At ease, sailor," Darrow said. "I'd imagine you'd be Lt. Johnson?"

"Yes, sir. I arrived from Honolulu on the *Malolo* this morning, sir." The young lieutenant handed Darrow a legal file, one of those cardboard expanding jobs, tied tight in front; the lieutenant's manner was so grave the thing might have contained military secrets. "I trust these documents will satisfy your requirements."

"I'm sure they will, son. You don't look old enough to be either a sailor *or* a lawyer."

"Well, I'm both, sir."

"Good for you."

"Admiral Stirling sends his regards."

Darrow nodded. "I'll thank him for these, and give him my own regards, personally, in a few days."

"Very good, sir." Lt. Johnson returned the nod and disappeared into the fog.

"Something pertaining to the case?" Leisure ventured, hope dancing in his eyes.

Darrow said, matter of factly, "Transcript of the rape trial, the Ala Moana trial, they call it. Also some affidavits from our clients."

Leisure grinned. "Splendid!"

"You have more faith in documents than I do, George," Darrow said. "We'll have to size our clients up, face to face, to know whether we're in the clover, or in the soup. Speaking of which, let's get out of this pea soup and into the lap of luxury."

Darrow and Ruby went up the gangway first, with the Leisures and me following.

"Why's everybody dressed to the nines?" I asked Leisure.

"So they won't have to change," Leisure said. "Formal dress at dinner, almost immediately after we board."

I winced. "*Formal* dress?"

"Didn't bring your tux along, Nate?"

"No. But I brought both my ties."

Soon we were up on deck, lined along the rail, but no one was seeing us off, and if anyone had, they'd have been shadows lost in the fog. No *bon voyage*, here. So I took my leave of the Darrow party and got a steward's help in finding my quarters.

In my cabin—Number 47, right across from First Class, where the grown-ups were staying—I found formal attire awaiting me on a hanger—white jacket, black tie, white shirt, black trousers, even a cummerbund and, tucked in a pocket, cuff links. Clarence Darrow had provided; he may not have been a fiend for preparation, but the absolutely necessary arrangements got made.

As if by magic, my bag had beaten me aboard: it was already on a luggage rack just inside the door. The cabin itself would suffice, particularly since it was larger than my one-room apartment back at the Hotel Adams, with considerably classier furnishings: bamboo bed, bamboo writing table and chair, cut flowers in a vase on the bamboo nightstand. The lighting had a soft, golden, nightclub aura, courtesy *deco* fixtures that echoed the leaf design of the green and black carpet, and the windows—that is, the portholes—had half-shutters. Unlike the Hotel Adams, where I shared facilities with other "guests," I had a bathroom to myself, tub and all.

So what the hell, I took a bath; with luck, no one would notice one was missing.

The ship cast off as I was bathing—there was a lurch that sent my bathwater sloshing—and then the engines settled into a steady throb and I just soaped and soaked as the ship and I enjoyed friendly waters.

Before long, wearing formal attire for the first time in my young roughneck life, I went wandering smoothly down a wide stairway into a movie set of a dining room, a vast hall of glossy veneers, chrome trim, deep-pile carpeting and over six hundred wealthy passengers. Plus one pauper. I informed the maître d' I was with the Darrow party, and he put me in the charge of a red-jacketed waiter, who bid me follow him.

None of the Haves seemed to notice a Have-not was strolling in disguise amongst them, as they sat chatting and chewing at elegant round tables whose white linen tablecloths were arrayed with fine china, crystal, and gleaming silverware.

I leaned in and whispered in Clarence Darrow's ear: "You look like the head waiter at the Ptomaine Hilton."

Darrow craned his big shaggy head around. "You look like a bouncer at the best bordello in Cicero."

Ruby said, "Clarence, please!" But it was, as usual, a good-natured scold. She was in a white-patterned navy silk dress with a cloth corsage and a navy felt hat with a dip brim; nice as she looked, she was underdressed for the room. The Darrows shopped at Sears.

Leisure, looking dapper in his own white jacket and black tie, half-stood as I took my place at the table; his wife looked lovely in a black chiffon frock with a Spanish-lace bodice, her hat a matching tam turban with jaunty bow. The Leisures shopped Fifth Avenue.

I still shopped at Maxwell Street, but old habits are hard to break.

The two attractive lawyers' wives were no competition, however, for the newest member of our party, a woman-child with a heart-shaped face blessed with china-blue eyes, button nose, and Clara Bow Kewpie lips, haloed by a haze of blond, near-shoulder-length waves.

For a fraction of an instant, and a quick intake of breath, I thought she was nude: the satin gown encasing her high-breasted slender form was a pale pink, damn near the shade of her bare arms, its halter neck coming to a point at the ruby brooch at the hollow of her throat.

Best of all, the chair awaiting me was next to this vision of youthful pulchritude.

Ruby, her mouth twitching with amusement at my open admiration for the girl, said, "Isabel Bell, this is Nathan Heller—my husband's investigator."

"Charmed I'm sure," she said. She didn't look at me.

Isabel Bell was studying a menu whose cover depicted a slender island beauty with blossoms in her hair; the glowing airbrushed blues and yellows and oranges were a dreamy promise of the Polynesian paradise presumably awaiting us at Oahu.

Darrow said, "Miss Bell is Thalia Massie's cousin. I've invited her to join our little group—she's on her way to lend her cousin some moral support."

"That's swell of you," I said cheerfully to this beauty who had not yet deigned to cast her baby blues upon me. "Are you and Mrs. Massie close?"

"Langouste Cardinal," she said, still gazing at the menu. "That sounds yummy."

I took a look at the menu. "I was hoping for lobster, on a fancy barge like this."

"Langouste *is* lobster, silly," she said, finally looking at me.

"I know," I said. "I just wanted to get your attention."

And now I had it. Whether she'd been pretending not to notice the best-looking (and one of the few) unattached males in the room, I can't say; but those big blue eyes, and long natural fluttery lashes, were suddenly locked on yours truly.

"*Very* close," she said.

"Huh?"

With a snippy sigh, she turned her attention back on the menu. "Thalo and I, we're very close.... That's her nickname, Thalo. We practically grew up together. She's my dearest friend."

"You must be torn up about all this."

"It's been simply dreadful. Ooooo . . . coconut ice cream! That ought to get us in a tropical mood."

I could have written her off right then as a trivial shallow little creature. But because she was probably no older than twenty, and a product of her heredity and environment, I decided to cut her some slack. Her pretty puss and swell shape had nothing to do with it. Or everything. One of the two.

"Actually," I said, "Hawaii isn't really tropical."

She looked at me again; she may have been shallow, but those blue eyes were deep enough to dive into. "What is it, then?" she challenged.

"Well, while the Hawaiian Islands *do* lie between the Tropic of Cancer and the Equator, they simply aren't sultry or hot. There's always a breeze."

Darrow said, "Mr. Heller is right. A land of no sunstroke, no heat prostration—just trade winds sweeping in continuously from the Pacific."

"From the northeast, more or less," I added sagely.

"This is my first trip to the Islands," she admitted, as if ashamed.

"Mine, too."

She blinked, cocked her head back. "Then what makes you so darn knowledgeable?"

"The *National Geographic*."

"Are you making fun of me?"

"What do you think, sister?" I asked.

There were smiles all around the table—except from Miss Bell. In fact, she didn't speak to me again through dinner; but I had a feeling she was interested. Cute stuck-up kids love it when you needle them . . . unless they're completely hopeless and humorless. In which case, even a pretty puss and swell shape wouldn't make it worth the trouble.

We were halfway through our coconut ice cream when Leisure—who'd seemed distracted throughout the endless sumptuous courses of dinner—asked Darrow, "When you've had a good look at those transcripts and affidavits, could I have some time with them?"

"Take 'em tonight," Darrow said, waving offhandedly. "Stop by my stateroom, take 'em away, and pore over 'em to your heart's content."

"I'd like a look at them myself," I said.

"You can have 'em after George," Darrow said magnanimously. "I love to be surrounded by well-informed people." He turned to his wife, next to him. "They've a full orchestra and a nightclub, dear . . . and there's no Prohibition at sea. A fully appointed bar awaits us." He patted her hand and she smiled patiently at him. "What a wonderful, decadent place this is. You up for some dancing?"

We all were.

The ship's cocktail lounge—the size of which redefined the meaning of the phrase—was a streamlined *moderne* nightclub ruled by indirect lighting and chrome trim; with its cylindrical barstools and sleek decorative touches, we might have been on the Matson Line's first spaceship.

The dance floor was a glossy black mirror so well polished, remaining upright was a challenge, let alone exhibiting any terpsichorean grace. The orchestra had an ersatz Crosby, and, as I danced with Ruby Darrow, he was singing Russ Columbo's tune "Love Letters in the Sand" while a ukulele laid in the main accompaniment.

"They seem determined to get us in the island mood, don't they?" I asked.

"When are you going to ask Miss Bell to dance? She's the prettiest girl here, you know."

"You're the prettiest girl here. . . . I might get around to it."

"You've danced with me three times, and Mrs. Leisure four."

"Mrs. Leisure's pretty cute. The way her husband's all caught up in this case, maybe I can make some time."

"You've always been a bad boy, Nathan," Ruby said affectionately.

"Or maybe I'm just playing hard to get," I said, glancing over at Miss Bell, who was dancing with Darrow, who was windmilling her around and occasionally stepping on her feet. She was wincing with pain and boredom.

I felt sorry for her, so when they played "I Surrender, Dear," with the would-be Crosby warbling the lyrics, I asked her to dance.

She said, "No thank you."

She was sitting at our table, but everyone else was out on the dance floor; I sat next to her.

"You think I'm Jewish, don't you?"

"What?"

"The name Heller sounds Jewish to you. I don't mind. I'm used to people with closed minds."

"Who says I have a closed mind?" She turned her pouty gaze out on the dance floor. "Are you?"

"What?"

"Of the Jewish persuasion?"

"They don't really persuade you. It's not an option. It comes with the birth certificate."

"You *are* Jewish."

"Only technically."

She frowned at me. "How can you be 'technically' Jewish?"

"My mother was Irish Catholic. That's where I got this Mick mug. My father was an apostate Jew."

"An apost . . . what?"

"My great-grandfather, back in Vienna, saw Jew killing Jew—over their supposed religious differences—and, well, he got disgusted. Judaism hasn't been seen in my family since."

"I never heard of such a thing."

"It's true. I even eat pork. I'll do it tomorrow. You can watch."

"You're a funny person."

"Do you want to dance or not? Or did Darrow crush your little piggies?"

Finally she smiled; a full, honest, open smile, and she had wonderful perfect white teeth, and dimples you could've hidden dimes in.

It was the kind of moment that can make you fall in love forever—or for at least as long as an ocean voyage.

"I'd love to dance . . . Nathan, is it?"

"It's Nate . . . Isabel. . . ."

We danced to the rest of "I Surrender, Dear," then snuggled close on "Little White Lies." We left in the middle of "Three Little Words" to get some air out on the afterdeck. We leaned against the rail near a suspended lifeboat. The fog of San Francisco was long gone; the stars were like bits of morning peeking through holes punctured in a deep blue night.

"It's cool," she said. "Almost cold."

The thrum of the engines, the lapping of the ocean against the luxury liner cutting through it, made us speak up a little. Just a little.

"Take my jacket," I said.

"No . . . I'd rather just snuggle."

"Be my guest."

I slipped my arm around her and drew her close; her bare arm did feel cold, gooseflesh tickling my fingers. Her perfume tickled my nose.

"You smell good," I said.

"Chanel," she said.

"What number?"

"Number Five. You've been around, haven't you?"

"I didn't just fall off a turnip truck."

She laughed a little; it had a musical sound. "I can't help liking you."

"Why fight it? Do you do anything?"

"What do you mean?"

"I mean, go to school, or . . . do rich girls like you ever work?"

"Of course we work! If we want to."

"Do you?"

"I don't want to. . . . But maybe I'll have to, someday. I'm not so rich, you know. We got hit hard in the Crash."

"I didn't feel a thing."

She flashed me a quick frown. "Don't be smug. It's not a joke, people jumping out of windows."

"I know it isn't. How old are you?"

"Twenty."

"Are you in school?"

"I might go to college. I wasn't planning to, but . . ."

"What happened?"

"I was engaged to this boy."

"You were?"

"He met someone else."

"Not someone prettier. That wouldn't be possible."

Her eyes studied the dark water. "He went to Europe. Met her on the *Queen Mary*."

"Ah. Shipboard romance."

"Maybe it started that way. He's engaged to her, now."

"I know an excellent way for you to get back at him."

"How's that?"

And when her head was tilted up to look at me while she asked that question, I kissed her. It started out gentle and sweet, but then it got hot and deep, and when we parted, we were both damn near panting. I leaned over the rail and caught my breath and watched whitecaps rolling over the inky sea.

"You kissed fellas before," I noted.

"Once or twice," she said, and she kissed me again.

Her stateroom was just across the hall from mine, but as we paused there, I took a moment from us pawing each other and said breathlessly, "I gotta get something from my room."

She blinked. "What?"

"You know . . . something."

"What . . . Sheiks?" She swatted the air. "I have some in my train case."

I guess you've guessed by now she wasn't a virgin. But she wasn't all that experienced, either; she seemed surprised when, after a while, deep inside of her, I rolled with her, moving her around and up on top. I had a feeling her former fiancé had been strictly a missionary position sort of guy.

But she soon got the swing of it, and was liking riding rather than being ridden. Her eyes were half-hooded, as if she were tipsy with desire, her body washed with ivory from the porthole, the shadows of the half-open shutters making an exquisite pattern on the smooth planes of her body as she leaned forward, hips grinding, breasts swaying. Those breasts, lovely, perfectly conical, not big, not small, were peaked with large, swollen aureoles, like those of an adolescent girl just entering puberty. She was well out of puberty, however, and the smooth warmth of her around me, the movie star loveliness of her hovering over me, turned me tipsy, too. . . .

She slipped out of bed, and into the bathroom while I plucked a tissue from the nightstand to dispose of the lambskin armor she'd provided me. Two or three minutes later, she returned, and slipped the compact curves of her flawless young body into her undergarment, a creamy little teddy, got herself a Camel from her purse on a bamboo chair, and lighted the ciggie up with a tiny silver lighter.

"You want a tailor-made?" she asked.

"No. It's one bad habit I haven't got around to."

"We used to roll 'em, back at girls' school." She inhaled, exhaled, the blue smoke drifting like vapor. "You got anything to nip at?"

"There's a flask in my jacket pocket . . . no, the other pocket."

Cigarette dangling from the Kewpie mouth, she unscrewed the cap on the silver flask and had a jolt. "Ah! Demon rum. Want some?"

"Sure. Bring it back to bed with you."

And she did, passing me the flask as she eased under the covers next to me.

"You must think I'm terribly wicked," she said. "Just a little tramp."

I sipped the rum. "I certainly won't respect you in the morning."

She knew I was kidding, but she asked anyway, "You won't?"

"Not some little trollop who sleeps with the first good-lookin' kike who comes along."

She yelped a laugh, and grabbed a pillow and hit me with it; I protected the flask so as not to spill any of its precious contents.

"You're an awful person!"

"Better you figure that out now than later."

She put her pillow back in place, and snuggled against me, again. "I suppose you think we'll be doing this every night of the trip."

"I have nothing else planned."

"I'm really normally a very good girl."

"Good, hell. You're great."

"You want me to hit you again?" she asked, reaching for the pillow. But she left it in its place, and settled back against it and me and said, "You just pushed the right button, that's all."

I slipped a hand over one silk-covered bosom and touched a forefinger to a puffy nipple ever so gently. "Hope to shout . . ."

"Awful person," she said, and blew out smoke, and French-kissed me. It was a smoky, rum-tinged kiss, but nice. And memorable. Funny how much this rich little good girl kissed like some of the poor little nasty girls I'd run across.

"Poor Thalo," she sighed, taking the flask from me.

"What?"

"Sex relations can be so wonderful. So much fun."

"I couldn't agree more."

She swigged, wiped her mouth with a hand. "To have it ru-ined . . . by some awful greasy native beasts." She shuddered. "Just to think of it makes me want to run and hide. . . ."

"What was she like?"

"Thalo?"

"Yeah."

"You mean, growing up together?"

"Yeah. Docile, quiet . . . ?"

"Thalo! Not hardly! You think it's a bowl of cherries, being rich. But you more or less have to raise yourself. Not that I'm complaining. Those days at Bayport, they were something. . . ."

"Bayport?"

"It's a little community on the South Shore of Long Island. Thalo's parents have a summer home there. It's like a park, really—that big house, lake, woods. . . . We used to go bareback riding . . . and I do mean *bare*."

"No parents around to object to such shenanigans?"

Another swig. "They were gone most of the time—social functions, foreign jaunts. The house was run by the Filipino domestics, who Thalo didn't have to answer to. Glorious days, really."

"You went to school together, too?"

"Yes—Hillside in Norwalk, then, later, National Cathedral, in Washington. Strict schools, but summers were madcap; we ran wild. Lived in our bathing suits all summer."

She handed me the flask and got out of bed; a lovely thing in that teddy, completely unselfconscious in her near nudity.

"We had this old Ford," she said, fishing another smoke from her purse, "that we painted up with all sorts of colors and crazy sayings. Rode around with our feet and legs hanging out of the car. Tore around, regular little speed demons."

"Never got picked up? Never lost your license?"

She lighted up the new ciggie. "Oh, we didn't have licenses. We weren't old enough."

Soon she was back in bed with me, the orange eye of her cigarette staring in the darkness.

"I shouldn't say this, but . . . she used to love it."

"Love what?"

"It. You know—*it*? Doing it? Boys from our set, visiting their own parents, they'd come to that big house . . . we had the run of the place . . . come midnight we'd go skinny-dipping in the lake. . . ."

"With the boys?"

"Not with the gardener! I don't think Tommie . . . nothing."

"What?"

"It's just . . . I shouldn't say."

"Something about her husband?" I asked, passing her the flask.

She took another slug, then said, "I haven't seen Thalo since she and Tommie were stationed at Pearl Harbor almost two years ago. I don't have a right to say anything about it."

"About what?"

"I . . . don't think he could satisfy her."

"In what way?"

"In whatever way you think. He's so . . . ordinary, dull, unexciting. She's a romantic, fun-loving girl, but her letters to me. . . . She was bored with being a Navy wife. He was off on submarine duty all the time, she was lonely . . . no fun. No attention. And now this."

"It's nice of you to go to her side in this dark hour."

"She's my best friend," Isabel said, and took another slug of rum from my flask. "And anyway, I've never been to Hawaii before."

She fell asleep in my arms; I removed the glowing cigarette stub from her fingers, crushed it out in a glass ashtray on the nightstand, placed my flask there, and allowed the motion of the ship, plowing its way through the Pacific, to lull me.

But I didn't go to sleep for a long time. I kept thinking about Thalo and Isabel, fun-loving girls skinny-dipping with boys.

And how Thalia Massie's dull husband had helped kill a man to preserve his wife's honor.

THREE

I leaned against the starboard rail with Isabel on one side of me, and Leisure on the other. Mrs. Leisure was next to her husband, and the Darrows were just down the rail from her, as our little group peered across deep blue waters. A balmy breeze ruffled hair, rustled dresses, fussed with neckties; the sky was as blue as Isabel's eyes, the clouds as white as her teeth. She was a foolish girl, but I would love her forever, or at least till we docked.

"Look!" Isabel cried; it was a cry that would have made sense, a hundred and fifty years ago, when spying land meant fresh water and supplies and the first solid ground in weeks or even months.

But at the end of a modern four-and-a-half-day ocean voyage, it was just plain silly—so why did my heart leap at the sight of an indistinct land mass, dancing in and out from the morning clouds? Gradually revealing itself, growing larger and larger on the horizon, was the windward shore of Oahu, and as the *Malolo* rounded the point, we got a gander at a cracked gray mountain.

"Koko Head," seasoned traveler Leisure informed us.

Maybe so, but it was a head with no more natural growth than a bald old man—a disappointing, and inaccurate, envoy of the island, as very soon the grayness of Koko dipped into a valley of luxuriant green foliage, including the expected gently waving palms and occasional flower-blossom splashes of color.

"There's Diamond Head!" Queen Isabel squealed, pointing, as if informing Columbus of the New World.

"I see you've read the *National Geographic*, too," I said, but I didn't even get a rise out of her. Her blue eyes were wide and her smile that of a kid with a nickel viewing a well-stocked penny candy counter; she was even jumping up and down a little.

And Diamond Head was a magnificent sight, all right, even if a city kid like me wasn't about to tip as much to my society page cutie-pie. After all, I came from the town that invented the skyscraper, and some paltry seven- or eight-hundred-foot natural wonder wasn't about to earn oooh's and ahhh's from a hardboiled boyo like me.

So why was I staring goofy-eyed, like a hypnotist's watch was waving in front of my mug? What was the magic of this long-dead crater? Why did its shape demand study, call out for a metaphor? Why did I see Diamond Head as a crouching beast, its gray fur furrowed, its blunted sphinx head lifted ever so gently, paws extended into the ocean, a regal, wary sentinel to an ancient land?

"See that small depression, on the ledge of the crater?" Leisure asked, though he was really instructing.

"Near the peak there?" I offered. Beneath the lower, greening slopes of the volcano nestled a lushness of trees and a scattering of residences that were pretty lush themselves.

"Exactly. The natives say an enormous diamond once perched there, snatched away by an angry god."

"Maybe they couldn't find a virgin to sacrifice," I said. "Scarce commodity, even back then."

That got me a nudge from Isabel. I wasn't sure she'd been listening.

As the natural barrier of the volcanic sentry gradually drew away, the supple white curve of Waikiki Beach began revealing itself.

"That's the Moana Hotel," Leisure said, "oldest on the island."

It was a big white Beaux Arts beach house got out of hand,

with a wing on either end bookending the main building; a massive banyan tree and a pavilion fronted the hotel's stretch of beach. Beyond this turn-of-the-century colonial sprawl was an explosion of startling pink in the form of a massive stucco Spanish-Moorish structure, a cross between a castle and a mission, spires and cupolas lording it over landscaped grounds aswarm with ferns and palms.

"The Royal Hawaiian Hotel," Leisure said. "Also known as the Pink Palace."

"Hot dog," I said.

"Why so chipper?" Isabel wondered.

"That's where I'm staying. The Royal Hawaiian. . . ."

"I'll be with Thalo, in her little bungalow in Manoa Valley," Isabel said glumly. "She says it's no bigger than the gardener's cottage back at Bayport."

"Well, the posher crowd stays at that pink flophouse, there. Drop by anytime. Feel free."

Leisure was looking at me through those ever-narrowed eyes; he wore a mild frown, and whispered, "You're staying at the Royal Hawaiian?"

"That's what C.D. said."

"Funny," he said, still sotto voce. "He told me the party's lodgings are at the Alexander Young. Anne wasn't any too thrilled."

"What's wrong with the Young?"

"Nothing, really. A sound choice. Downtown, close to the courthouse. More of a commercial hotel."

"I'm pretty sure he said Royal Hawaiian," I shrugged. "Want me to ask him?"

"No! No. . . ."

Waikiki Beach appeared to be a narrow strip of sand, rather than the endless expanse I'd imagined; but room enough for dabs and smidgens of bathing suit and beach umbrella color to paint the shore, as bathers bobbed in the water nearby. A few hundred yards out, occasional bronze figures would rise out of the water like apparitions: surf riders, gliding in, in a spray of white, shooting toward the beach, occasionally kneeling to paddle up some extra speed, mostly just standing on their boards as casually as if they were waiting for a trolley. Was that a *dog* riding with one of them?

"Could that be as easy as it looks?" I asked Leisure.

"No," he said. "They call it the Sport of Kings. Get crowned by one of those heavy boards, and you'll know why."

Sharing the surf, but keeping their distance from its riders, were several long, narrow canoes, painted black, trimmed yellow, warlike-looking hulls supported by spidery extensions to one side ("outrigger canoes," according to Leisure). The four-man crews were paddling in precision, stroking through the water with narrow-handled fat-bladed paddles.

Just to the left of the Pink Palace was a cluster of beach homes and summer hotels; then the low-slung severe structures of a military installation peeked out among palms; in the fore was an incongruous water playground of floats, diving platforms, and chutes, in use at this very moment by sunners and swimmers.

"Fort De Russey," Leisure pointed out. "The Army dredged the coral and came up with the best stretch of beach in town. Civilians are always welcome."

"Not always."

"What do you mean?"

"Isn't that near where Thalia Massie was abducted?"

Leisure's tour guide spiel suddenly stalled. He nodded gravely. Then he said, "Best not to forget why we're here."

"Hey, don't let me spoil the party. I'm eatin' up this sunshine and ocean spray, too." I nodded toward the dazzling coastline. "But you know how sometimes a girl looks gorgeous from a distance? Then when you get close up—pockmarks and bad teeth."

A shrill siren split the air, the sort of breathy whistle that might announce a shift change at a factory, or an air raid.

"What the hell . . ."

Leisure nodded toward the shore. "We're being greeted—and announced. That's the Aloha Tower's siren, letting locals know it's a 'steamer day.'"

A clock tower did indeed loom above the harbor, like a beacon, ten stories' worth of sleek white *art deco* spire, topped by an American flag. Not everyone on this ship was aware they were visiting a United States territory; I'd even overheard the ship's purser being approached by one well-to-do imbecile wanting to exchange his U.S. currency for "Hawaiian money."

When the whistle let up, Leisure said, "Can you see the word above the clock face?"

"No."

"There's actually a clock face on all four sides, and the word *aloha* is over each one. It means hello—and good-bye."

"Who's idea was that? Groucho Marx?"

The ship was slowing down; then it came to a stop, as several small launches drew up alongside it.

"What's this about?" I asked Leisure.

The attorney shrugged. "Harbor pilot, health officers, customs officials, reps from various hotels booking rooms for any passengers that didn't plan ahead. It'll be at least another forty-five minutes before we dock."

The mainland reporters who had traveled with us had long since given up on getting anything out of Darrow (other than anti-Prohibition spiels); but a small rabid pack of local newshounds, who had just clambered aboard, sniffed us out at the rail.

They wore straw fedoras and white shirts with no jackets, pads and pencils in hand, bright eyes and expectant white smiles in tanned faces. At first I thought they were natives, but on closer look, I could see they were white men, darkened by the sun.

"Mr. Darrow! Mr. Darrow!" were among the few words that could be culled from their overlapping questions. "Massie" and "Fortescue" were two more words I made out; also "rape" and "murder." The rest was noise, a press conference in the Tower of Babel.

"Gentlemen!" Darrow said, in a courtroom-quieting fashion. He had stepped away from our little group, turning his back on the view of Honolulu's white buildings peeking around the Aloha Tower. "I'll make a brief statement, and then you will leave Mrs. Darrow and me to make our preparations to disembark."

They quieted.

"I would like you kind gentlemen to do me the small favor of informing the citizens of Honolulu that I am here to defend my clients, *not* white supremacy. I have no intention of conducting this trial on a basis of race. Race prejudice is as abhorrent to me as the fanatics who practice it."

"What *will* be the basis, then?" a reporter blurted. "The 'unwritten law' of a husband defending a wife's honor?"

A smirk creased his face. "I have trouble enough keeping up with the laws that've been written down. Altogether too many of 'em, don't you think, gentlemen? People can't be expected to obey 'em all, when there's such a surplus. In fact, I think the imminent removal of a certain law—I believe it's known as the Volstead Act—is a case in point."

Another reporter took the bait. "What do you think will be accomplished by the repeal of Prohibition?"

"I think it will be easier to get a drink," Darrow said soberly.

One of the reporters, who hadn't been taken in by Darrow's shift of subject, hollered out, "Do you expect Mrs. Fortescue to be acquitted?"

He chuckled silently. "When did you last see an intelligent, handsome woman refused alimony, let alone convicted of murder? No more on this subject, gentlemen."

And he turned his back to them, settling in next to Mrs. Darrow at the rail.

But a reporter tried again, anyway. "Are you aware your autobiography has been selling like hotcakes here in Honolulu? Looks like the locals are checking up on you, Mr. Darrow. Any comment?"

Darrow arched an eyebrow as he glanced back in mock surprise. "It's still on sale here, is it? I would've thought it would be sold out by now!"

For perhaps ninety seconds they hurled more questions at his back, but the old boy ignored them, and the pack of 'hounds moved on.

Soon the ship had gotten under way again, shifting its nose toward the harbor, slowly making its way to the dock; from the starboard side, we had a fine view of the city, and it was bigger than I expected, and more contemporary—not exactly a scattering of grass huts. White modern buildings were clustered beneath green slopes dotted with homes, all against an unlikely backdrop of majestic mountains. It was as if a twentieth-century city had been dropped by mistake, from a plane perhaps, onto an exotic primordial isle.

Down the rail from us, other passengers were squealing and laughing; something more than just the scenic view was getting their attention. Isabel, noticing this, glanced at me, and I nodded, and we moved quickly down there to see what was going on.

Finding another place at the rail, we saw brown-skinned boys down below in the drink, treading water; others were diving off the approaching pier to join this floating assemblage. Silver coins flew through the air, flipped and pitched from passengers down from us a ways, the metal catching the sun and winking, then plinking into the amazingly clear blue water. You could actually see the coins tumbling down. Then the white soles of feet pointed skyward as the boys dived for the nickels and dimes.

Somebody tapped me on the shoulder.

It was a good-looking college kid we'd met in the *Malolo's* indoor swimming pool the other day. In a setting fit for a Roman orgy, rife with Pompeian Etruscan columns and mosaic tile, the sharp-featured handsome kid had been swimming with quick authority and caught my—and Isabel's—attention.

He must've seen us watching him, because he had finally come over and struck up a conversation. He wanted to meet Darrow, who was sitting on a marble bench nearby, fully clothed, watching pretty girls swim (Ruby was off with the Leisures someplace). The affable kid, toweling off his tanned muscular frame, had introduced himself to Darrow as a fellow Clarence and a prelaw student in California. He'd grown up on a pineapple plantation on Oahu and was taking a semester off to spend some time at home.

"With a name like Clarence you'll never need a nickname," Darrow had told him.

"Oh, I've got a nickname, and it's sillier than Clarence," the good-natured kid said.

And he had told us, and it was a silly nickname all right, and we'd all had a laugh over it, though we'd never run into the kid on the ship again—he wasn't traveling first-class. Now here he was, interrupting my view of native boys diving for nickels.

"Would you do me a favor?" he asked. "I can't ask any of these stuffy rich people, and you seem like a regular guy."

"Sure." If I'd said no, I'd have been denying being a "regular guy."

And the son of a bitch began taking off his clothes.

Isabel had noticed, by now, and was smiling with pleasure as the damn Adonis stripped to red swim trunks.

"Be a pal and keep these for me," he said. "I'll catch up with you up on the dock."

And he thrust the bundle of shirt, pants, shoes, and socks into my arms, stepping out onto the deck just behind the passengers ogling the native divers.

"Who's got a silver dollar?" he called.

Faces turned toward him.

"I'll dive from the deck," he said, "for a silver dollar!"

"Here!" a mustached fellow called, digging into his pocket and holding up the silver coin; the sun caught it and a reflection lanced off it.

And I'll be damned if this kid didn't climb over the rail, and position himself, yelling "Now!" following the pitched coin into the deep blue waters, in a high perfect dive that cleaved the water with the assurance of God parting the Red Sea.

Before long, he emerged with a toss of wet dark hair and a happy, infectious grin, holding the coin up as he bobbed there. The sun caught it again, and both the smile and the coin dazzled his audience on deck, who began to applaud and cheer. Isabel put two fingers in her mouth and let loose a whistle the Aloha Tower might have envied.

Then he stroked off toward the pier as our boat continued making its way there.

"Wasn't that the damnedest thing," I said.

"What a man," Isabel sighed.

"Thanks," I said, and we grinned at each other, going arm in arm after the rest of our party.

When the ship slipped gracefully into Pier 9, a mob was waiting; a band in white uniforms performed syrupy renditions of Hawaiian tunes while colored streamers and confetti were hurled, and shapely dark hula girls in grass skirts and floral-print brassieres swayed, their slender necks bedecked with wreaths of brightly colored flowers. The citizens who'd come to greet us were less a melting pot than a list of racial ingredients: Japanese, Chinese, Polynesian, Portuguese, and Caucasian faces were among the locals on hand to greet the tourists they depended on for their livelihoods.

As we walked across the gangway into this mad merriment, I had to wonder if there wasn't an undercurrent of hysteria at this particular "steamer day," an edge provided by the tension and turmoil of the most controversial criminal matter that had ever faced the Islands.

Just as Darrow stepped onto the cement of the pier, an attractive native woman in a loose dress, the tropical version of the Mother Hubbard known as a muumuu, transferred one of the half-dozen flower garlands she was wearing from her neck to Darrow's. The battery of press photogs lying in wait—one of whom had no doubt put the woman (who was a seller of the things) up to it—jockeyed for position to record Darrow's chagrin for posterity.

But C.D. wasn't having any.

"Hold off there!" he said, shifting the wreath to his wife's neck. "You're not catching me wearing those jingle bells—I'll look like a damned decorated hat rack."

"*Lei*, mister?" the native woman asked me cheerfully.

"No thanks," I said. Then to Isabel: "They don't waste any time here, do they?"

"That's what those flowers are called, silly," she said. "A *lei*."

"Really?" I asked innocently, and then she knew I was teasing her. And joining the ranks of every mainlander male who ever set foot on Oahu, in making that particular pun.

Darrow was leading the way through the crowd—the old boy seemed to know what he was doing and where he was going. I still had that kid's clothes tucked under my arm, and was looking around for him. His head popped up above the throng, and I held up till he angled through, still in his trunks but pretty well dried off, now. The climate, though pleasant, was warm enough to be his towel.

"Thanks!" he grinned, taking his stuff from me.

"Hell of a dive, for a dollar."

That great grin flashed. "When I was a kid, I was right in there with the other beach boys, divin' for nickels. Gotta raise the ante a little, when ya get older. Where you staying? I'll drop by and use the buck to buy you lunch."

"I think the Royal Hawaiian."

"A buck doesn't go far there, but I know some people on the staff—maybe they'll cut me some slack. Heller, isn't it? Nate?"

I said it was as we shook hands, and he tossed me a "See ya," and disappeared back into the crowd.

Leisure leaned in and said, "You know who that is?"

"Some crazy college kid. Buster, he said they call him."

"That's Clarence Crabbe. Hawaii's great white hope in the Olympics comin' up this summer. He took two bronze medals in '28, at Amsterdam."

"Diving?"

"Swimming."

"Huh," I grunted. "No kiddin'."

A Navy driver was waiting for us at the curb; his seven-passenger black Lincoln limousine could have handled all of us, but Darrow sent Ruby and Mrs. Leisure on to the hotel, on foot; it was easy walking distance, and our baggage would be delivered. Isabel (looking lovely in a *lei* I'd bought her) started to go with the two women, and Darrow stopped her, gently.

"Come with us, dear," he said, "won't you?"

"All right," Isabel said.

So we all got in the back of the limo, where Isabel and I sat facing Darrow and Leisure; everyone but Darrow was confused.

"I thought we were staying at the Royal Hawaiian," I said.

"You're staying there, son," Darrow said, as the limo rolled smoothly into traffic. How odd it seemed for this city to be such a . . . city. Buses and streetcars and traffic cops, with only the predominance of various shades of brown and yellow faces to let you know this wasn't Miami or San Diego.

"Why's Nate staying at the Royal Hawaiian?" Leisure wondered, just a slight touch of cranky jealousy in his tone.

"For two reasons," Darrow said. "First, I want to keep our investigator away from reporters, keep him off the firing line. They'll only bother him about the Lindbergh business, for one thing, and I want him someplace where he can invite various witnesses and others involved in the case, for a friendly conversation over lunch or fruit punch, without the prying eyes of the press."

Leisure was nodding; jealous or not, it made sense.

"It won't hurt," Darrow continued, "to have an opulent setting to entice the cooperation of these individuals. Also, I can sneak off there myself, if I need to confer with someone, away from journalistic meddlers."

"Despite all the lawyerly bypaths you just took," I said, "that's just one reason. You said two."

"Oh. Well, the other reason is, I was offered a free suite at the Royal Hawaiian, and this was a way to take advantage of that invitation."

And he beamed at me, proud of himself.

"So the taxpayers of Chicago pay for my services," I said, "and the Royal Hawaiian provides my lodging. You couldn't afford *not* to bring me along, could you, C.D.?"

"Not hardly. Mind if I smoke, dear?"

"No," Isabel said. "But where are we going?"

"I was just wondering that myself," Leisure said. He still wasn't used to Darrow's offhand way of doing things.

"Why, taking you to your lodgings, child," Darrow said grandly to the girl, as his steady old hands emptied tobacco from a pouch into a curl of cigarette paper.

"I'm staying with my cousin Thalia," she said.

"Yes," Darrow said. "She's expecting us."

FOUR

The Navy limousine slipped into the stream of leisurely traffic on King Street; the Oriental and Polynesian drivers of Oahu, and even the Caucasians for that matter, seemed more cautious, less hurried than mainlanders. Or maybe the seductive warm climate with its constant cool breeze encouraged a tempo that to a contemporary Chicagoan seemed more appropriate for horse carts and carriages.

Nonetheless, Honolulu remained resolutely modern. There were trolley cars, not rickshaws, and on side streets, frame houses were in evidence, not a native hut in sight. The stark modern lines of white office buildings were softened by the soothing greenery of palms and exotic flora, and once we'd left the clustered heart of the business district, the urban landscape was calmed by occasional stretches of park or by a school or a church or some official-looking building resplendent on verdant manicured grounds.

Coca-Cola signs, Standard Oil pumps, drugstore window posters advertising Old Gold Cigarettes were a reminder that this was America, all right, despite the coconut trees and foreign faces.

Soon we were climbing into an area that Leisure labeled Manoa Valley, and that our youthful Navy chauffeur further identified as "The Valley of Sunshine and Tears."

"There's a legend," the driver said in a husky voice, turning his head to us but keeping an eye on the road, "that in olden days, a maiden who lived in this valley met with tragedy. Lies were told about her virtue, and it made her man jealous, and all involved came to a bad end."

"Such stories often turn out thus," Darrow said gravely.

Right now we were moving through a silk-stocking district, spacious near-mansions with beautifully maintained gardens and spacious golf-course-perfect lawns. We were on the incline that was well-shaded Punahou Street, and the college of that name was off to our right, up-to-date buildings on lavish royal palm-flung grounds.

"Somebody has money," I said.

Leisure nodded toward a stately mansion that might well have been an estate outside London. "This is old white money—they call them *kaimaaina haoles* . . . missionaries, Yankee traders, and their descendants. We're talking second- and third-generation, now. You've heard of the 'Big Five'?"

"Isn't that a college football conference?"

Leisure's narrow lips pursed a smile. "Hawaii's Big Five are the plantation, shipping, and merchandising companies that own these islands. Matson Lines money, Liberty House, which is the local version of Sears . . ."

"The white man came to Hawaii," Darrow intoned suddenly, as if from a pulpit, "and urged the simple natives to turn their eyes upward to God . . . but when the natives looked down to earth again, their goddamn *land* was gone."

We rose into the upper portion of Manoa Valley, where the estates gave way to a network of shady lanes and a concentration of cottages and bungalows. Though we were on a steep gradient, the boundaries of the valley were steeper still—mountainous slopes providing a dark blue backdrop; it was as if this were a stadium scooped from the earth by nature, and we were down on the Big Five's playing field.

I posed a question to the driver. "How far are we from Pearl Harbor?"

"A good half an hour, sir."

"Is it common for a Navy officer to live this far from the base?"

"Yes, sir," the driver said. "In fact, quite a few Navy officers live in Manoa Valley—Army as well. Lt. Massie and a number of other younger officers live within close proximity of one another, sir."

"Oh. That's nice. Then they can get together, socialize . . ."

"I wouldn't know about that, sir," the driver said, strangely curt.

Had I touched a nerve?

Number 2850 on the narrow slope of Kahawai Street was a precious white Tudor-style bungalow, its gabled roofs decorated with vertical and diagonal slashes of brown trim, and large brown-striped canvas awnings so determined to keep out the sun that they almost hid the windows. Though the yard was tiny, foliage was plentiful, well-trimmed boxcar-shaped hedges hugging the little house, several oriental trees like absurdly large bushes providing sheltering green. I wasn't sure whether the effect was one of coziness or concealment.

There was a driveway, where the Navy driver pulled in; the street was too narrow to park along. Soon, Isabel and I, heads craned back, were standing in the street, admiring the way the mountains provided a misty green backdrop to the little house.

The Navy chauffeur was helping Darrow out of the backseat as the sound of a screen door closing announced a lanky guy of about thirty, in white shirt with sleeves rolled back and crisp canary trousers, legs knifing as he rushed out to greet us. His brown hair was rather thin, but his smile was generous; he was bestowing it on Darrow, who was standing in the drive next to Leisure.

"Pleased to meet you, sir—I'm Lt. Francis Olds, but my friends call me Pop. I'd be honored if you'd pay me that compliment."

The enthusiastic Olds was extending a hand, which Darrow took, shook, saying, "Much as I'd like to please you, Lieutenant, I'm afraid I couldn't quite bring myself to that. This suit I'm wearing is older than you."

"Well," the lieutenant said, folding his arms, grinning, "at thirty, *I'm* the old man around here—Tommie and the rest, they're just a buncha fresh-faced kids barely outta college."

Darrow's gray eyes narrowed. "You're a friend of Lt. Massie's?"

"I'm sorry! I haven't explained myself. I run the Ammunition Depot, out at Pearl. My wife and I have been taking turns keeping Thalia company, making sure the press and any curiosity-seekers don't bother her here, during the day. We post armed guards at night."

Darrow frowned. "The situation's that severe?"

He nodded. "There have been bomb threats. Word of gangs of Japs and native trash driving around Manoa Valley in their junker cars. . . . You know, I'm afraid you have *me* to blame for your involvement in this, Mr. Darrow."

"How is that, Lieutenant?"

The lieutenant pointed at himself with a thumb. "I'm the one brought up your name. I'm the one encouraged Mrs. Fortescue to hit up her rich friends on the mainland for the dough it would take to get a really *top* lawyer. And I *knew* you were the only man for this case."

Wry amusement creased Darrow's face. "You have excellent judgment, young man."

"And, well . . . I'm also running the fund-raising drive, at the base, to raise your fee to cover Lord and Jones."

"Who?"

"The two enlisted men you're defending!"

The accomplices to Mrs. Fortescue and Tommie Massie in the killing of Joseph Kahahawai. I didn't think C.D. had spent much time going over those transcripts and statements back on the *Malolo*. Leisure was wincing.

"Well, then," Darrow said, with no apology for forgetting the names of two of the clients he'd come thousands of miles to defend, "I guess I will have to capitulate to your request . . . Pop."

Darrow introduced Isabel, Leisure, and myself to Pop Olds, who greeted us warmly, glad to see anybody who was part of the great Darrow's team. He walked us behind the hedge to the front door.

_____

"We're friends of the Massies," he explained. "My wife and I were in a play with Thalia and Tommie, at the local Little Theater." He grinned shyly. "Actually, Thalia and *I* are the hams. . . . I arranged walk-ons for our spouses so we could all spend some time together."

So Thalia Massie was an actress; I'd have to keep that in mind.

Darrow was laying a hand on the lieutenant's shoulder. "I'm grateful for your attentiveness to Mrs. Massie, Pop . . . but I have to ask you a courtesy."

"Anything, Mr. Darrow."

"Wait out here while I speak to Mrs. Massie. I view her as a client in this case, and wish to limit the audience for the painful memories I must go probing after."

Olds seemed a little disappointed to be left out, but he said, "Certainly, sir—certainly. I'll just catch a few smokes out here. . . ."

A maid in a brown uniform with white apron met us as we stepped inside; she was Japanese, petite, quietly pretty, without an ounce of makeup, her shiny black hair in a Louise Brooks bob.

"Miss Massie resting," she said, lowering her head respectfully. She was addressing Darrow, who stood at the head of our group, crowding into the little living room. "But she ask I wake her when you arrive."

And she went quickly off.

The place was pretty impersonal; my guess was they'd rented the bungalow furnished—with the possible exception of a new-looking walnut veener console radio-phonograph in one corner. This was dark, functional, middle-class nicked-up stuff whose point of origin was probably Sears—or, rather, Liberty House. They'd dressed it up a little—the wine-color mohair davenport and matching armchair had antimacassars; the occasional tables had doilies but almost no knickknacks.

On one table were a few family photos, including a wedding portrait of a very young, pasty-faced couple, the pretty bride slightly taller than the fetus of a groom, whose formal naval attire seemed sizes too big for him; another photo, in an ornate silver frame, depicted an attractive, long-faced matron with frozen eyes and a long string of pearls.

A painting over the stuffed horsehair couch depicted the sun setting over Diamond Head, but the frame was ornate European, and nothing else in the room was remotely Hawaiian, not even the faded pink floral wallpaper, or the well-worn oriental rug on the hardwood floor.

From the living room, through a wide archway, was a dining room with more dark nondescript furnishings; I could catch a white glimpse of the kitchen, the next room over. The bedroom must have been off the dining room, to the right, because that's the way the pretty bride in the wedding portrait—Thalia Massie—came in.

She wore black—black dress, black beaded necklace, black sideways turban—as if in stylish mourning for her normal life that had died late last summer. Blades of blondish-brown hair arced around the round smooth contours of her oval face; the faint outline of a scar touched her left cheek, near her mouth, trailing to the jawline. She looked quite a bit like Isabel, the same cupid's-bow mouth, small well-formed nose and big blue eyes, but Thalia's were what unkind people in the Midwest call cow's eyes—wide-set and protuberant.

Still, the overall effect was a pretty girl, and with a nice shape, too—a little pudgy, perhaps. And her shoulders were stooped—she was rather tall, but it took you a while to realize it. Had she always had that uncertain gait? She almost shuffled in, as if in a perpetual state of embarrassment. Or shame.

And yet those clear eyes met us all directly, blinking only rarely, the result being a languid, remote expression.

Isabel rushed forward and took her cousin in her arms, gushing words of sympathy; but as they embraced, Thalia Massie looked blankly at me over Isabel's shoulder. Thalia patted Isabel's back as if her cousin were the one who needed comforting.

"I should have come sooner," Isabel said.

Thalia twitched her a smile in response as Isabel took her cousin's hand, and the two girls stood there side by side, Isabel looking like Thalia's blonder sister.

Darrow stepped forward with a fatherly smile and clasped one of Thalia's hands in both of his big paws; Isabel receded, giving Thalia center stage.

"My dear, I'm Clarence Darrow," he said, as if there were any doubt, "and I've come here to help you and your family."

"I'm very grateful." Her smile seemed halfhearted; her voice low, throaty, but barely inflected. She was twenty-one—married at sixteen, according to what I'd read on the *Malolo*—but I'd have guessed her at least twenty-five.

Darrow introduced Leisure ("my distinguished co-counsel") and me ("my investigator—he's just returned from working with Colonel Lindbergh"), and Thalia granted us nods. Then Darrow led her to the couch under the Diamond Head painting. Isabel sat next to her, close to her, taking Thalia's hand supportively.

Leisure drew the couch's matching armchair around for Darrow, so that he was facing Thalia. I found a caneback wing chair—by the way, was a more uncomfortable chair ever invented?—and pulled it to one side of Darrow. Leisure preferred to stand; arms folded, he watched the unfolding scene through those all-seeing narrowed eyes of his.

Thalia drew her hand away from Isabel's, doing so with a little smile, but her cousin's hand-holding clearly made her uncomfortable. She folded her hands primly in her lap and looked at Darrow with the big languid eyes. There was weariness in her gaze, and distaste in her tone.

"I'm more than willing to talk to you, of course," Thalia said. "I will do anything to help Tommie and Mother. But I hope it won't be necessary to ... dredge up all that other unpleasantness."

Darrow sat forward in the chair; his smile, and tone, remained fatherly. "Would that I could spare you, child. But if we're to defend—"

"This is a different case," Thalia said, almost snippily. "Those rapists aren't on trial and, for that matter, neither am I. This is about what Tommie and Mother and those sailors did."

The smile turned regretful. "Unfortunately, dear, the two cannot be separated. What they did flowed out of what was done to you. . . . And without an understanding of what happened to you, a jury would view what your husband and mother did as, simply . . . murder."

Her forehead furrowed in irritation, but the eyes remained wide. "Who's better aware of that than I? But you were provided transcripts of what I said in court. Isn't that enough?"

"No," Darrow said firmly. "My staff and I need to hear these words from your own lips. We need to ask our own questions. There's no stenographer, here, though Mr. Heller will take some notes."

I took that prompt to get out my notepad and pencil.

"And," Darrow continued, pointing at her gently, "you need to be prepared, young lady—because it's very likely you'll be taking the witness stand to tell your story yet again."

Her sigh was a rasp from her chest, and she looked toward a side wall, away from Isabel, who was watching her with sympathy but also confusion. Finally Thalia turned her head back to Darrow.

"I'm sorry," she said. "I do want to help. Please ask your questions."

But her face remained an oval mask, devoid of emotion, marked only by that white line of scar down her jaw.

Darrow leaned forward and patted her hand. "Thank you, dear. Now, I'll try to make this as painless as possible. Let's begin with the party. You didn't want to be there, I understand?"

The cow eyes went half-hooded. "When these Navy men get together, they drink too much, and embarrass themselves, and their wives—though the *women* drink too much, too. And I didn't really care for that tawdry place, anyway."

"The Ala Wai Inn, you mean?" I asked.

She glanced at me noncommittally. "That's right. Loud music, frantic dancing, bootleg liquor . . . I found it in poor taste *and* depressing, to be quite frank about it. Every Saturday night at the Ala Wai is 'Navy Night'—the management give the Navy boys the run of the place, and it can get wild."

"Did it that night?" I asked. "Get wild?"

She shrugged a little. "Not really. Just dreary. Boring."

"Then why did you go?" I asked.

"I only went because Tommie and Jimmy . . . Lt. Bradford . . . and another officer had made a reservation for a table for their wives and themselves, and how would it look if Tommie went alone? But once I got there, it didn't take long for me to get tired of all that nonsense."

Darrow asked, "What time did you leave, dear?"

"Shortly after 11:30. But I wasn't leaving, really. I just decided to go for a walk and get some air."

"Was someone with you?"

"No. I was alone. I walked along Kalakaua Avenue and crossed the canal and I turned down John Ena Road, walked a block or so down, toward the beach."

"How far did you walk?"

"To a spot within, oh, twenty feet of where the road turns into Fort De Russey. I was just going to walk a little ways down the road, then turn back and stroll back to the Ala Wai Inn."

"Just getting some air," Darrow said, nodding.

"That's correct."

"What happened then, dear? I'm sorry, but I have to ask."

She began twisting her fingers in her lap, as if she were trying to pull them off; her gaze drew inward, and glazed over.

"A car drove up behind me and stopped, a Ford touring car. Two men got out and grabbed me and dragged me toward it. I was struggling, and the one called Joe Kahahawai hit me in the face, in the jaw. Hard."

Next to her, Isabel gasped, drew a hand to her mouth.

But Thalia remained emotionless. "The other one, Henry Chang, placed his hand over my mouth and pulled me into the backseat. I begged them to let me go, but every time I spoke, Kahahawai hit me. Chang hit me, too."

"Was the car still parked," I asked, "or was it moving?"

"Moving," she said. "As soon as they dragged me in there, they pulled away; there were two or three other boys in the front seat."

"What nationality?" I asked.

"Hawaiians, I thought at the time. Later, I learned they were a mixed-race group."

According to the materials I'd read, the motley crew of

young island gangsters included Joe Kahahawai and Ben Ahakuelo, pure-blooded Hawaiians; Horace Ida and David Takai, Japanese; and Henry Chang, Chinese-Hawaiian.

"Go on, dear," Darrow said.

"I offered them money, I told them my husband would give them money if they would let me go. I said I had some money with me they could have. I had my purse, and I said, 'Take my pocketbook!' One of them in the front seat, Ahakuelo, turned around and said, 'Take the pocketbook,' and Chang took it from me. I got a good look at this Ben Ahakuelo—he turned around several times and grinned at me. He had a gold tooth, a big filling about here." She opened her mouth and pointed.

"How far did they take you?" I asked.

"I don't really know. I know they were driving along Ala Moana Road, heading towards town. Maybe two or three blocks. They drove the car into the underbrush on the right-hand side of the road, and Kahahawai and Chang dragged me out and away from the car and into the bushes and then Chang assaulted me. . . ."

Thalia said all this as calmly, and detachedly, as if she were reading off a laundry list; but Isabel, next to her, was biting her fist and tears were streaming down her face, streaking her makeup.

"I tried to get away, but I couldn't. They hit me so many times, so hard, I was dazed. I couldn't imagine that this was happening to me! I didn't know people were capable of such things. . . . Chang hit me, and the others were hovering around, holding my arms."

Isabel gasped.

Thalia didn't seem to notice. "Then the others . . . did it to me. I was assaulted five or six times—Kahahawai went last. I started to pray, and that made him angry and he hit me very hard. I cried out, 'You'll knock my teeth out,' and he said, 'What do I care? Shut up!' I asked him please not to hit me anymore."

Isabel, covering her mouth, got up and ran from the room.

"There were five men," I said. "You think you may have been assaulted as many as six times?"

"I lost count, but I think Chang assaulted me twice. I remember he was standing near me, and he said, 'I want to go again.' That was all right with the others, but one of them said, 'Hurry up, we have to go back out Kalihi way.' "

"They spoke in English?" I asked.

"To me, they did; sometimes they talked to each other in some foreign language. They said a lot of filthy things to me, in English, which I don't care to repeat."

"Certainly, dear," Darrow said. "But you heard them call each other by name?"

"Yes, well, I heard the name Bull used, and I heard the name Joe. I heard another name—it might have been Billy or Benny, and I heard the name Shorty."

"You must have got a good look at them," I said.

She nodded. "Kahahawai had on a short-sleeved polo shirt, blue trousers. Ahakuelo, blue trousers, blue shirt. Horace Ida, dark trousers, leather coat. And Chang—I think Chang had on dark trousers."

This was the kind of witness a cop dreams of.

"Now, dear, after they'd had their vicious way with you," Darrow said, "what happened next?"

"One helped me to sit up, Chang I think. He said, 'The road's over there,' then they bolted for their car, got into it, and drove away. That's when I turned around and saw the car."

I asked, "Which way was it facing?"

"The back of the car was toward me. The car's headlights, taillights, were switched on."

"And that's when you saw the license plate?"

"Yes. I noticed the number. I thought it was 58-805, but I guess I was off a digit."

The actual license, belonging to Horace Ida's sister's Ford touring car, was 58-895. Easy mistake, considering what she'd been through, confusing a 9 with a 0.

Darrow said, "Dear, what did you do after the attack?"

"I was very much dazed. I wandered around in the bushes and finally came to the Ala Moana. I saw a car coming from Waikiki and ran toward the car, waving my arms. The car stopped. I ran to it, half blind from their headlights, and asked the people in it if they were white. They said yes, and I told them what had happened to me and asked them to take me home. They wanted to take me to the police station, but I asked them to bring me here, which they did."

Darrow asked, "What did you do when you got home?"

"I took off my clothes and douched."

No one said anything for several long moments.

Then, gently, Darrow asked, "Did this procedure prove . . . successful?"

"No. A couple of weeks later I found I was pregnant."

"I'm very sorry, dear. I understand your physician performed a curettage, and eliminated the, uh, problem?"

"Yes, he did."

Isabel, on shaky legs, reentered the room; she smiled embarrassedly and sat on the couch, giving Thalia plenty of room.

Darrow said, "Returning to that terrible night . . . When did you next see your husband?"

"About one o'clock in the morning," Thalia said. "He called me from a friend's, looking for me, and I told him, 'Please come home right away, something awful has happened.' "

"When your husband returned home, did you tell him what these men had done to you?"

"Not at first. I couldn't. It was too awful, too horrible. But he sat with me on this couch and kept asking. He knew something was terribly wrong. Even though I'd cleaned myself up, my face was all bruised and puffy; my nose was bleeding. He begged me to tell him."

"And you did?"

She nodded. "I told him everything—how they'd raped me. How Kahahawai broke my jaw when I tried to pray. How all of them attacked me. . . ."

"I understand your husband called the police, took you to the hospital . . ."

"Yes. Eventually I identified four of the five boys, who'd been picked up on another assault that same night."

Darrow gently inquired about the ordeal that had followed, the weeks of medical treatment (teeth pulled, jaw wired shut), the "travesty" of the trial of the five rapists that had resulted in a hung jury, the flurry of press interest, the racial unrest manifested by several incidents between Navy personnel and local island youth.

"The worst part was the rumors," she said hollowly. "I heard Tommie hadn't believed me and was getting a divorce. That I was assaulted by a naval officer and that Tommie found him in my room and beat him and then beat me up . . . all kinds of vile, nasty rumors."

"How did your husband withstand these pressures, dear?"

"I told him not to worry about these rumors, but he couldn't sleep and he got so very thin. Then I would wake up at night, screaming, and he would be right there, soothing me. He was so wonderful. But I was worried."

"Why?"

"He didn't sleep, he had rings around his eyes, he'd get up at night and walk up and down the living room, smoking cigarettes."

"And your mother—all of this was very difficult for her, obviously."

"Yes. When she arrived from Bayport, in response to the first cablegram that I'd been injured, she didn't even know about the . . . true nature of what had happened to me. She was outraged, indignant, vowed to do whatever it took to help."

"How did that help manifest itself, dear?"

"Well, at first, she took over the household duties—Tommie had been acting as both housekeeper and my nurse, in addition to his normal naval duties."

"But that wasn't all she did, was it?"

"No. Mother was relentless in urging both Admiral Stirling and the local civil authorities to see that my attackers were brought to trial, and punished."

"She wasn't living with you," I said, "when . . ."

"No," she interrupted. "No. When I got up and around, and was feeling better, this little house was just too small for all of us. My younger sister, Helene, was with her . . . Helene's since gone back to Long Island, to be with my father, who was too ill to travel here . . . and Mother rented a place of her own."

Leisure spoke, for the first time since the interrogation had begun. "Did you have any part in the abduction of Joseph Kahahawai, Mrs. Massie?"

Thalia looked at him sharply. "None! The first I knew anything of it was when Seaman Jones came to my door, the morning of the incident."

"Before or after the killing?" I asked.

"After! He rushed in and handed me a gun and said, 'Here, take this—Kahahawai has been killed.' And I said, 'Where's Tommie?' And he said he'd sent Tommie off with Mother to . . . to dispose of the body."

And she just sat there impassively, with no more expression on her face than a bisque baby's.

"Then what did this seaman do?" Darrow asked.

"He asked me to make him a drink, a highball. And I did."

"A man had been killed, Mrs. Massie," I said. "By your husband and your mother."

"I'm sorry the man was shot," she said, and shrugged. "But it was no more than he deserved."

Then she apologized for her "earlier rudeness" and asked if we'd like anything to drink. Her maid had made a pitcher of iced tea, if anyone was interested.

"Beatrice!" she called.

And the pretty, efficient little maid came in with a pitcher of tea with floating lemons and a tray of glasses.

"You know," Thalia said, "I sometimes wonder why they didn't just kill me—it would have been so much easier for all concerned, in the long run. . . . I hope you like your tea sweetened, in the Southern style."

FIVE

Isabel needed some fresh air, so we stepped outside while Darrow chatted with Thalia Massie—nothing directly to do with the case, just small talk about naval life at Pearl and her experiences taking courses at the University of Hawaii, even garnering recommendations from her about restaurants in Honolulu. Darrow liked to make his clients feel comfortable with him, think of him as a friend.

And while Thalia wasn't exactly a client, her role in this case was crucial. Darrow was turning on his charm, his warmth, on this apparently cold-blooded girl.

"How's Thalo doing?" Pop Olds asked. The lieutenant was sitting on the steps of the front stoop, several ground-out cigarette butts on the sidewalk nearby.

"All right I think," I said. "Hard to tell—she's a very self-contained young woman."

Olds got to his feet, shook his head. "Hard on her, out here. She gets pretty lonely."

"Isn't she spending any time with her husband?" I asked. "I understand he and the others are in custody of the Navy, not the local coppers. Can't she get access to him?"

"Oh, yes," Olds said. "That part of it's fine, anyway. Tommie and Mrs. Fortescue and the two sailors are on the U.S.S. *Alton*."

I frowned. "What, out at sea?"

He chuckled. "No. It's an old warship stuck in the mud in the harbor. It's used as temporary living quarters for transient personnel."

"I don't think this is healthy," I said, "her being stuck out here in seclusion. She puts up a hell of a front, but . . ."

Isabel hugged my arm. "Maybe she'll be better with me around."

"Maybe. The last thing we need is our chief witness committing suicide."

Isabel drew in a fast breath. "Suicide . . ."

"I've had some experience in that area," I said. "She needs some company. Some companionship."

"Well," Olds said thoughtfully, "the ammunition depot's located on a little island in the middle of the harbor, and that's where my quarters are. My wife and I have one of the few houses on base."

"Do you have room for Thalia?" I asked.

"Certainly. I'm not sure we could accommodate Miss Bell, here, as well. . . ."

I patted Isabel's hand. "I think Mr. Darrow could arrange housing for Miss Bell at the Royal Hawaiian."

Isabel kept her face troubled, but she was hugging my arm enthusiastically now. "Well," she said, trying to sound disappointed, "I really would like to be at Thalo's side, through this . . ."

"You'd be welcome at Pearl, anytime," Olds said. "You could spend every day with your cousin, if you like. You'd just have to find someplace else to sleep."

"We can manage that," I said with a straight face. "I'll run this idea past Mr. Darrow, and let you know before we leave."

Darrow was delighted by the suggestion, and Thalia liked the idea, too. Pop Olds said he'd put the plan in motion— Admiral Stirling was sure to give his okay—but for the time being, Isabel would stay behind with Thalia. This was where Isabel's belongings were being delivered.

She walked me to the limo, where the Navy driver was helping Darrow back in. The breeze was wafting her lovely haze of blond hair. Her arm in mine, she pulled me down, leaned in, her lips almost touching my ear.

"I can't decide whether you're wonderful or terrible," she whispered.

"No one can," I whispered back. "That's my charm."

In the limousine, I said, "Where to now, C.D.?"

"Pearl Harbor," he said, "to meet our clients."

"Might I make a suggestion?"

Darrow looked toward Leisure, who was sitting beside me in the roomy back of the limo. "You've probably noticed, George, this boy is not shy about making his thoughts known."

Leisure gave me a sideways smile. "I've noticed that. And I respect it. We three have a considerable challenge ahead, and I don't believe we should hold anything back."

"Agreed," Darrow said. "What's your suggestion, Nate?"

"Let's make a slight detour. Mrs. Fortescue's rented bungalow is only a few blocks from here. We probably won't be able to get in, but let's at least have a look at the outside of it."

Less than three blocks away, just one house off the East Manoa Road intersection, on Kolowalu Street, was a nondescript, even dingy little white frame number, a charmless cottage set back amid some scroungy trees with untended hedges along the side. With its intersecting pitched roofs, it was like a parody of the Massies' little dream house. The yard was slightly overgrown, making it a mild eyesore in this modestly residential section.

No question about it: if you had to pick a house on this street where a murder might have happened, this was the place.

The Navy driver parked the limo across the way, and we got out, crossed the quiet street, and had a look around.

Darrow, hands on hips, was studying the bungalow like a doctor looks at an X-ray. He stood ankle-deep in the gently riffling grass, like an oversize lawn ornament.

"Wonder if it's been rented out yet," Leisure said.

"Sure doesn't look like it," I said. "Unless Bela Lugosi moved in. . . . But I'll find a neighbor to ask."

The *haole* housewife next door stopped her vacuuming to

come to the door. She was an attractive brunette in a blue housedress, hair pinned up under an island-print kerchief; she thought I was cute, too. She wiped some perspiration from her upper lip and answered my questions.

No, it hadn't been rented, the place was still empty. The real estate agent *was* starting to show it, though. They'd left a key with her, if I was interested. . . .

I came back grinning, my prize dangling from a key chain.

Soon we were inside the little place, and it *was* little: only four rooms and bath—living room, kitchen, two small bedrooms. More rental furniture, but of a lower quality than at the Massies'; not a framed picture on the walls, not a knickknack in sight. No radio, no phonograph. Dusty as hell, and only the crusty dried remains of two fried eggs in a skillet on the stove, and a place setting for two at the kitchen table, indicated anyone had ever lived here at all.

The rust-colored outline of bloodstains in the master bedroom indicated somebody had died here, however. Odd-shaped stains on the wooden floor, like maps of unchartered islands . . .

The bathroom was spotless—including the tub where the body of Joseph Kahahawai had been dumped for cleaning and wrapping purposes.

"Mrs. Fortescue didn't live here," Leisure said from the bathroom doorway as I studied the gleaming bathtub.

"What do you mean?" I asked.

"She just *stayed* here. Like you stay in a hotel room. I don't think there's anything for us to learn in this place."

"Do you see anything useful, son?" Darrow asked me, from the cramped hall.

"No. But I smell something."

Darrow's brow furrowed in curiosity. Leisure was studying me, too.

"Death," I said, answering the question in their eyes. "A man was murdered here."

"Let's not use that word, son—'murder.' "

"Executed, then. Hey, I'm all for getting our clients off. But, gentlemen—let's never forget the smell of this place. How it makes your goddamn skin crawl."

"Nate's right," Leisure said. "This is no vacation. A man died, here."

"Point well taken," Darrow said, his voice hushed, somber.

The seven-mile stretch that separated Honolulu from the naval base at Pearl Harbor was a well-paved boulevard bordered by walls of deep red sugarcane stalks on either side. The breeze rustled the cane field, making shimmering music.

"I like Thalia," Darrow said, after a long interval of silence. "She's a clever, attractive, unassuming young woman."

"She's awfully unemotional," Leisure said.

"She's still in a state of shock," Darrow said dismissively.

Leisure frowned. "Seven months after the fact?"

"Then call it a state of detachment. It's her way of dealing with tragedy, protecting herself; she's erected a kind of wall. But she spoke the truth. I can always tell when a client's lying to me."

"Two things bother me," I said.

Darrow's brow furrowed. "What would those be?"

"She kept describing herself as 'dazed,' and painted a nightmarish picture . . . convincingly."

Darrow was nodding sagely.

"But for a woman in a daze," I said, "she noted a hell of a lot of details. She gave us everything but the laundry marks on their damn clothes."

"Perhaps the awful event is frozen in her memory," Darrow offered.

"Perhaps."

Leisure asked, "What's the other thing that bothered you, Nate?"

"It's probably nothing. But she talked about her mother taking over the housekeeping for her . . ."

"Yes," Leisure said.

"And that when she got back on her feet, the place was suddenly too small for them, and Thalia could handle the housekeeping herself again, so her mother moved out."

Darrow was listening intently.

"Only in the meantime," I continued, "housekeeper Thalia's taken on a full-time maid."

"If there's room for the maid," Leisure said, raising an eyebrow, "why not room for Mom?"

I shrugged. "I just think relations between Thalia and her mother may be a little strained. Isabel told me Thalia practically raised herself, that her mother was never around. I don't think they were *ever* close."

"Yet the mother faces a murder charge," Darrow said, savoring the irony, "for defending her daughter's honor."

"Yeah, funny, isn't it? Let's say they don't get along—can't be under the same roof together—then why does Mother Fortescue go out on this limb for her little girl?"

"Maybe she was defending the family name," Leisure suggested.

"Or maybe Mrs. Fortescue feels guilty about neglecting her kid," I said, "and cooked up a hell of a way to finally make it up to the girl."

"Mother and daughter needn't love each other," Darrow said patiently, as if instructing children, "for a mother's instincts to take hold. Among many species, the mother forgets herself, in protecting the life of her offspring. It's purely biological."

At Pearl Harbor Junction, our limousine bore straight ahead, pulling up to the entrance to the naval station, an innocuous white-picket gate between fieldstone posts in a mesh-wire fence that couldn't have kept out a troop of Campfire Girls. Our driver checked in with the Marine MP there, who checked us off on a clipboard, and gave us admittance into a surprisingly shabby facility.

Not that the Navy Yard didn't have its impressive points. Like the immense battleship bed of the cement pit labeled DRY-DOCK—14TH NAVAL DISTRICT; or the coaling station with wharf, railroad, and hoisting towers. Or Ford Island (as our driver identified it), with its seaplane station and battery of ungainly planes.

But the wooden shacks labeled, variously, GYRO SHOP, ELECTRICAL SHOP, MESS HALL, DIESEL SHOP looked more like a rundown summer camp than a military base. Sheet-iron shelters housing sailors' automobiles had a cheap, temporary look; and the submarine base, with what should have been a grand array, was a couple dozen tiny subs at a wobbly wooden network of finger piers.

The fleet was definitely *not* in. No great warships loomed in the harbor. The only ship in sight was the *Alton*, perpetually stuck in the mud, aboard which our clients were in custody.

But our first stop was at the base headquarters, another unassuming white building, if better maintained. Our young Navy chauffeur was still our guide, and he led Darrow, Leisure, and me into a large waiting room. Venetian blinds on the many windows were letting in slashes of sunlight as men in white bustled in and out with paperwork; the chauffeur checked us in with the reception desk. We had barely sat down when an attaché pushed open a door and summoned us with, "Mr. Darrow? The admiral will see you now."

The office was spacious, its paneling light brown, masculine, touched here and there with an award or a plaque or a framed photograph; one wall, at our left as we entered, was taken up almost entirely by a map of the Pacific. Behind the admiral was a wall of windows with more blinds, but these were shut tight, letting no sun in at all; an American flag stood at ease, to the admiral's right. His mahogany desk, appropriately enough, was as big as a boat, and it was shipshape: pens, papers, personal items, arranged as neatly as if prepared for inspection.

The admiral was shipshape, too—a narrow blade of a man in his late fifties, standing behind the desk with one fist on a hip. In his white uniform with its high collar, epaulets, brass buttons, and campaign ribbons, he looked as perfectly groomed as a waiter in a really high-class joint.

Pouches of skin slanting over grayish-blue eyes gave him a relaxed expression that I doubted; his weathered countenance was otherwise rather dour: prominent nose, long upper lip, lantern jaw. He was smiling. I doubted the smile, too.

"Mr. Darrow, I can't tell you how pleased I am," the admiral said in a mellow voice gently touched by the South, "that Mrs. Fortescue took my advice and acquired your good services."

Second Navy man today who'd taken credit for that.

"Admiral Stirling," Darrow said, shaking the hand his host extended, "I want to thank you for your hospitality and help. May I introduce my staff?"

Leisure and I shook hands with Admiral Yates Stirling, exchanged acknowledgments, and at the admiral's signal took the three chairs opposite his desk. One of them, a leather padded captain's chair, was clearly meant for Darrow, and he took it grandly.

The admiral sat, leaning back in his swivel chair, hands resting on the arms.

"You will have the full cooperation of my men and myself," Stirling said. "Full access to your clients, of course, twenty-four hours a day."

Darrow crossed his legs. "Your dedication to your people is commendable, Admiral. And I appreciate you giving us your time, this afternoon."

"It's my pleasure," the admiral said. "I think you'll find that, despite the grim nature of your mission, these beautiful islands have much to commend them."

"We couldn't have asked for a lovelier day for our arrival," Darrow said.

"Merely a typical Hawaiian day, Mr. Darrow—the sort of day so magnificent it's almost enough to make one forget the existence of certain sordid people permitted to exist on these heavenly shores by a too-trusting Providence. . . . If you'd like to smoke, gentlemen, please go right ahead."

The admiral was filling an ivory meerschaum with tobacco from a wooden humidor with an anchor carved on it; he didn't drop a flake of stray tobacco on the spotless desk.

"I imagine you refer," Darrow said, as he began casually building a cigarette, "to Mrs. Massie's five assailants."

"They're only a symptom of the disease, sir." Stirling was lighting up the pipe with a kitchen match. He puffed at it, got it going, like a tugboat's smokestack. Then he leaned back in the chair and spoke reflectively.

"When I first visited Hawaii, well before the turn of the century, long before I dreamed a naval command here would be mine, these beautiful gems of the Pacific were ruled over by a dusky Hawaiian queen. Since then, a once-proud Polynesian race has been displaced by Orientals, coming from the coolie class chiefly, the lowest caste in the Orient. That picturesque simple Hawaiian civilization has well nigh passed away, never to return. . . ."

I knew racial rot like this was anathema to Darrow; but I also knew he needed to stay on the admiral's good side. Still, I knew he wouldn't let this pass. . . .

"Yes, it is a pity," Darrow said as he lighted his cigarette from a matchbook, neither sarcasm nor recrimination in his tone, "that so many waves of cheap yellow labor were brought in to work on the white man's plantations."

The admiral only nodded, puffed at his pipe solemnly. "The large number of people of alien blood in these islands is a matter of grave concern to the government; nearly half the population here is Japanese!"

"Is that a fact."

"Even factoring in our twenty thousand military personnel, Caucasians number barely over ten percent. The dangers of such a polyglot population are obvious."

"I should say they are," Darrow said. "Now. Admiral . . ."

"Hawaii is of prime strategic importance—she must be made invulnerable from attack, or an enemy would have a sword to the throat of our Pacific coast. And that's why, strange as it may seem, this unfortunate Massie affair may provide an unexpected blessing."

Suddenly Darrow was interested in Stirling's racist editorializing. "In what way, Admiral?"

"Well, as I've already made clear, I'm no advocate of the melting pot experiment. I've been lobbying for some time that the U.S. needs to limit suffrage in Hawaii. I've long expressed my firm belief that the controlling government here should be under the jurisdiction of the Navy, and Army."

"The reports in the mainland press," Darrow said gently, "of women unsafe on your streets at night, that a hoodlum element here is holding Honolulu in its grip . . . these have opened the door to Washington considering martial law?"

The mildest frown grazed the admiral's face. "That may yet

happen, though I take no pleasure in the fact, Mr. Darrow. Until this affair, I'd always had congenial and cordial relations with Governor Judd.... We've often gone out in a mutual friend's motor sampan, to different parts of the islands, for deep-sea fishing."

Wasn't that just peachy.

"But," the admiral was saying, "it is the irresponsibility of the Territorial government, and the corruption, and incompetence, of the local police, that transformed the Massie case from a mere crime into a major tragedy."

"Admiral," I said, risking a question, "do you mind telling us how you think that happened?"

"Yes," Leisure said, "we've made ourselves familiar with the facts of the case, but we're burdened with an outsider's point of view."

The admiral was shaking his head; smoke curled out of his pipe in corkscrew fashion. "It's hard to describe how hard the news hit this base . . . that a gang of half-breed hoodlums on the Ala Moana had ravaged one of our younger set. Thalia Massie is a friend of my daughter's, you know—Mrs. Massie is a demure, attractive, quiet-spoken, sweet young woman."

"We've met with her," Darrow said, nodding. "I concur with your assessment, sir."

His pipe in hand waved a curl of smoke in the air. "Imagine thousands of young officers, sailors and marines, on the naval base, in ships, who as American youth had been taught to hold the honor of their women sacred."

Well, I knew more than a few sailors on leave in Chicago who hadn't held the honor of women so very goddamn sacred. . . .

"My first inclination," he continued, his eyes hard under the pouches, "was to seize the brutes and string them up on trees. But . . . I set that impulse aside, to give the authorities a chance to carry out the law."

Darrow seemed about to say something; he seemed about to burst, and the admiral's endorsement of lynch law wasn't something he was likely to let ride, even when he needed to. . . .

So I jumped in with, "You gotta give the local coppers *some* credit, Admiral Stirling—they sure picked those hoods up in a hell of a hurry."

"That was a kindly Providence," the admiral said. "Were the particulars of their capture in the materials you were provided?"

Darrow glanced at me; he didn't know.

"No," I said. "Just that the assailants had been involved in another assault, earlier that night. Was that another rape?"

The admiral shook his head, no. His pipe had gone out. He relighted it as he said, "About forty-five minutes past midnight, only about an hour and a quarter after Mrs. Massie left that nightclub, an automobile with four or five dark-skinned youths bumped bumpers with a car driven by a white man and his *kanaka* wife."

"*Kanaka?*" I asked.

"Hawaiian," the admiral said, waving out his kitchen match. "Interracial couples are, unfortunately, all too common here. At any rate, one of the dark men got out of the car, saying, 'Let me at that damn white man!' But the woman, apparently a husky Island gal, jumped out and confronted the bully. Smacked him a few times, and he scurried away, and he and the other cowards drove off. But the woman got their license number and reported the collision at once to the police. By three o'clock that morning, the five hoodlums who'd been the occupants of that car were rounded up and placed under arrest."

"Sounds like pretty good police work to me," I said.

"There are a number of competent officers on the force," the admiral admitted. "Perhaps you've heard of Chang Apana— he's something of a local celebrity. The fictional Chinese detective Charlie Chan was based on him."

"Really," I said. I'd read several Chan serials in *The Saturday Evening Post*; and there was a pretty good talkie with Warner Oland, the title of which escaped me, which I'd seen last year, at the Oriental. Appropriately enough.

"Unfortunately, Chang Apana is approaching retirement age," the admiral said, "and his involvement in the Massie case was minimal. But could even *his* judgment be less than suspect?"

I couldn't hold back a smile. "You mean, even Charlie Chan can't be trusted?"

The admiral lifted an eyebrow. "He's Chinese. His sympathies might well be with the colored defendants. And the vast majority of policemen are Hawaiian, or have Hawaiian blood—there's a longstanding patronage system giving such individuals an inside track on police jobs."

If I was supposed to get indignant about police patronage, the admiral was telling the wrong boy: how did he think I got my job on the Chicago PD?

"The Honolulu police department," the admiral was saying, "is divided against itself in the Massie matter. During the six long weeks it took Mrs. Massie to recover to the point where she could undergo the rigors of a trial, many officers were said to be making reports to the *defense* attorneys, instead of the DA's office!"

Darrow gave me a sideways glance that all but said, *Where can I find some coppers like that back home?*

"And," continued the admiral, "those hoodlums had the best legal minds in the Territory—William Heen, a Territorial senator and former circuit judge, and William Pittman, brother of U.S. Senator Kay Pittman."

I asked, "How could a bunch of kid gangsters afford top talent like that?"

The admiral sighed. "Two of the five culprits were of pure Hawaiian blood, so it was no surprise the acknowledged head of their race, Princess Abby Kawananakoa, gave them financial support. After all, her own son is a hoodlum beach boy, in Oahu Prison on a second-degree murder charge."

"So a defense fund was raised?" Darrow asked.

"Yes. And, keep in mind, both Hawaiian defendants were professional athletes, and local gate-receipt attractions. Managers of sporting contests helped finance the defense as well."

"Two of the assailants were *sports* heroes?" I asked. "But you've been saying they were hoodlums . . ."

"They are," the admiral said crisply, teeth tight around the stem of his pipe. "Ben Ahakuelo is a popular local boxer—he also was convicted with his crony Chang on an attempted rape charge in 1929. . . . Governor Judd paroled him so he could represent the Territory at the National Amateur Boxing Championship at Madison Square Garden last year. The late Joseph Kahahawai was a football star—*and* a convicted felon . . . he did thirty days on a first-degree robbery charge in 1930."

"What about the other two boys?" Darrow asked.

"They had no criminal records," the admiral said with a shrug, "but they were known as bad characters by the police, with no visible means of support. And all five were soon out on bail, thanks to Princess Abby and the defense fund. Ahakuelo and Kahahawai continued playing football each Sunday, their names emblazoned in headlines on the sports pages of our Honolulu papers. . . ." He sighed, shook his head. "In spite of the discipline I maintain on this base, I half-expected to find those savages swinging by the neck from trees up Nuuana Valley or at the Pali."

"And of course," Darrow said gravely, "one of the defendants *was* seized and beaten by Navy men. . . ."

The admiral nodded matter-of-factly. "Yes. Horace Ida, severely so, and I believe that the discipline our men were under prevented more drastic action being taken upon him. They were trying to obtain a confession . . ."

Darrow asked, "Did they succeed?"

"Rumor is, yes . . . but the duress involved would negate it. By the way, I allowed Ida to be brought around, to have a look at the sailors on liberty that night, and he was able to make no identification."

Not surprising. You know what they say—all white boys look alike.

The admiral continued, "And this wasn't the only clash between Navy men and the hoodlum element. . . ."

"How badly did things get out of hand?" Leisure asked.

"Well, to give security to the isolated naval people in Manoa Valley and the other suburbs, I established more foot patrols of sailors, and established Navy radio cars in districts where Navy families lived."

"Why weren't the cops doing that?" I asked.

"All I can tell you is that this was done at the request of the mayor and the sheriff. And the pressure I've brought to bear has resulted in a major shake-up of the force, finally . . . a new chief of police, practically the entire department put on a year's probation."

"How did you manage that?" I asked, impressed.

The admiral's smile was tiny but bespoke large smugness. "There is certain . . . leverage the Navy has been able to apply."

"What kind of leverage?" Darrow wondered.

The admiral's eyes damn near twinkled. "We have, from time to time during this unfortunate affair, cancelled shore leave. When the fleet is in, gentlemen, income for many businesses in Honolulu is up. By withholding that from the community, well . . . you can imagine the results."

"You obviously tried to exert a positive influence on this case from the beginning," Darrow said. Even I couldn't detect the sarcasm.

The admiral's pouchy eyes tightened. "This degenerate sex criminal Kahahawai would be alive today, if Governor Judd and the attorney general had listened to me."

Darrow frowned thoughtfully. "How so?"

"After the trial ended in a hung jury, I suggested they keep those rapists locked up, until a second trial could be held. But they insisted it was *illegal* to raise bail above what an individual could pay. It would violate their civil rights, don't you know. You see, by accident of birth, these creatures are technically 'Americans'. . . . Well—I suppose you gentlemen are anxious to meet with your clients."

"With your kind permission," Darrow said, rising. "By the way, Admiral—how did you manage to keep our clients under your benign influence?"

"You mean, why aren't they in jail?" He allowed himself a broader smile. "Cristy, the trial judge, had no stomach for the responsibility of what might happen to Mrs. Fortescue and the others, what with threats of terrorism and mob violence. I suggested the judge swear one of my officers in as a special officer of the civil court, to supervise their confinement aboard the

Alton. And I promised to produce the defendants wherever and whenever the Territory might need them."

"Nicely handled," Darrow said, meaning it.

The admiral was standing now, but he stayed back behind his desk. "You know, Mr. Darrow, in the trial against those hoodlum rapists, the jury deliberated for ninety-seven hours. . . . Deadlocked at seven for not guilty, five for guilty. The *exact* proportion of yellow and brown to white members of the jury. You will undoubtedly face a polyglot jury in this case, as well. . . ."

"There will be no hung jury in this trial," Darrow predicted.

"You're up against Prosecutor John C. Kelley—he's a young firebrand. He'll attack ferociously . . ."

"And I'll counterattack with an olive branch," Darrow said. "I'm here to heal the breach that's opened between the races in these garden islands, sir. Not to gouge open that gaping wound further."

And we left the admiral to ponder Darrow's words.

Six

Our limo driver remained our chaperon as we were led to that obsolete, decommissioned, rundown old cruiser sitting high and dry on a mudflat in Pearl Harbor, the U.S.S. *Alton*. The driver turned us over to the two armed Marine sentries at the mouth of the seventy-five-foot gangplank that separated the ship and the shore. One of the sentries escorted us aboard, leading the way as we danced across to the rickety wooden gangplank's tune.

Above this screaky melody, Leisure managed to be heard, whispering to Darrow, "The admiral gives quite a ringing endorsement of lynch law, wouldn't you say?"

But if racial champion Darrow was expected to provide a biting condemnation of Stirling (now that our host was absent), he disappointed. Well, he disappointed Leisure. I knew C.D. well enough to have predicted he'd say something like: "Admiral Stirling is a Navy man, and a Southerner, and his statements are naturally prejudiced."

Which is exactly what he said.

Our Marine escort led us to the top deck. "The *Alton*'s used as a general mess hall," he said over the echo of our feet on metal, "and Officers' Club."

He led us into a wardroom, in the stern of the ship, saying,

"Mrs. Fortescue and Lt. Massie are staying in the captain's cabin, just through here."

We were moving past a large mess table where a number of officers watched us with curiosity, several obviously recognizing Darrow as he shambled by. The interior of the ship, at least judging by this mess hall, was nothing like its sorry exterior: the walls were mahogany paneled, with framed oil paintings of admirals, display cases of trophies, and shining silver ornamentation.

Darrow asked, "The captain was so kind as to vacate his quarters for my clients?"

"No, sir—Captain Wortman lives in Honolulu with his wife. This stateroom is usually reserved for visiting admirals."

Or very special guests, like defendants in murder trials.

Our escort knocked at the door, saying, "Mrs. Fortescue? Your guests are here."

"Show them in," a cultured, Southern, feminine voice responded.

The Marine opened the door and Darrow stepped in first, followed by Leisure and myself. The door clanged shut behind us, as if a reminder we'd entered a jail cell of sorts; but what a hell of a jail cell this was.

Mahogany paneled, spacious, with a big round mahogany table at the center of the room, this might have been a first-class cabin on the *Malolo*—dark attractive furnishings including wardrobe, chest of drawers, a single bed. Here and there, colorful Hawaiian flowers in vases and bowls gave a woman's touch to these resolutely male quarters.

And greeting us like an elegant hostess was Mrs. Grace (née Granville) Fortescue, her hand extended to Darrow as if she expected him to kiss it.

So he did.

"What a pleasure and honor it is to meet you, Mr. Darrow," she said.

Her Southern accent was as refined as she was: tall, slim, Grace Fortescue might have been hostessing a tea in her cherry-colored suit and jaunty matching hat, pearls looped around her rather long, slender, somewhat crêped neck, single matching pearls dangling from her earlobes. Her dark blond hair (the same color as Thalia's) was cut short, in a youthful, stylish bob, and she might have been as young as forty, or as old as (approaching) sixty—it was hard to say; but she was definitely at that age where a woman is no longer pretty but handsome, and despite her bright eyes (the same light blue as Isabel's), there was no discounting a certain drawn, weary look to these finely carved features. There were lines in this haughty face etched by recent events.

Darrow introduced Leisure, and Mrs. Fortescue warmly offered him her hand—although he merely clasped it, not kissed it—and then Darrow turned to me and said, "And this is the young man we discussed, on the telephone."

"The young detective Evalyn recommended!" she said with a lovely smile.

"Nathan Heller," Darrow said, nodding, as I took the hand Mrs. Fortescue offered. I didn't kiss it either.

"Evalyn?" I asked, thoroughly confused.

"Evalyn Walsh McLean," she explained. "She's one of my dearest friends. In fact, if I may be frank . . ."

"You're definitely among friends, Mrs. Fortescue," Darrow intoned with a smile.

". . . Mrs. McLean is helping finance my defense. Without Evalyn's help—and Eva Stotesbury's—I honestly don't know where I'd be."

"You didn't tell me . . ." I began to Darrow.

Darrow shrugged. "Didn't seem pertinent."

Here I'd thought the idea to use me on this case had been purely C.D.'s. In Washington, D.C., recently, I'd encountered Evalyn McLean—whose (estranged) husband owned the *Washington Post*, and who herself owned the Hope Diamond; Evalyn had been involved by a scam artist—knowing of her sympathy for Colonel Lindbergh (Evalyn having lost a child by tragedy herself)—in one of the numerous dead-end ransom schemes that plagued that case.

Evalyn was a very attractive older woman, and we'd hit it off famously. So famously, it had apparently gotten around. . . .

"Evalyn suggested I inquire of Mr. Darrow if he was

acquainted with you," Mrs. Fortescue said, "seeing as how you're both Chicagoans and in a criminal line of work."

That was the best description of the common ground between lawyers and cops I'd ever heard: a criminal line of work.

"And imagine my surprise and delight," she continued, "when Mr. Darrow said he'd known you since you were a lad."

I wasn't sure I'd ever been a "lad," and I just kind of gave her a glazed smile. One thing about working with Clarence Darrow: the surprises just kept coming.

"Tommie is resting," she said, gesturing to a closed door. "Should I wake him?"

"I don't think that will be necessary," Darrow said, "just yet."

"Please sit down," she said. "Would you gentlemen like some coffee, or perhaps tea?"

We settled on coffee, and she went to the door and called out, "Oh, steward!"

A mess hall sailor approached her and she asked him to fetch four cups of coffee with sugar and cream. He responded with a nod, and she shut the door. We all half-stood as she took her place at the round table.

"Now, Mrs. Fortescue," Darrow began, getting his shipwreck of a self settled in his chair, "my associate, young Mr. Heller here, is going to take some notes. He's not a stenographer, mind you—just some informal jotting down of this and that, to back up this feeble old memory. No objection?"

She beamed at me, fluttering her lashes. "That would be just fine."

I wondered how much her friend Mrs. Walsh had told her about me.

"And just how are you bearing up, Mrs. Fortescue?" Darrow asked gently.

"Now that the worst is over," she said, "I feel more at ease than I have in months. My mind is at peace. I'm satisfied."

"Satisfied?" Leisure asked.

"Satisfied," she said stiffly, sitting the same way, "that in our efforts to obtain a confession from that brute, we weren't breaking the law, but attempting to aid it. I've slept better since the day of the murder than I have for a long time."

A frown had tightened Darrow's face on the word "murder," but now he affected a benign, almost saintly smile as he patted her hand. "We'll not be using that word 'murder,' Mrs. Fortescue. Not amongst ourselves, and certainly not to anyone with the press."

"You must have read that interview in the *New York Times*," she said, putting a hand to her chest, her expression mildly distressed. "I'm afraid I *was* indiscreet."

His smile was lenient, but his eyes firm. "You were. I don't mean that unkindly . . . but you were. No more talk of 'murder.' Or of your only regret being that you 'bungled the job.' "

"That did look . . . clumsy in print, didn't it?" she asked, but it was an admission, not a question.

"Are you really sleeping better now?" I asked her. "Pardon me for saying so, ma'am, but I would think the stress of this situation would have to take its toll."

She raised her chin, nobly. "It's much better with everything all out in the open. They suppressed my daughter's name, in the first case, but that only made it worse. Rumors ran rampant. People would stare at her poor bruised cheek, and whisper and wonder." Her face tightened, pinched; suddenly she looked sixty. "Lying gossip, filthy stories—a campaign calculated to drive my child out of Honolulu, or short of that, defame her character, and prejudice jurors if she dared to prosecute a second time. Not long before the . . . what *shall* I call the murder, Mr. Darrow?"

This time his smile was a twitch. "Let's use the word 'incident,' shall we?"

She nodded. "Not long before the . . . incident . . . a few days, I think . . . I went to Judge Steadman—he'd been very kind to us, during the trial. I told him I feared for my daughter's life. Not only were those five rapists running wild and free, this escaped criminal Lyman was reported to be in Moana Valley."

"Who?" Darrow asked.

"Daniel Lyman," Leisure said. "A murderer and rapist who walked out of Oahu Prison with a burglar pal of his on a New Year's Eve pass. They've since ravished two more women, one of them white, and committed numerous robberies. The partner was captured but Lyman's still at large. It's been a major embarrassment to the Honolulu police."

"But a boon to Admiral Stirling," I said, "in his efforts to shake out the department."

Darrow nodded, as if he knew what we were talking about. To Leisure he posed: "Was this in the materials Lt. Johnson provided us, before we boarded the *Malolo*?"

Leisure nodded.

I turned to our client. "Mrs. Fortescue, were you afraid this Lyman might attack your daughter . . . ?"

"No," she said, with a bitter little smile, "but he would have made a convenient scapegoat, had she been found dead, would he not? And without Thalia, there is no case against those five defendants." She frowned to herself. "Four defendants, now."

Darrow leaned forward, brow furrowed. "Tell me—how did your son-in-law hold up under all of this pressure?"

She glanced toward the closed door behind which Lt. Massie napped. She lowered her voice to a whisper and said, melodramatically: "As much as I feared for Thalia's life, I feared for Tommie's sanity."

Darrow arched an eyebrow. "His sanity, dear?"

"I feared he couldn't withstand the strain—he'd become sullen, he wasn't sleeping or eating well, he became uncharacteristically withdrawn. . . ."

A knock at the door interrupted, and Mrs. Fortescue imperiously called, "Come!" and a galley gob came in with a silver tray bearing cups of coffee, a creamer, and a bowl of cube sugar.

As the sailor served us, I sat studying this proud, rather dignified society matron and tried to picture her masterminding the kidnapping of a brutal Hawaiian rapist. I could picture her serving *hors d'oeuvres*; I could picture her playing bridge. I could even picture her, just barely, inside that dusty bungalow on Kolowalu Street.

But picture her party to guns and blood and naked dead natives in bathtubs? I couldn't form the image.

"You had no intention of taking a life," Darrow said ever so gently, "did you, dear?"

"Absolutely not," she said, and sipped her coffee, pinkie poised genteelly. "My upbringing is Southern, but I assure you, I am no believer in lynch law. I cannot state that too emphatically. My upbringing, my family traditions, early religious training, make the taking of another's life repugnant to me. Like you, sir, I am opposed to capital punishment."

Darrow was nodding, smiling. He liked the sound of this. I didn't know if he bought any of it, but he liked the sound.

"Then exactly how did this happen?" I asked.

"Incrementally," she said. "As you probably know, after the first trial ended in a hung jury, the five defendants were required to report to the Judiciary Building every morning. I think it may have been Judge Steadman's hope that they would violate his edict, and he could issue orders for their imprisonment . . . but they were reporting regularly."

"Who told you this?" I asked.

"Judge Steadman himself. I was also friendly with the clerk of the court, Mrs. Whitmore. She was the one, I'm afraid, who planted the seed."

"The seed?" Leisure asked.

"Mrs. Whitmore's the one who told me the second trial was being delayed indefinitely. The district attorney's office was afraid of another hung jury—and after another mistrial, the accused could not be tried again—those beasts would go free! The prosecution, Mrs. Whitmore said, had made such a mess of things in the first trial, it was going to be impossible to bring about a conviction unless one of the defendants confessed."

"So you decided," I said, "to get a confession yourself."

She gestured with a flowing hand, as if she were explaining why it had been necessary to postpone this afternoon's flute recital, and substitute a string quartet.

"I had no sudden inspiration, Mr. Heller," she said. "The notion emerged gradually, like a ship from the fog. I asked Mrs. Whitmore if the five men were still reporting to the courthouse, and she said they were. She mentioned that the big Hawaiian reported every morning."

"By 'the big Hawaiian,' " Leisure said, "she meant Joseph Kahahawai?"

Mrs. Fortescue nodded, once. "I lay awake that night thinking about what the clerk of court had said."

"And the ship," I said, "emerged from the fog."

"With remarkable clarity," she said. "The next day I went around to see Mrs. Whitmore again. I told her I'd heard a rumor that two of the accused rapists had been arrested, over at Hilo, for stealing a motor. She said she doubted that, but checked with the probation officer, a Mr. Dickson, who came out and spoke to me, assuring me that Kahahawai had just been in that morning. I asked, don't they all come in together? And he told me, no, one at a time, and at specific hours—he couldn't have them dropping in on him at just any old odd time."

"So you established the basic time that Kahahawai reported in to his probation officer," I said.

"Yes. Then I went to the office of the *Star-Bulletin* to get copies of newspapers with Kahahawai's picture. I began studying his features in a clipping I carried with me. That evening, I spoke with Tommie about my idea. He admitted to me he'd had similar notions. And he'd heard a rumor that Kahahawai had confessed the rape to his stepfather! I suggested perhaps we might inveigle the brute into a car on some false pretense, whisk him to my home, and frighten him into confessing."

"And what," Darrow asked, "was Tommie's reaction?"

"At first he was enthusiastic—he'd spoken to Major Ross of this newly formed Territorial Police, and to several others, who gave him the same impression I had gotten—that without a confession, there would be no second trial, certainly no conviction. But then he wavered—how, he wondered, might we manage to get the native into our car? I wasn't sure myself, quite frankly—but I said, 'Can't we display at least as much cunning as these Orientals?' And then I remembered Seaman Jones."

"Jones?" Darrow asked.

"One of the two enlisted men we're defending," Leisure prompted.

"Ah yes. Please continue, Mrs. Fortescue."

"In December, this young enlisted man, Jones, had been assigned to act as a sort of bodyguard to Thalia, my daughter Helene, and myself, while Tommie was away on sea duty. When

Tommie returned, young Jones remained in the neighborhood as one of the armed sentries who patrolled Manoa Valley."

Part of Admiral Stirling's efforts to protect Navy personnel and their families against the "hoodlum element" roaming suburban streets.

"Jones became friendly with your family?" I asked.

"Oh yes. When he was guarding us, he'd often provide a fourth for bridge; when he was patrolling, he'd stop in for coffee. Occasionally we'd provide a couch or a chair for him to take a nap. Such a sweet, colorful boy with his tales of adventures in the Far East."

"So you enlisted his aid in your plan?" I asked.

"I merely reminded Tommie," she continued, "that Jones had often said he wanted to help us, in any way. I knew we could trust this boy. I suggested to Tommie that he confide in Jones, seek his ideas, his assistance."

"Go on, Mrs. Fortescue," Darrow said kindly.

"Well, the next morning I continued exploring the lay of the land, as it were. I parked in front of the Judiciary Building on King Street, at eight o'clock, and watched the hands of the clock creep to ten. I would open my purse, to peek in at the clipping of Kahahawai I had pinned, there. I wanted to make sure I would recognize him. Much as it disgusted me, I sat studying that brutal, repulsive black face. But at ten-thirty, there had been no sign of him, and I was forced to leave."

"How so?" Darrow wondered.

She shrugged. "I was expecting guests for a little luncheon party."

Darrow, Leisure, and I exchanged glances.

"My little Japanese maid wasn't up to making the preparations all by her lonesome, so I gave up my vigil, for the moment, and—"

"Excuse me." The voice was male—soft, Southern, unassuming.

We turned our attention to the doorway to the adjacent cabin, where Lt. Thomas Massie stood in shirtsleeves, hands in the pockets of his blue civilian trousers in a pose that should have seemed casual but only looked awkward.

Short, slender, dark-haired, Massie might normally have seemed boyishly handsome, but his oval face—with its high forehead, long sharp nose, and pointed chin—showed signs of strain. His tiny eyes were dark-circled, his complexion prisoner pallid, his cheeks sunken. And his mouth was a thin tight line.

He was twenty-seven years old and looked easily ten years older.

We rose and he came over to us, introduced himself, and Darrow made our introductions; we shook hands. Massie's grip was firm, but his hand was small, like a child's.

He took a seat at the table. "I am embarrassed," he said, "sleepin' through my first meetin' with my counsel."

Darrow said, "I instructed Mrs. Fortescue not to wake you, Lieutenant."

"Tommie. Please call me Tommie. Just because we're Navy doesn't mean we have to stand on ceremony."

"That's good to hear," Darrow said, "because we need, all of us, to be friends. To trust each other, confide in one another. And, Tommie, I let you sleep because I thought it best to hear Mrs. Fortescue's version of this incident."

"Judgin' by what I overheard," Tommie said, "you're pretty well into it."

"We're up to the afternoon before," I said.

"That was when I brought Jones and Lord around to the house on Kolowalu Street." Massie's speech was an odd mixture of clipped and casual, his staccato delivery at odds with his Southern inflection.

"Lord is the other enlisted man?" Darrow asked Leisure, and Leisure nodded.

"Out at the base that mornin', while Mrs. Fortescue was stakin' out the courthouse," Massie said, "I called Jones over . . . he's a machinist's mate, we were involved in athletics on the base—I used to be a runner, and I offered my services helpin' him train the baseball team? Anyway, I called Jones over and said I'd heard Kahahawai was ready to crack. And Jones said, 'But he just needs a little help, right?' Kinda winked at me as he said it. I said that was so; was he willin' to help? He thought it over for a second, then he said, 'I sure as hell am.' If you'll excuse the language, Mrs. Fortescue, that is what he said."

Mrs. Fortescue nodded regally, her smile benign.

"I asked Jones if he knew of anyone else who might help, somebody we could count on. And he said, 'Yeah, let's go up to the gym' . . . that was on the third floor of the barracks? 'Let's go up to the gym, I'll introduce you to Eddie Lord. He's all right. If you think he's all right, too, well, hell—we'll bring 'im along!' Sorry about the language."

"I'm the wife of a military man, Tommie," Mrs. Fortescue said with a ladylike laugh. "I'm not easily shocked."

"Lord was in the ring," Massie continued, "sparrin' with another gob. A strappin' specimen for a lightweight; you could see right away he could handle himself. Lord—that's Fireman First Class Edward Lord? Jones called him over, and we chatted a little bit. He seemed like a regular guy."

"Did you fill Lord in, on the spot?" I asked.

"No. I talked to Jones first, said, 'Can he be trusted?' And Jones said, 'Eddie and me was shipmates for five years.' That was all I needed to know. Jones said he'd fill Lord in, and we arranged to meet at Mrs. Fortescue's, no earlier than three."

"After my luncheon," Mrs. Fortescue explained.

"We stopped in town, at the YMCA," Massie said, "and changed into civilian clothes. Then we drove to Kolowalu Street, where we introduced Mrs. Fortescue to Eddie Lord, and she told us of this idea she had to use a false warrant from Major Ross, to lure Kahahawai into the car."

"My little Japanese maid was still in the kitchen," Mrs. Fortescue said, "so I paid her her weekly wages a day early, and gave her the next day off. And then I suggested to Tommie and his boys that we drive down to the courthouse."

"To case the joint," Massie said, with a wry little smile. It would have seemed flippant if his eyes hadn't been so haunted.

"That night," Mrs. Fortescue said, "I sent my daughter Helene to Thalia's, to spend the night, and we reviewed our plans, the four of us. Kahahawai would be brought to my house. We would get a confession from him. We would make him sign it, and take it to the police."

"What if the police dismissed the confession as coerced?" I asked. "Nothing came of it when those Navy boys grabbed Horace Ida."

"Then we'd take it to the newspapers," Massie said. "They'd surely print it, and at least that way these damned rumors about my wife's honor would be put to rest."

"Who rented the blue Buick?" Leisure asked.

"Jones and Lord," Massie said. "I went on home, and they returned to Mrs. Fortescue's, where they slept in the livin' room, on the couch, on the floor. So we'd be ready to go, bright and early."

"And the two guns?" Leisure asked.

"The .45 was mine," Massie said. "The .32 Colt was Lord's . . . it's missing. I don't know what became of it."

Kahahawai had been killed with a .32.

I asked, "You prepared the fake summons, Mrs. Fortescue?"

She gestured gracefully again. "Yes, and I would have preferred to use a typewriter on the warrant, but the machine was at Thalia's. So I hand-printed it—'Territorial Police, Major Ross Commanding, Summons to Appear—Kahahawai, Joe' . . . putting his last name first made it seem more official. Tommie provided a gold seal from a diploma of his . . ."

"Chemical warfare," Massie said, "at Edgewood Arsenal in Maryland. The diploma wasn't of any use to me, so I just snipped off the gold seal and Mrs. Fortescue glued it on the paper."

Mrs. Fortescue sipped her coffee, then said thoughtfully, "But the piece of paper still looked . . . insufficient somehow. Lying on my desk was that morning's paper . . . I spied a paragraph that seemed about the right size, clipped it, and pasted it on the warrant. It looked better."

Leisure asked, "Were you aware of the implicit irony in the words of that clipping?"

"No," she said with a faint smile. "It was an accident of fate, the philosophical nature of that paragraph . . . but those words have been so widely quoted, I can reel them off to you now, if you like: 'Life is a mysterious and exciting affair and anything can be a thrill if you know how to look for it, and what to do with opportunity when it comes.' "

Darrow, Leisure and I exchanged glances again.

"The next mornin'," Massie said with a grim smile, "we all had a laugh over it, at breakfast."

Leisure asked, "You ate breakfast before you went out on your . . . mission?"

"I cooked up some eggs for the sailors," Mrs. Fortescue said, "but they didn't seem to have any appetite. All they wanted was coffee. I suggested we leave, so we'd be at the courthouse by eight o'clock."

"We were wearing civilian clothes," Massie explained, "and I had a chauffeur's cap and dark glasses on, as a disguise. I gave Lord the .45—he was going to watch the back entrance—and he and Jones and I got in the rented Buick and drove to the courthouse. Mrs. Fortescue followed in her roadster."

"I parked in front of the courthouse," she said. "Why not? I had nothing to conceal. Tommie parked in front of the post office, nearby; the two sailors got out, Tommie staying behind the wheel of the parked sedan. I left my car and gave Jones the picture of the native I'd cut from the paper; he already had the sham summons. Jones went to the main entrance, to await our man, and I returned to my car. Mrs. Whitmore noticed me and stopped and we had a friendly little chat."

"Perhaps a minute after Mrs. Whitmore went inside," Massie said, picking it up, "we saw two natives crossin' the courthouse grounds. One of them was a little guy, but the other one was big, heavy—Kahahawai, wearin' a blue shirt and a brown cap. I pulled up the sedan alongside the curb just as Lord was approachin' the two natives. He showed Kahahawai the summons, and Kahahawai wanted the other fella to come along, but Jones grabs him and says, 'Just you,' and shoves Kahahawai in back of the car. Jones got in after him and we headed out King Street, toward Waikiki."

"I saw Lord coming around the side of the courthouse," Mrs. Fortescue said. "The sedan was already out of sight when I picked him up and . . ."

"Excuse me for interrupting," Darrow said. "But I need to back things up a tad, to ask Tommie here a few pertinent questions."

Why was Darrow cutting in, just when it was getting good? Just when we were about to find out what had happened behind the closed doors of the house on Kolowalu Street that resulted in Joseph Kahahawai's demise, courtesy of a .32 slug under the left nipple?

"Your mother-in-law indicates," Darrow was saying to Massie, "that you suffered a mental strain due not only to the heinous crime committed upon your sweet wife, but to these foul rumors flying about."

Massie didn't understand this interruption, either. There was confusion in his voice as he said, "Yes, sir."

"Did you seek any medical help? For your restlessness, your insomnia . . ."

"I talked to several doctors, who seemed concerned about my physical state."

"And your mental state?"

"Well, I was advised by Dr. Porter to take Thalia and leave the islands, for both our sakes . . . but I was adamant that my wife's honor be cleared, and that flight from this island would be seen as an admission that these slanders were of substance. . . ."

Darrow, behind a tent of his hands, was nodding, eyes narrowed.

"If I might continue," Massie said, clearly wanting to get on with his story and get it out of the way, "we arrived at the house on Kolowalu Street and—"

"Details, at this point, won't be necessary," Darrow said, with a wave of the hand.

I looked at Leisure and he looked back at me; I wonder which of us had the more startled expression.

"Why bother, right now, with the sordid particulars—I think we all know what happened within that house," Darrow said. "I think it's obvious whose hand held the weapon that took Joseph Kahahawai's life."

"It is?" Massie said, with a puzzled frown.

"Well, it can't be this lovely lady," Darrow said with a gracious gesture. "She is too refined, too dignified, too much a picture of motherhood touched by tragedy. And it could not have been either of those two sailor boys, because after all, that would be murder, plain and simple, wouldn't it?"

"It would?" Massie asked.

"It most certainly would. We're very fortunate that neither of them pulled the trigger, because you, as an officer, enlisting their aid, well, that would amount to incitement."

Mrs. Fortescue wasn't following any of this. Massie, however, had turned even paler. Whiter than milk, though not nearly so healthy.

Darrow was smiling, but it was a smile that frowned. "Only one person could possibly have pulled that trigger—the man with the motive, the man whose wife's good name had been defiled even as had she herself been so woefully defiled."

Massie squinted. "What . . . what do you think happened in that house?"

"What I would imagine happened," Darrow said, "was that Joseph Kahahawai, confronted by the righteousness of the man he had wronged, blurted a confession, and in so doing, sparked an inevitable reaction from that righteous wronged man, in fact provoked an insane act . . ."

"You're not suggesting I construct a story . . ." Massie began.

Darrow's eyes flared. "Certainly not! If you don't remember shooting Kahahawai, in fact if everything is a sort of haze, that would only make sense, under these circumstances."

Darrow clapped his hands together, and we all jumped a little.

"Well, now," he said, "I certainly don't mean to put words in your mouth. . . . Why don't we come back to the events within that house, at a later date . . . tomorrow, let's say, after you've had a chance to collect your thoughts . . . and perhaps speak with Mrs. Fortescue, and your two sailor friends, and compare your recollections—not to come up with a unified story, of course, but rather to see if, among you, your collective memory might be jogged."

Massie was nodding. Mrs. Fortescue was quietly smiling; she got it—now, she got it.

"Now," Darrow said, rising, "let's go meet those sailor boys, shall we? Let's just get acquainted. I don't think I'll want to question them about the incident . . . not just yet. Then perhaps we can have a bite of late lunch in the mess hall, Mrs. Fortescue, and if you're up to it, you can relate your adventures with the police."

Those "adventures," of course, had to do with the attempt the conspirators had made to dump Kahahawai's sheet-wrapped naked body; they'd been caught by the cops with the corpse in the backseat of the rental Buick on the way to Hanauma Bay.

It seemed the other native, the "little guy" who'd been walking across the Judiciary Building grounds with Joe Kahahawai when the fake summons was served, was Joe's cousin Edward Ulii, who had been suspicious about Joe getting shoved into that Buick, and immediately reported it as a possible abduction. When a radio car spotted the Buick speeding toward Koko Head, shades drawn, Mrs. Fortescue's jig was up.

"I'd be delighted, Mr. Darrow," Mrs. Fortescue said.

And soon we were walking along the old gun deck of the cruiser, past empty weapon ports; up ahead Darrow was walking along with his arm around Mrs. Fortescue, Massie following like a puppy.

"This may be the most straightforward case of felony murder I ever encountered," Leisure whispered to me. "Premeditation all the way . . ."

I let out a short laugh. "Why do you think C.D. pulled that temporary insanity rabbit out of his hat?"

"I have to admit I was shocked," Leisure said, shaking his head. "He stopped just short of suborning perjury. I've never witnessed a more blatant display of questionable ethics in my career."

"Come to Chicago," I advised. "We got plenty more where that came from."

"You're not offended?"

"Hardly." I nodded up toward Massie and his mother-in-law as they walked with Darrow. "Do you think those two misguided souls deserve life in prison?"

"They probably deserve a good thrashing, but . . . no."

"Neither does C.D. He's just doing what it takes to give them the best goddamn defense he can muster."

We followed echoing laughter to where Jones and Lord were playing a spirited round of Ping-Pong in a room that could have handled ten times as many cots as the two unmade ones on its either side. No guard was watching them. Both were short, muscular, good-looking gobs in their early twenties.

Jones was a wiry wiseguy with his brown hair slicked back on a square head, and Lord a curly-headed Dick Powell type with a massive build for a little guy. Seeing us enter, they stopped their game and doffed their seamen's hats.

Mrs. Fortescue rather grandly said, "Allow me to introduce Mr. Clarence Darrow."

There were handshakes all around, and Darrow made our introductions as well, and informed the sailors he wasn't here to talk in depth about the case just yet, merely to say hello.

"Boy, are we glad to see you," Jones said. "I feel sorry for the other side!"

"It's an honor meeting you, sir," Lord said.

"Show them your memory book!" Mrs. Fortescue urged Jones.

"Sure thing, missus!" Jones said, and dragged out a thick scrapbook from under one of the unmade cots. "I just pasted in some more today."

Lord and Massie were off to one side of the room, lighting up cigarettes, chatting, laughing, kidding each other. I found a chair to sit on while Leisure leaned against a bulkhead, silently shaking his head.

And Clarence Darrow was sitting on the edge of the cot next to the grinning Jones, who turned the pages of the scrapbook, already overflowing with clippings, while Mrs. Fortescue stood with hands fig-leafed before her, watching with delight as her savior and one of her servants conferred.

"I ain't never got my name in the papers before," the proud sailor said.

I wondered if sports star Joe Kahahawai had kept a scrapbook, too; he'd made the papers lots of times. Mostly the sports page. He'd make it again, in the coming weeks.

Then it was pretty likely to taper off.

SEVEN

You might have found the Alexander Young Hotel—a massive block-long brownstone with two six-story wings bookending a long, four-story midsection—in downtown Milwaukee or maybe Cleveland. Like so many buildings built around the turn of the century, it straddled eras—stubbornly unembellished, neither modern nor old-fashioned, the Young was a commercial hotel whose only concession to being located in paradise was a few potted palm plants and occasional half-hearted vases of colorful flowers in an otherwise no-nonsense lobby.

The reporters were waiting when we arrived midafternoon, and they swarmed us in a pack as we moved steadily toward the elevators in the company of the hotel manager. The mustached little man had met us at the curb not only to greet us, but to let C.D. and Leisure know the numbers of the suites where they would find their wives.

"I've spoken to my clients," Darrow said to the reporters as we moved along, "and have heard enough to decide upon my line of defense. And that's all I have to say about the subject at present."

The overlapping requests for further clarification were pretty much unintelligible, but the words "unwritten law" were in there a good deal.

Darrow stopped suddenly, and the reporters tumbled into each other, like an auto pileup.

"I'm down here to defend four people," he said, "who have been accused of a crime that I do not think is a crime."

Then he pressed on, while the reporters—stalled momentarily by that cryptic comment—lagged behind as the old boy deftly stepped onto a waiting elevator. And Leisure and I were right there with him, while the hotel manager stayed out, holding back the press like a traffic cop.

One newshound yelled, "The Hawaiian legislature must agree with you—they've just made rape a capital offense."

"And isn't that a magnificent piece of lawmaking," Darrow said bitterly. "Now a man committing a rape knows he'll receive the same punishment if he goes ahead and kills his victim, too. He might as well go all the way, and get rid of the evidence!"

The elevator operator swung the door shut, and the cage began to rise.

Slumped next to me, Darrow shook his big head, the comma of gray hair flopping on his forehead. "That goddamn Lindbergh case," he muttered.

"What about the Lindbergh case, C.D.?" I asked. I'd spent enough time on that crime to have a sort of proprietary attitude.

"It got this wave of blood thirst going among the populace. Whoever snatched that poor infant opened the door for capital punishment for kidnappers ... and how many kidnap victims are going to die because of that?"

Ruby Darrow met us at the door of the suite; her smile of greeting turned immediately to one of concern.

"Clarence, you look terribly tired ... you simply must get some rest."

But Darrow would hear none of it. He invited us into the outer sitting area of the suite, where again the Hawaiian influence was nil: dark furnishings, oriental rug, pale walls with wooden trim. We might have been in a suite at the Congress on Michigan Avenue, though the seductive breeze drifting in the open windows indicated we weren't.

"These were waiting at the desk for you," Ruby said testily, and handed him several envelopes.

He sorted through them, as if this were his morning mail at home, tossed them on a small table by the door. Then he removed his baggy suit coat and flung it over a chair; Leisure and I took his lead and removed our suit coats, but draped them more carefully over a coffee table by a comfortable-looking sofa whose floral pattern was the only vaguely Island touch in the suite.

C.D. settled into an easy chair, put his feet up on a settee, and began making a cigarette. Leisure and I took the couch as a clearly distressed Ruby, shaking her head, disappeared off into the bedroom, shutting the door behind her, not slamming it, exactly.

"Ruby thinks I'm going to die someday," Darrow said. "I may just fool her. George, you've been remarkably silent since Pearl Harbor. Might I assume you're displeased with me?"

Leisure sat up; it was the kind of sofa you sank down into, so this took effort. "I'm your co-counsel. I'm here to assist, and follow your lead."

"But . . ."

"But," Leisure said, "taking Tommie Massie by the hand like that, and steering him into a temporary insanity plea—"

"George, we have four clients who quite obviously caused the death of Joseph Kahahawai due to their felonious conspiracy. They face a second-degree murder charge, and a reasonable argument could be made that they're lucky the grand jury didn't slap them with murder in the first."

"Agreed."

"So we have no choice: we have to prove extenuating circumstances. What extenuating circumstances avail themselves to us? Well, there's no question that Tommie Massie's stress-ravaged mental condition is our best, perhaps our only, recourse."

"I certainly wouldn't want to try to prove Mrs. Fortescue insane," Leisure said with a smirk. "She's about as deliberate and self-controlled an individual as I've ever met."

"And those two sailors aren't nuts," I said. "They're just idiots."

Darrow nodded. "And idiocy is no defense . . . but temporary insanity is. All four were in agreement to commit a felony—kidnapping Kahahawai, the use of firearms to threaten and intimidate their victim . . ."

"No question about it," I said, "Tommie's the best shooter for the jury to pin its sympathy on."

"I agree," Leisure said, and he whapped the back of one hand rhythmically into the open palm of the other, as he made his point. "But the felony murder concept still prevails—all four are equally guilty, no matter who fired the shot."

"No!" Darrow said. "If Tommie Massie, while temporarily insane, fired the shot, he is *not* guilty . . . and if Tommie is not guilty, then none of them are, because there *is* no crime! The felony evaporates and so does the concept of felony murder right along with it."

Leisure's eyes were open wide; then he sighed and began nodding. "Obviously these clumsy fools had no intention of murdering Kahahawai."

"They're as much victims in this as Kahahawai," Darrow said gravely.

"I wouldn't go quite that far, C.D.," I said. "Mrs. Fortescue and the boys aren't in the ground."

The only sound in the room was the gentle whir of a ceiling fan.

"I have misgivings myself," Darrow admitted, sighing heavily. "After all, I've never employed the insanity defense. . . ."

"Sure you did, C.D.," I said. Was his memory completely gone? How could he forget his most famous trial?

"Loeb and Leopold, you mean?" He smiled patiently, shook his head, no. "I pleaded those boys guilty, and merely used insanity as a mitigating circumstance, in seeking the judge's mercy. No, this is a full-blown insanity defense, and we're going to need experts in the field of psychiatry."

Leisure nodded. "I agree. Any ideas?"

Darrow gazed at the ceiling fan's blades. "Did you follow the Winnie Ruth Judd trial?"

"Certainly," Leisure said. "Who didn't?"

"Those alienists who testified on behalf of Mrs. Judd made a hell of a good case that she had to be crazy to have dismembered those two gals, and stuffed 'em in that trunk."

Leisure was nodding. "Williams and Orbison. But Mrs. Judd was convicted . . ."

"Yes," Darrow said with a winning smile, "but I wasn't defending her. I was impressed by their testimony; will you track them down by telephone, George?"

"Certainly, but I doubt they take charity cases. . . ."

"Establish their availability and fee. When I confer privately with Mrs. Fortescue and Tommie, tomorrow, I'll let them know how important bringing in alienists is to their defense. They'll find the money, amongst their rich friends. Could you start on that right now?"

Leisure nodded and stood. "I'll call from my own suite; Anne's probably wondering what's become of me."

"Be back by four-thirty, if you can, George. We're meeting with those local fellows for further briefing."

Darrow was referring to Montgomery Winn and Frank Thompson, the Honolulu attorneys who had handled the case before Darrow came aboard. Winn had prepared much of the material we'd looked at on the *Malolo*.

With Leisure gone, Darrow said, "I think we may have offended George's delicate legal sensibilities."

"Tough finding out your hero has feet of clay," I said.

"Is that what I have?"

"Up to about the knees."

He let out a horse laugh. Then he sat forward, putting his cigarette out in an ashtray on the small table by his chair; he rested his hands on his thighs and gazed at me sleepily.

"Let's get down to it, son," he said. "I'm going to be making a lot of noise, with the press boys, about how it doesn't matter whether Joe Kahahawai and his cohorts were *really* guilty of raping Thalia Massie or not. That it doesn't matter a ding-dong diddly damn whether it was some other carload of Island hoodlums, or Thalia Massie's overactive imagination, or Admiral Stirling and the entire Pacific fleet. What matters is that

Tommie Massie and Mrs. Fortescue and those two sailor boys
believed Kahahawai to be one of her attackers . . . the brute who
broke that poor girl's jaw and wouldn't let her pray. And I will
be trumpeting from Honolulu to doomsday that we are not,
and *will* not, retry the Ala Moana case in that courtroom."

"That's what you'll be saying to the press."

"Right. And it's a boxcar of bullshit. Oh, in a technical legal
sense, it's sound enough, but what we really need to free
our clients is proof that they killed the right man. It gives
them moral authority for this immoral, senseless act they
perpetrated."

"Which is where I come in."

He narrowed his eyes, nodded slyly. "Exactly. This rape
case, this so-called Ala Moana case, I want you to dig into it. Interview the witnesses, naval personnel, local officials, the goddamn man on the street if you have to." He thrust out his arm
and his finger pointed right at me; it was like having a lightning
bolt almost hit you. "If you can find new evidence of the guilt of
those rapists—and I *believe* Thalia Massie, I *believe* her, based
upon her words and her demeanor and, if nothing else, that
goddamned license plate number that she missed by only a
single goddamned digit—then we can make a hero out of the
sorry human unit that is Thomas Massie. And we can spring
'em all!"

I was sitting forward, loosely clasped hands draped between my open knees. "What do we do with this new evidence,
should I find it?"

He winked. "Leave that to me. I'll make sure the jury hears
about it, and the papers. Of course, I *will* in this trial be retrying
the Ala Moana case, because it speaks to the motivation and the
mental condition of Tommie Massie. No prosecutor can keep
that out of the record. . . . Now—I'm going into court tomorrow
morning, and I'm going to ask for a week to prepare my case;
the judge'll give it to me, too."

"Of course he will. You're Clarence Darrow."

"And that's about all the consideration I expect my fame to
get me in this case, but I'll damn well take it. Then I expect it'll

take a good week to select a jury . . . I intend to make sure it does."

"So you'll buy me two weeks."

He nodded. "I would expect, during the trial, you'll be at my side, at my table. That's where I'll want you, and need you, not running around chasing girls down some snow white beach."

"Is that how you figure I'll spend my time?"

"Some of it. Of course, you've already landed this Bell girl. Fine-looking young woman. You bagged that filly the first night aboard ship, didn't you?"

"Admitting that wouldn't be gentlemanly."

He tilted his head; his eyes had a nostalgic cast. "Does she look as good out of a bathing suit as she does in one, son?"

"Better."

Darrow sighed with pleasure at the thought of that, then hauled his weary body to its feet; quite a process, sort of like re-assembling himself. He was fishing for something in his baggy pants pocket as he motioned for me to rise, and I did, and he walked me to the door. He slipped his arm around my shoulder. With his other hand, he pressed some keys in my palm.

"There's a car waiting for you in the hotel garage. Mrs. Fortescue's provided it."

"Any special car, or do I just start trying keys in ignitions?"

"A blue Durant roadster. It'll get you in the mood of the case: it's her own car, the one she drove to the courthouse the day they snatched Kahahawai."

I grunted a laugh. "At least it isn't the car they hauled that poor bastard's body in."

He moved away to pluck one of the envelopes off the table by the door. "This is for you, too, son—it's your temporary private investigator's license, and permission to carry a firearm in the Territory of Hawaii."

"What the hell," I said, having a look at the document, signed by the chief of police. "I'm legal."

He patted my shoulder. "I'll be holed up here, mostly, working with George. Check in with me by phone and we'll meet every day or so. Now, I want you to stay away from this hotel—I don't want the reporters getting after you." He dug in his pocket. "Here's some expense money. . . ."

I took the five tens he was offering, and said, "Whose idea was it, hiring me? Yours or Evalyn Walsh McLean's?"

"Does it matter where a great notion first rears its head?"

"Don't tell me *she's* paying my expense money. . . ."

He touched his caved-in chest with splayed fingers. "Now that injures me, it really does. You know I dote upon you—as if you were my own son!"

"Is having me around costing you *anything*?"

"Certainly, Nate. That was my pocket you saw me reach into, wasn't it?"

"Yeah, but I don't know whose money you dug out."

His gray eyes were impish. "Why, your money, Nate. Your money, now."

I grunted another laugh. "I'd put you under oath, but what difference would it make?"

"What do you mean?"

"What good's it do, having an agnostic swear on a Bible?"

He was chuckling over that as he closed the door behind me.

The top was down (and I left it down) on the Durant, a two-tone blue number with wire wheels that was surprisingly sporty for a society matron like Grace Fortescue, even if she was an accomplice to murder. The buggy handled nicely and the three-and-a-half-mile drive from Honolulu to Waikiki—straight down King Street, right on Kalakaua Avenue—was a pleasant combination of palm-shaded drive, strolling locals, and budding commerce. I tossed my fedora on the floor on the rider's side, because the motor-stirred breeze would have sent it sailing, and it felt good, getting my hair mussed. The steady stream of traffic was divided by a clanging trolley, and halted occasionally by Polynesian traffic cops with stop-go signs—no traffic lights in Honolulu, though they had streetlamps. Pretty soon the coral-pink stucco spires of the Royal Hawaiian began emerging up over the trees, like a mirage playing peek-a-boo.

Turning right off Kalakaua into the hotel driveway, I was

swept into lushly green, blossom-dabbed, meticulously landscaped grounds along a palm-lined gentle curve of asphalt that
wound around to the Pink Palace's porte cochere, where my
rubbernecking damn near ran me smack into one of the massive pillars at the entryway.

The doorman, a Japanese, wore a fancier white uniform and
cap than Admiral Stirling. When he leaned his smooth round
face in, I asked him where the parking lot was, and he told me
they'd park "the vehicle" for me.

I left the motor running, grabbed my bag out of the back,
took the claim stub (imagine giving an automobile to somebody like you were checking your damn hat!), tipped the doorman a nickel, and headed inside. A Chinese bellboy in an
oriental outfit tried to take my bag as I bounded up the steps,
but I waved him off; I only had so many nickels.

The lobby was cool and open, with doorless doorways letting in lovely weather, chirping birds, whispering surf. The
massive walls with their looming archways and the high ceiling
with its chandeliers dwarfed the potted palms and fancy lamps
and wicker furnishings, not to mention the people, who seemed
mostly to be staff. There were enough bellboys—some in those
oriental pajamas, others in crisp traditional red jacket and white
pants, all in racial shades of yellow and brown—to put together
a football team; and room enough to play, without stepping off
the Persian carpet.

But there were damn few guests. In fact, as I moved to the
registration desk at left, I was the only guest around at the moment. As I was signing in, a honeymooning couple in tennis
togs strolled by arm in arm. But that was about it.

Even the fancy lobby shops—display windows showing off
jade and silk and high fashions, for the moneyed man or
woman—were populated only by salesclerks.

An elevator operator took me up to the fourth floor, where I
found a room so spacious and beautifully appointed, it made
my cabin on the *Malolo* look like my one-room flat back home.
More wicker furniture, ferns and flowers, shuttered windows,
and a balcony that looked out on the ocean. . . .

It was late afternoon, and the sunbathers and swimmers

were mostly indoors; a spirited game of surfboard polo was under way, but that was all. No outrigger canoes in sight; no surf-riding dogs.

The day was winding down and I was, frankly, exhausted. I dropped the sort of immense window shade that was the only thing separating the balcony from the room itself, and adjusted the shutters till the room was as dark as I could get it, stripped to my shorts, and flopped on the bed.

Ringing awoke me.

I turned on the bedside lamp. Blinking, I looked at the telephone on the nightstand and it looked back at me, and rang again. I lifted the receiver, only half-awake.

" 'Llo."

"Nate? Isabel."

"Hi. What time is it?"

"Eight-something."

"Eight-something at night?"

"Yes, eight-something at night. Did I wake you? Were you napping?"

"Yeah. That old man Clarence Darrow wore me the hell out. Where are you? Here in the hotel?"

"No," she said, and there was disappointment in her voice. "I'm still at Thalia's. She's not moving out to Pearl Harbor till tomorrow, so I'm staying with her, tonight."

"Too bad—I could use the company. I seem to have this whole barn to myself."

"That doesn't surprise me. I hear business at the Royal Hawaiian is terrible since the Crash."

I sat up. "Listen, I'd like to talk to Thalia again—without C.D. and Leisure around. There's hardly anybody at this damn joint—maybe you and she could come around for breakfast. I don't think there'll be too many gawkers."

"Let me ask her," Isabel said. She was gone for a minute or so, then came back: "Thalia would love to get away. What time?"

"How about nine? Just a second, let me look at this . . ." There was an information card on the nightstand with room service and other restaurant info. "We'll meet at the Surf Porch. Just ask at the desk and they'll shoo you in the right direction."

"This sounds delightful, Nathan. See you tomorrow. Love you."

"Back at ya."

I rolled out of bed. I stretched, yawned loudly. I was hungry; maybe I'd put my pants on and go down and charge a great big fancy meal to my room. That was one way to stretch fifty bucks a week expenses.

Yanking the cord, I lifted the big window shade and let the night air roll in off the balcony. Then I wandered out there in my shorts and socks to drink in the night. The sky was purple and scattered with stars; the moon, full and almost golden, cast glimmering highlights on the ebony ocean. Diamond Head was a slumbering silhouette, barely discernible. I drew in the sea breeze, basked in the beauty of the breakers rolling in.

"Please excuse intrusion," a quiet voice said.

I damn near fell off the balcony.

"Did not wish to disturb you." He was seated in a wicker chair, to the left, back away from the ledge of the balcony, a skinny little Chinese guy in a white suit with a black bow tie, a Panama hat in his lap.

I stepped forward, fists balled. "What the hell are you doing in my room?"

He stood; he was no more than five foot. He bowed.

"Took liberty of waiting for you to wake up."

His head had a skull-like appearance, accentuated by his high forehead and wispy, thinning graying hair. His nose was thinly hawkish, his mouth a wide narrow line over a spade-like jaw; but his most striking feature was his eyes: deeply socketed, bright and alert, and the right one had a nasty scar above and below it, the entire socket discolored, like an eye patch of flesh. Knife scar, I'd wager, and he was lucky he didn't lose the eye.

"Who the hell are you?"

"Detective First Grade Chang Apana. Care to see badge?"

"No thanks," I said, letting out a half-laugh, half-sigh. "It would *take* Charlie Chan to sneak in here and not wake me. Any special reason you dropped by unannounced?"

"Roundabout way often shortest path to correct destination."

"Who said that? Confucius?"

He shook his head, no. "Derr Biggers."

Whoever that was.

I asked, "You mind if I put on my pants?"

"By all means. You mind if I smoke?"

We sat on the balcony in wicker chairs. As we spoke, he chain-smoked. That wasn't a very Charlie Chan–like thing to do; and, as I recalled, the fictional detective was roly-poly. But maybe Chang Apana and his storybook counterpart had other things in common.

"What are you doing here, Detective Apana?"

"You're working with famous lawyer—Clarence Darrow. On Massie case."

"That's right. But I haven't even started poking around yet. How did you know . . . ?"

"Chief of police showed me paperwork giving you permission to carry weapon and investigate, here. You're Chicago policeman?"

"That's right. I took a leave of absence to help Mr. Darrow out. We're old friends."

A tiny smile tickled the line of a mouth. "You're not old at all, Mr. Heller. I have been detective for thirty-seven years."

That surprised me, but looking at the crevices on that skeletal mug, I could believe it.

"You still haven't told me what brings you here, Detective Apana."

"Please. Call me Apana, or Chang. I am here to offer aid and information to brother officer."

"Well, then, why don't you call me Nate, Chang. Why do you want to help me? Where do you stand on the Massie case, anyway?"

His eyebrows lifted. "Depends which case. Tommie Massie and his mother-in-law and sailors, law is clear. Man they kidnapped was killed."

"It's not quite that simple. . . ."

"Not simple at all. Heavy cloud hangs over this island, Nate. Will we be stripped of self-government? Will dream of statehood burst like bubble? Outcome of trial will determine these things . . . and yet these things have nothing to do with law, or justice."

"Where do you stand on the other case? The Ala Moana rape case?"

"I stand in embarrassment."

"Why?"

"Because department I serve for thirty-seven years have disgraced self in committing many blunders. Example—Inspector McIntosh arrest five boys because they were involved in another 'assault' same night . . . that assault was minor auto mishap and scuffle. Not rape. But McIntosh arrest them on this basis, _then_ he build his case. This is same inspector who drives suspect's car to scene of crime to examine tire tracks, and wipes out tracks in process."

"Yeah, I read about that in the trial transcript. That does take the cake."

"Cake taken by Thalia Massie when her memory makes remarkable improvement. Night she was attacked, she tell police she leave Ala Wai Inn between twelve-thirty and one a.m. Later, when Inspector McIntosh cannot make this work with suspects' strong alibis, Mrs. Massie change time to eleven-thirty. Night she was attacked, she tell police she can't identify rapists, too dark. Tell police also she didn't see license plate number. Later, memory miraculously improve on all counts."

"You think Kahahawai and the others are innocent?"

He shrugged. "Unlike Inspector McIntosh, Chang Apana prefer making mind up after investigation complete. 'Mind is like parachute, only function when open.' " He withdrew a card from his suit jacket pocket and handed it to me. "If you wish my aid, call me at headquarters, or at my home on Punchbowl Hill."

"Why would you want to help the defense in this case?"

"Perhaps I only wish to help a brother officer from the great city of Chicago. Perhaps fame of Clarence Darrow has reached these shores. Clarence Darrow, who is defender of men regardless of shade of skin."

"My understanding was, you weren't directly involved in this case."

The wide thin line of his mouth curved into a glorious smile. "No. Chang Apana nears retirement. He is grand old man of department. Sits at his desk and tells his stories—but he also hears stories. Stories of drunken Navy officer the night of rape picked up near Massie house with fly open. Stories of Mrs. Massie telling Navy officer not to worry, everything be all right. Stories of how the police had to fire gunshots at Mrs. Fortescue's car before it pull over. Stories of Lt. Massie's pride when body of Kahahawai is found in back of car. . . ."

He stood.

"Should you wish to talk to officers who witnessed these events, Chang Apana can arrange. Should you wish to discover the truth, Chang Apana can open doors."

I stood. "I just may take you up on that, Chang."

He bowed again, and placed the Panama on his head; its turned-up brim seemed ridiculously wide, like an oversize soup bowl. A smile tickled the wide straight line that was his mouth.

"Welcome to Paradise," Chang said, and went out as quietly as he must have come in.

EIGHT

The next morning, on the Surf Porch of the Royal Hawaiian, I sat at a wicker table, sipping pineapple juice, awaiting my guests for breakfast, enjoying the cooler-than-yesterday's breeze. Off to the left, Diamond Head was a slumbering green and brown crocodile. Beyond a handful of palms watching, leaning, and a narrow band of white beach bereft of bathers, the shimmer of ocean was a gray-blue interrupted occasionally by the lazy roll of whitecaps. The overcast sky seemed more blue and white than gray, low-slung clouds hugging the horizon, making the gentle graduations of blue so subtle it was hard to tell where the sea ended and the sky began.

Just as the coolness and the overcast had nixed most beach activity this morning, the Surf Porch itself was lightly attended. Maybe a third of the canopied swinging chairs along the back wall were in use by the well-to-do few who were sharing this palatial hotel with a certain Chicago representative of the hoi polloi. I seemed to be the only one on the porch who wasn't in white; in my brown suit, I felt like a poor relation hoping to worm into the will of a wealthy invalid uncle I was visiting at a very chic sanitarium.

"Excuse please," the waitress said. A lovely Japanese girl in a colorful floral pattern kimono, she bore a pitcher of pineapple juice and wanted to know if I wanted more.

"No thanks," I said. I didn't really like that bitter stuff; I'd accepted the first glass just out of civility, not wanting to insult the Island beverage or anything. She was about to depart when I stopped her: "Say, you could bring me some coffee?"

"Cream? Sugar?"

"Black, honey," I said, and grinned.

She smiled a little and floated off.

All the waitresses here wore kimonos—like the wenches who wore them, each garment was as lovely, delicate, and different as a snowflake; these little geishas were so attentive, it stopped just short of driving you batty. Maybe that was because the help at the Royal Hawaiian—Oriental and Polynesian, to a man (and woman)—seemed to outnumber the patrons.

I glanced back at the archway entry, to see if my guests were here; after a moment, as if I'd willed it, there they were, eyes searching for, and finding, me.

Waving them over, I admired all three women as they crossed the porch—Thalia Massie, pudgy but pretty in a navy blue frock with big white buttons, the lenses of her sunglasses like two big black buttons in counterpoint under the shade of the brim of her white-banded navy chapeau; Isabel, her face glowing in a hatless haze of blond hair, fetching in a white frock with red polka dots that lifted nicely around her knees as the breeze caught the wispy fabric, and which she only half-heartedly pushed down; and finally, a surprise visitor, Thalia's Japanese maid, Beatrice, as slender and daintily pretty as any of the kimono girls serving us, but wearing a white short-sleeved blouse and ankle-length dark skirt, her jaunty white cuff-brim turban a pleasant contrast with her bobbed black hair, a small white clutch purse in one hand.

None of the guests, rocking in their porch chairs, enjoying the study in blues and grays before them, gave an inkling of reaction to the celebrity who had just entered, though a few of the males sneaked a peek at the three pretty girls.

I rose, gestured toward the three chairs—I'd only been expecting Thalia and Isabel, but this was a table for four, luckily—

and Thalia held up a hand, stopping her two companions from sitting just yet. Not till she'd gotten something straight.

"We'll be going to my new quarters at Pearl Harbor, from here," Thalia said in her low husky near-monotone, "and my maid Beatrice is accompanying me. I hope you don't mind my bringing her along, Mr. Heller. I believe in treating servants like people."

"Damn white of ya," I said, smiling at Beatrice, whose mouth didn't return the smile, though her eyes did; and I gestured again, for all of them to sit, and, finally, they did.

The geisha brought my coffee, and filled Thalia and Isabel's coffee cups; Beatrice had turned hers over. Then the kimono cutie stayed around to take our breakfast order. I went for the fluffy eggs with bacon while Isabel and Thalia decided to share a big fruit plate. The waitress seemed confused as to whether to take Beatrice's order, and Beatrice wasn't helping by sitting there as mute and expressionless as Diamond Head itself.

"Are you having anything?" I asked her.

"No thank you," she said. "I'm just along."

"You mean like a dog?"

This immediately made everybody uncomfortable, except me, of course.

"Well, if you expect me to feed you under the table," I said, "forget about it. You don't like coffee? Get her some, what? Juice? Tea?"

"Tea," Beatrice said softly. Her eyes were smiling again.

"And why don't you bring us a basket of goodies we can all share," I suggested to the waitress. "You know, muffins and what-have-you."

"Pineapple muffins?" the geisha asked.

"Anything *without* pineapple," I said with a wince.

That seemed to amuse all the women, and I sipped my coffee and said, "I'm glad you girls could make it this morning."

"I'm going to stop by the desk," Isabel said, beaming, "and see about my suite."

"I talked to C.D. this morning," I said. "It's all arranged. They have a key waiting for you."

"Swell," she said, hands folded, smile dimpling that sweet face. It was pretty clear I had a date tonight. A hot one.

"It's lovely here," Thalia commented, rather distantly, the black lenses of her sunglasses looking out on the blues and grays and whites of that vista whose horizon you had to work to make out. Wind whipped the arcs of her dark blonde hair.

"Would you like to wait till after breakfast?" I asked.

She turned the big black eyes of her glasses my way; the rest of her face held no more expression than they did. "Wait till after breakfast for what?"

"Well, I need to ask you some things. Didn't Isabel mention the reason for my invitation?"

A single eyebrow arched above a black lens. "You and Mr. Darrow already questioned me, yesterday."

I nodded. "And he'll question you again, and again, as will Mr. Leisure. And they'll have their agenda, and I have mine."

"And what, Mr. Heller," she asked crisply, "is yours?"

Isabel, the breeze making her headful of blonde curls seem to shimmer, frowned in concern and touched her cousin's wrist. "Don't be mad at Nate. He's trying to help."

"She's right," I said. "But I'm not a lawyer, I'm an investigator. And it's my job to go over details, looking for the places where the prosecution can make hay."

Thalia shifted in her wicker chair; the surf was whispering and her monotone barely rose above it. "I don't understand. This trial isn't about me. It's about Tommie, and Mother . . ."

She'd said much the same thing to Darrow.

I sipped my coffee. "This case begins and ends with you, Thalia . . . may I call you Thalia? And please call me Nate, or Nathan, whichever you prefer."

She said nothing; her baby face remained as blank as the black lenses. Isabel seemed uneasy. Beatrice had long ago disappeared into herself; she was just along.

Thalia took a deep breath. "Mr. Heller . . . Nate. Surely you can understand that I'm not anxious to go into court and tell this story again. I hope that's not the road you and Mr. Darrow intend to go down."

"Oh but it is. It's the only way a jury can be made to understand what motivated your husband."

She leaned forward; it was getting eerie, staring into those black circles. "Wasn't the Ala Moana trial enough? You know, many women hesitate to report a case of assault because of the awful publicity and the ordeal of a trial. But I felt it was my duty to protect other women and girls. . . ."

Isabel patted her cousin's hand again. "You did the right thing, Thalo."

She shook her head. "I couldn't bear to think that some other girl might have to go through what I did," she said, "at the hands of those brutes. From a personal standpoint, the punishment of these creatures was secondary to just getting them off the street—only the ordeal of that trial didn't accomplish that, did it?"

"My investigation may," I said.

She cocked her head. "How do you mean?"

I shrugged. "If I can gather enough new evidence, they'll be put away."

Her laugh was throaty and humorless. "Oh, wonderful! *Another* trial, after this one! When will this end? No one who hasn't undergone such an experience can possibly imagine the strain upon not just the *victim*, but their *family*. . . ."

"Isn't that why we're here?" I suggested.

"I would imagine you're here because of money," she snapped.

"Thalo!" Isabel said.

"I know," she said resignedly, and sighed. "I know. Your Nate is only trying to help. Well, if going to court again, and testifying as to the details of that terrible night, will help my family . . . and save other girls from similar horrifying experiences . . . then I feel the end will justify the means."

I might have pointed out that the end justifying the means was the kind of thinking that got her hubby and mumsy in such hot water; but since she seemed to have just talked herself into cooperating with me, I let it pass.

"Good," I said. "Now—I was up late last night . . ." I took out my notebook, thumbing to the right page. ". . . going over the court transcripts and various statements you made. . . . Please understand that I'm only asking questions that the prosecution is likely to bring up."

"Go ahead, Mr. Heller." She forced a smile. "Nate."

"Normally," I said, "a witness's recollections decrease geometrically with the passage of time. But your memory, about this unfortunate event, seems only to improve."

Her mouth twitched, as if it were trying to decide whether to frown or smile; it did neither. "My recollection of the 'unfortunate event' is all too clear, I'm afraid. I suppose you're referring to the statements I made that night, or rather in the early morning hours that followed. . . ."

"Yes," I said. "You were questioned by an Inspector Jardine, also a cop named Furtado, and of course Inspector McIntosh, within hours of the assault. And several other cops, as well. You even spoke to the nurse at the emergency hospital, a Nurse Fawcett. . . ."

"That's right. What of it?"

"Well, you told these various cops, and Nurse Fawcett, that you couldn't identify your assailants. That it was too dark. But you thought that maybe you could identify them by voice."

Thalia said nothing; her Kewpie doll mouth was pursed as if to blow me a kiss. Somehow I didn't think she had that in mind.

"Yet now your recollections include physical descriptions of the assailants, down to the clothes they were wearing."

"I'm telling the truth, Mr. Heller. As I recall it now."

"Make it Nate." I took another sip of the coffee; it was a strong, bitter brew. "You also said, initially, that you were convinced the boys were Hawaiian, as opposed to Chinese, Japanese, Filipino, or whatever. You said you recognized the way they spoke as Hawaiian."

She shrugged one shoulder. "They *were* all colored, weren't they?"

"But only Kahahawai and Ahakuelo were Hawaiian, and two of the boys were Japanese and the last one Chinese."

Another throaty laugh. "And you can tell the difference?"

"In Chicago we know the difference between a Jap and a Chinaman, sure."

I was watching Beatrice out of the corner of an eye, and she didn't flinch at my racial crudity.

"Is that right?" Thalia said. "Does that hold true even when you're being raped?"

Isabel looked very uncomfortable. She clearly didn't like the way this was going.

I leaned in. "Thalia—Mrs. Massie—I'm playing a sort of devil's advocate here, okay? Looking for the weak spots that the prosecution can kill us with. If you have any explanations besides knee-jerk defensive smartass remarks, I'd appreciate hearing them."

Now Isabel leaned in—frowning. "Nate—that's a little forward, don't you think?"

"I didn't go to finishing school," I said. "I went to school on the West Side of Chicago where first graders carry knives and pistols. So you'll have to pardon my lack of social graces . . . but when you're in a jam, I'm the kind of roughneck you want to have around. And, Mrs. Massie—Thalia—you're in a hell of a jam, or anyway, your husband and mother are. They can do twenty to life on this rap."

There was silence—silence but for the chirping of caged birds out in the nearby lobby, and the gentle but ceaseless surge of the surf on the shore.

Thalia Massie, the black lenses of her glasses fixed upon me, said, "Ask your questions."

I sighed; flipped a notebook page.

"In the hours after the rape," I said, "you went through your story six times, and you consistently said you hadn't been able to make out the license plate number of the car. You said as much to four different police investigators, and a doctor and a nurse."

She shrugged.

"Then," I said, "in Inspector Mcintosh's office at police headquarters, on your seventh pass at the story, it suddenly came to you."

"Actually," she said, chin lifted, "I got it wrong by one number."

"Horace Ida's car was 58-895, you said it was 58-805. Close

enough. Missing one number makes it more believable, somehow. But there are those who say you may have heard that
number in the examining room at Queens Hospital."

"Not true."

My eyebrows went up. "A police car with its radio on, full
blast, was parked right outside the windows of the examining
room. An officer testified that he heard an alarm for car 58-895,
in possible connection with your assault, broadcast three
times."

"I never heard it."

I sat forward. "You do realize that the only reason that car
was really being sought was its involvement in a minor accident and scuffle earlier that evening, which had also been clas-
sified an assault?"

"I'm aware of that, now."

"You also said, on the night of the assault, that you thought
the car you'd been pulled into was an old Ford or Dodge or
maybe Chevrolet touring car, with a canvas top, an old ripped
rag top that made a flapping noise as they drove you along?"

Another shrug. "I don't remember saying that. I know it
came up at the trial, but I don't remember it."

And then sometimes her memory wasn't so hot.

"Thalia, Horace Ida's car . . . actually, it was his sister's car, I
guess. . . . Anyway, Ida's car was a 1929 Model A Phaeton. A
fairly new car, and its rag top wasn't torn. Yet you identified it."

"It was the car, or one just like it. I knew it when I saw it."

Breakfast arrived, our geisha accompanying a waiter who
was delivering it on a well-arranged tray, and Thalia smiled
faintly and said, "Is that all? Do you mind if we eat in peace?"

"Sure," I said.

There was quite a bit of awkward silence as I dug into my
eggs and bacon, and the two girls picked at a lavish plate of
pineapples, grapes, papaya, figs, persimmons, bananas, cubed
melon, and more. They small-talked as if I weren't there, discussing (among other things) how Thalia's father the major was
recuperating from his illness, and how nice it was that Mrs.
Fortescue's mother—vacationing in Spain—had sent a support-
ive wire to her daughter.

"Grandmother said she was so convinced of Mother's innocence," Thalia said, "there was no need to come, really."

We were all having a second (or in Thalia's case, third) cup of coffee when I started in again.

"What can you tell me about Lt. Jimmy Bradford?"

"What do you want to know?" Thalia was holding her coffee cup in patrician style—pinkie extended. "He's Tommie's friend. Probably his best friend."

"What was he doing stumbling around your neighborhood, the night of the rape, drunk and with his fly open?"

"Nathan!" Isabel blurted, her eyes wide and hurt.

"I would imagine," Thalia said, "having had rather too much to drink, he found a bush to relieve himself behind."

"Relieve himself in what way?"

"I won't dignify that with a response."

"Why did you say to him that everything would be all right, just before the cops hauled him in for questioning?"

"He was cleared," she said. "Tommie vouched for him. Tommie had been with him every second all evening."

"That wasn't what I asked."

"Nate," Isabel said, "I'm getting very perturbed with you. . . ."

Perturbed. That was how rich people got pissed off.

I said to Thalia, "If you don't want to answer the question—"

"He's a friend," she said. "I was reassuring him."

She had just been beaten and raped by a bunch of wild-eyed natives, and *she's* reassuring *him*.

"I think this charming breakfast has lasted quite long enough," Thalia said, bringing her napkin up from her lap to the table, pushing her chair back.

"Please don't go," I said. "Not until we talk about the most crucial matter of all."

"And what would that be?"

"The time discrepancy."

Another flinch of the mouth. "There is no time discrepancy."

"I'm afraid there is. The activities of the five rapists are fairly well charted—we know, for example, that at thirty-seven minutes past midnight, they were involved in the accident and scuffle that made them candidates for suspicion in the first place."

"I left the Ala Wai Inn at eleven thirty-five, Mr. Heller."

"That's a pretty exact time. Did you look at your watch?"

"I wasn't wearing a watch, but some friends of mine left the dance at eleven-thirty and I left about five minutes after they did. My friend told me later that she had looked at her watch and it'd been eleven-thirty when they left."

"But your statement that night said you left between half past midnight and one."

"I must have been mistaken."

"And if you did leave between half past midnight and one, those boys didn't have time to get from the intersection of North King Street and Dillingham Boulevard, where the minor accident and scuffle took place . . ."

"I told you," she said, rising, "I must have been mistaken, at first."

"Your memory improved, you mean."

She whipped the sunglasses off; her grayish-blue eyes, normally protuberant, were tight and narrow. "Mr. Heller, when I was questioned that night, in those early morning hours, I was in a state of shock, and later, under sedation. Is it any wonder that I saw things more clearly, later on? Isabel—come along. Beatrice."

And Thalia moved away from the table, as Isabel gave me a withering look—two parts disgust, one part disappointment—and Beatrice followed. I noticed the maid had left her little purse behind and I started to say something, but she signaled me not to with the slightest shake of the head.

When they were gone, I sat there wondering, waiting for Beatrice to tell her mistress that she had to go fetch something she'd forgotten.

And soon she was back, picking up the purse and whispering, "I have tonight off. Meet me at Waikiki Park at eight-thirty."

Then she was gone.

Well. Hotcha.

Looked like even with Isabel mad at me, I still had a date tonight.

NINE

The gentle rustle of palms and the exotic fragrance of night-blooming cereus gave way to the insistent honk of auto horns and the pungent aroma of chop suey as quietly residential Kalakaua Avenue turned suddenly, noisily, commercial. And even the star-flung black velvet sky and its golden moon were eclipsed by the glittering gaudy lights of Waikiki Amusement Park, engulfing the corner of Kalakaua and John Ena Road like a bright spreading rash.

Signs directed me to turn left on Ena for entry into the parking lot; across the way were shack-like businesses catering to the amusement park overflow, cheap cafes, a beauty parlor, a barbershop. Locals, *kanakas* and *haoles* alike, were walking along in the yellow glow of streetlamps, couples strolling the sidewalk hand in hand, drinking bottles of pop, nibbling sandwiches, licking ice cream cones; just a block or two down was the beach. A few native girls in their teens and twenties, looking both absurd and sexy in flapperish attire, were trolling for sailors and soldier boys; this was the sort of typically sleazy but seemingly safe area you might expect to find outside any amusement park.

I wheeled Mrs. Fortescue's Durant roadster into the pretty nearly filled lot, in the shadow of a roller coaster, Ferris wheel, and motorcycle death loop. The music here wasn't the Royal

Hawaiian's lazy steel guitar and ukulele mix designed to lull rich tourists away from their money: it was the familiar all-American song of the midway—bells dinging and kids screaming and the calliope call of a carousel. And this tune, too, was designed to part a fool from his money.

She was waiting around front, at the arcaded entrance on Kalakaua, just under the A of the looming white bulb WAIKIKI PARK sign, leaning against an archway pillar, a cigarette poised in fingers whose nails were painted blood red. The white blouse and long dark skirt were gone, replaced by a clingy bare-armed tight-in-the-bodice knee-length Japanese silk dress, white with startling red blossoms that seemed to burst on the fabric; her shapely legs were bare above white sandals out of which peeked the red-painted nails of her toes; her mouth was lip-rouged the same bright red as the flowers on the dress; and a real red blossom was snugged in her ebony hair, just over her left ear. Only her white clutch purse remained of this morning's mundane wardrobe.

"Mr. Heller," she said, and her smile set her face aglow. "Nice see you."

"Nice see you," I said. "That dress is almost as pretty as you are."

"I didn't know if you show up," she said.

"I never stand up pretty girls who ask me out."

She drew on the cigarette, emitted a perfect round smoke ring from a perfect round kiss of a mouth. Then, smiling just a little, she said, "You flirting with me, Mr. Heller?"

"It's Nate," I said. "And with the way you look in that dress, any man with a pulse would flirt with you."

She liked that. She gestured with her hand holding the cigarette. "You want smoke?"

"Naw. Might stunt my growth."

"Don't you got your full growth, Nate?"

"Not yet. But stick around."

The white flash of her smile outshone the flickering lights and neons of Waikiki Park. I offered her my arm and she tossed her cigarette in a sparking arc, then snuggled awfully close for a first date. Was Thalia Massie's little maid attracted by my he-man charms, or was she tricking on the side?

I wanted desperately to think that this curvy little chopstick cutie was irresistibly attracted to me; I hated to think she might be a hooker who knew a horny mainlander when she saw one. I was certainly irresistibly attracted to *her*—the intoxicating scent of her (was it perfume, or the flower in her hair?), the way the pencil-eraser tips of the full little handfuls of her breasts poked at the silk of her dress (it was just cool enough to inspire that), and of course the lure of the unfamiliar, the allure of the Far East, the unspoken promise of forbidden pleasures and unspeakable delights. . . .

We didn't say much, for a while. Just strolled arm in arm through a crowd of mostly locals, a yellow woman on the arm of a white man no big deal in this melting pot. Other than the racial hodgepodge, this could have been the midway of the Illinois State Fair—very little of the park seemed uniquely Hawaiian. The merry-go-round with its seahorse mounts, the giant clapboard Noah's ark with its gangway up to a petting zoo, had vague ocean ties; and there was an ersatz Island flavor to the hula dolls and paper *leis* and toy ukuleles the shooting galleries offered up for marksmanship. But mostly this was the same world of sawdust and sideshows that any American would recognize as foreign only in the sense that it transcended the ordinary humdrum of life.

We had cotton candy—shared a big pink wad of it, actually—as she guided me toward a sprawling two-story clapboard shed.

"I can't believe it," I said.

"What?"

"No bugs. No gnats or skeeters, no nothin'."

She shrugged. "They leave when swamp drained."

"What swamp?"

"Swamp where Waikiki is now."

"Waikiki used to be a swamp?"

She nodded. "Go down to Ala Wai Canal, you wanna find some bugs."

"No, that's okay. . . ."

"Years ago, they drain Waikiki to make room for more sugarcane. All the swamps and ponds, all the little farmers and fisherman, gone. The beach and all this tourist trade, that was just happy accident."

"Like the bugs that left."

She nodded. "No snakes in Hawaii, either. Not even down at Ala Wai."

"They got driven out, too?"

"No. They never here."

I gave her a little smirk. "No serpents in Eden? I find that hard to believe."

She raised an eyebrow. "Just human kind. They everywhere."

She had a point. The building we were heading to was jumping with music and kids. The closer we approached, the more the night throbbed with a very American jazz band version of "Charley, My Boy"—with the strum of a guitar and some steel guitar thrown in, to make it nominally Hawaiian style. Kids yellow, white, and brown stood out front and along the side of the clapboard pavilion, sharing snorts of hooch from flasks, catching smokes and smooches. I was definitely overdressed in my suit and tie—the boys wore silk shirts and blue jeans, the girls cotton sweaters and short skirts.

I paid at the door (35 cents admission, but couples got in for half a buck), got a ticket stub in return, and we squeezed past the packed dance floor and found a table for two. Up on an open stage, the band—the Happy Farmers (according to the logo on the bass drum head), Hawaiians in shirts almost as loud as their music—had segued into a slow tune, "Moonlight and Roses." The sight of these couples—here a yellow boy with a white girl, there a brown girl with a white boy, locked together in sweaty embrace under a rotating mirrored ball catching flickering lights of red and blue and green—would have given a Ku Klux Klan member apoplexy.

"You want a Coke?" I asked her.

She nodded eagerly.

I went off to a bar that served soft drinks and snacks, got us two sweaty cold bottles of Coke and a couple glasses, and returned to my beautiful Oriental flower, who was zealously chewing gum.

Sitting, I sneaked my flask of rum from my pocket and asked her, "Can we get away with this?"

"Sure," she said, pouring Coke into her glass. "You think Elks don't like their *oke*?"

Oke, I gathered, was Hawaiian for white mule.

I poured some rum into her glass of Coke. "This is an Elks Club?"

She stuck her gum under the table. "Naw. But local fraternal orders, they take turn sponsoring dances. It was Eagles, that night."

By "that night" she meant the night Thalia Massie was assaulted.

"This is the joint where the rapists went dancing," I said, making myself my own rum and Coke, "before they snatched Thalia."

She looked at me carefully. "You really think that?"

I slipped my flask away. "What do you mean?"

"Why do you think I ask you here?"

"My blue eyes?"

She didn't smile at that. "You were giving Mrs. Massie hard time today."

"That's my job."

"Giving her hard time?"

I shook my head, no. "Trying to shake the truth out of her."

"You think she lying?"

"No."

"You think she telling truth?"

"No."

She frowned. "What, then?"

"I don't think anything—yet. I'm just starting to sort through things. I'm a detective. That's what I do."

"You haven't made mind up?"

"No. But somebody *did* do something to your boss lady. I mean, she didn't break her own jaw. She didn't rape herself."

She thought about that. Sipped her drink. "Crimes like that

don't happen here. Violence—it not Hawaiian. They a gentle race. Tame like dog or cat in house."

"Well, only two of these dogs were Hawaiians. One cat was Japanese."

Something flickered in her eyes, like a fire that momentarily flared up. "Two are Hawaiian. The Chinese boy, he half-Hawaiian. This not a crime that make sense, here. Rape."

"Why not?"

"Because girls here . . ." She shrugged. ". . . you don't have to force them."

"You mean, all you have to do is buy 'em a Coke? Maybe put a little rum in it? And you're home free?"

That made her smile, a little; like I'd tickled her feet. But then, like the flare-up in her eyes, it disappeared. "No, Nate. That not it . . . hard to explain to mainlander."

"I'm a quick learner."

"Before missionaries come, this friendly place. Even now, only rape you hear of is . . . what do you call it when the girl is underage?"

"Statutory rape?"

She nodded. "Young girls give in to older boys, then parents find out, or baby is on way . . . then you hear about 'rape.' Colored man forcing himself—on a *white* woman? Not happen here."

"There's a first time for everything," I said. "Besides, are you telling me the racial line doesn't get crossed under the sheets?" I nodded toward the polyglot parade of lust out on the dance floor. "What's that, a mirage?"

"It get crossed," she said. "Beach boys—Hawaiian boys who teach surf at hotel beach? Their pupils usually female tourists, sometimes lonely Navy wives . . . but this sex is, what's word?"

"Consenting."

She nodded.

"Is that what you think? Your boss lady had a fling with a beach boy and it got out of hand? And she concocted a story that—"

"Didn't say that. You must . . . you must think I'm terrible."

"I think you're a livin' doll."

She avoided my fond gaze. "But terrible person. Traitor to employer."

I shrugged my eyebrows, sipped my spiked Coke. "I don't think a rich person paying a servant a few bucks a week buys any great sort of loyalty. If it did, guys like me couldn't ever get the dirt on anybody."

"You honest man."

I almost choked on the Coke. "What?"

"You say what you think. You don't hide nothing."

Often I hid everything, but I said, "That's right."

"Will you dance with me?"

"Sure."

The Happy Farmers had just begun "Love Letters in the Sand," and the steel guitar was pretty heavy on this one, and as I held Beatrice near to me, the fragrance of the flower in her hair made me giddy—or was it the rum?

"I thought you might not come," she said, "because of Miss Bell."

"We're just friends, Isabel and me."

"She told her cousin you sweethearts."

"That's an, uh . . . exaggeration. We just met on the ship. Besides, she's mad at me."

"Because you hard on Mrs. Massie today."

"That's right."

I held her close.

"Nate."

"Yes."

"You at your full growth now?"

"Damn near."

The next tune was fast. I adjusted my trousers, as best as possible, and we headed back to the table. But before we sat, Beatrice said, "You have a car?"

"Of course."

"We can't go my place. I live with my mother and two sister and two brother. Over Kapalama way."

"I'm at the Royal Hawaiian."

"No. Not there. Miss Bell might see."

Good point.

She touched my hand. Softly, slyly, she said, "I know place where couples go. Down beach road. To park?"

"Lead the way," I said.

Soon we were pulling out of the Waikiki Park parking lot.

"See that barbershop?" she asked, pointing across the way to the line of dingy shops. "See that *saimin* wagon?"

I glanced: a somewhat ramshackle two-story building (living quarters above) was given over to a barbershop with a traditional pole and a window that said ENA ROAD BARBERSHOP; through the window could be seen a woman barber snipping at a white male customer's locks; next door, in the direction of the beach, was a vacant lot with a food cart (SUKIYAKI DINNER, SAIMIN, HOT DOGS) and some picnic tables scattered around, couples eating noodles out of bowls; a few cars were parked up on the lot, getting served by white-aproned Orientals, drive-in style.

"That where Mrs. Massie seen by witnesses," Beatrice said. "Walking along with white man trailing after."

"And that," I said, nodding toward the big white two-story store—GROCERIES—COLD DRINKS AND TOBACCO—that sat just ahead, on the corner of Hobron Lane and Ena, "is the building that obscured the witnesses' view, when Thalia was grabbed."

"If that true," Beatrice asked, "what happen to the white man following after? Did he disappear around that corner?"

I looked over at her. "Beatrice—what's your stake in this, anyway?"

"Before he die last year, my father work at the same cannery as Shorty's father," she said.

"Shorty?"

"Shimitsu Ida. Horace Ida. Turn here."

"Huh?"

"Turn right. If you still wanna go lover's lane."

I still wanted to go to lover's lane. Just as I was turning onto the beach road, the landscape of Ena Road had shifted somewhat: the eating joints and other small shops gave way to bungalows—little more than wooden shacks—and two-story ramshackle apartment houses clustered together.

She noticed my giving the area the once-over. "Bachelor officer from Fort De Russey rent those."

I snorted a laugh. "You'd think they'd want something nicer."

"Out of the way, for taking native girl. Close to the beach where they can meet female tourist. And Navy wife. Only not all officer are bachelor, hear tell."

As we headed down the beach road, the landscape again shifted; we were on a narrow blacktop, and right now we were the only car on it. The road in some disrepair, rather bumpy, its coral underlayer glowing white in the moonlight. Though the ocean was nearby—you could hear and smell and sense it but not see it—we might have been driving through a desert, what with the algarroba thickets and scrubby underbrush and wild cactus. No palms, here—the closest things were the telephone poles lining this sorry roadway.

"They use to fight," she said suddenly.

"Who did?"

"Mr. and Mrs. Massie."

"Like how?"

"He swear at her and tell her to shut up. Sometimes she walk out."

I frowned. "Do you know what these fights were about?"

"She didn't like it here. She was bored. She drink too much. He tell her to stop, he said she drive his friends away. She has sharp tongue, Mrs. Massie."

"How long did you work for them?"

"Over two year."

"Then you didn't come aboard after Mrs. Fortescue moved out, to help with the housekeeping?"

"No. I was there when Mother Fortescue moved in."

"How did she and Thalia get along?"

"They didn't. She use to scold Mrs. Massie for not doing more housework, more cooking, for sleeping too much."

"*That's* why Mrs. Fortescue moved to her own bungalow?"

Beatrice nodded. "And the fights between Mr. and Mrs. Massie. They disturb Mother Fortescue. Here—pull in, here."

We'd come maybe a mile and a half. A small lane led into a

clearing, and I turned the nose of the Durant in; my headlights picked up the cement foundations of a torn-down building poking through weeds. Scattered rubbish, broken bottles, cigarette stubs, and the tracks of tires designated this as a make-out spot.

I cut the engine, and the lights. The moon was full enough to allow us to see each other plainly. The red of her lips and the flowers on her dress were muted in the moonlight. I was staring at her, part of me just admiring her, another part trying to figure her out; she looked away.

"What else do you know, Beatrice?" I asked. "What do you know that troubles you so much you sought me out?"

Her head swiveled on her neck and she turned her dark steady eyes on me. Without inflection, as matter of fact as a bored clerk behind a store counter, she said, "I know that Mrs. Massie was seeing other man."

"What other man?"

"Some officer. When Mr. Massie was away, he would come. At first, once a week. Then in May last year, he come oftener. He stay all week, when Mr. Massie was away on submarine duty."

I let some air out. Behind us, lurking behind the brush, the ocean was crashing on a reef. "This sounds pretty brazen, Beatrice."

"They don't kiss or touch in front of me. They sleep in separate rooms—at least, they start night and begin morning, in separate rooms."

"Still pretty bold . . ."

"They would go swimming at Waikiki, go picnic at Kailua, Nanakuli Beach. Sometimes she would stay away, two, three days—take sheets, pillow slips, towels, and nightclothes."

"Who was this officer?"

"Lt. Bradford."

Jimmy Bradford. The guy stumbling around with his fly open; the guy Thalia made assurances to before she was taken to the emergency room. . . .

"You never came forward," I said.

Her brow tightened. "And I'm ashamed. I need this job. My

mother is widow with five kids. I'm just one generation away from coolie labor, Nate. I couldn't risk . . ."

I moved closer to her. Touched her face. "You got nothing to be ashamed of, honey."

"You don't know what it's like. My father came from Hiroshima, too many people, too many poor people. Here in cane fields, on plantation, my father make nine dollars a month plus food. To him that was big step up. He made more at cannery, but eighteen-hour day for so many year, kill him."

I stroked her hair. "Honey, I grew up on Maxwell Street. I'm a slum kid, myself. But every generation has it a little easier— your kids'll go to college. Wait and see."

"You're a funny one."

"How so?"

"Selfish but sweet."

"Sweet, huh?" I ran my hand from her hair down onto the coolness of her bare arm. "Then why don't we quit talking about all this depressing malarky and find something better to do. . . ."

I kissed her. She put herself into it, and gave a very nice kiss, though it was pretty much standard issue; I mean, the secrets of the Orient didn't open up to me, even if her mouth did and our tongues danced the hootchie-koo. Still, it was doing the trick, all right—I was getting my full growth again.

I was leaning in, for another kiss, when she said, "You know where we are, Nate?"

"Sure—lovers' lane."

"That's right. Ala Moana."

And I started to kiss her, then pulled away.

"Shit," I said. "Pardon my French. . . . This is where it happened. *This* is where it *happened*!"

She nodded. "This is old Animal Quarantine Station."

I drew away, looking out the windshield at the weeds and rubble and cement slabs. "Where Thalia says she was taken . . . and raped. . . ."

She nodded again. "Wanna get out? Look around?"

I was torn between the two great needs of my life: the yearning between my legs, and the curiosity between my ears.

And the damn curiosity won.

"Yeah, let's get out for a second."

I got out on my side, and came around and opened the door for her.

"See those bushes over there?" she asked. "That's where she say they drag her."

And I turned and stared at the darkness of the thicket, as if it could tell me something; but the moonlight didn't hit the thicket, and there was nothing to see.

But I could hear something.

Someone.

"There's somebody else here," I whispered, holding a protective arm in front of her. "Get in the car!"

More than one someone—I could hear them moving, crunching the weeds underfoot, and I hadn't brought my damn gun! Who would have thought I'd need a goddamn nine-millimeter Browning to go on a goddamn date with a geisha girl housemaid?

Then one by one they emerged from the darkness—four faces, belonging to four men, sullen faces that looked white in the moonlight, but they weren't white faces, oh no.

They were the faces of the four men, the surviving four, who had brought Thalia Massie to this place to rape and beat her.

And as they advanced toward me like an army of the Island undead, I reached for the handle of my car door, only to feel it slip from my grasp.

The car was pulling out of this lover's lane, without me.

From the window as she drove, hands with blood-red nails clutching the wheel, Beatrice called out, "I've done what you ask. Now leave me out!"

And somehow I didn't think she was talking to me.

TEN

As I backed away, they encircled me, four skulking boys in denim slacks and untucked silk shirts; the shirts were of various dark colors, which had helped them blend into the darkness of the underbrush as they waited. But as I moved backward into the moonlit clearing, and they moved in lockstep with me, four Islanders dancing with the only white mainlander at the colored cotillion, blossoms emerged on the dark blue and dark green and deep purple shirts, flowers of yellow, of ivory, of red, strangely festive apparel for this brooding bunch of savages to have worn on this mission of entrapment.

I stopped, then wheeled within the circle, not liking having any of them behind me. From the pictures in the files I knew them: David Takai, lean as a knife blade, dark-complected, his flat features riding an elongated oval face, sharp bright eyes shining like polished black stones, black hair slicked back; Henry Chang, short, solidly built, eyes bright with resentment, curly hair sitting like an unruly cap atop a smooth, narrow face whose expression seemed on the verge of either tears or rage; Ben Ahakuelo, broad-shouldered boxer, light complected, matinee-idol handsome in part due to heavy eyebrows over dark sad eyes; and Horace Ida, who was a surprise to me, as the photo had shown only the round pudgy face with its slits for eyes and an unruly black shock of pompadour—I was not prepared for that fat-kid puss to sit atop a short, wiry, lean, power-ful frame, nor for those eyes to burn with such intelligence, such alertness, such seriousness.

"What the hell do you want with me?" I asked. I did my best to sound indignant, as opposed to scared shitless.

For several moments, the only response came from the nearby surf crashing on the reef, and the rustle of leaves shaking in the wind. Like me. Ida looked over at Ahakuelo, as if seeking for a prompt; but the broad-shouldered mournful-eyed boxer said nothing.

Finally Ida said, "Just wanna talk." He was facing me now, as I did my slow turn within their circle.

I planted my feet. "Are you the spokesman?"

Ida shrugged. I took that for "yes."

"If you wanted to talk," I said, "you should've just stopped by my hotel."

Ida grunted a laugh. "We draw reporters and coppers like shit draws flies. You think Ala Moana boys can go waltzing into Royal Hawaiian?"

Henry Chang was smirking; the expressions of the other two remained grimly blank. These four—with the late Kaha-hawai—were of course the so-called "Ala Moana boys," named for this lonely stretch of ruined blacktop along which their crime was supposedly committed.

"Besides," Ida said with a little shrug, "how we know you pay attention? Here you pay attention."

He had a point.

"What do you fellas want from me?"

"If we want to fuck you up, we could, right?"

I started turning in a circle again; my hands balled into tight fists. "It might cost you more than you think. . . ."

Now Henry Chang spoke, only it was more of a bark: "But we could, right, *haole*?"

"Yeah," I admitted; my stomach was jumping—the first guy who hit me in the stomach was getting a cotton candy facial. "Yeah, I think the four of you got me sufficiently outnumbered. What do you say we go one at time, just to be sporting?"

Ida slapped his chest and the thump echoed in the night. "You hear *our* side, okay?"

"Huh?"

His voice was so quiet, the sound of the breakers on the reef almost drowned it out. "We not gonna fuck you up. We ain't gangsters like *haole* papers say. We just want you hear our side."

Tentative relief trickled through me. "I, uh, don't mind talkin' to you boys—but isn't there someplace a little less cozy . . . ?"

"Yeah." Ida nodded, smiled, and there was something unsettling about the smile. "I know a *good* place. We take you for a ride. . . ."

To a guy from Chicago, that phrase had a certain unhappy resonance.

But I couldn't see trying to make a break for it; at least one of these guys, brawny Ahakuelo, was a top athlete, a boxing champ and a star of the local variety of football, which was played barefoot. What were my odds of outrunning *him*?

Besides, I was feeling increasingly *not* in danger. Melodramatic as this stunt may have been, luring me by way of an Oriental siren to this weed patch in the boonies between Waikiki and Honolulu, this didn't seem to be about harming me. Scaring me, yes. Harming me—maybe not. . . .

Ida was gesturing around him. "This is where Massie woman say we bring her and screw her and beat on her."

Henry Chang said bitterly, "You think I got to force a woman? You think Benny here gotta force a woman?"

What was I going to do, disagree?

"This doesn't seem like too tough a town to get laid in," I granted them.

"We can kill you," Ida said. "We can beat shit outa you. But we ain't gonna." He turned to Takai. "Mack, get the car."

The lean Japanese nodded and headed out of the clearing onto the blacktop.

Ida said, "You know what the cops do? When they not find my tire tracks here, they bring my car out and drive it around and *make* tracks. But they not get away with it."

"I heard," I said. "But I also heard you've got supporters in the department."

Ida nodded and so did Ahakuelo; Chang was studying me with apparent hatred.

"Lemme tell you how far *that* help go," Ida said. "That just means when some cop is doin' things to frame us, another cop warn us."

Nearby, an auto motor started up. In a few moments, headlights came slicing into the clearing as Takai pulled up and, leaving the engine running, hopped out of the tan Ford Phaeton, its top down.

"The infamous car," I said.

"Come for ride," Ida said.

Soon our little group had piled into the Phaeton, Takai, Chang, and Ahakuelo in back, Ida behind the wheel in front with me in the rider's seat.

"We didn't rape on that woman," Ida said over the gentle rumble of the well-tuned Model A engine. We were tooling down Ala Moana smoothly, but for the occasional pothole.

"Why don't you tell me about that night, Horace?"

"My friends call me Shorty," he said.

So we were pals now?

"Fine, Shorty," I said. I turned my head to look back at the three unfriendly faces in the backseat. "You guys call me Nate."

Takai pointed to himself. "They call me Mack." He pointed to dour Henry Chang. "He's Eau." It sounded like he was saying, "He's you." But I figured it out after a second.

Ahakuelo said, "Call me Benny."

And I'll be damned if he didn't extend his hand. I reached around and shook with him. No similar offer came from the others.

"That Saturday night last September," Ida said, "I was just fooling around. Go to Mochizuki Tea House, no action. Try a Filipino speak over in Tin Can Alley, run into Mack and Benny. Some beer, some talk."

The lights of Honolulu were up ahead, and the nearly jungle-like area was thinning out. The ocean was visible at left, endless black glimmering gold, stretching to a purple starry sky overseen by a golden moon.

"Benny knew about a wedding *luau* we could crash," Ida said.

Behind me Benny said, "We weren't invited but the son of the host, Doc Correa, he's a friend of mine."

"We had beer, some roast pig. We run into Eau and Joe Kahahawai at the *luau*. Then things got kinda slow, and somebody say, how 'bout we go to dance at Waikiki Park?"

We were passing by a Hooverville, a city of shacks fashioned from flattened tin cans, scrap sheet metal, crates and boxes ... nothing uniquely Hawaiian about this squatter's town, except that it was oceanfront property.

"We get to dance at eleven-thirty. We don't wanna pay for tickets 'cause we know at midnight, it *pau*, over. So we bum a couple ticket stubs off some friends who was leaving the dance, and Joe and Eau take the stubs and go in, I wait in parkin' lot."

Ahakuelo said, "Plenty of witnesses saw us in there."

"Yeah," David Chang said, "like that *wahine* you slapped on the ass."

Takai laughed. "Glad he did! That way she remember him."

Chang said bitterly, "She remembered you were drunk."

"*Kulikuli*," Ahakuelo snapped at Chang with a scowl.

The landscape along Ala Moana had a marshy look, now; I had a hunch I could find those mosquitoes here that had been driven out of Waikiki.

"It does sound like a lot of drinking was going on that night," I said. "How much did you boys have?"

"Benny hit the *oke* a little hard," Ida admitted. "Joe, too. Rest of us, couple beers. Joe and Eau run into Benny and Mack at dance, then after while, Joe come out to parking lot and pass off a ticket stub to me. I go inside a while, and he wait in lot."

To the left were tiny wharves where small boats were tied, mostly fishing boats, distinctive low-slung sampans, with a few sleek yachts interspersed, looking as out of place as white tie and tails at a country hoedown.

"Midnight," Ida said, "dance over, stand around lot talkin'

to people maybe five minutes—then we pile in the Ford and go back to the *luau*."

"How long were you there?"

"Ten minutes maybe. Somebody was playing music in the house, but no action, it was *pau*. They was singing 'Memories.' They was outa beer. Benny wanna go home, he have football practice next day, so I drop him off and he head home, over on Frog Lane."

The buildings of Honolulu up ahead, the ships and lights of the harbor over at left, were distinct before us now.

"You must've had that little fender-scraper with that white woman," I said, "along about then."

"I show you where it happen," Ida nodded, turning to the right onto Sheridan Street, the first opportunity to turn onto any street in some time.

Soon we were turning left onto King Street, a magnificent old plantation on the right, glimpsed through shrubs, foliage, a stone-and-wire fence, and the spreading branches of palms protecting it and its grounds from the tourists frequenting the Coconut Hut, a tacky grass-shack souvenir shop directly oppo- site—its sign boasting "A BIT OF OLD-TIME HAWAII IN THE HEART OF HONOLULU."

Before long, courtesy of the least likely tour guides Oahu might have provided, I was getting my first glimpse at the heart of Hawaiian government. Ida slowed down so I could have a nice look. At right was the Iolani Palace, set back far enough from the street to look like a dollhouse in the moon- light. A boxy Victorian affair with towers on the corners and in the middle (both front and rear) and plenty of gingerbread trim, almost ridiculously grandiose on its manicured grounds with its palm tree sentinels, the palace was a building that tried very hard not to look Hawaiian.

And across from the palace, on my left, was the Judiciary Building, another quaint monstrosity with balustraded bal- conies, Grecian pillars, and a central clock tower. Several schools of architecture seemed to be doing battle, none a win- ner, yet there was a comic-opera grandness about it.

In front of the building, on a stone pedestal, stood a golden statue of a native warrior, a spear in hand, a feathered cloak about him, his build powerful, his features proud.

"King Kamehameha," Ida said. "Kinda looks like Joe."

Joe Kahahawai, he meant; his murdered friend.

"Joe was proud he look like Kamehameha. Almost as proud of that big toe he kick football with.... That's where they kidnap him."

Yes it was: when Kahahawai had approached the courthouse that morning last January to report to his probation officer, he had walked in the shadow of the statue of the Island monarch he resembled into the false summons and waiting arms of Tommie Massie and company. There, next door to the Judiciary Building, across a side street, was the modern structure of the post office, where Mrs. Fortescue had parked, and watched, and waited.

We drove through downtown Honolulu—within spitting distance of the Alexander Young Hotel—and had I wanted to call out for help or jump out, I could easily have done it. I wasn't quite sure why these boys wanted me to hear "their side" of it; but I didn't think I was in danger, and besides, I *wanted* to hear their side of it. . . .

Beyond the downtown, in a working-class residential neighborhood, Ida pulled over to the curb, leaving the engine thrumming. We were at the arterial intersection of King and Liliha streets, with Dillingham Boulevard curving off to the left, toward Pearl Harbor.

Ida was pointing over toward Liliha, at the STOP sign. "I just dropped Eau off, and pull out on King when this big damn Hudson come roarin' down King, headin' toward town, goin' like hell. I yank the wheel around and we both slow down and just touch fenders."

"A little *haole* guy was driving," Henry Chang said, "but it was his big fat *wahine* mama that cussed us."

Ida said, "She yell out the window, 'Look the hell where you're goin'!' And I yell back, 'What's the matter with you?' "

Ahakuelo said, softly, some regret in his voice, "It make Joe mad, seein' that white man with that big-mouth *kanaka* gal. Big

Joe jump out and yell, 'Get that damn *haole* out here, and I'll give him what's coming to him.' "

"But the little guy stay behind the wheel," Ida said. "He look real scared. The big fat mama didn't—she got outa the car, damn big woman, almost tall as Joe. She come over cussin', smellin' of *oke*, drunk as hell. We all jump outa the car but she and Joe already at each other. She grab Joe by the throat and scratch him and Joe shove her offa him, and she fall on the runnin' board of her car. Big fat wildcat, we had enough of that, even Joe, and we scramble back in car and drive off like hell, laughin' about it."

"Only it was no laughing matter," I said, "after she went to the cops, and reported it as an assault."

Ida's expression was confused, frustrated. "*She* hit *Joe*."

"And Joe hit her." I decided to risk the following: "I hear he punched her in the face—like Thalia Massie got punched in the face."

Behind me, Henry Chang snarled, "*Haole pi'lau!*"

Which I didn't imagine was a term of endearment.

Ida looked at me, eyes steady. "He just push her, on side of head. If Joe punch her in face, are you kidding? He woulda break her damn jaw!"

I said nothing. I didn't have to: Ida suddenly realized what he'd said, swallowed thickly, and put the Phaeton in gear and, with care, pulled back out onto King, heading back toward town. Before long he took a left on Nuuanu Street.

Ida didn't say anything for a while; maybe he was wondering how different his life—and Joe Kahahawai's—might have been if that little fender-bender with Agnes and Homer Peeples (that was the couple's name) hadn't seen epithets escalate into rough stuff.

Finally I asked, "Why did you lie, Shorty?"

He gave me a quick, startled glance. "What?"

"You lied to the cops, when they came around and rousted you out of bed, in the early morning hours after the rape."

He was stopping, just beyond a lush park, where Nuuanu Street forked, a road off to the right labeled Pacific Heights.

"I didn't know any *haole* woman got attack," Ida said. "All I know was Joe hit that fat *wahine* bitch, and I didn't wanna get mixed up in it."

"So you told the cops you didn't go out that night. And that you loaned the car to some Hawaiian pal of yours—a pal you knew by sight but not by name?"

Ida nodded glumly; his smirk had no humor in it. "Not very good lie, huh?"

"One of the worst I ever heard," I said cheerfully.

"I told truth later same night. . . ."

"Sure, after they grilled you—but you got off to a bad start with that whopper." When the first thing out of a suspect's mouth is a lie, a cop never believes another word.

"That cop McIntosh, he drag me into his office where Mrs. Massie sit, face banged up, and say to me in front of her, 'Now look at your beautiful work!' *Then* he ask her if I am attacker!"

Christ, talk about prompting—why didn't Mcintosh just stencil the word RAPIST on the poor bastard's shirt? What happened to the standard practice of placing a suspect like Ida in a lineup?

"But she didn't identify me," Ida said. "Next afternoon, Sunday, coppers take Mack, Eau, Big Joe, and me to Massie house in Manoa Valley."

"Why in hell?" I asked.

"So she could identify us."

Not a lineup downtown where the real suspects were intermingled with bogus ones, under the watchful eye of the DA's office—but home delivery of the coppers' prime suspects!

"Sunday, cops ain't picked Benny up yet," Ida was saying. "So Benny, he wasn't there. Funny thing, Mrs. Massie said to Big Joe—'Don't they call you Ben?' But she say she recognize Eau and Joe. She don't pick me out. Don't even know me from the night before at police headquarters."

For several miles now, we'd been gliding along the valley road with fabulous estates on either side, their lavish gardens lorded over by royal palms. It was as if we were passing through an immense open-air nursery.

"They take Mrs. Massie back to hospital," Ida said, "later that same afternoon. And Benny, cops pick him up at the football field, where he practice, and take him to hospital and ask Mrs. Massie if he is one of attackers."

From the backseat, Ahakuelo's voice reeked frustration. "She said didn't know me!"

Even with the cops tying these boys in red ribbons and depositing them in her lap, Thalia Massie had failed to identify them during that crucial forty-eight-hour period after the crime. Only later did she come to know them down to their shoe size.

"We innocent men," Ida said proudly, as the Phaeton seemed to float past a cemetery.

"Maybe you did get railroaded on this one," I said. "But don't kid a kidder: your pal Joe was convicted on a robbery charge ..." I looked over my shoulder and directed my next comment to Ahakuelo, who seemed to have warmed to me some; Henry Chang was still glowering. "And Benny, you and Eau here did time on a rape charge."

"Attempted rape!" Chang spat.

"Sorry. That makes all the difference. . . ."

"We got parole," Ahakuelo said, "and the charge got dropped down to 'fornication with a minor.' I was eighteen, Eau just a kid, too—we was at a party and there was lots of *oke*, lots of fucking."

"Some of the girls was under sixteen," Ida further explained.

So the prior rape charges against Ahakuelo and Chang, which had produced such indignation on Admiral Stirling's part, were *statutory* rape busts?

"And Joe wasn't convicted on no robbery beef, either," Ida was saying.

"He wasn't?"

Ida shook his head, no; we were passing by another park—according to a wooden sign, Queen Emma Park. "Joe loaned some money to this friend of his, Toyoko Fukunaga. Fukunaga owe Joe this money too long, and wouldn't pay. After time, Big Joe shake the cash outa Fukunaga, and Fukunaga file a complaint. They have trial, but jury can't make up their mind."

These guys seemed to inspire hung juries.

"DA say they skip 'nother trial if Joe plead guilty on assault and battery," Ida continued. "He do thirty days."

So Big Joe Kahahawai's criminal record consisted of a dis-agreement between him and a friend over a debt.

A rambling country club clubhouse marked the spot where the streetcar line ended, and private residences began to thin out to nothing as the valley road began to wind. Ida took a fork to the right, about a mile past the country club, and we sailed along the bank of a stream, briefly, before the road plunged into a tunnel of trees, shutting out the moonlight.

I was getting uneasy again. "Where are you taking me, Shorty?"

"We see Pali," he said, as if that meant anything to me.

The eucalyptus-tree forest gave way to sheer ridges of stone, and the sides of the valley seemed to gradually close in on us as we climbed. My ears were popping. The air had turned chill, the wind kicking up.

"Gettin' a little cold, isn't it?" I asked. "You wanna put the top up on this buggy?"

Ida shook his head no. "Pali might rip canvas top right off."

What was Pali, a goddamn Cyclops?

"Who the hell is Pali?" I growled.

"Pali is cliff," Ida said, "where Kamehameha and warriors drive Kalanikupule's warriors back over edge. Long drop."

From the backseat came Henry Chang's helpful voice: "Two-*thousand*-foot drop, *haole*."

"It's thoughtful of you fellas to try to make me feel at home," I said. "But maybe any more sight-seeing oughta wait till daylight. . . ."

We had rounded a final curve and now a breathtaking panorama stretched out before us; the golden glow of the moon had been replaced by silver, and it was with this gleaming paint-brush that the greens and blues of the vista were touched, muted into an unreality like that of a hand-painted postcard, mountains, cliffs, bays, strands of coral, ivory endless sea under a starry black-blue dome. God, it was lovely. Christ, it was far down.

And shit, the wind! It was a cold howling gale up here, whipping hair, flapping clothing, flapping *skin*, it was a goddamn hurricane, formed, I supposed, by wind funneling through the ridges of these cliffs. My body was immediately overtaken by a flu-like chill.

"Get off car!" Ida yelled at me. These guys seemed to say "off" where a normal person would say "out"; but somehow it didn't seem like the time for a semantic discussion.

And we all piled out, that nasty air current making fluttering human semaphore signals out of all our clothing, the dark flowered silk shirts flying like the absurd flags of several silly nations. My tie was a waggling tattletale tongue.

Suddenly Henry Chang was on one side of me, and Benny Ahakuelo on the other, and each gripped me just above either elbow. Ida was facing me, his pudgy face set in a stern fearsome mask, his black hair waving, whipping. David Takai stood just behind him, his slicked-back hair having more success against the wind than the rest of us, his flat face blank, dark stone eyes unreadable.

"Last December," Ida shouted, "big buncha sailors grab me, haul my ass up here, wanna make me confess I rape that white woman."

Ida began unbuttoning the shirt even as the silk flapped around his hands.

I glanced out at the view: rolling hills, the even lines of a pineapple plantation, cattle fields, rice paddies, banana-tree groves, and the seas striking, curling, foaming over the distant reef. All of it, silver in the moonlight. Lovely. I wondered how lovely it would look as I was windmilling through the air on my way to the rocks two thousand feet below.

Or was Henry Chang exaggerating? Was it only fifteen hundred feet?

Ida had the shirt off and he handed the fluttering garment to Takahi, who was attending him like a servant. Was Ida freeing himself up to administer me a beating? And I would have to take it; the other three could hold onto me and I'd just have to fucking take it. . . .

But now, in the ivory bath of the moonlight, Ida's surprisingly lean body revealed streaks of white scars, a sea of them, slashing his flesh, and he turned like a model showing off a new frock, and revealed a back that was even more brutally striped with welts that had graduated to scar tissue. He had been brutally whipped—front and back.

Then Ida wheeled, and he came very close to me, as Henry Chang and Benny Ahakuelo held me. Yelling to be heard over the gale, he said, "They work me over pretty good, whaddya think?"

"Not bad," I managed.

"And I not confess. Bleed like hell, pass out after while, but goddamn, *not* confess! Nothin' *to* confess!"

Chin high, his proud point made, Ida held his hand out to his attendant Takai and took back his flapping garment, got it on, and buttoned up, despite the wind.

"You tell Clarence Darrow," Ida said. "You tell him we innocent men. Joe was innocent, too. You tell him he's on wrong side of courtroom. Wrong side!"

"I'll tell him," I said. No smart talk or disagreement from these quarters: Henry Chang and Ahakuelo were still holding onto me; I was still seconds away from being a flung rag doll bouncing my way down to a rocky death.

"He supposed to help *little* people!" Ida shouted indignantly. "He supposed to be colored man's defender! Not rich goddamn murderers! You tell him we wanna talk to him. We want his ear! You *tell* him!"

I nodded numbly.

And then they dragged me back into the car and took off.

It was a six-, seven-mile drive, but not another word was spoken, not until they dropped me by my car in the Waikiki Park parking lot, where Beatrice was sitting on the running board, her legs stretched out; she was smoking, a bunch of butts scattered on the gravel near her pretty red-painted toenails. When she saw us pull in, she got to her feet, tossed me the keys without a word or expression, and climbed in the front seat with Ida, where I'd been sitting.

"Tell Darrow," Ida said.

And the Phaeton was gone.

ELEVEN

Clarence Darrow, wrapped in a white towel like a plump Gandhi, his comma of gray hair turned into wispy exclamation marks by the wind, his smile as gleeful as a kid Christmas morning, was seated in the outrigger canoe, positioned midway, like ballast, two berry-brown beach boys in front of him, three behind. They paddled the boat and their joyful passenger over an easy crest of surf as news photographers on the beach—invaders in suit and tie amongst the swimming-attired tourists—snapped pictures.

One of Darrow's tanned escorts—the one paddling right at the front of the boat—was the king of the beach boys himself: Duke Kahanamoku, a "boy" in his early forties. An infectious white smile flashed in the long dark handsome face, and sinewy muscles rippled as the Duke stroked the water.

"Took Tarzan to beat him," Clarence Crabbe said.

We were sitting under a beach umbrella at a little white table on the sand with the pink castle of the Royal Hawaiian looming beautifully behind us. The young Olympic hopeful looked like a bronze god in his black trunks with matching athletic T-shirt. I was in tourist mode—white slacks with sandals and one of those colorful silk shirts like my kidnappers of the night before had worn: a red print with yellow and black parrots, short-sleeve and sporty and loud enough to attract attention back in Chicago's Bronzeville. This wardrobe—which also included a wide-brimmed Panama hat and round-lensed sunglasses that turned the world a soothing green—was courtesy of various shops in the hotel, and charged to my room. If there's anything a detective knows how to find, it's ways to pad an expense account.

Crabbe had called this morning; I didn't place him at first, but when he offered to buy us lunch with his silver dollar, it came to me: the kid who dived from the *Malolo* deck! We'd had lunch on the *lanai* (that's "porch" for you mainlanders) outside the hotel lounge, the Coconut Grove, only I didn't let him pay for the tab, which the buck wouldn't have covered, anyway—I signed it to my room.

Now we were spending the early part of the afternoon watching Darrow caper on the beach for the press, giving them plenty of frivolous photos and the occasional questionable tidbit ("There is no racial problem whatsoever in Hawaii"), while along the way paying the Royal Hawaiian back for my room with the publicity his famous presence attracted.

"Huh?" I asked, in response to Crabbe's statement about Tarzan beating Duke Kahanamoku.

"Johnny Weismuller," Crabbe explained. He was watching Kahanamoku wistfully. "He's the guy who finally took Duke's title away, as world's fastest swimmer. In Paris, in '24."

"And '32's gonna be your year?"

"That's the plan."

Though the Royal Hawaiian was way under capacity, its beachfront was aswarm with sunbathers, swimmers, and would-be surf riders. Here and there, a muscular Hawaiian in a bathing suit was attending a female—either conducting a friendly class in surfing, or sitting on the beach beside her, rubbing coconut oil on pale flesh.

"These beach boys," I said to Crabbe, "do they work here?"

"Some do. But all the beaches in Hawaii are public—the boys can come and go as they like. Hey, I used to be one of them."

"A *haole* like you?"

He flashed me a grin as white as Kahanamoku's. "You're

picking up on the lingo, Nate. Yeah, there are a few white boys out there hustling surfing lessons."

"And hustling the women?"

His grin turned sly. "Since I never pay for sex, I make a general of policy of not charging for it, either."

"But some beach boys do charge for their stud services?"

He shrugged. "It's a point of pride. Say, what's Clarence Darrow foolin' around with Duke and the boys for? Shouldn't he be waist-deep in the case?"

Right now Darrow was ankle-deep in surf. Kahanamoku was helping Darrow out of the boat and onto the sand, the reporters and photographers scuttling in like crabs, snapping shots, hurling questions.

"He *is* working on the case," I said. "On the public relations front, anyway—not to mention race relations. Hanging out with Duke Kahanamoku, he's sending a message that he doesn't think all the beach boys are rapists."

"Those Ala Moana defendants," Crabbe said, "aren't beach boys. Just typical restless Honolulu kids, drifting through life."

He said this with a certain sympathy.

"Guys in their late teens, early twenties," I said, "are restless everywhere, not just Hawaii."

"Yeah, but a lot of kids here are *really* adrift. All these different races tossed together here, their cultures, their traditions, in tatters."

"Then you don't think the Ala Moana boys are 'gangsters'?"

"No, and I don't think they're rapists, either."

"Why's that?"

Crabbe sighed. The cool wind was cutting through the warmth of the afternoon, making his dark blond hair dance; handsome damn kid—if he wasn't so affable, I'd have hated his guts.

His gaze was steady. "There's an old Island saying— 'Hawaiians will talk.' But the cops couldn't get anything out of the boys."

"So what? Lots of suspects in all kinds of cases keep their traps shut."

He shook his head. "Not Hawaiian suspects. If the cops and

their billy clubs and blacksnake whips didn't get the story out of 'em, *oke* and curious friends and relatives would. And the word would spread across the Island like the surf rolling over that beach."

"And it hasn't?"

"Nope. Why do you think support among the colored population is so overwhelmingly on the side of the 'rapists'? Besides, you don't have to rape a woman on Oahu. There's too much good stuff ready for the asking."

Maybe if you looked like this kid, there was.

"That area Thalia Massie was walking along when she got grabbed," I said, "was a red-light district. Maybe Horace Ida and his pals were riding along and mistook her for a chippie and decided to tear off a free piece."

He thought about that. "That's the best case anybody's made for the prosecution so far. That's certainly the way it could've happened. But not by the Ala Moana boys."

"Why?"

"Because Hawaiians will talk! Word around town, among the colored population, is it was *another* gang of boys. How many dozen convertibles full of Island boys looking for a party d'you suppose are prowling around on a given Saturday night?"

This kid would've made a good lawyer. Maybe after he got this Olympic stuff out of his system, he'd finish up law school.

"You got the time, Nate?"

I checked my watch. I told him it was getting close to two.

He stood; his musculature had the same sinewy rippling quality as the Duke's. "Guess I better scoot. I'm supposed to be over at the Natatorium by two."

"The what?"

"Natatorium. It's a saltwater pool over near Diamond Head. It's where I'm training."

"Good luck to you," I said and offered my hand.

He shook it and was gathering his towel to go when I asked casually, "Why'd you wanna have lunch with me today, Buster?"

That was his nickname, wasn't it? Isn't that what he told me on the pier after the *Malolo* docked?

Must've been, because he answered, "Why, I just wanted to repay your kindness on the ship the other day—"

"You ever met any of the Ala Moana boys?"

He blinked. "Yeah, uh . . . I knew Joe Kahahawai. I know Benny Ahakuelo, too."

"Local athletes, like you."

"Yeah." Now he gave me an embarrassed grin. "And you caught me at it—trying to put in a good word for my friends, without letting you know they are my friends. . . ."

"I'm a detective. They pay me for catching people at things."

"I'm sorry. I really didn't mean to mislead you—"

"Don't apologize for trying to help out your friends. Listen, Buster—you didn't tell me any lies, did you?"

"No. Just that one little sin of omission. . . ."

I grinned at him. "That makes you a hell of a lot more reliable than most people I talk to. Thanks for the information. Good luck in Los Angeles."

That was the upcoming Olympics site.

"Thanks, Nate." He flashed another embarrassed grin, waved, and was gone.

Darrow was moving up onto the beach. Duke Kahanamoku was heading back out with his pals in the outrigger, probably to duck the reporters. Before, the sound of Darrow's voice had been muffled in the gentle roar of the waves and the happy chatter of the sunbathers and swimmers, running in and out of the surf, or sprawled on the white sand on towels to broil like lobsters. But now, as C.D. and the reporters moved toward the hotel and the row of tables with beach umbrellas, where we sat, I could pretty well make out what they were saying. . . .

"Worried you're gonna get a racially mixed jury, Judge?" one reporter asked. The newshounds tended to call Darrow "Judge," even though he'd never been one; it was a way to kid and compliment him at the same time.

"Oh, I've no doubt we'll have a racially mixed jury, and no misgivings about it, either. I would embrace that as an opportunity in establishing a bridge between white and brown and yellow."

"I don't think you can use the same tactics you usually use, Judge," another reporter chimed in. "If the court tells a Hawaiian jury that shooting a man is against the law, and the jury thinks your clients did the shooting, well that's all there is to it: they'll find 'em guilty."

"That's the damned trouble with trials," Darrow growled. "Everybody thinks about the law and nobody thinks about people! Now if you'll excuse me, gentlemen, that's all for today. . . ."

Darrow answered a few parting questions as the reporters and their photographers slowly withdrew, and he sent me a tiny glance that said "Stick around" as he went to the table down a ways from me, where Ruby, Mrs. Leisure, and Isabel were sitting. He joined them and began chatting amiably.

No doubt in anticipation of possible press pictures, Mrs. Darrow's pleasantly stout frame was decked out in a sporty white-trimmed blue dress and hat, Mrs. Leisure attractively casual in belted beach pajamas—beige blouse and blue trousers—and blindingly blond Isabel a knockout in her white skirt with blue polka dots and a matching hat; her blouse was actually the nicely filled upper half of her white swimming suit. Isabel wasn't speaking to me, but I intended to mend that fence—when I got around to it.

George Leisure wasn't present—somebody had to prepare for the coming court case.

"Excuse me, suh."

The voice was mellow, male, not quite a drawl, but nonetheless touched by Southern inflection.

I turned. Straw fedora in hand, his white linen suit immaculate, a pleasant-featured man in his thirties, his brown hair touched lightly with gray at the temples, sharp eyes under lazy lids behind wire-framed glasses, half-bowed to me. His manner was almost courtly.

"You are Nathan Hellah?"

"Yes," I said, somewhat warily; despite the cordial, civilized bearing, this guy could after all be a reporter.

"Mr. Darrow requested ah speak with you. I'm Lt. Commander John E. Porter. I've been assigned by Admiral Stirlin' to be at Mr. Darrow's disposal. May ah sit down?"

Half-standing, I gestured to the chair Crabbe had vacated. "Of course, Doctor. C.D.'s mentioned you. You two seem to have hit it off."

"Clarence is easy to like." He placed his hat on the little table as he sat. "And it's an honor bein' associated with such a great man."

"I notice you're out of uniform, Doctor."

"Since ah'm spendin' so much time, bein' Mr. Darrow's personal physician, Admiral Stirlin' decided it might not be wise."

Might not be the best press relations, at that, Mr. Darrow being seen in the ongoing company of a naval officer.

"If we're going to discuss the case, Doctor," I said, "do you mind if I take notes?"

"Not at all."

But before turning to a fresh page in my little notebook, I was first checking to see if a memory the doctor's name had jogged was correct: yes. Here he was in my notes from the *Alton* interview with Mrs. Fortescue and Tommie Massie: Porter was the doctor who, before the first trial, had advised Tommie to take Thalia and leave the Island.

"What's your normal duty, Doctor?"

"I'm a gynecologist, Mr. Hellah, assigned to the care of dependent wives."

"Gynecologist—isn't that a doc that gets paid by women to look at what they won't show just any ol' man?"

"Quaintly but accurately put, yes."

"So you were Thalia's doctor, before the rape? For female problems?"

"Yes, suh, and general health concerns. And after the incident, Admiral Stirlin' asked to look after Lt. Massie, as well, suh."

This pleasant-looking professional man had tight, troubled eyes. It was the look of somebody who knew things he'd rather not.

"I attended Mrs. Massie the night of the incident, as well. I can give you the details if you like, suh."

I noticed he never quite used the word "rape."

"Please," I said.

He didn't have to consult his notes: "I found a double fracture of the lower jaw so severe her jaw had been displaced and her upper and lower jaws could not meet. Three molars on the right side of her jaw were in such proximity to the fracture, extraction was necessary. Both her upper and lower lips were swollen, discolored, and her nose was swollen. I also found small cuts and bruises about her body."

"All of this supports Thalia's story that she was beaten and raped, wouldn't you say, Doctor?"

The raising of one eyebrow was barely perceptible; his gentle Southern-tinged voice was hardly audible above the rolling surf and beach noise.

"Mistah Hellah, that is the fact. However, it is also a fact that her clothes were not torn, nor was there any trace of semen on her dress or undah-garments. And my examination of her pelvic area indicated no abrasions or contusions. She had douched when she arrived home, which could be the reason there was no indication that she had been raped."

I sat forward. "Is there some doubt that she was raped at all?"

"Let us say that there is no doubt she was beaten. Her jaw will probably never be the same; it will always have a little lump, there. And there is certainly nothin' to indicate she was *not* raped. She is a married woman, Mistah Hellah, and her vagina, uh, opens quite a bit."

"In other words, you could drive a truck in there and not leave any tire tracks."

His eyes widened behind the wire frames. "I might not have put it quite so . . . colorfully . . . but ah believe you have grasped my point."

"Why did you advise Lt. Massie to take his wife and leave the Island?"

That surprised him. "I wasn't aware you were aware of that, Mistah Hellah. I did so advise the lieutenant. I even offered to go to Admiral Stirlin' and advise a transfer on grounds that he and Mrs. Massie's health was sufferin'. I felt the publicity would be harmful to both the Navy and the Massies, and ah could see no useful purpose bein' served by that trial."

"No useful purpose in putting some vicious rapists away? If Mrs. Massie *was* raped—and your examination neither confirmed nor ruled that out—she and her husband might quite naturally want to see justice done."

His expression was dismayed, but then as the eyes behind the wire frames studied me, his face blossomed into a knowing smile. "You're goin' fishin', aren't you, Mistah Hellah?"

I grinned back at him. "They do that around these parts, I understand. Look, Doctor—Darrow asked you to talk to me, and you obviously want to share some things with me. What is it that's creasing your patrician brow?"

Now he sat forward; and his voice was so hushed I had to work to filter out the beach noise and discern the troubled words in his tranquil tone.

"I mentioned ah attended Mrs. Massie as her physician, prior to this incident. Only because Mrs. Massie's attorney has requested ah share this knowledge with you am ah doin' so, and then only reluctantly."

"As Mr. Darrow's paid and licensed investigator," I said, "I'm bound by the same client confidentiality code as he is. And as you are."

Dr. Porter sighed, swallowed, spoke. "Mrs. Massie had a preexisting condition when ah first began attendin' her—preeclampsia, which manifests itself through hemorrhages in the liver and kidneys. Left unattended, eclampsia is often fatal. The symptoms are rapid weight gain, high blood pressure . . . and secondary hemorrhages in the retinas."

"The eyes, you mean?"

"That is correct, suh. This generally leads either to blindness or at least badly impaired vision."

My grunt was sort of a laugh—an amazed laugh. "Are you saying Thalia Massie is blind as a bat?"

"No. No. But her . . . visual acuity is drastically reduced.

Specifically, her eyesight has been impaired by preeclamptic toxemia. She is particularly impaired in low-light situations."

"Like at night. In the dark."

"Precisely."

"Christ. She identified these guys, and she's fucking blind?"

"You are overstating, suh. Somewhat. There *is* a question whether she could recognize these people in the dark, since she practically couldn't see in the daytime."

"Jesus. You testified in the first trial, didn't you?"

"Yes, suh."

"But not to this."

"No, suh. I would have had ah been asked—but ah was not questioned on this subject."

And as a loyal naval officer, under Admiral Stirling's thumb, the chance of Porter volunteering this information was unlikely, to say the least. But now that Joseph Kahahawai had been killed, Porter's conscience was clearly bothering him.

"There is somethin' else, Mistah Hellah."

Wasn't this bombshell enough?

"After ah performed a curettage, my analysis of the uterine scrapings did not indicate pregnancy."

I blinked. "You mean, Thalia didn't get pregnant by her rapists?"

"Or by anyone—despite what she said on the witness stand."

And to her attorneys and their investigator.

"You might find it illuminatin', as well, to know that the figures Admiral Stirlin' and others have consistently provided to the press, regardin' the high incidence of rape in Hawaii, are grossly inflated."

I nodded. "I'd kind of come to that conclusion on my own, Doc. They're mostly statutory rapes, right?"

"Yes, what the law refers to as 'carnal abuse of a minor.' With the exception of Mrs. Massie, the only rape of a white woman here in the past year is an unfortunate incident in-volvin' an escaped prisoner."

I thumbed through my notebook; hadn't Mrs. Fortescue mentioned something abut this? Yes.

"Daniel Lyman," I said.

"That is correct, suh," Porter said. "And ah believe this miscreant is still at large, further inflamin' public indignation."

"Well, I certainly appreciate you sharing this information with me, Dr. Porter."

"I only hope ah'm not required to take the stand in this second trial. If ah have to get up and tell everything ah know, it'd be awful—it'd make monkeys out of everybody."

A familiar raspy voice to one side of us said: "No fear of that, Dr. Porter."

Darrow, his potbelly like a beach ball he was hiding under the top of his black bathing costume, pulled up a third chair and sat.

"In the first place," Darrow said, "I've already suffered through one 'monkey' trial. In the second, I would never dream of calling you to the witness stand—you're one of the two honest physicians I've ever met."

I said to Porter, "And how many honest lawyers do you know, Doc?"

Porter's only response was a little smile.

We kept our voices down; the continuing beach noise created privacy in this crowd.

Darrow asked, "Can I assume you've filled my young friend in on what you know, Doctor?"

Porter nodded.

Darrow fixed his gray gaze on me as he jerked a thumb toward Porter. "John here has provided some remarkable insights not only into the Ala Moana case, but the psychology of the various racial groups on Oahu. I'd imagine we'd be hard pressed to find another naval officer with the doctor's intimate knowledge of Hawaii's social strata."

"You flatter me, Clarence," Porter said.

Darrow turned his gaze on the doctor. "Now I must risk insulting you, John, because I need to ask you to withdraw from this little gathering—I need a few moments alone with my investigator."

Porter rose, and in one graceful gesture swept his straw

fedora from the table even as he gave a little half-bow. "I'll be in the Coconut Grove, Clarence, enjoyin' an iced tea."

"Be sure to ask for sugar," I told him. "It's not automatic in this part of the world."

Porter snugged on his hat and smiled. "Whereas a slice of pineapple, rather than lemon, is. These Island customs are curious. Good afternoon, Mistah Hellah."

And Porter strolled inside.

"After hearing the doc's story," I asked, "have you changed your opinion about Thalia?"

Darrow's smile was a wavy crease in his rumpled face. "I still find her a clever girl."

"You just don't believe her story."

A grand shrug. "It's not important that I believe her; it's important that her mother and her husband *believed* her."

On the phone, I had told Darrow about my encounter last night with Horace Ida and company.

He leaned back in his chair, folded his hands on his round tummy. "You weren't the only one that spent some time yesterday with Island luminaries. Know who Walter Dillingham is?"

"Somebody important enough around town to get a street named after him."

"That's his father's street. Walter Dillingham is the president of a dozen companies, an officer or board member of a dozen or so more. He had me for luncheon yesterday at his home on Pacific Heights. Speaking for not only himself but the entire so-called *haole* elite, Dillingham expressed his belief in the guilt of the Ala Moana boys."

"So what?"

"So," Darrow drawled, "if all those important rich white people think those boys are guilty, I figure there's a damn good chance they aren't."

I nodded, relieved by Darrow's line of thinking. "It's starting to seem possible, maybe even probable, that those boys—including Joe Kahahawai, the man our clients murdered—didn't abduct and attack Thalia Massie."

His smile turned crooked. "I ascertain that those young fellows were apparently fairly convincing in last evening's melodrama . . . but the fact remains, on the way to making their point, they did kidnap you."

"Granted. But they had their reasons, and it sure got my attention. Are you going to see them? They desperately want to talk to you."

He shook his shaggy head no. "Conflict of interest. Perhaps after Mrs. Fortescue, Lt. Massie, and the sailor boys are free, I might be able to meet with them—until then, simply not possible."

"What if they grab me again?"

He grunted a laugh. "Those sweet innocent boys? Perish the thought."

"Look, they're Island roughnecks, slum kids, but I don't think they're rapists, and I don't think you do, either, C.D. Hell, these damn police used identification methods abandoned half a century ago by any civilized police department."

His expression turned mock curious. "When and where was it you encountered a civilized police department? I don't remember ever having the pleasure."

"You know what I mean. Three times, they dragged the defendants in front of Thalia, as good as telling her, 'These are the parties we suspect, and we want you to ID 'em.' "

He was shaking his head, no. "The issue is not whether Joe Kahahawai was innocent or guilty. The real point to consider is that our clients *believed* Kahahawai attacked Thalia. They committed an illegal, violent act but are justified by the purity of their purpose."

"Are you kidding?"

The gray gaze was steady. "No. I believe in taking into account cause and effect, not succumbing to hatred, fear, and revenge."

"You mean the way Mrs. Fortescue and Tommie did?"

He twitched a frown. "I was referring to our court system."

"Then do you want me to stop looking into the attack on Thalia?"

His eyes flared. "No! Just because our clients didn't know the truth when they committed this act doesn't mean we shouldn't know the truth when we set out to defend them. If

Joe Kahahawai *was* guilty, that is helpful to us. Our moral ground is higher, our case is stronger."

"So I'm to keep at it."

A slow nod. "You're to keep at it."

"What if I find out Kahahawai was innocent?"

One eyebrow flicked up. "Then we hope to hell the prosecution doesn't know as much as we do. . . . In a few days, jury selection begins."

"And then the fun."

Now a little smile. "And then the fun. Speaking of which, I bear unhappy tidings from Miss Bell."

"Yeah?"

He put on a sad mask. "It seems she has the nastiest little sunburn. Isn't that tragic? She was wondering if you would meet her at her room at three o'clock, to rub lotion on her poor red skin."

"I think I could manage. How is it she's willing to associate with me again?"

His hand gesture was a flippant flip. "I explained that your job is, in part, to play devil's advocate for me; that you are in fact *helping* poor dear Thalia, not hindering her."

I laughed, once. "You know, I knew sooner or later it would come to this, C.D."

"What's that, son?"

I scooted my chair back in the sand, and stood. "You pleading my case."

And I padded into the Royal Hawaiian, mind spinning with thoughts of Dr. Porter's revelations, but other parts of me anticipating a reunion with Miss Bell.

I was no beach boy, but I knew all about applying suntan lotion to the shoulders of a beautiful woman.

TWELVE

Set back a ways from Kalakaua Avenue, the former tourist hotel turned nightclub that was the Ala Wai Inn sat perched on the rocky shore of the fetid drainage canal whose name it had taken. Spotlights nestling in palm trees called attention to the two-story white frame trimmed black and brown would-be pagoda, its occasional octagonal windows glowing yellow in the night like jack-o'-lantern eyes.

"It's a roadhouse posing as a Jap tearoom," I said, tooling Mrs. Fortescue's sporty Durant down the drive.

"Looks like fun to me," Isabel said next to me, puffing prettily on a Camel. She'd gone hatless this evening, the better to show off her new hairdo courtesy of the Royal Hawaiian beauty shop; it was shorter and curlier, a cap of platinum curls, vaguely reminiscent of Harpo Marx but one hell of a lot sexier.

I pulled the roadster into a packed parking lot and invented a place next to a grass-shack toolshed. We were nestled in pretty snug, and Isabel had to slide over and get out on my side. I helped. She was a bundle of curves draped in Chanel, and smelled much better than that swampy drainage ditch nearby.

She was in my arms, then, and we kissed, another of her smoky, deep kisses, her tongue tickling my tonsils. We'd spent much of the last couple days (except for when I was tracking down witnesses to talk to) patching up our romance. Very little discussion of our differences was involved.

Her crêpe de chine dress had sideways blue and white stripes, as if she were standing in the slanting shadows of venetian blinds. It was slinky and would have looked vampy, but she was a little too nicely rounded for that.

Hand in hand, we walked to the brightly lighted entryway of the Ala Wai, pausing as Isabel crushed her Camel out under her high heel on the cinders. I must have looked pretty jaunty in my Panama hat, untucked red silk shirt with the parrots, and lightweight tan trousers. Or like a complete fool.

"So this is where Thalo's trouble began," Isabel said.

"Guess so," I said, but I was starting to think Thalia Massie's troubles had begun a lot earlier than that Saturday night last September. Which was why I was here. There were, after all, nicer places in Waikiki I could have taken the lovely Miss Bell dining and dancing.

As we stepped inside the smoky, dimly lighted joint, with its phony bamboo-and-hibiscus decor, a swarthy, stocky fellow in an orange shirt with flowers on it that made my parrots pale came forward with the ready smile and appraising eye of the doorkeeper he was.

"Evening, folks," he said over the steel-guitar–dominated music, and the giddy chatter of customers. "Little crowded. Dine tonight, or jus' dance?"

"Just dance," I said.

He winked. "Sol Hoopii Trio tonight. Those boys keep it hoppin'." He gestured with his hand toward the circular dance floor. "Some booths lef' in back."

"Is the Olds party here?"

"Ah yes. I get a girl show you."

He called over a Japanese cutie in a kimono affair that, un-like the geisha garb of the waitresses at the Royal Hawaiian, was cut in front to show some leg. She was pretty, and pretty sweaty, tendrils of her piled-up black hair snaking loose; she had an order pad in hand, a pencil tucked behind her ear.

"Olds party," the doorkeeper told her.

She blew hair away from her face, and grunted, "This way," swaying off.

The doorkeeper grinned and pointed to himself with a thumb. "Need anything, jus' ask for Joe—Joe Freitas!"

And we followed our sullen leggy geisha along the edge of the jammed dance floor. That the dance floor opened onto the terrace meant only that the mugginess and buggy, fishy odor of the canal could wend its way in to intermingle with the tobacco smoke, greasy food smells, and perspiration odor.

Two tiers of teakwood-lattice booths circled the dance floor but stopped at the terrace wall, making a sort of horseshoe; the upper tier extended out a few feet, making the floor-level booths cozier. Dark booths they were, each lighted by a single candle, deep booths that were damn near alcoves, lending privacy to conversations and assignations.

The Sol Hoopii Trio had a tiny stage to one side of the open terrace; they wore pink shirts and matching trousers with red cummerbunds and leis—three guitars, one of them a steel played in a lap, one of the guitar players singing into a microphone. No drummer, but the dancers didn't mind—those guitarists were laying down a jazzy beat behind the falsetto gibberish.

With the exception of the Sol Hoopii Trio and other hired help, the Ala Wai Inn was conspicuously white this evening. White faces, white linen suits on many of the men, only the dresses of the white women to splash a little color around.

The geisha showed us to the booth where Lt. Francis Olds, in white linen, sat with a cute plump green-eyed redhead in a blue dress with white polka dots.

"Good evening, Pop," I said to the lieutenant. "Don't get up—we'll slide in."

And we did, Isabel getting in first, Olds scooching around the square table, closer to the redhead.

"This is Doris, the little woman," Olds said, gesturing to the redhead's generous bosom, making his description seem less than apt. "Doris, this is Nate Heller, the detective who works for Mr. Darrow I was telling you about."

"Pleased to meetcha," she said. She was chewing gum, but

it wasn't off-putting; it just made her seem enthusiastic, like the flirty green eyes she was flashing at me.

Olds didn't have to introduce Doris to Isabel, because with the Olds' baby-sitting Thalia at their home on that ammo-depot island out at Pearl, Isabel had been a frequent visitor.

"Thanks for helping me out," I said to Olds.

"Not a problem," Olds said. "Anything to help Thalia. She's on the *Alton* tonight, by the way, playing bridge with Tommie, Mrs. Fortescue, and either Lord or Jones, Jones I think."

Honey, we're having the conspirators over for cards!

Brother.

I had told Olds out at Pearl Harbor yesterday that I needed to talk to a number of Tommie's fellow officers, but that I hated to do it under Admiral Stirling's nose. Was there somewhere more informal, where I might be able to get looser, straighter answers out of them?

He had suggested stopping by the Ala Wai on Saturday night.

"Why Saturday?" I'd asked him.

"Saturday night is Navy Night at the Ala Wai. *Kanaka* locals know to stay away. So do enlisted men. Strictly junior officers and their wives, out dancing and dining and drinking. They can't afford the dining rooms at the Royal Hawaiian or Moana, you know, where the upper ranks go. But the food at the Ala Wai is passable and affordable, the music's loud, the lights are low. What else would a Navy man ask?"

Olds had agreed to meet me and introduce me to some of his—and Tommie's—friends. The way flasks of liquor and local moonshine were passed around freely, he assured me, I'd find my subjects well lubricated and talkative.

"Besides," Olds had said, "if you're going to question them about the night Thalia was raped, what better place to talk to them than the place where they spent that very evening?"

He'd had a point, but now that I was here, I wasn't so sure it'd been a good idea. The loud music, the crowded dance floor, the smoky heat . . . None of it seemed all that conducive to conducting interviews, even informal ones.

The level of activity here was just this side of frantic: on the dance floor, there was continual cutting in during songs and swapping of partners at the end of them; men and women (seldom couples) were table-hopping, the laughter shrill and drunken. The smudgy shadows of couples necking could be seen in booths and corners, and there was fairly bold pawing going on, on the dance floor.

"You sailor boys sure know how to have a good time," I said.

"A lot of us go way back."

"You're the oldest one here, Pop—and you ain't thirty. How the hell far back *can* they go?"

Olds shrugged. "Annapolis. Every Saturday night at the Ala Wai is like a damn class reunion, Nate. You gotta understand something, about sub duty ... you risk your life every day down there, crowded into those unventilated cramped metal coffins. Any second you can sink to the bottom, no warning, no hope of rescue. Hardship like that breeds loyalty among men, forges friendships deeper than family." He shook his head. "Hard to explain to a civilian."

"Like it's hard to explain why Jones and Lord helped Mrs. Fortescue and Tommie snatch Joe Kahahawai?"

Olds looked at me like he wasn't sure whose side I was on; of course, neither was I.

"Something like that," he said.

"Is Bradford here?"

"That's him, there." Olds nodded toward the dance floor. "With the little blonde. That's Red Rigby's wife."

Dark-haired, slender, blandly handsome, Lt. Jimmy Bradford was doing the Charleston with a good-looking blonde. He was grinning at her and she was grinning back.

"You guys ever dance with your own wives?"

Olds grinned. "Maybe on our anniversaries."

"Is that why, that night, Tommie didn't notice Thalia was missing till one a.m., when the party was shutting down and it was time to go home?"

A disappointed frown creased his friendly face. "That's not fair, Nate."

"I'm just trying to make sense out of this. Thalia and

Tommie come to Navy night for the weekly party, Thalia claims she leaves at eleven-thirty, and it's an hour and a half later before Tommie notices his lifemate is gone."

"He noticed a lot earlier than that."

"When *did* he notice, Pop?"

Olds shrugged; he didn't look at me. "After that little fuss."

"What little fuss?"

Doris chimed in, giggly: "When Thalia got slap-happy."

"Zip it," Olds snapped at her, shooting daggers.

But I pressed. "What do you mean, Doris? What are you talking about?"

Doris, wincing with hurt feelings, shook her head no and gulped at her *oke*-spiked glass of Coke.

"Pop," I said quietly, "if you don't level with me, I can't help Tommie."

He sighed, shrugged. "Thalia just had a little argument with somebody and went storming off. Nobody I know of remembers seeing her after that—it was maybe eleven-thirty, eleven-thirty-five at the time."

"Argument with who?"

"Lt. Stockdale. Ray Stockdale."

"Is he here? That's one guy I'd really like to talk to."

Olds shook his head, no. "I don't think so. At least I haven't seen him."

I glanced at Doris and she looked away. She was chewing her gum listlessly now.

"But there's plenty of guys who *are* here," Olds said brightly, "who'll be willing to talk to you, once I vouch for you."

"Why don't you take me around, then?"

"Sure. Doris, you keep Miss Bell outa trouble, okay?"

I said to Isabel, "Don't fall in love with some sailor while I'm gone, baby."

Her Kewpie mouth pursed in a mocking little smile. She was lighting up another Camel. "Ditch a girl in a joint like this, big boy, you take your chances."

I arched an eyebrow. "You take your chances just stepping inside a joint like this."

I blew her a kiss and she blew me one back, and no sooner had we departed the booth than a pair of officers in white linen mufti sauntered over, and in a flash, Olds's wife and my date were out on the dance floor fighting for their honor.

"They don't waste much time here," I commented.

"It's a friendly place," Olds allowed.

And by way of proof, over the next hour, he introduced me to half a dozen friendly brother officers of Tommie Massie's, all of whom spoke highly of Thalia. Smoking cigarettes and cigars, drinking bootleg hootch, arms slung around giggling women who might or might not be their wives, they slouched against the bar or sat in booths or leaned against walls, glad to cooperate with Clarence Darrow's man. Phrases recurred, and because of the circumstances, I took no notes, and even later that night, looking back on it, I found the youthful submariners in white linen mufti blurring into one indistinguishable mass of high marks for Thalia ("nice kid," "sweet girl," "kinda quiet but a swell gal," "she's crazy about Tommie") and scorn for the rapists ("*all* them niggers should be shot").

Finally I told Olds I had all the info I needed, and sent my chaperon back to the booth. I'd told him I needed to take a leak, which was true enough. What I didn't tell him was that I'd seen Jimmy Bradford slipping into the men's room a moment or two before.

Soon I was sidling up to the urinal next to Bradford and we were both pissing as I said, "Don't forget to button up, after you're done."

He frowned at me in confused irritation. "What?"

"That's what got you in trouble with the cops, isn't it? Walking around with your fly open, the night Thalia Massie was assaulted?"

The frown turned into a sneer. "Who the hell are you, mister?"

"Nate Heller. I'm Clarence Darrow's investigator. I'd offer to shake hands, but . . ."

He finished before I did, and I joined him at the sink, waiting for him to finish washing up so I could have my turn.

He looked at me in the streaky mirror; his features may

have been bland, but the blue eyes were sharp—and he didn't seem as drunk as his brother officers. "What do you want?"

Looking back at him in the mirror, I shrugged, smiled a little. "I want to talk to you about the case."

He used a paper hand towel. "I had nothing to do with the killing of Kahahawai."

"Nobody said you did. I want to talk to you about what happened to Thalia Massie last September."

He frowned. "What does that have to do with the case Darrow's trying?"

"Well, it does seem just the slightest little bit connected, since it's the goddamn murder motive. But maybe you don't want to help."

He turned and looked at me; his eyes narrowed, like he was aiming a rifle at me. "Of course I'll talk to you," he said. "Anything to help Tommie and his wife."

"Good." I stepped up to the sink and washed my hands. "Why don't we take some air?"

He nodded, and we exited the john and went out past the stocky doorkeeper into the warm night; the air this close to the drainage canal seemed muggy, and there was no sign of the trade-wind breeze that made the Hawaiian heat so bearable. He leaned against a Model A and fished a pack of Chesterfields from his pocket. He shook out a smoke, then held the pack toward me.

"Want one?"

"No thanks," I said. "It's the only bad habit I haven't acquired."

He lighted up with a match. "You know, all you had to do was ask. I'm willing to help. You didn't have to crack wise."

I shrugged, leaned against a parked Hupmobile coupe, facing him. "I left four messages for you at Pearl—two with your captain, two with your wife. You never returned my calls. I figured maybe you were ducking me, Lieutenant."

"I'm just busy," he said, waving out the match.

"Is that why you didn't testify at the Ala Moana trial?"

He blew out smoke. "Nobody asked me to testify. Besides, I was on sub duty."

"Did somebody arrange that?"

The eyes tightened again. "What are you getting at, pal?"

"Nothing. Just, when I went over the court transcripts, you seemed like a pretty important witness to turn into the little man who wasn't there."

"I've cooperated right down the line. Tommie's my best friend. I'd do anything for him."

"You mean, like sleep with his wife?"

He pitched the cigarette and lurched forward, grabbing me by my parrot shirt. He was close enough I could tell it was bourbon he'd been drinking; couldn't make out the brand, though, but definitely not home brew.

"You got a filthy mouth, Heller."

I looked down toward his clenched fists clutching my shirt. "That's silk. It damages easily."

He blinked and let go. Backed off. "It's a dirty damn lie. Thalia is a—"

"Nice girl. She loves Tommie. Quiet, though. Yeah, I heard the story. You guys all got it down pat—that's probably why none of you were called at the first trial."

"What are you talking about?"

"DAs don't like it when groups of witnesses use identical language; they're afraid some smart defense lawyer will crack through the hooey and get at the truth—like how you sub-mariners pass your wives around like other guys pass around a ciggie or a bottle."

He was sneering again. "You're a cocky son of a bitch, aren't you? You really want your teeth handed to you, don't you?"

"You want to try, Jimmy? Or do you only break women's jaws?"

He blinked. "Is that what you think? You think *I* hit Thalia . . . ?"

"Lovers' quarrel turns ugly—a girl needs somebody to blame. Who better than a bunch of 'niggers'?"

His face was reddening. "You're crazy—there was *nothing* between Thalia and me . . ."

"I have witnesses that place you in Thalia's house, last May, when her husband was away, on sub duty. Witnesses who say you also went on overnight trips to the beach."

He was shaking his head, no, violently, no. "That's just small filthy minds talking. Thalia and my wife Jane and Tommie and I, we're close friends, that's all. It was completely innocent."

"Separate bedrooms, you mean? Now tell me about how Santa Claus is a real guy."

"Go to hell! My wife went back home, last May, to Michigan, to take care of her sick mama. I was alone, Thalia was alone . . . lonely. I kept her company. Out of friendship to both her and Tommie."

"Oh, I believe this. This sounds real likely."

"I don't give a damn what you believe! There was nothing between Thalia and me except friendship. And if I didn't want to help her _and_ Tommie, I wouldn't be putting up with this horseshit interrogation!"

"Okay," I said calmly, patting the air with my hands. "Okay. Then let's just back up a few steps. Tell me what happened that night. The night Thalia was assaulted."

He let out a sigh, then shrugged. "It was just another Navy Night at the Ala Wai. Dancing, drinking, laughing. Husbands and wives do tend to split up on Navy Night, go their separate ways—nothing wrong with that. We're not swapping wives! It's just a damn party."

"Okay. Did you see Thalia leave?"

"No."

"Did you leave yourself, at any time?"

"No."

"Well, you eventually _did_ leave. . . ."

Another shrug. "Party lasted longer than usual. I even slipped a couple bucks to the orchestra to play past midnight, we were having so much fun. I took off my shoes and danced. Everybody stood around and clapped in rhythm and . . ."

"Everybody saw you, you mean."

Another rifle-aim narrowing of the eyes. "What's that supposed to mean?"

"It means you might have slipped out, then slipped back,

and made yourself conspicuously seen, to build an alibi."

"I don't want to talk to you anymore."

"What were you doing walking outside Thalia's house with your fly unbuttoned, Jimmy?"

"I was a little drunk. I took a piss in the bushes. Some cops came along and I got smart with 'em and they hauled me in."

"That's how you became a suspect in the rape."

He scowled. "It was just a stupid mix-up. Tommie told 'em he'd been with me all night. Thalia vouched for me, too."

"What were you doing there? You don't live next door to the Massies or anything."

"Tommie and me left the Ala Wai around one o'clock; when he couldn't find Thalia, he assumed she'd gone on to the Rigbys—it was kind of an after-party tradition to go over to Red's for a nightcap and scrambled eggs, and when Tommie called home from the Ala Wai and got no answer, he figured Thalia must've caught a ride over there. Tommie drove us over to the Rigbys, but there was no Thalia. So Tommie called home again—and this time she was there, and that's when she told him about the . . . you know."

"The rape."

"Right. Tommie rushed out and took off in his Ford, and then I started gettin' worried. . . . I'd only heard his half of the phone conversation, but it was clear something was terribly wrong at home. So I walked over."

"And stopped to take a piss along the way."

"Yeah. And forgot to button my fly, and that's how the stupid mix-up with the cops happened."

"I see. Do you know anything about Thalia having an argument with Lt. Stockdale?"

He shrugged. "I was just on the fringe of that. It was nothing special."

"What was it about?"

"I don't really know. When people are drinking, they don't need an excuse to bicker."

"I guess they don't."

We stood staring at each other. The muffled sound of the band and the gaiety within the Ala Wai mingled with the call of birds and the rustle of trees; these sounds, which neither of us had noticed while we were talking, seemed suddenly deafening.

Finally he asked, "Is that all?"

I nodded. "Thanks for the information."

His smile was nervous. "Look, uh . . . sorry I grabbed your shirt. I know you're just doing your job."

"Forget it. I was provoking you."

"You admit that?"

I nodded. "I've been getting canned stories from everybody I talked to here, tonight. I had to find a way to cut through the bullshit, so I gave you the needle." I held out my hand. "No hard feelings?"

He took it; we shook.

"No hard feelings," he said.

I smiled at him, and he smiled back, but I didn't mean it, and neither did he. This bastard had been fucking Thalia Massie, and we both knew it.

We wandered back inside together, and split off faster than the marrieds around this joint did. I went over and buttonholed the stocky doorkeeper, Joe Freitas.

"You wouldn't happen to know Lt. Stockdale, would you, Joe?" I was asking this question over the edge of a shiny half-dollar.

Joe snatched the half-buck and jerked a thumb upward. "Booth upstairs. Tall good-lookin' fella. Short curly yella hair."

Stockdale was, as the doorkeeper had promised, a blond-haired bruiser, ruggedly handsome; he had a flask and two glasses, an ashtray with two burning cigarettes, and a skinny but pretty brunette he was nuzzling. Both he and his lady friend were tipsier than a three-legged table.

"Sure, I'll talk to you!" he exploded, good-naturedly drunk. "Sit yourself down. This is Betty. She's Bill Ransom's wife— except for tonight." And he let out a horse laugh and Betty's giggle evolved into an unladylike snort.

I slid into the booth. "I hear the night Thalia Massie was assaulted, you and she had a little run-in."

"Hey, first off," he said, overcompensating with his

enunciation in an effort to be soberly serious, "I'm as against niggers raping white women as the next guy."

"That's an admirable view."

"Just because Thalia Massie is a lousy stuck-up slut is no reason niggers should go around raping her. That character, Joe Ka-ha-what's-it? *I'da* shot that black bastard myself, if they'd invited me to the party. Tommie Massie is my pal."

"What happened that night, Ray? Between you and Thalia, I mean."

He shrugged. "We was eatin', and me and the wife and another coupla couples." He gestured vaguely off to the right. "Over in one of the private dinin' rooms. Thalia come stumblin' in, drunk as skunk, uninvited." He leaned forward conspiratorially. "Nobody liked Thalia, snooty little bitch. Little Miss Sassiety Butter-Wouldn't-Fucking-Melt-in-Her-Pussy."

Ah yes. As Olds had said, you make special friends on submarine duty.

"She come waltzin' in here, and we just ignore her. She wasn't invited! And she just stands there with her goddamn nose in the air, and clears her throat and says, 'Don't you know a lady's entered the room.' I says, 'I don't see any.' About then, Jimmy Bradford comes in, lookin' for her I guess . . . they used to be kind of an item, y'know. Anyway, pouty little bitch says, 'You're no gentleman, Lt. Stockdale,' and Bradford says, 'Take it easy, baby, this is a public place.' But Miss Sassiety Bitch struts up and sticks her chin in my face and says, 'I don't care! You're no gentleman, Lt. Stockdale, talkin' to me like that!' I says, 'Well, Thalia, who gives a shit what a lousy slut like you thinks, anyway.' Which is when she slapped me."

"*Slapped* you. . . ."

This hadn't been in the transcript material I'd been provided! No wonder Doris Olds had referred to Thalia as "slap-happy."

"Yeah." He touched his jaw. "She whaled me a good one."

"Then what happened?"

He shrugged. "She stormed outa there. Good thing, too. I'da kicked her fat ass, if she hadn't, and the other fellas hadn't been holding me back. I was well and truly pissed off. Then, I guess somebody went looking for Tommie, to tell him what happened. He come looking for her, but she was long gone, o' course."

"When was this?"

"I dunno. Eleven-thirty, maybe."

I thanked Stockdale and left him to his guzzling and nuzzling, and searched out the doorkeeper again.

"Joe, did you hear anything about a fuss upstairs involving Mrs. Massie, the night of the assault?"

"She slap some sailor, I hear."

"Did you see her leave? I mean, did she come flying down the stairs and go rushing out?"

Joe shook his head, no. "That was a busy night. I was showin' people to their seats, not always watchin' the door."

"You didn't see her leave, sometime between eleven-thirty and midnight?"

"No . . . but I did see somethin' else."

"What?"

His smile was friendly but his eyes were mercenary. "I'm tryin' to remember, boss."

I dug out a dollar for him. "Does this jog it?"

"Comin' back to me, boss. I remember her, that girl in the green dress. When her party come in that night, it was the first big party to arrive, and she walk ahead of others, with her head bent over. I thought maybe she was mad at somebody, or maybe drunk already."

"That's not worth a buck, Joe. Keep trying."

"Okay. But I think maybe this is worth two dollars."

"Try me and see."

"Oh-kay. I remember seein' her standin' by the doorway about midnight, little after, maybe. She was talkin' to Sammy."

That perked me up. "Who's Sammy?"

"Sammy's worth two dollars, easy."

"Two bucks it is. Who's Sammy, Joe?"

"He's a music boy."

"What?"

"Hawaiian boy, he play music with Joe Crawford's band, over on Maui. But when he's home, on Oahu, he like to come over to the Ala Wai, and listen to the music, here. We always got good music here, boss."

"What were Sammy and Mrs. Massie talking about?"

"I couldn't hear 'em." He shrugged. "Not even for 'nother dollar."

"Were they friendly?"

"She seem a little worked up."

"Arguing, then?"

"No. Jus' talkin', boss."

"Has Sammy been back since?"

"Sure. Now an' then, once in while."

"Lately?"

"Not sure."

"Look—this is where you can reach me." I got out my notebook, jotted down my name and the Royal Hawaiian's phone number, tore off the paper. "If Sammy shows up, no matter what time of day, Monday through Sunday—you call me. There's a fin in it for you—and I don't mean a shark, get me?"

Grinning, he snatched the slip of paper from my hands like it was the five-spot. "Got you, boss."

The rest of the evening I spent dancing with Isabel to the syrupy but rhythmic music of the Sol Hoopii Trio.

And when we went out to the car, hand in hand, she said, "Did you find anything out?"

"Nothing particularly useful," I said.

It was a lie, of course, but I didn't feel like being the only guy who went to the Ala Wai Inn tonight who didn't get laid.

THIRTEEN

In a land redolent of exotic blossoms, the second floor of the old Kapiolani Building at King and Alakea streets offered a mingling of pungent cockroach-repelling creosote and stale tobacco smoke. It was not an unfamiliar bouquet. I was, after all, a Chicago copper, and this was, after all, the temporary headquarters of the Honolulu Police. The central station house at Bethel and Merchant was getting a facelift, Chang Apana had explained.

They'd moved a few things in to turn this place into headquarters—the big open room you entered had a high counter for the desk sergeant to shuffle reports behind, a handful of desks against one wall with blue-uniformed cops talking to citizens at them, a few file cabinets, a scattering of straight-back chairs. Ceiling fans whirred lazily, throwing shadows, rustling papers.

The desk sergeant told me the assembly room of the detective bureau was on the second floor. At the top of the stairs, I found Chang Apana in another big open room. The midmorning sun was filtering in through high windows, giving a golden glaze to greenish plaster walls and hardwood floor; like a lethargic cook beating eggs, ceiling fans stirred the air. At one end, an area was set up with chairs and a blackboard for roll call, and some glassed-off offices were along the right wall.

Otherwise, it was desks and one central table where cops could gather for a conference or to just shoot the bull.

At that table—which had an oddly decorative top, a dragon fashioned from black and white dominoes and mah-jongg tiles—sat Chang Apana, again in white linen and black bow tie, and a swarthy hawk-faced character who was either a cop or a hood. Under the ridge of a snapbrim that would have done George Raft proud, keen dark eyes tracked me as I approached. His suit was brown and rumpled, his tie red and snug, and he wasn't as small as Chang, but he wouldn't have met the Chicago PD's height requirement, or the mob's for that matter.

They were smoking cigarettes and drinking coffee. This wasn't exactly a bustling squadroom. Only about a third of the desks were filled, and anybody who wasn't seated wasn't in a hurry. There was no more sense of urgency here than on the beach at the Royal Hawaiian.

On second thought, there was more urgency at the beach: that surfboard polo could get pretty intense.

Chang stood politely and, half a beat later, so did the other guy. Smiling like a skull, Chang half-bowed; his companion didn't.

"Detective Nate Heller, Chicago police," Chang said, with a gesture to his hawk-faced friend, "Detective John Jardine, Honolulu police."

We shook hands; the guy had a firm grip but he didn't over-play it. He was studying me with the cold unblinking eyes of a cop assessing a murder suspect.

Chang called a secretary over—a round-faced Hawaiian girl with a nice shape under her businesslike blouse and skirt—and instructed her to bring me some coffee. How did I want it? Chang wondered. Black, I said. She nodded and went after it.

"Whose side are you on, Detective Heller?" Jardine asked.

I pulled out a chair and sat. "Why, same as any cop—my own."

A tiny grin flashed in the dark face. He sat, and then Chang did, too.

"This is quite a table." I gestured to the black and white domino–mah-jongg mosaic.

"It's Detective Apana's handiwork," Jardine said.

I arched an eyebrow Chang's way. "A carpenter and a great detective?"

"I did not make table," Chang said, lighting up a fresh cigarette. "But I provide makings."

"This is all stuff Chang confiscated in Chinatown gambling raids," Jardine said, with a nod toward the black and white dragon. "Like to see Charlie Chan go wading into *that* crowd."

"Detective Jardine is too generous with praise," Chang said. But he obviously was eating it up.

The secretary brought me the coffee. I thanked her and we exchanged smiles and I watched the hula sway of her hips as she wandered back to her desk, efficient but in no hurry. Hawaii was the most distracting damn place.

"So, Detective Jardine," I said, "whose side are *you* on? Besides your own . . . in the Massie case, I mean."

His mouth twitched; his hawkish face remained otherwise blank, though his eyes were sharp as needles. "I do my job. Gather evidence. Report what I see. It's not up to me who gets prosecuted."

"Would you have prosecuted the Ala Moana boys?"

Another twitch. He exhaled smoke. "Not without a better case."

I sipped my coffee; it was hot and bitter and good. "Do you think they did it?"

A shrug. A deep suck-in on the cigarette. "I don't know. There are some pretty persistent rumors floating around town that another gang was roving around that night."

"Any leads on who they might be?"

Jardine shook his head, no. "But then we didn't pursue any."

Frowning thoughtfully, Chang said, "Something puzzling. There is saying on Islands—'Hawaiians will talk.' "

"So I hear," I said. "But nobody's even *whispering* about who this second gang might be. What do you make of that?"

Jardine shrugged again, taking a sip of his coffee. "Maybe there is no second gang."

Chang lifted a forefinger. "Confucius say, 'Silence big sister of wisdom.' "

"You mean, anybody who knows who this second gang is," I said, "is smart enough to keep quiet about it."

"What happened to 'Hawaiians will talk'?" Jardine asked grouchily.

I lifted a forefinger. "Capone say, 'Bullet in head little brother of big mouth.' "

That made Chang smile. Smoke from the cigarette between his fingers drifted up like a question mark before his skeletal, knife-scarred face.

"Well," Jardine said, "*somebody* took Thalia Massie to the old Animal Quarantine Station. I don't know who it was or what they did to her, but she was there."

"How do you know?"

"We found things of hers."

"Oh, yeah," I said, remembering, "some beads."

I had dismissed this, knowing how easily they could have been planted.

"A string of jade-colored beads," Jardine said, "and some Parrot matches and Lucky Strike cigarettes Mrs. Massie identified as hers."

"Her purse was found, too, wasn't it?"

"A green leather purse, yes, but not by us. The Bellingers, the couple that Mrs. Massie flagged down for a ride after it happened, found the purse on the road, later, when they were on their way home."

I sipped my coffee, said casually, "Weren't you one of the first detectives to talk to Thalia? Weren't you there that night, at the house in Manoa Valley?"

Jardine nodded. "She didn't want to get medical attention, refused to go to the hospital, really put her foot down. Of course, I knew in a rape case how important a pelvic examination was. But she wouldn't hear of it. Finally I convinced her husband, and he convinced her."

"What sort of shape was Tommie in?"

"Pretty well in his cups."

Chang said, "Tell Detective Heller about Lt. Bradford."

Jardine frowned. "You read too much into that, Chang."

"Tell him."

I knew Bradford's version of the "mix-up," but was eager to hear the cops' side. Strangely, Jardine seemed hesitant to get into this.

"Lt. Massie corroborated Bradford's story," Jardine said. "Bradford spent the evening at the Ala Wai Inn in Massie's company. He's not a suspect in the rape and beating."

"But you did arrest him that night," I said.

Jardine nodded. "For mopery. He was drunk, he had his fly open, he told us to go to hell when we pulled alongside him."

"That gets you more than arrested in Chicago," I said.

Jardine was stabbing his cigarette out in an ashtray that sat on one of the dragon's limbs. "He told us we should leave him alone, he was an officer with the Shore Patrol. We told him if he was in the Shore Patrol he should know better than to give another cop a hard time."

"Tell him," Chang said.

Jardine sighed. "When I brought Mrs. Massie out to drive her to the hospital, Bradford was being shown to a patrol wagon. They spoke. I heard her say to him, 'Don't worry, Jack—it's going to be all right.' It was . . . it was like *she* was comforting *him*."

Chang looked at me with both eyebrows raised. The ceiling fans whirred above us. Jardine might have been a cigar-store Indian in a fedora, he was sitting there so motionless, so expressionless.

"Is there anything else about the case," I asked, "you can share with me?"

Jardine shook his head, no. "I got pulled off the investigation, when Daniel Lyman and Lui Kaikapu broke out of Oahu, New Year's Eve."

Chang Apana's tone was almost scolding. "How can prisoner break out of cage with no door?"

"What d'you mean?" I asked.

Chang said, "Most guards in Oahu prison, like most prisoners, are Hawaiians. Big on honor system. You in jail but have urgent business on outside, just ask for pass. You want to know how murderer Lyman and thief Kaikapu 'broke out'? Chang will tell you: guards send them out to get big supply of *okolehao* for prison New Year's Eve party."

This reminded me of Cook County jail, who let the likes of the bootlegging Druggan brothers in and out at will, and neither the jailers nor the Druggans were Hawaiians.

"But the trustees didn't bother to come back," I said.

"Once they got out," Jardine said, "they decided to split up and take their chances on their own. We caught Kaikapu the next day."

"But Lyman's still at large."

Jardine's mouth twitched again. "The bastard mugged a couple out parking, tied the guy up to a fence with fishing line, raped the woman, took a buck and a quarter out of her purse, and then drove her home."

"Thoughtful fella."

"And he's been leading us a goddamn merry chase ever since."

"You're still on the case?"

Jardine sipped his coffee. "Sort of."

"What does that mean?"

Jardine dug in his pocket for a pack of Lucky Strikes— presumably not the ones found at the crime scene. "The governor appointed Major Ross to head up a Territorial Police Force."

"Just to track this jailbird down?"

"No." He lighted up the Lucky, exhaled smoke through his nose, echoing the dragon on the table. "We're in the middle of a departmental shake-up here, most of it due to the screwups in the Massie case. Heads are rolling daily. This Territorial Force is supposed to pick up the slack."

"Who are these temporary coppers?"

"Major Ross has a group he's picked from his National Guard members plus some Federal Prohibition Agents and a few American Legion volunteers."

Funny. Joe Kahahawai had served in the National Guard under Major Ross; it had been Mrs. Fortescue's fake summons from Ross that summoned Big Joe to his death.

Jardine continued, "I'm liaison between Major Ross's group and the PD."

I grunted a laugh. "Only all the king's horses and all the king's men haven't found this raping murderer."

Jardine nodded. "But we'll get him."

"Any sightings? Any other crimes?"

"Enough sightings to believe Lyman hasn't left the Island. No more rapes, no major thefts credited to him. He's gone way underground. Probably in the hills."

"Well, if you're off the Massie case, does that mean I can't ask you to chase down a lead for me?"

Jardine's eyes flashed. "Not at all. What'd you come up with?"

I sat forward and smiled just a little. "Are you aware that right before she went out the Ala Wai door, Thalia had a little chat with a *kanaka*?"

Jardine frowned in interest. "New one on me. Where you'd get this?"

"I'm a detective."

That amused Chang; at least, he smiled a little.

"His name's Sammy," I went on, "and he's some kind of musician with a band on Maui." I got out my little notepad and read off the name: "Joe Crawford's band. Are there any coppers on Maui you can check with?"

Jardine was nodding, getting out his own notebook to write down the names.

"Excuse me," a male voice intoned from behind us; it was deep and rang with authority.

The big man standing in the doorway of one of the glassed-in offices behind Jardine had the leanly muscular frame of a football linebacker and the pleasant, patient smile of a parish priest. Angularly handsome, kindly features rode a bucket skull, Brylcreemed black hair touched at the temples with gray. Whereas most of the detectives wandering through the Detective Bureau were Hawaiian, their ill-fitting wrinkled Western suits looking like costumes they were uneasily wearing, this guy was strictly Anglo-Saxon, and his dark brown suit looked neat and natural.

Both Chang and Jardine scooted their chairs back and stood, and I followed their lead.

"Inspector McIntosh," Chang said, "may I introduce honorable guest from Chicago Police, Nate Heller."

Never losing the kindly smile, he ambled over to me, held out his hand, as he said, "You've wandered off your beat."

We shook; his grip was surprisingly soft, though his hand was like a catcher's mitt.

"I do that from time to time," I said. "Actually, Clarence Darrow is an old family friend. He's come out of retirement for this case and doesn't have an investigator on staff anymore, so I'm helping him out."

"I'll bet Mr. Darrow had to pull some strings to arrange that."

"He knows how. I'm pleased to meet you, Inspector. I mentioned to Detective Apana that I hoped to speak with you."

"Chang said as much. Isn't the trial getting under way? I'd figure you to be at Mr. Darrow's side."

"Jury selection began Monday. I'm still doing legwork till the trial proper begins."

"Ah." He gestured like a gracious host. "Why don't you step into my office, Detective Heller." He cast his benignly beaming face upon Chang and Jardine. "I'll speak to our guest privately."

The two detectives nodded and sat back down.

Moments later, door shut behind us, I was taking the seat across from McIntosh's big desk; other than filing cabinets, the oversized cubicle was bare: no photos or diplomas on the wall, only a few personal items on the desk to tide its occupant over till these temporary quarters were behind him.

McIntosh settled his rangy frame into the wooden swivel chair behind the desk and sat nervously rubbing his forefinger against one graying temple as we spoke.

"I wanted to speak to you one on one," McIntosh said. "Chang Apana is a living legend around here, and Jardine is one of our best, most dogged investigators. But they're Chinese and Portuguese, respectively, and I wanted to be able to level with you."

"What does their race have to do with anything?"

The patient smile widened condescendingly; the lids of the world-weary, worried eyes went to half-mast. "Everything in Honolulu has to do with race, Detective Heller."

"Well, then . . . how, specifically, in this instance? We have more than one race in Chicago, by the way. I've seen colored people before."

"I didn't mean to patronize. But even the sharpest detective from the biggest city force is going to find himself, well, frankly, in over his head in these waters."

"Maybe you can toss me a life buoy."

He chuckled mildly, even as he continued rubbing his temple nervously. "Let's start with the Honolulu Police Department. We're under terrible political pressure right now, and are in the midst of a reorganization. Our authority is being chipped away at, with this Territorial Force under Major Ross. And do you know why?"

"I have a hunch, but I don't really want to seem impertinent."

"Speak frankly."

"It would seem you screwed up the Massie case."

He swallowed; rubbed his forehead. "Race and politics, Detective Heller. Some years ago, white and Hawaiian political factions here threw in together, to keep the Japs and Chinese from dominating local government. Part of the deal was, the whites tossed lesser governmental jobs to Hawaiians. There are two hundred and eighty men on the force, Detective Heller—and two hundred and forty of them are Hawaiian, or of mixed Hawaiian blood."

"What's the difference, as long as they're good men."

McIntosh nodded, bringing his hands before him, folding them prayerfully. "Most of them *are* good men—they're just not good cops. For most patrolmen and even detectives, no other qualification is needed but Hawaiian blood. Oh, and an eighth grade education."

"Isn't there any kind of testing, training . . ."

"Certainly. Cops here are trained to be able to give tourists directions. They have to be able to spell the names of the outer islands, and recommend points of interest."

"Are they cops or tour guides?"

McIntosh's mouth flinched. "I don't like to bad-mouth my men, Detective Heller. Some of them—like Chang and Jardine—could rival any cops you could find anywhere. My point is that there are political pressures on this Island that undermine the department's performance."

"And how would you rank your performance on the Massie case?" I purposely used "your" ambiguously.

"Under the circumstances, we performed well; there was the blunder at the Quarantine Station, with the tire tracks, that simply can't₌be excused. But there was pressure to prosecute, even though the case was weak."

"You admit it's weak?"

"We needed more time, we weren't ready for trial. There were too many damn chinks in the government's case that hadn't been filled."

I presumed he didn't mean "chinks" in a racial sense, but it was an interesting choice of words.

"All we had was Thalia Massie's story," he said, ticking items off on his fingers. "Then the supporting story of Eugenio Batungbacal that he'd seen a woman dragged into a car at about twelve-fifteen. Then, Mrs. Massie's identification of the suspects, and her recollection of the license number. Plus the discovery of her necklace and other items at the crime scene, and then there's the police records of Ahakuelo and Kahahawai."

"Every one of those points is, to some degree, vulnerable," I said, ticking them off on my fingers. "Thalia could be lying, witnesses other than Batungbacal seem to contradict him, Thalia originally said she couldn't identify the assailants or remember the license plate, finding Thalia's beads and such at the scene doesn't place the suspects there, and Ahakuelo and Kahahawai's 'records' are minimal at best."

"Do you expect me to disagree? But I will say this, the fact that Mrs. Massie initially said she couldn't identify them—

when she was half-hysterical, in shock, or under sedation—
bothers me not in the least. Those boys did it, all right."

That sat me up straight. "You really believe that?"

The world-weary eyes tightened. "Absolutely. Look at it
this way—when we picked Ida up, he lied through his teeth.
He said he hadn't driven that car when in fact he'd been out all
night in it. Then, without prompting, Ida blurted out that he
hadn't attacked the white woman—*before anybody had told him
about the Massie rape!*"

I frowned in thought. "So how in hell did he know about a
white woman being attacked?"

"Precisely. Belated or not, Mrs. Massie did identify four of
the five boys, and she came up with that license number, just
one little digit off. I don't know how you do it in Chicago, Detective Heller, but in Honolulu, once a man lies to me twice, I
don't have to take his damn word for anything."

I couldn't argue with that.

"No, those are guilty boys. We just didn't have proper time
to build a case." He sighed, smiled tightly. "Is there anything
else I can help you with?"

"No. No, you've been generous with your time."

"I've instructed Detective Apana to make himself available
to you as needed. While we are technically on the side of the
prosecution in the Fortescue case, we have great admiration for
Mr. Darrow and a certain sympathy for his clients."

"Thank you."

We shook hands again, and I found my way back to Chang
and Jardine, who stood as I approached. McIntosh was shut
back inside his office.

"Doesn't surprise me the inspector wanted to talk to you
privately," Jardine said glumly.

"Oh?"

"There's a faction of the force—Hawaiian and Portuguese,
mostly . . . and I'm Portuguese myself—who were suspected of
leaking information to the defense, in the first trial. And to the
Japanese-English newspaper, the *Hochi*, which was sympa-
thetic to the Ala Moana boys."

"I see."

The dark eyes under the brim of the George Raft fedora were mournful. "Just disappoints me the inspector doesn't trust me."

"He spoke highly of you, Inspector Jardine."

"Good to hear. You need any backup, Chang knows where to find me."

We shook hands again, and Jardine sauntered over to a desk and got to some paperwork.

Chang, who was on his way home to his wife and eight kids on Punchbowl Hill, walked me downstairs and out onto King Street, where a balmy breeze kissed us hello.

"McIntosh seems like a good man," I said.

"Good man," Chang agreed. He snugged on his Panama. "Poor detective."

"Why do you say that?"

"He arrested Ala Moana boys on hunch, then stubbornly stuck with it."

"He says Ida lied to him. That Ida blurted out something about not attacking the 'white woman.' "

"Ida lied to protect self over *other*, minor assault when he and friends bump bumpers with *kanaka* gal and *haole* husband. And Ida was in station house, when he said that about not attacking white woman. He could easy have heard about Mrs. Massie by then . . . station was jumping with the news."

"I see."

Chang laughed humorlessly. "McIntosh is like carpenter who build straw house on sand: first strong wind bring disaster."

"Who said that?" I asked.

"I did," Chang said, and he tipped his Panama and went his way.

FOURTEEN

The Sunday evening before the first day of the trial, Isabel and I piled into Mrs. Fortescue's Durant roadster with the top down, Isabel's short Harlow hair fluttering as we drove out along the cliffs of Diamond Head, winding up the slopes past a lighthouse, pulling over to the edge of the cliff, stopping, getting out, crossing the lava rock alongside the road to stand hand in hand watching the surf beat against the coral reef below. Bronze fishermen with bare chests, long trousers, and shoes (the reefs were sharp, jagged) were down in the water with hand nets and three-pronged spears, now and then hauling in shimmering slithering catches, silver, red, blue fish, some solid, others striped, eels and squirming squid, too. As we watched this native ritual dance against the expanse of amethyst ocean and white breakers, the red setting sun began tinting the waves pink, until the sun slipped over the horizon and purple night fell like an enormous shadow over the sea, the moon a stingy sliver now, the stars more generous but the darkness intimidating, Isabel clutching my hand tight, glad she wasn't alone, and suddenly blossoms of orange light burst below, then began flittering about, like giant fireflies. They were fishing by torchlight down there, now.

Back in the blue roadster, rather intoxicated by this lovely dark night, we began down the other side of the rise, gliding by expensive beach houses and estates; coming down, you could see the swimming pools of the rich cut out of the lava and coral rock above sea level, kept filled, washed clean, by the high tide. Scrub brush gave way to exotic foliage and coconut palms on the Kahala Road as we skimmed past more fancy beach houses, until we reached the entry of the Waialae Golf Club, which was under the Royal Hawaiian's control and open to hotel guests.

This time of evening, the eighteen-hole golf course was of no interest; we parked and went into a clubhouse smothered in palms and tropical shrubbery and were served an Italian supper on a spacious *lanai* on the edge of the ocean. Isabel was wearing a blue-on-white polka-dot beach ensemble; with her jaunty little matching cap, you'd never guess her blouse was the upper part of her white swimsuit. I had my trunks on under my tan linen trousers; my second acquisition of an aloha shirt (as the loud silk shirts were locally baptized) got a few looks even in this determinedly casual touristy crowd. This time it was dark blue with white and red blossoms. Maybe I'd start a trend.

After supper, we lounged on deck-style chairs on the *lanai* in the light of Japanese lanterns, sipping a fruity punch that was greatly improved by the rum from my hip flask (my supplier was a Japanese bellboy at the Royal Hawaiian to whom I'd made it clear the local home brew wasn't good enough, and damned if he didn't come up with Bacardi).

Isabel said, "We haven't talked about the case."

And we hadn't, at least hardly at all; my devil's advocacy only seemed to rile her. We'd been spending the evenings together, and then the nights, with her scurrying back to her room across the hall at dawn and me meeting her a few hours later downstairs for breakfast. She had rented a little Ford coupe and, each day, drove to Pearl Harbor to spend the day with Thalia and company, at the Oldses' and/or on the *Alton*.

But the evenings were devoted to dining and dancing and strolling along the white sand while palms swayed and ukuleles thrummed before retiring to my room, screwing our brains out on the bed in the breeze blowing in from the balcony. It was a honeymoon I could never afford with a woman who would never have me, in real life.

Fortunately, this wasn't real life: it was Waikiki.

"What do you want to know about the case?" I asked, knowing the exchange that followed might cost me my conjugal rights for the evening.

"How do *you* think it's going to go?"

"Well . . . C.D. has a racially mixed jury. That was probably inevitable, considering the makeup of the population. He's got his work cut out for him."

"They didn't mean to kill that brute."

"They meant to kidnap him. And when the cops turned on their siren, Mrs. Fortescue kept right on going. The coppers had to fire two shots out the window at the buggy, before the old girl finally pulled over."

Her heart-shaped face was a delicate mask, as pretty and blank as a porcelain doll's. "We're going to be heading up the same road, you know. For our moonlight swim?"

"I hadn't really thought about it," I said, lying. I'd meant to get out here and have a look all along. The plan (whether devised by Mrs. Fortescue, Tommie, or one of the sailor boys had never been established) had been to drive Kahahawai's body out to Hanauma Bay and dispose of it in something called, colorfully, sinisterly, the Blowhole.

"They were foolish, weren't they, Nate?"

"Not foolish, Isabel. Goddamn stupid. Arrogant."

She turned her delicate features toward the ocean. "Now I remember why I stopped asking you about the case."

"They killed a man, Isabel. I'm trying to help them get off, but I'll be damned if I know why."

She turned back to me, her eyes smiling, her Kewpie-bow mouth blowing me a kiss as she said: "I know why."

"You do?"

A little nod. "It's because Mr. Darrow wants you to."

"It's because I'm being paid to do it."

"That's not it at all. I've heard you two talking. You're hardly getting anything out of this; just your regular police salary and some expenses."

I touched her downy arm. "There *are* a few dividends."

That made the Kewpie lips purse into a little smile. "You look up to him, don't you, Nate? You admire him."

"He's a devious old bastard."

"Maybe that's what you want to be when you grow up."

I frowned at her. "What made you so smart all of a sudden?"

"How is it you know him, a famous man like Clarence Darrow?"

"A nonentity like me, you mean?"

"Don't be mean. Answer the question."

I shrugged. "He and my father were friends."

"Was your father an attorney?"

"Hell no! He was an old union guy who ran a bookstore on the West Side. They traveled in the same radical circles. Darrow used to come in to buy books on politics and philosophy."

She was looking at me as if for the first time. "So you've known Mr. Darrow since you were a kid?"

"Yeah. Worked in his office as a runner when I was going to college."

"How much college do you have?"

"Started at the University of Chicago, had some problems, finished up a two-year degree at a junior college."

"Were you going to be a lawyer?"

"That was never my dream."

Her eyes smiled again. "What was your dream, Nate?"

"Who says I had a dream?"

"You have a lot of dreams. A lot of ambitions."

"I don't remember telling you about 'em."

"I can just tell. What was your dream? What *is* your dream?"

I blurted it: "To be a detective."

She smiled, cocked her head. "You made it."

"Not really. Not really. You about ready to get out of here? Catch that swim up the roadway?"

"Sure." She gathered her things and we headed for the parking lot, where she started in again.

"You've been looking into what happened to Thalo, haven't you?"

"Yes."

"Have you found anything helpful to Mrs. Fortescue and Tommie, in your search?"

"No."

I opened the rider's-side door on the Durant, shut her in, and that was all the conversation for a while. We were soon tooling along the edge of the club links. Before long we were passing groves of coconut palms and papaya orchards, truck gardens, chicken ranches, a campground, a large modern dairy. Then we wound through more coconut groves along the foot of the hills, at our left a looming black crater, at our right a cliff— Koko Head—projecting out into the sea. A sign at a fork in the road promised us the Blowhole if we took the dirt road to the left; I braved it.

Isabel started back in, working her voice above the rumble of the engine, the bump of the tires on hard dirt, and the top-down wind. "Surely you don't think Thalo is lying about what happened to her."

"Something happened to her that night last September. Something violent. Like she said to Tommie on the phone— something awful. I'm just not sure what."

"You think those terrible colored boys are innocent?"

"I think they're not guilty. There's a difference."

"What do you mean?"

"They may have done it; they're roughnecks and borderline disreputable characters. 'Innocent' is a moral term. 'Not guilty' is the legal term, and that's what they are: there just isn't enough evidence to convict them."

"But that was why Tommie and Mrs. Fortescue had to try to get a confession!"

I didn't feel like pressing the point. But in almost two weeks of trying, I'd certainly come up with nothing to give Darrow even the most dubious moral high ground for his clients to oc- cupy. Having talked to every major witness in the Ala Moana case over the past two weeks, I had accumulated nothing but doubts about Thalia, her story, and her identification of Horace Ida, Joseph Kahahawai, and the rest.

Young, personable George Goeas, a cashier with Dillingham Insurance in Honolulu, had taken his wife to the dance at

Waikiki Amusement Park that night. About ten minutes past midnight, he and the missus crossed the street to John Ena Road, and drove down to the *saimin* stand for a snack of noodles. A young woman in a green dress, her head lowered, walked by.

"She seemed to be under the influence of liquor," Goeas told me. "About a yard and a half from her, we saw a white guy following directly in back of her. He kept trailing after her for maybe twenty-five yards. . . . The way she held her head down, and him working to catch up with her, I kinda thought maybe they'd had a lovers' quarrel or something. Then they walked out of view, a store blocking the way."

"What did the guy trailing her look like?"

"Like I said, white. Five feet nine, hundred and sixty-five pounds maybe, medium build. Trim appearance. Looked like a soldier to me."

Or a sailor?

"What was he wearing?"

"White shirt. Dark trousers. Maybe blue, maybe brown, I'm not sure."

Mrs. Goeas had a better eye for fashion detail. She gave a precise description of the dress Thalia had been wearing, right down to a small bow in back, and described her as, "Mumbling to herself, swaying as she walked, I would even say stumbling."

I met with Alice Aramaki, a tiny, pleasant girl of perhaps twenty, in the barbershop on John Ena Road, opposite the amusement park. Alice was one of Honolulu's many Japanese lady barbers; her father owned the shop and she lived upstairs. She had seen a white woman in a green dress walk past her store at a quarter past midnight.

"What color hair did this woman have?"

"She was dark blond hair."

"Anybody walking near her at the time?"

"A man was walking. He was a white man."

"How was she walking, this woman in the green dress?"

"Hanging her head down. Walking slowly."

"What did the white man wear?"

"No hat. White shirt. Dark pants."

A group of men from various walks of life—a local politician, a greengrocer, two partners in a building supply company—had gone to the dance at the amusement park that night. They were headed down John Ena Road toward the beach at about twelve-fifteen when one of them, former city supervisor James Low, spotted "a woman in a blue or maybe green dress walking like a drunken person." A man was trailing after her, but Low wasn't sure of the man's race. The woman and man seemed to be heading toward a car parked at the curb.

As Low and his friends drove on by, some girls on the street called out to Low, and he spoke out the window to them, while his friends saw something that caught their attention.

The driver, Eugenio Batungbacal, said, "I see about four or five men with one girl, two mens holding the woman with hands and one is following. They look like they force the woman on their car."

He meant "in" the car—the odd Island usage of "on."

"She looked like she was drunk," he continued, "because two mens hold her arms and she tried to get away."

"What did this girl look like? Was she white?"

"I don't know, 'cause she is not facing to me. If she is facing to me, I tell you whether she is nigger or white or Portuguese."

"What color dress was she wearing?"

"I don't know. Long dress, though."

"Like an evening gown?"

"Like that."

But others in the same car hadn't perceived this as a struggle. I asked Charles Cheng, greengrocer, if he wasn't alarmed by what he'd seen.

"No, I thought they were just a bunch of friends."

"You didn't get excited when these guys were dragging a girl into their car?"

"No. I thought she was drunk and they were helping her."

None of them heard screams or saw a punch thrown.

Still, this conformed to some degree to Thalia's story—except that another carload (this one of guys and gals) at about the same time put Horace Ida and his pals elsewhere. Accord-

ing to Tatsumi Matsumoto—his friends called him "Tuts"—
Ida's car had followed his out of the amusement park.

The story—which included one of the boys from Tuts's car
jumping over onto Ida's bumper and riding for a while, talking,
even tossing Ahakeulo some matches—was confirmed by the
other boy and two girls in the car, and it put the suspects at
Beretania and Fort streets at around twelve-fifteen.

Husky Tuts—a former college football star who was finan-
cially independent, having inherited his father's estate—hung
around the sporting scene, hobnobbed with athletes and gamblers, and was friendly with Benny Ahakeulo. It was possible
he and his friends were helping cover up for Benny.

But I didn't think so. Tuts was affable and open and unre-
hearsed, telling his story, and the two girls were just flighty
young Hawaiian gals who lacked the details a more contrived
story would have contained.

"Did you see your friend Benny earlier, at Waikiki Park,
Tuts? At the dance?"

"I did more than see him. We both went up to the same girl
and asked her to dance."

"Who won?"

Tuts smirked. "She turned us both down."

Middle-aged salt-of-the-earth George Clark, an office manager with the Honolulu Construction and Draining Co., and his
matronly missus, had been playing bridge all evening with the
Bellingers, from their neighborhood; half an hour or so after midnight, they all set out to Waikiki in one car for a late-night snack.
On their way to the Kewalo Inn on Ala Moana, just past the
Hooverville squatters' shacks, the car's headlights caught the
frantic form of a woman in a green dress, flagging them down.

It was Thalia, of course, who (once ascertaining that these
were white people) begged for a ride home. Her hair was di-
sheveled, her face bruised, her lips swollen.

"She was about our daughter's age," Clark told me, "and I
guess we kind of felt for the girl. But she had a funny attitude."

"How so?" I asked him.

"She seemed angry, not upset, kind of . . . indignant. Not

tears. It was more like, how could anyone dare do such a thing to her."

"What did she say had been done to her?"

"She said a gang of Hawaiian hoodlums had grabbed her, pulled her into their car, robbed and beat her, and tossed her back out again."

"She didn't say anything about sexual assault?"

"Nothing. And she only wanted a ride home. She was adamant about no hospital, no police. Just get her home. Her husband would take care of her, she said."

Mrs. Clark made an interesting addition to her husband's observations: "We all noticed her evening gown seemed undamaged. Later, George and I read about five boys . . . assaulting her . . . and we both wondered how her gown could be in such good condition."

At the lookout, I parked the car just off the dirt road and, hand in hand, Isabel and I moved to the edge of the cliff and, prompted by the sound of crashing surf and whooshing air, peered down at the fabled Blowhole, a shelf of rock extending like the deck of a ship into the sea, silvery gray in the modest moonlight, white breakers rolling up over it. The opening toward the front of the ridge of rock looked small from up here, but it had to be three or four feet in diameter. Nothing happened for a while; then finally several waves surged in with increasing force and, like the whale blowhole for which it was named, the rocky spout geysered water, trapped in the cave below and propelled out in fountains of foam, streams of spray, twenty or thirty feet high.

Isabel held on tightly to my arm. "Oh, Nate—it's breathtaking . . . so lovely. . . ."

I didn't say anything. Its beauty hadn't occurred to me; what had was how you could walk right out on that shelf and, between geysers, drop something into the cave below. Something or someone.

Over to our right was a tiny bay within high shelves of rock, a small pocket of beach beckoning us. Towels tucked under our arms, we went looking for a footpath, found it, and, hand in hand, with me in the lead, made our way down the steep, rocky slope, treading gingerly in our sandals, laughing nervously at each misstep.

Finally we were down on the pale sand, between high walls of rock, a tiny private beach at the foot of the vast ocean. We spread beach towels, and I stripped to my trunks as she shed her polka-dot skirt and jacket down to her form-fitting white suit. Pale as her flesh was, in the glow of the muted moonlight, she might have been nude, the wind rustling her boyishly short blond hair. The only sound was the lazy surf rolling in and the wind surfing through foliage above.

She stretched out on her towel, her slender, rounded body airbrushed by moonlight. I sat on my towel, next to her; she was drinking in the beauty of the night, I was drinking in hers.

Finally she noticed my eyes on her and then she settled her gaze on me. She propped herself up on an elbow; at this angle, her cleavage was delightful.

"Mind if I pry some more?" she asked innocently.

"You can try."

"I can understand your admiration for Mr. Darrow. I understand family ties. But this is more than that."

"I don't get you."

"He's taken you under his wing. Why?"

"I'm cheap help."

She shook her head, no, and the blond hair shimmered. "No. Look at Mr. Leisure. He's a top Wall Street attorney, and I get the feeling he's working for peanuts, too."

"Your point being?"

"Clarence Darrow can finagle just about anybody into helping him out. It's like the President asking you for help, or Ronald Colman asking you to dance."

"I wouldn't care to dance with Ronald Colman, thanks."

"Why you, Nate?"

I looked out at the ocean; the little beach had small rock formations here and there that the gentle surge of surf splashed over idly.

"Let's go for a swim," I said.

She touched my arm, gently. "Why you?"

"Why do you care?"

"I care about you. We're sleeping together, aren't we?"

"How exclusive a list is that?"

She grinned, chin wrinkling. "You're not going to get out of it by making me mad. Like the gangsters in the movies say— spill."

She looked so cute, her eyes taking on an oddly violet cast in the non-light, that I felt a sudden surge of genuine affection for the girl wash over me in a tide of emotion.

"It's because of my father."

"Your father."

"He and Darrow were friends."

"You've said that."

"My father didn't want me to be a cop. Neither does Darrow."

"Why not?"

"Darrow's an old radical, like my father. He hates the police."

"Your father?"

"Darrow."

She frowned, trying to sort it out. "Your father *doesn't* hate the police?"

"Hell, he hated them worse than Darrow."

"Is your father dead, Nate?"

I nodded. "Year, year and a half now."

"I'm sorry."

"Nothing for you to be sorry about."

"So Mr. Darrow wants you to quit the police force and work for him. As his investigator."

"Something along those lines."

She squinted in thought. "So it's all right, being a detective . . . as long as you're not a *policeman*."

"That's it."

"I don't get it. What's the difference?"

"The cops represent a lot of bad things to people like Darrow and my father. The government abusing citizens. Graft, corruption . . ."

"Aren't there any honest cops?"

"Not in Chicago. Anyway . . . not Nate Heller."

"What did you do, Nate?"

"I killed my father."

Alarm widened her eyes. *"What?"*

"You know that gun you asked me about the other night? That automatic on the dresser?"

"Yes. . . ."

"That's what I used."

"You're scaring me, Nate. . . ."

I swallowed. "I'm sorry. Look, I did something that disappointed my father. I told lies in court and took money to get a promotion, then I used the money trying to help him out . . . his store was in trouble. Shit."

Her mouth was trembling, her eyes wide not with alarm but dismay. "He killed himself."

I didn't say anything.

"With . . . with your gun?"

I nodded.

"And you . . . and that's the gun you carry? You still *carry*?"

I nodded again.

"But, why . . . ?"

I shrugged. "I figure it's the closest thing to a conscience I'll ever have."

She stroked my cheek; she looked like she was going to cry. "Oh, Nate. . . . Don't do that to yourself. . . ."

"It's all right. It helps remind me not to do certain things. Nobody should carry a gun lightly. Mine's just a little heavier than most people's."

She clutched me, held me in her arms like a baby she was comforting; but I was fine. I wasn't crying or anything. I felt okay. Nate Heller didn't cry in front of women. In private, deep into a sleepless night, awakened from a too-real dream of me finding my father slumped over that table again, well, that's my goddamn business, isn't it?

Taking my hand, she led me across the sand into the surf and we let the soothingly warm water wash up around our ankles, then let it up to our waists, and she dove in and began swimming out. I dove after her, cutting through water as comfy as a well-heated bath.

She swam freestyle with balletic grace; rich kids get plenty of practice swimming. But so do poor ones, at least those with access to Lake Michigan, and I knifed my way alongside her, catching up, and thirty feet out or so we stopped, treading water together, smiling, laughing, kissing. We were buffeted gently by the tide, and I was just about to say we'd better swim back in when something seemed to yank at our feet.

I lurched toward Isabel, clutching her around the midsection, as the undertow sucked us down under, way under, in a funnel of cold water, fourteen feet or more, flinging us around like rag dolls, but I held onto her, I wasn't giving her up and the riptide tossed us around in our desperate embrace, until finally, after seven or eight seconds that seemed a lifetime, a wave thundering up from the ocean's floor deposited us on the shore, and I dragged her onto the beach and onto dry sand, before that wave could withdraw and pull us back out to sea, and down again into the undertow.

We huddled on one towel, teeth chattering, hugging each other, breathing fast and deep; we stayed that way for what seemed a long time, watching an incredibly beautiful wave crash onto the shore, reminding us how close we'd just come to dying.

Then her mouth was on mine and she was clawing off her swimsuit as desperately as we'd fought the riptide, and I was out of my suit and on top inside of her, the slippery velvet of her mingling with grating sand, driving myself into her, her knees lifted, accepting me with little groans that escalated into cries echoing off the ridges around us, heels of my hands digging wedges in the sand as I watched her closed eyes and her open mouth and the quivering globes of her heaving breasts as those puffy aureoles tightened and wrinkled with vein-pulsing passion, and then we were both sending cries careening off the canyon-like walls, drowning out the roar of the surf, before collapsing into each other's arms, and sharing tiny kisses, murmuring vows of undying love that in a few moments we'd both regret.

She was the first to have regrets. She trotted back out into where the water came to her knees and she crouched there, to wash herself out, her fear of the tide overriden by another fear. When she trotted back, and got back into her suit, she sat on her towel and gathered her arms about her, trying to disappear into herself.

"I'm cold," she said. "We should go."

We both got quickly dressed, and this time she led the way up the rocky footpath to where our car was parked near the Blowhole overlook.

As we drove back, she said nothing for the longest time. She was staring into the night with an expression that wasn't quite morose, more . . . afraid.

"What's wrong, baby?"

Her smile was forced and her glance at me was so momentary it hardly qualified. "Nothing."

"What is it?"

"It's just . . . nothing."

"What, Isabel?"

"That's the first time . . . you didn't use something."

"We were all caught up in it, baby. We damn near died out there. We got worked up. Who could blame us?"

"I'm not blaming anybody," she said reproachfully.

"It won't happen again. I'll buy a bushel of Sheiks."

"What if I get pregnant?"

"People try for years and don't make babies. Don't worry about it."

"All it takes is once."

We were gliding by fancy beach homes again; I pulled over in the mouth of a driveway. I left the motor running as I reached over and touched her hand.

"Hey. Nothing's going to happen."

She looked away. Pulled her hand away.

"You think I wouldn't make an honest woman of you, if it came to that?"

She turned and looked sharply at me. "I can't marry *you*."

Then it hit me.

"Oh. Oh yeah. My last name is Heller. Good Christian girl like you can't go around marrying Jews. Just fucking them."

She began to cry. "How can you be so cruel?"

"Don't worry," I said, putting the car into gear. "You can always tell 'em I raped you."

And I did what I should have done earlier: pulled out.

FIFTEEN

W as I the only one it struck odd? That the scene of the crime, or at least the scene where the crime began, was also the site of the trial?

Every morning of the proceedings, the quaintly neoclassical Judiciary Building, outside of which Joe Kahahawai had received his bogus summons, was guarded by a phalanx of dusky police in blue serge uniforms insanely unsuited for the sweltering heat. The baroque building itself was roped and sawhorsed off, helping the cops keep back crowds about two-thirds *kanaka* and one-third *haole*; whether it was the heat or the cops, the potentially volatile racial mix never ignited. These were gawkers attracted not by controversy or politics but good old-fashioned tabloid murder.

Only seventy-five seats inside were available for the general public, and these precious pews had the colored servants of the *kamaaina* elite camping outside the courthouse overnight to save their bosses a spot, while Navy wives (accustomed to early rising) showed up in the early morning hours, with camp stools, sandwiches, and thermoses of coffee. Still others— out-of-work *kanakas*, and there were plenty of those—planned to sell their seats for the going rate of twenty-five bucks a shot.

Each morning, the scream of sirens scattered birds in ban- yans and stirred the curious crowd as a caravan of motorcycle police leading and following two cars (two defendants per car, under Navy guard) made its delivery from Pearl Harbor. The two seamen rode together—Jones and Lord, short, burly, uncomfortable in suits and ties, tough little kids playing dressup—cigarettes drooping from nervously smiling lips as they emerged from the Navy vehicle into the waiting custody of uniformed cops, who escorted them into the courthouse. Tommie, dapper in his suit and tie, made a slight, sad-looking escort for his patrician mother-in-law (in a succession of dark tasteful frocks and matching tam turbans), who seemed at once aloof and weary. Like Joe Kahahawai's golden ghost, the statue of King Kamehameha took all this in, unamused.

Every day, everyone who went inside—from defendant to spectator, from reporter to Clarence Darrow himself (and the judge, too)—got patted down for weapons by cops. Next, they passed by an adjacent courtroom that had been turned into a bustling pressroom—desks, telephones, typewriters, telegraph lines, accommodating a dozen or more reporters from as far away as London—before entering the small courtroom with its dark plaster walls and darker woodwork, lazily churning ceiling fans, and open windows looking out on whispering palms and the Punchbowl's green hills set against a blue-sky backdrop, letting in streaming sun, traffic noises, and buzzing mosquitoes.

At each and every session, white women—well-to-do white women, at that—took the majority of the public seating; this was, after all, the social event of the season. Conspicuously absent from this group was Thalia and Isabel, but they were well represented in spirit. A collective moan of mournful sympathy would emerge from the gals of the gallery each morning as the defendants trouped down the aisle to their seats behind the lawyers' table. At particularly dramatic (or melodramatic) testimony, they would (according to what seemed called for) shed tears together, they would sigh as one, they would gasp in unison. They managed to do this without ever once eliciting the wrath of Judge Davis, a bespectacled New Englander of medium size and enormous patience.

On the other hand, they frequently received glares and even

an occasional rebuke from no-nonsense prosecutor John C. Kelley, a square-shouldered block of a man, ruddy-faced, bald but for a monkish fringe of reddish hair.

Kelley hadn't seen forty, but if finding himself pitted against the elder statesman of defense lawyers intimidated him, he didn't show it. Nor did he seem daunted by the presence, each day, of a Navy contingent headed up by Admiral Stirling Yates himself, no less imperial in civilian clothes.

Confident, almost cocky, crisp in tropical whites, Kelley fixed his piercing blue eyes on the all-male, mixed racial bag in the jury box: six whites (including a Dane and a German), a Portuguese, two Chinese, and three of Hawaiian ancestry.

"Gentlemen," he said, his hint of brogue lending authority to his words, "these defendants are charged with the crime of murder in the second degree."

Kelley's only gesture toward the defense table was a wag of the head, but the jury's twenty-four eyes went to the four defendants, whose backs were to the rail behind which were the tables of reporters. Lord and Jones were at left, with Tommie next, and next to him, Mrs. Fortescue. All four sat rigidly, never glancing around the courtroom, eyes straight ahead, Mrs. Fortescue's bearing as expressionlessly military as that of her lieutenant son-in-law and their two sailor accomplices.

Kelley continued with the indictment: "The Grand Jury of the First Judicial Court of the Territory of Hawaii do present that Grace Fortescue, Thomas H. Massie, Edward J. Lord, and Albert O. Jones, in the city and county of Honolulu, on the eighth day of January, 1932, through force of arms—to wit, a pistol loaded with gunpowder and a bullet . . ."

Next to Mrs. Fortescue sat Darrow, snarl of hair askew, his fleshy yet angular frame draped over his wooden chair as casually as his haphazardly knotted tie. A watch chain looped across the vest of a dark suit that looked a size too large for a body that wore skin that looked a size too large itself. Leisure, every bit the well-dressed Wall Street attorney, was next to Darrow, and I was next to Leisure.

". . . did unlawfully, feloniously, and with malice aforethought and without authority and without justification or extenuation . . ."

Kelley turned and, with another wag of his skinned-coconut skull, indicated—at the rail near the end of the jury box—a dark, husky, impassive rumpled-faced fellow in white shirt and dark trousers and a slender, equally dark woman in a long white Mother Hubbard, weeping into a handkerchief: the parents of Joseph Kahahawai.

". . . *murdered* Joseph Kahahawai, Jr., a human being. . . ."

The pugnacious prosecutor outlined his case in less than an hour, from Tommie renting the blue Buick to Mrs. Fortescue crafting the ersatz summons, from the abduction of Joe Kahahawai in front of this very building to the kidnappers' ill-fated attempt to dispose of the body, which had led to a high-speed chase in which the cops had been forced to fire at them to stop.

He saved the best for last: the murder itself. He piled up vividly disturbing details—bloodstained clothing, blood-streaked floorboards, a gun stuffed behind sofa cushions, spare bullets, rope with a telltale purple thread labeling it naval property, a bathtub where bloody clothes were washed, a victim who was allowed to bleed to death.

"We will show you," Kelley said, "that there was no struggle in the house that might allow these defendants to claim self-defense. Kahahawai was a strong athlete, capable of putting up a good fight, but there is no evidence of any such fight in that house."

Through it all, Mrs. Fortescue stared numbly forward, while Tommie seemed to be chewing at something—gum, I thought at first; his lip, I later realized. The two sailors seemed almost bored; if the gravity of all this had hit them, it didn't show.

Kelley leaned on the jury box rail. "When Joseph Kahahawai, reporting faithfully to his probation officer, stood in the shadow of the statue of King Kamehameha, under the outstretched arm of the great Hawaiian who brought law and order to this island, the finger of doom pointed at this youthful descendant of Kamehameha's people."

Suddenly Kelley wheeled toward Mrs. Fortescue, who seemed mildly startled, straightening.

"That finger was pointed by Grace Fortescue," Kelley said, and he pointed his forefinger at her as if he were on a firing squad aiming a rifle. "In today's vernacular, she was the finger man who put Kahahawai 'on the spot'!"

When Kelley sat down, Darrow did not rise. He remained slumped in his chair, merely uttering, "The defense will reserve its opening statement, Your Honor."

In three methodical but fast-moving days, the scrappy Kelley built his case, brick by brick: Kahahawai's cousin Edward Ulii, as light as Joe had been powerful, told of the abduction; Dickson, the probation officer, told of telling Mrs. Fortescue about Kahahawai's obligation to report to him each day; Detective George Harbottle, a young, ruggedly handsome specimen who looked like Hollywood's notion of a cop, told of the car chase and capture, and the corpse wrapped in the bloody white sheet in the backseat.

"Detective," Kelley said, "would you mind stepping from the witness stand and identifying the parties you arrested?"

The brawny dick stepped down and touched Jones, then Lord, then Tommie on the shoulder; but when he approached Mrs. Fortescue, she rose regally and stared directly at him, chin lifted.

Harbottle didn't touch her; he just backed away, pointing with a thumb, muttering, "This lady was driving."

As Mrs. Fortescue took her seat, Harbottle settled himself back on the stand, and Kelley asked, "Did Lt. Massie appear to be in shock, Detective?"

Darrow, doodling on a pad, seemingly paying scant attention, said, "Calls for a conclusion, Your Honor."

Kelley turned toward the judge with a patently placating smile. "Your Honor, as a police officer, Detective Harbottle has been called to the scene of many crimes, many accidents. His opinion as to the state of mind of—"

Darrow raised his eyes and his voice. "The detective hasn't been called as an expert in human behavior, Your Honor."

Judge Davis, his expression blank as the Sphinx, said, "Sustained."

"Detective Harbottle," Kelley said, leaning on the witness

chair, "did Lt. Massie speak to you, after you arrested him and the others along the roadside?"

"In a roundabout way, yes, sir."

"What do you mean, 'in a roundabout way,' Detective?"

"Well, Patrolman Bond came over to me and said, 'Good work, kid,' you know, congratulating me on the arrest. But Lt. Massie, who was sitting in back of the radio patrol car, thought the comment was meant for him—"

With weary patience Darrow called out, "The witness doesn't know what Lt. Massie was thinking, Your Honor."

"The comment about what Lt. Massie was thinking will be stricken," the judge informed the court stenographer.

Kelley said, "What did Lt. Massie say?"

Harbottle shrugged. "He said, 'Thank you,' and raised his hands like this . . ." Harbottle lifted his clasped hands and shook them in the end-of-the-game gesture of victory common to boxers and other athletes.

Kelley smiled nastily at the jury. "Thank you, Detective. That will be all. Your witness."

Darrow didn't rise as he smiled up at the detective. "When my associate Mr. Heller spoke with you, on Thursday last, didn't you describe Lt. Massie's demeanor as follows: 'Very stern, sitting straight up, just staring straight ahead, never saying a word.' Do you recall that?"

"I do," Harbottle admitted.

"What was Mrs. Fortescue doing at that time?"

"Sitting on a rock alongside the road."

"What was her demeanor?"

Kelley rose and arched an eyebrow. "I hope counsel isn't asking this witness for expert testimony on human behavior."

Darrow's smile was grandfatherly. "I'll rephrase—was she talkative? Was she smiling and chatty and gay?"

"She was staring straight ahead," Harbottle said. "In a kind of daze. Silent as the rock she was sitting on."

Darrow nodded sagely. "No further questions."

With the exception of such occasional skirmishes, Darrow continued to pay little apparent heed to Kelley and his case; he mostly declined cross-examining Kelley's witnesses, allowing

Leisure to ask a few questions now and then. Darrow had never denied the crime; cross-examining would only prolong such prosecution theatrics as waving before the jury the bloody garments found in a wet bundle in the rental Buick.

The latter display, however, in conjunction with the testimony of one of the patrolmen who found them, elicited tears from Mrs. Kahahawai, sending Darrow to his feet.

"With all due respect to this fine lady," Darrow said, "I must request that she be removed from the courtroom on the grounds that her emotion might sway the jury."

The judge shook his head, no. "She has a right to be present, Mr. Darrow."

Kelley's parade of witnesses continued: the garage clerk who rented Tommie the Buick; the hardware store counterman who sold a revolver to Mrs. Fortescue and an automatic to Jones; the neighbor who heard "an explosion" coming from Mrs. Fortescue's house at 9:00 A.M. January 8; Detective Bills, in whose expert opinion the coil of rope around the dead man's body came from the submarine base; County Coroner Dr. Faus, who established that the path of the bullet through Kahahawai's heart had been diagonal, at an angle indicating the victim was lunging defensively forward when he was shot; Inspector McIntosh, who reported that Jones "acted drunk" when apprehended at the Fortescue bungalow, but "seemed quite sober" when questioned at the station house; other cops who, searching the bungalow, found Mrs. Fortescue's purse with Kahahawai's picture tucked inside, Tommie's automatic under a sofa cushion, Kahahawai's cap, two pearl buttons in the bathroom from Kahahawai's undershorts, and a spare box of .32 shells wrapped up in the fake summons (these Jones had kept stuffed under his shirt!).

The fake summons, of course, made for effective courtroom reading by Kelley.

" 'Life is a mysterious and exciting affair,' " the prosecutor said, reading from the document itself, " 'and anything can be a thrill if you know how to look for it and what to do with opportunity when it comes.' "

A lot of people thought of Darrow as a great showman, but I

have to admit, Prosecutor John C. Kelley could have taught Barnum and Bailey a trick or two: he displayed a huge full-color anatomical chart of a male torso with the bullet path in red; he exhibited glossy photos of bloodstains in the bungalow; he passed out bloody towels, bloody clothes to the jury for them to personally handle; and the bloody sheet; and the rope, and a glittering array of bullets and cartridge shells.

Through all this, Darrow slumped in his chair and doodled and played with his pencil, occasionally objecting, almost never cross-examining. Mrs. Fortescue remained aloof, impassive, but Tommie began biting his nails.

Kelley's last witness was inevitable: Esther Kahahawai, Joe's mother, coming back to haunt Darrow for his objection to her presence.

As the dark, thin, frail gray-haired woman in the Mother Hubbard approached the stand, Darrow arose and raised his hands gently, blocking the way, turning to the judge.

"We will concede everything this witness has to say," he said gravely. "We will stipulate that she is the mother of Joseph Kahahawai, that she saw him that morning when he left—anything. . . ."

Kelley was on his feet. "There are two mothers in this court-room, Your Honor. One is a defendant, but the other has no defense—her son is dead. We think both these women should be allowed to testify."

"Withdrawn," Darrow said, softly; he smiled with sympathy at Mrs. Kahahawai and removed himself from her path, taking his place.

Her voice was low, difficult to hear, but no one in the court-room missed a word. She wept into her handkerchief almost continuously during her testimony; many of the spectators—even the white wealthy women whose sympathy was with the defendants—wept along with her.

"Yes, that was his shirt," she said, as Kelley somberly showed her the bloody clothing. "And those, his socks. And his dungarees . . . yes. Yes. I just washed them, and sewed the buttons on."

"Was Joe in good health that morning when he left you?"

"Yes."

"When did you see him again?"

"Saturday. At . . . at the undertaker's."

"That was the body of your son Joseph?"

"Yes."

"Thank you, Mrs. Kahahawai. No further questions."

Darrow's voice was barely audible: "No questions, Your Honor."

Sobs echoed in the courtroom as Kelley, in an almost courtly fashion, led her down from the stand.

Darrow leaned over to me, his stringy locks tumbling carelessly, and whispered: "I guess we had that coming. The sympathy can't be all on one side."

He looked very old to me at that moment; tired and old.

Kelley looked fresh as a daisy. He was prancing toward the prosecution table, talking as he went: "The prosecution rests, Your Honor."

The court recessed for lunch, and as usual, Darrow, Leisure, his clients, and I went over to the Alexander Young. C.D., accompanied by Ruby, passed up luncheon for a nap in his room, while the rest of us took the elevator to the roof garden restaurant. No one expected our clients to make a break for it, and we had arranged for the grand old man of the department, Chang Apana, to have the honor of being the nominal police guard.

Because of Chang's presence, conversation was kept superficial and nothing related to the case was discussed. Leisure's wife joined us, as usual, and the couple talked amongst themselves. Neither Tommie nor Mrs. Fortescue said much of anything, having finally fallen into a morose understanding of the gravity of their situation.

But Jones and Lord, smoking, laughing, were a cheerful pair of imbeciles. Curly-haired Lord didn't say much, but square-headed Jones was a cocky, chatty son of a bitch.

"You see the shape on that girl reporter from New York?" he asked me.

"It got my attention," I admitted, nibbling at my bacon-lettuce-and-tomato sandwich.

"I think she likes me." He was cutting his minute steak eagerly. "She's always wanting to talk to me."

"You don't think being a defendant in a murder trial could have something to do with it?"

"She's got four of us to choose from, don't she? And it's me she flashes her peepers at, ain't it?"

"Good point."

"Did you see that little Chinese girl over by the wall, on the left? She's a doll. And there's some good-looking American girls in that courtroom, believe you me."

This bastard was a bigger lecher than I was.

I looked at him with a tiny smile. "You mind a little advice, Deacon?"

"Not at all, Nate."

"I saw you ogling those gals. Smiling at them. I don't think smiles are all that appropriate in a situation like the one you're in."

He shrugged, spearing a chunk of O'Brien potato. "I don't see the harm. Don't I want people to know I'm a nice guy?"

Chang Apana, seated next to me picking at a small bowl of chow chow, said quietly, so only I would hear, "Owner of face cannot always see nose."

After recess, Darrow led our contingent down the aisle, court resumed, and America's most famous trial lawyer, in a wrinkled, baggy double-breasted white linen jacket, rose and addressed the bench.

"I waive my opening statement, Your Honor," Darrow said, a rasp underlining the deceptive casualness of his drawl.

A ripple of disappointment rolled over the gallery at being denied their first extended sampling of the Darrow courtroom oratory.

" . . . And call my first witness, Lt. Thomas Massie."

The disappointment disappeared in a rush of excitement as Tommie popped to his feet, jack-in-the-box style, and strode quickly to the stand, where he almost shouted his oath to tell the truth.

Tommie wore a dark blue suit with a light tan tie, an ensemble suggested by Darrow to seem vaguely naval, slightly military. The sharp features of his boyish face had fixed into a tight expression that fell somewhere between scowl and pout.

In a manner that may have been intended to relax the obviously tense Tommie, and lull the jury, Darrow began an unhurried journey through Tommie's early years—born, Winchester, Kentucky; military school; Naval Academy; marriage on graduation day to sixteen-year-old Thalia Fortescue. On through his naval duties—the U.S.S. *Lexington*, the sub base at New London, Connecticut, his two years of further sub duty out of Pearl Harbor.

Then, in the same soothing, casual tone, Darrow said, "Do you remember going to a dance last September?"

"How could I forget it?" Tommie said.

Kelley was already on his feet.

"Where was that party?" Darrow asked.

"The Ala Wai Inn," Tommie said. "My wife didn't feel like goin', but I persuaded her to."

Kelley was standing before the bench, now. "Your Honor, I don't intend to interrupt with constant objections," he said quietly, earnestly, "but I feel entitled to know the relevance of this testimony."

Darrow had drifted to the bench too, and Kelley turned to the old boy and asked, point blank, "Is it your intention to go into the Ala Moana case?"

"I do so intend."

"Then, Your Honor, the prosecution should be informed at this time if one of the defendants will make an insanity plea—in which case, we will not oppose this testimony."

"We do intend," Darrow said, "to raise the question of insanity in relation to the one who fired the pistol."

Kelley frowned and bit off the words: "Is a plea of insanity to be offered in behalf of Lt. Massie?"

Darrow smiled. "I don't think it's necessary at this time to single out any particular person."

Kelley was shaking his head, no. "Unless the prosecution is informed that a plea of insanity is to be made on Lt. Massie's behalf, I will object to any further testimony along these lines, by this witness."

Darrow made a gesture with two open hands as if he were holding a hymnal. "Your Honor, Mr. Kelley in his opening statements linked all the defendants together as equally guilty. Now he wishes me to separate them for his convenience."

The judge, pondering this, looked first from one attorney to the other, like a man watching a tennis match.

"It is common knowledge, Your Honor," Kelley said, "that the defense has imported prominent psychiatrists from the mainland." The prosecutor gestured first to Tommie, then to the other three defendants. "The prosecution has the right to know which of these four Mr. Darrow will claim insane."

"I'll gladly tell you," Darrow said.

Kelley glared at him. "Which of them, then?"

Darrow beamed. "The one who shot the pistol."

Kelley's face was reddening. "The prosecution has the right to know the person for whom this insanity plea is to be made so that *our* alienists may also examine this individual."

"These alienists of yours," Darrow said, "would appear as rebuttal witnesses, of course."

"Of course," Kelley said.

"Now I'm a stranger here in your lovely land, Mr. Kelley, but if my rudimentary understanding of procedure in Hawaii is correct, I'm under no obligation to submit my clients to examination by rebuttal witnesses."

"Your Honor, this is outrageous. I object to this line of questioning on grounds of relevance."

"Now," Darrow said, as if Kelley's words were harmless gnats flitting about, "if the prosecution wishes to seat its alienist experts as spectators in the gallery, I'd certainly have no objection."

Why would he? Any opinion they might offer on the witness stand would be followed by the obvious, and devastating, defense query: "Doctor, have you examined the accused?"

Next to me Leisure was smiling. This was his handiwork, but Darrow's delivery was priceless.

"Your objection is overruled, Mr. Kelley," Judge Davis said. "You may continue questioning along these lines, Mr. Darrow."

And he did. Probing gently, Darrow withdrew from

Tommie his tale of the Ala Wai Inn party and his search for his wife, as the party wound down; how he'd finally reached Thalia by phone to hear her cry, "Come home at once! Something awful has happened!" And in excruciating detail, Tommie told of Thalia's description to him of the injuries and indignities she'd endured.

"She said Kahahawai had beaten her more than anyone," Tommie said. "She said when Kahahawai assaulted her, she prayed for mercy and his answer was to hit her in the jaw."

At the defense table, Mrs. Fortescue's stoic, noble mask began to quiver; tears rolled down her flushed cheeks, unattended, as her son-in-law described her daughter's suffering.

"She said over and over again," Tommie was saying, "why hadn't the men just killed her? She wished they'd killed her."

Many of the women in the gallery were weeping now; sobbing.

"The followin' day," Tommie said, "when she was in the hospital, the police brought in the four assailants."

Kelley, remaining seated, said quietly, "Your Honor, I object to the use of the word 'assailants.' "

Darrow turned to Kelley, shrugged, said, " 'Alleged assailants,' then. Or suppose we call them four men?"

"She said these four men were the ones," Tommie said, lips twisting as if he were tasting something foul. "I said, 'Don't let there be any doubt about it,' and she said, 'Don't you think if there were any doubt I could never draw another easy breath?' "

This slice of melodrama seemed a little ripe to me; I didn't know how the rest of the room was taking it, but to me Tommie's Little Theater background was showing. And in trying too hard, he had introduced, at least vaguely, Thalia Massie's possible doubts about the identity of Ida and company.

Darrow steered Tommie gently back on course, drawing from him a description of the faithful days and nights he'd spent at the hospital and at home, nursing his beloved bride back to health. Tommie described nightmares of Thalia's from which she awoke screaming, "Kahahawai is here!"

"Could you ever get the incident out of your mind?" Darrow asked.

"Never! And then the rumors started . . . vile . . . rotten! We were gettin' a divorce, I'd found my wife in bed with a fellow officer, I'd beaten her myself, a crowd of naval officers assaulted her, she wasn't assaulted at all . . . every stupid foul variation you could imagine. It got to where I couldn't stand crowds, couldn't look people in the face. I couldn't sleep, I would get up and pace the floor and all I could see was the picture of my wife's crushed face. . . . I felt so miserable I wanted to take a knife and cut my brain out of my head!"

Considering what Tommie had just said, Darrow's next question seemed almost comical. "Did you consult a doctor?"

"Yes, but I was more concerned with what a lawyer thought. I was advised that the best way to stop these vicious rumors was to get a signed confession from one of the . . . four men. I'd heard Kahahawai was gettin' ready to crack, and spoke to my mother-in-law. . . ."

"Other than these rumors," Darrow asked gently, "did anything else prey upon your mind?"

"Y-yes. We knew an operation was necessary to . . . prevent pregnancy."

This was dangerous ground. I knew that Darrow knew Thalia had not been pregnant; I wasn't sure if Tommie knew, and God only knew if Kelley knew. . . .

Yet Darrow pressed on: "Were you sure she was pregnant?"

"There could be no doubt."

Kelley was going through some papers; did he have the medical report signed by Darrow's friend Dr. Porter?

But still Darrow continued: "Could the pregnancy have been due to you?"

"No. It couldn't have been."

"Was it done, the operation?"

"Yes. I took her to the hospital and Dr. Porter performed it. This . . . this had a strange effect on my mind."

And Tommie began to weep.

Kelley wasn't making a move; if he did have the card, he'd

decided not to play it. It was clear Tommie believed Thalia had been pregnant; he wasn't *that* good an actor.

"It's getting late in the day, Your Honor," Darrow said sorrowfully. "Might I request an adjournment until tomorrow?"

The judge accepted Darrow's suggestion with no objection from Kelley. Mrs. Fortescue bolted from the defense table to guide her son-in-law off the stand. With her arm around the child-man's shoulder, the tall woman walked up the aisle of a courtroom filled with teary-eyed *haole* women as Chang Apana led Tommie and Mrs. Fortescue and the two gobs to their Shore Patrol escorts.

At the next session, as Tommie again took the stand, Darrow faced the judge and dropped a bombshell that blew Kelley immediately to his feet.

"Your Honor," Darrow said, a thumb in one of his suspenders, "there seems to be a little misunderstanding between the prosecutor and myself and I'd like to set it right. We are willing to state that Lt. Massie held the gun that fired the fatal shot."

A tidal wave of reaction rolled over the gallery and the judge gaveled the courtroom to silence.

Darrow continued, as if he hadn't noticed the stir he'd caused: "Now, Lieutenant, if we can get back to these rumors that had been plaguing you and your wife . . ."

Kelley said in a machine-gun burst of words: "Even with this admission, Your Honor, this line of questioning involving the Ala Moana case is admissible only under a plea of insanity, and even so, any information supplied to Lt. Massie by his wife and others in reference to that case is hearsay and should be stricken from the record."

"Your Honor," Darrow said patiently, "we expect the evidence to show that this defendant was insane. I did not say that he would testify that he killed the deceased. We will show that the gun was in his hand when the shot was fired . . . but whether Lt. Massie knew what he was doing at the time is another question."

Judge Davis thought about that, then said, "Mr. Kelley, it appears that the defense is relying on the defense of insanity and that the witness now on the stand fired the fatal shot. This opens the door for testimony bearing on the defendant's state of mind."

"My objection has been met, Your Honor," Kelley said. "However, we feel we're entitled at this time to know the type of insanity Lt. Massie is alleged to have been laboring under when he fired the shot."

Darrow said, "Come now, Mr. Kelley, surely you're aware that even leading experts use different terminology for identical psychological disorders. Your Honor, may I resume my examination of the witness?"

"You may," the judge said.

Kelley, seeming for the first time flustered, returned to his seat.

Darrow patiently took Tommie through the formation of the abduction plot, from discussions with his mother-in-law to his first meetings with Jones and Lord.

"Was the purpose of your plan to kill the deceased?"

"Certainly not!"

Finally Darrow had reached the point in Tommie's story where, back on the *Alton* in that first interview, C.D. had refused to let his client continue.

Now, here in court, I would finally hear the "true" story.

"I drove to Mrs. Fortescue's house, up into the garage," Tommie said. "When I got inside, in the kitchen, I took Jones's gun from the counter."

"That was a .32?"

Tommie was almost motionless, and machine precise as he testified. "A .32, yes sir. And I called out and said, 'All right, come in—Major Ross is in here.' Kahahawai still believed he was on his way to see the major. I took off my dark glasses and gloves—the chauffeur apparel—and then we were all in the livin' room, Kahahawai sittin' down in a chair. Mrs. Fortescue and Lord came in. Stood nearby as I went over and confronted Kahahawai. I had the gun in my hand."

"And where was Jones?"

"Mrs. Fortescue told him to wait outside and see that we weren't disturbed. I pulled back the slide of the gun and let it click in place—I wanted to scare him. I said, 'Do you know who I am?' He said, 'I think so.' I said, 'You did your lyin' in the courtroom but you're going to tell the whole truth now.' He looked nervous, tremblin'. He said, 'I don't know nothin'.' I asked him where he was on the night of September twelfth and he said the Waikiki dance. I asked him when he left the dance and he said he didn't know, he was drunk. I said, 'Where did you pick up the woman?' He said, 'We didn't have no woman.' I told him he'd better tell the truth. Who kicked her? 'Nobody kicked her.' I said, 'Tell me how you drove home,' and he rattled off a bunch of streets and I don't know their names but I let him go on awhile, then I said, 'You were a prizefighter once, weren't you?' And he nodded, and I said, 'Well that explains how you knew where to hit a woman one blow and break her jaw.' He looked really nervous now, he wet his lips, he was squirmin' and I said, 'All right, if you're not goin' to talk, we'll make you talk. You know what happened to Ida out at Pali?' He didn't say, but he was nervous, tremblin'. I said, 'Well, what he got was nothin' to what you're going to get if you don't tell the whole story, right now.' And he said, 'I don't know nothin',' and I said, 'Okay, Lord, go out and get the boys. After we work him over, he'll talk all right.' Kahahawai started to rise up and I pushed him back down and said, 'Ida talked and told plenty on you. Those men out there, they're comin' in and beat you to ribbons.' "

Tommie's voice began to quaver.

"Kahahawai was tremblin' in his chair," Tommie said, "and I said, 'Last chance to talk—you know your gang was there!' And he must've been more afraid of a beatin' than the gun I was holdin' on him, 'cause he blurted it out: 'Yeah, we done it!' "

Darrow paused to let the courtroom savor the moment. Finally he asked: "And then?"

"That's the last I remember. Oh, I remember the picture that came into my mind, of my wife's crushed face after he assaulted her and she prayed for mercy and he answered her with a blow that broke her jaw."

"You had the gun in your hand as you were talking to him?"

"Yes, sir."

"Do you remember what you did?"

"No, sir."

"Do you know what became of the gun?"

"No, sir."

"Do you know what became of you?"

"N . . . no, sir."

Tommie swallowed hard; he seemed to be holding back tears.

Darrow stood before the jury box, arms folded, shoulders hunched. He gave his client a few moments to compose himself, then said, "Do you remember anything of the flight to the mountains?"

"No, sir."

"What's the first thing you recall?"

"Sittin' in a car on a country road. A bunch of people were comin' up to us, sayin' something about a body."

"Do you remember being taken to the police station?"

"Not clearly."

Darrow sighed, nodded. He went over and patted Tommie on the arm, then ambled toward the defense table, saying, "Take the witness, sir."

Kelley rose and said, "Are you proud of your Southern heritage, Lt. Massie?"

Darrow almost jumped to his feet. "Objection! Immaterial, and intended to imply racial bias."

"Your Honor," Kelley said, "if the defense can explore the defendant's state of mind, surely the prosecution has the same privilege."

"You may do so," the judge said, "but not with that question—it is misleading as it presupposes all Southerners are bigots."

Kelley moved in close to Tommie. "Do you remember Mrs. Fortescue telling a reporter that you and she 'bungled the job'?"

"Certainly not."

"Did Joseph Kahahawai seem frightened?"

"Yes."

"Did he plead for mercy?"

"No."

"Did he put up a fight?"

"No."

Kelley began to pace slowly up and down in front of the jury box. "Later, did Mrs. Fortescue or Jones or Lord, did any of them tell you how you behaved, or what you did, after the shot was fired?"

"Mrs. Fortescue said I just stood there and wouldn't talk. She took me into the kitchen and tried to get me to take a drink, but I wouldn't."

"What did Jones say about what you'd done?"

"He wasn't very complimentary."

"Really?" Kelley's tone was boldly arch. "Why? Because you only shot Kahahawai once?"

"No. He said I acted like a damn fool."

Kelley feigned shock. "An enlisted man spoke to *you* in such a fashion?"

"Yes—and I resented it."

Kelley sighed. Paced. Then he turned back to Tommie and said, "Did any of your fellow conspirators tell you why they took you along on the ride to Koko Head?"

"Yes ... Mrs. Fortescue said she wanted me to get some fresh air."

Kelley rolled his eyes and waved dismissively at Tommie. "This witness is excused."

Tommie stepped off the stand and walked with head high over to the defense table, where Darrow smiled at him and nodded as if he'd done a wonderful job. Some of it had been pretty good, but the little-boy business about resenting his enlisted-man accomplice's remark, and the lame notion that he'd been along on the corpse-disposal run to get some "fresh air," were not shining moments.

In fact, Darrow would need to follow up with something re-markable to make the jury forget those lapses.

"The defense calls Thalia Massie," Darrow said.

SIXTEEN

When the courtroom doors opened, Thalia Massie stood framed there as flashbulbs popped in the corridor, the packed gallery turning its collective head toward the surprisingly tall, astonishingly young-looking woman in the black crepe suit. Judge Davis didn't bother banging his gavel to silence the stirring, the whispering; he allowed it to run its course as Thalia moved down the aisle in an awkward slouch, her slightly pudgy, pale, pretty face framed by fawn-colored hair, her protuberant blue-gray eyes cast downward, advancing in the uncertain manner that witnesses had reported of her as she walked along John Ena Road one night last September.

Her husband met her as she moved between the defense and prosecution tables; she paused as Tommie took and squeezed her hand. A murmur of approval rose from the mostly female, predominantly white spectators; I caught Admiral Stirling (seated with a woman I assumed to be his wife) casting his approving gaze on the noble couple as they exchanged brief, brave smiles.

But even smiling, Thalia had an oddly glazed, expressionless look, the vaguely wistful cast of someone mildly drugged.

She approached the stand stoopingly and was fumbling toward the chair when the judge reminded her there was an oath to take. She straightened momentarily, raising her hand, swearing to tell the truth, then settled down into the seat, knees together, hands in her lap, shoulders slouched, a posture at once prim and reminiscent of a naughty little girl sent to sit in the corner.

Darrow, his demeanor at its most grandfatherly, approached the witness stand and leaned against one arm. He pleasantly, calmly elicited from her the mandatory points of identification: her name, Thalia Fortescue Massie; her age, 21; age at the time of her marriage, 16, to Lt. Massie on Thanksgiving Day, 1927; they had no children; she would say they were happy, yes.

Thalia's voice was a low, drawling near-monotone, nearly as expressionless as her face; but she was not emotionless: she twisted a handkerchief nervously in her hands as she answered.

"Do you remember going with your husband to the Ala Wai Inn on a certain night last September?"

"Yes. We went to a dance."

"Did you have anything to drink?"

"Half of a highball. I don't much care for liquor."

"When did you leave the dance?"

"About eleven-thirty-five at night."

"And where were you going?"

"I planned to walk around the corner and back."

"Why did you leave?"

"I was tired and bored."

"Where was Tommie?"

"When I saw him last he was dancing."

"And where did you go?"

"I started walking toward Waikiki Beach."

"I see. And tell me, where were you when something . . . unusual happened?"

Kelley was on his feet. "Once again, Your Honor, we are not here to retry the Ala Moana case. I must object to this line of questioning."

Darrow's smile was a mixture of benevolence and condescension. "Your Honor, all of this has bearing on Lt. Massie's state of mind."

Kelley was shaking his head, no. "What happened to this

witness has no direct bearing on the sanity issue—the only pertinent question, Your Honor, is what she told her husband."

A hissing arose from the gallery. The judge slammed his gavel twice, and frightened the snake into silence.

"Mr. Darrow," Judge Davis said, "you will confine your questions to what Mrs. Massie told her husband, and what he told her."

"Very well, Your Honor. Mrs. Massie, when did you next see Tommie? After you left the Inn?"

"About one o'clock in the morning. I'd finally reached my own home, and Lt. Massie telephoned me and I said, 'Please come home right away, because something awful . . .' "

But that's as far as she got. She buried her face in her hands, and her sobs echoed in the chamber. There was nothing Little Theater about it: this was real agony, and sent the ladies of the gallery dipping for their hankies in their purses.

Darrow's expression was cheerless, but I knew within that sunken old breast, he was jumping for joy. Thalia's cold-fish demeanor had transformed into the open sorrow of a wronged young woman.

Down from me at the table, Mrs. Fortescue, who'd been watching her daughter, eyes bright, chin up, reached for the sweating pitcher of ice water on the defense table and poured a glass. She pushed it down to Leisure, who nodded and rose, taking the glass up to Thalia. Leisure stayed up there, with Darrow, waiting for their witness to compose herself; it took a couple minutes.

Then Leisure took his seat, and Darrow resumed his questioning.

"What did you tell Tommie when he came home?"

"He asked me what happened. I . . . I didn't want to tell him because it was so terrible. . . ."

But she had told him, and now she told the jury, in all its awful detail, how she'd been beaten and raped, how Kahahawai had broken her jaw, how she'd not been allowed to pray, how one after another, they had assaulted her.

"I said, 'You will knock my teeth out!' He said, 'What do I

care, shut up, you . . .' He called me something filthy. And the others stood around and laughed—"

"Your Honor," Kelley said, sighing, not rising, "I don't want to be interjecting constant objections, but she's only allowed to say what she told her husband. That was your ruling."

Darrow turned toward Kelley with startling swiftness for such an old man, and his tone was hard and low. "This is hardly the time to be making objections."

Kelley's voice had equal edge: "I haven't been making *enough* of them!"

"Mr. Darrow," the judge began, "confine yourself to . . ."

But Thalia took that cue to break down again. Judge Davis and everyone else waited for her sobs to subside, and then Darrow patiently led her through a recital of how she'd identified her attackers at the hospital, and how "wonderful" and "attentive" Tommie had been to her during her recovery.

"He took such good care of me," she said, lips quivering. "He never complained about how often I woke him at night."

"Did you notice any change in your husband's behavior?"

"Oh yes. He never wanted to go out—the rumors bothered him so—and he didn't sleep, he'd pace up and down the living room smoking cigarettes. He barely ate. He got so thin."

"Did you know what he and your mother and the two sailors were planning?"

"No. Absolutely not. Once or twice Tommie said it would be wonderful to get a confession. I mean, it was always worrying him. I wanted him to forget about it, but he couldn't."

"On the day Joseph Kahahawai died, how did you learn what had happened?"

"Seaman Jones came to my door around ten o'clock."

"Before or after the killing?"

"After! He came in and said all excitedly, 'Here, take this,' and gave me a gun, 'Kahahawai has been killed!' I asked him where Tommie was and he said he'd sent Tommie off with Mother in the car."

"Did he say anything else?"

"He asked me for a drink. I fixed him a highball. He drank it and said, 'That's not enough,' so I filled his glass again. He was as pale as a ghost."

So was she.

The tears of the witness and those of the gallery had ebbed; the emotional tenor had finally evened out. It was a good stopping place, and Darrow dismissed the witness.

"Your Honor," Darrow said, "may I suggest we recess for the day, and not subject this witness to cross-examination at this time?"

Kelley was already approaching the witness stand. "Your Honor, I just have a few questions."

"We'll proceed," the judge said.

Thalia shifted in her seat as Kelley moved in; her body seemed to stiffen, and her face took on a defiant cast, her mouth taking on a faint, defensive smirk. Darrow, taking his seat at the defense table, smiled at her, nodding his support, but I knew the old boy was worried: I could see the tightness around his eyes.

"Mrs. Massie, do you remember Captain McIntosh and some other police coming to your house?"

"Yes." Her tone was snippy.

"Did a telephone call come in that was answered by Jones?"

"No." The smirk turned into a sneer.

Before our very eyes, the noble wronged wife was transmuting herself into an angry, bitchy child.

"Are you quite sure, Mrs. Massie?" Kelley stayed coldly polite.

She shifted stiffly in the chair. "Yes."

"Well, perhaps you answered it and Jones asked who was calling."

"No."

"Who is Leo Pace?"

"Lt. Pace is commander of the *S-34*."

"Your husband's submarine commander."

"Yes."

"Do you remember Jones going to the telephone and saying, 'Leo—you've got to help Massie cover this up. Help us all cover this up.' Words to that effect."

"No! Jones would never address an officer by his first name."

"Didn't Jones refer to your husband as 'Massie' in front of the police?"

"He didn't dare do it in *my* presence!"

I looked down at Darrow; his eyes were closed. This was as bad as Tommie's similar remark about resenting familiarity from the enlisted man who helped him pull a kidnapping.

"Mrs. Massie, didn't you instruct your maid, Beatrice Nakamura, to tell the police that Jones came over to your house not at ten, but at eight?"

"No."

"Really. I can call Miss Nakamura to the stand, if you wish, Mrs. Massie."

"That's not what I told her."

"What did you tell her?"

"I told her to say that he arrived a little after she came to work."

"And when is that?"

"Eight-thirty."

Thalia was displaying her remarkable ability to shift time; this was, after all, the same girl who had left the Ala Wai Inn at, variously, midnight, twelve-thirty, one o'clock, and (finally, at the cops' request to fit the needs of their case) eleven-thirty-five.

"What became of the gun Jones handed you?"

"I don't know."

"It's missing? Someone stole it from your house, do you think?"

"I don't know what became of it."

Kelley gave the jury a knowing smile, then turned back to the witness.

"You have testified, Mrs. Massie, that your husband was always kind and considerate to you—that you never quarreled."

"That is so."

"As a married man myself, I must compliment you. Marriages without conflict are rare. You're to be congratulated."

As he said this, Kelley was walking to the prosecution table, where his assistant handed him a document; Kelley perused the paper, smiled to himself, then ambled back to the witness stand.

"Did you ever have a psychopathic examination at the University of Hawaii, Mrs. Massie?"

"I did," she said, eyes tightening.

"Is this your handwriting?" Kelley handed her the sheet of paper, casually.

Thalia's pale face reddened. She was not flushed or blushing, but blazing with anger. "This is a confidential document! A private matter!" She waved the sheet at him. *"Where did you get this?"*

"I'm here to ask questions, Mrs. Massie, not answer. Now, is that your handwriting?"

The low monotone was replaced by a shrill screech. "I refuse to answer! This is a privileged communication between doctor and patient! You have no right to bring it into open court like this. . . ."

"Is the man who administered this questionnaire a doctor?"

"Yes, he is!"

"Isn't he just a professor?"

But Thalia said no more. Her chin raised, her eyes defiant, she began to tear the document down the middle. Kelley's eyes widened, but he said nothing, standing with folded arms, his mouth open in something that might have been a smile, as the petulant witness continued ripping the sheet up, tearing it to shreds. Then, with a flip of the wrist, she tossed the pieces to one side and they drifted like snowflakes as applause rang from the gallery and a few women cheered, whistled.

Judge Davis banged his gavel so hard the handle snapped. The courtroom was quiet. And while Thalia's white-women cheering section admired this display, the jury was sitting in stony silence.

Thalia, not yet dismissed from testimony, bolted from the stand and ran behind the defense table into the waiting arms of Tommie.

Kelley, savoring the moment, stood looking down at the scattered snowflakes of the confidential document.

"Thank you, Mrs. Massie," he said. "Thank you for at last revealing your true colors."

Darrow rose, waving an arm. "Strike that from the record!"

Judge Davis, frowning, the broken gavel still in hand, said, "It will be stricken. Mr. Kelley, the court finds your language objectionable."

But there was no contempt citing, though perhaps there might have been, had Thalia not taken center stage with one remark to the husband in whose arms she was enfolded, spoken in a way that would have reached the last row of the Little Theater.

"What right had he to say I don't love you?" she sobbed. "Everyone knows that I love you!"

Darrow closed his eyes. His client's wife had just revealed the contents of the document she'd destroyed.

Meanwhile, as Mrs. Fortescue looked on while dabbing her eyes with a hanky, Tommie was kissing Thalia, a lover's clinch that would have made a perfect romantic finish for a movie, only this courtroom drama wasn't over yet.

The next day Darrow closed his case with his two psychiatric experts imported from California, Dr. Thomas J. Orbison and Dr. Edward H. Williams, celebrated veterans of the Winnie Ruth Judd trial.

Orbison, ruddy, graying, portly, with wire-frame glasses and a hearing aid, described Tommie Massie's insanity as "delirium with ambulatory automatism."

Darrow grinned at the jury, raised his eyebrows, then turned back to his expert. "Translate it for those of us who didn't go to medical school, Doctor."

"Automatism is a state of impaired consciousness causing the victim to behave in an automatic or reflexive manner. In Lt. Massie's case, this was caused by psychological strain."

"In layman's terms, Doctor."

Orbison had a twitch of a nervous smile that damn near traveled to the corner of his left eye. "Lt. Massie was walking about in a daze, unaware of what was happening around him."

"You mentioned a 'psychological strain,' Doctor, that triggered this response. What was that?"

"When Kahahawai said, 'We done it,' it was as if a mental bomb had exploded in Lt. Massie's mind, inducing shock amnesia."

"He was insane just prior to, and after, the shooting?"

Orbison nodded and twitched his smile. "He became insane the moment he heard Kahahawai's last words."

Darrow said, "Thank you, Doctor. Your witness."

Kelley came quickly up, asking his first question on the move: "Isn't it possible a man might go through such 'psychological strain' and in a fit of anger kill a man and *know* it?"

The nervous smile twitched again. "The condition you call 'anger' would be anger with a delirium that is defined as insanity."

"You think it's improbable that Lt. Massie killed Kahahawai in a fit of anger?"

"Yes—because all of Lt. Massie's plans led up to getting a confession, and he killed the very person necessary to achieve this goal. This was an irrational, insane act."

"He was experiencing 'shock amnesia'?"

"That is correct."

"Are you aware, Doctor, that amnesia is not a legal insanity defense?"

Another twitch smile. "The amnesia aspect is not what labels Lt. Massie legally insane. The lieutenant was seized by an uncontrollable impulse when he was confronted by direct and final proof that Kahahawai was the man who assaulted his wife."

"I see. I see." Kelley gestured toward the defense table. "Well, Doctor, is Massie sane now?"

"Yes, of course."

"Ah," Kelley said, as if relieved. "Just a one-killing man, then. That's all, Doctor."

Darrow's second expert, Dr. Williams, tall, lean, stoic, his gray Van Dyke lending him a Freudish air of authority, basically concurred with Orbison, though he added a chemical slant to their shared diagnosis.

"The protracted worry Lt. Massie endured, the rumors on the street that troubled and frustrated him so, might bring out an actively irrational condition, resulting in pouring a secretion into the blood. Strong emotions can have an important effect on the suprarenal glands."

Darrow gestured toward the defense table. "Has Lt. Massie regained his sanity?"

"Quite fully."

"Thank you, Doctor. Your witness, Mr. Kelley."

Kelley strode forward. "Would you say it is possible that Massie might be telling a lie—that is, malingering in his testimony?"

"I suppose it's possible."

"Isn't it *usual* in cases of this sort for the defendant to simulate insanity and then hire expert witnesses who can testify in support of this pose?"

Williams frowned and turned toward the judge. "Your Honor, must I answer so disrespectful a question?"

"Withdrawn, Your Honor," Kelley said with a disgusted sigh. "No further questions."

Darrow rested his case, and Kelley—who had moments before sarcastically derided expert psychiatric testimony—called his own alienist, Dr. Joseph Bowers of Stanford University, by way of rebuttal. Bowers had testified for the prosecution in the Judd case; old home week.

The bearded, middle-aged, scholarly Bowers spoke for over an hour, showing off an encyclopedic grasp of the trial testimony thus far, detailing his study of Tommie's background, declaring, "Nothing in Lt. Massie's record indicates he was subject to states of delirium or memory loss—in my opinion, he was quite sane at the time of the killing."

Kelley was nodding. "What else has led you to this diagnosis, Doctor?"

Bowers had a habit of turning to face the jury as he gave his answers; with his air of professorial expertise, this was quite effective. "Well, I can't actually provide a diagnosis," he said, "because the defense has denied me access to the defendant."

Darrow growled, "I object to the witness's manner. Why

doesn't he face forward in the chair like any other witness? If he's going to address the jury, he might as well get up and make a speech to them. This is not the impartial attitude that—"

Bowers exploded; perhaps it was an uncontrollable impulse. "Do you mean to insinuate that I am not honest, sir? Well, I resent it!"

Darrow, hunkering over the table like a grizzly bear over a garbage can, grumbled: "Resent it, then."

"Please continue, Doctor," Kelley said, playing the voice of reason.

"Lt. Massie and these other three individuals," Bowers said, "knowing the consequences, took deliberate steps toward self-protection. They acted in a spirit of vengeance characteristic of persons who feel they've not obtained justice by legal means. Such individuals measure their acts, and consider the nature of and consequences of those acts. The steps of this plan were securing an automobile, wearing gloves and goggles, carrying guns, taking steps for disposal of the body, and so on."

Kelley was nodding. "Thank you, Doctor. That's all."

Darrow, remaining seated, asked only one question: "Doctor, may I assume you're being handsomely paid for coming down here and giving your testimony?"

"I expect to be paid," Bowers said testily.

"That is all."

Kelley, on his way back to his table, turned and said, "Prosecution rests, Your Honor."

"Summations begin tomorrow," Judge Davis said, and banged with his new gavel. "Court is adjourned."

And the next day summations did begin, but it was the second team up first, with Leisure making the case for the unwritten law ("You gentlemen of the jury must decide whether a man whose wife has been ravished, and who kills the man who did it, must spend his life behind dark prison walls, all because the shock proved too great for his mind"), and Kelley's tall young assistant Barry Ulrich lashing out against lynch law ("You cannot make Hawaii safe against rape by licensing murder!").

So it was on the following day, with police radio cars parked in front of the Judiciary Building, machine gun–toting patrolmen posted to stave off rumored native uprisings, in a the courtroom strung with wire and microphones to broadcast to the mainland what might be the Great Defender's last great oratory, the gallery packed even tighter than usual with Admiral Stirling and Walter Dillingham and other luminaries noticeably present, that Clarence Darrow rose from his chair behind the defense table where room had been made for his friend Dr. Porter, his wife Ruby, as well as Thalia Massie, seated holding hands with her husband, and shambled toward the jury. His suit was dark, baggy. His gray hair streamed haphazardly down his forehead. Fans hummed overhead. Palms rustled. Birds called. Traffic coursed by.

"Gentlemen, this case illustrates the working of human destiny more than any other case I've handled. It illustrates the effect of sorrow and mishap on human minds and lives, it shows us how weak and powerless human beings are in the hands of relentless powers."

He stood before the jury box as he spoke, his bony frame planted.

"Eight months ago Mrs. Fortescue was in Washington, well respected. Eight months ago Thomas Massie had worked himself up to the rank of lieutenant in the Navy, respected, courageous, intelligent. Eight months ago his attractive wife was known and respected and admired by the community. Eight months ago Massie and his wife went to a dance, young, happy. Today, they are in a criminal court and you twelve men are asked to send them to prison for life."

He began to slowly pace before them.

"We contend that for months Lt. Massie's mind had been affected by grief, sorrow, trouble, day after day, week after week, month after month. What do you think would have happened to any one of you, under the same condition? What if your wife were dragged into the bushes, and raped by four or five men?"

He paused, leaned against the rail of the box. "Thalia Massie was left on that lonely road in pain and agony and suffering. Her husband hears from her bruised lips a story as terrible, as cruel, as any I've heard—isn't that enough to unsettle any man's mind?"

He turned and walked toward the defense table; stood before Tommie and Thalia and said, "There have been people who have spread around in this community vile slanders. They concocted these strange, slanderous stories, and what effect did they have on this young husband? Going back and forth, nursing his wife, working all day, attending her at night. He lost sleep. He lost hope."

Darrow turned back to the jury as he gestured with an open hand toward Tommie. "Our insane asylums are filled with men and women who had less cause for insanity than he had!"

He ambled back to them, hands in the pockets of his baggy pants. "In time, five men were indicted for the crime. Tommie was in the courtroom during the trial of the assailants. A strange circumstance indeed that the jury disagreed in that case. I don't know why, I don't see why, but the jury did their work and they disagreed. Months passed, and still this case was not retried."

He again gestured toward the defense table, this time indicating Mrs. Fortescue. "Here is the mother. They wired to her and she came. Poems and rhymes have been written about mothers, but I want to call your attention to something more basic than that: Nature. I don't care whether it's a human mother, a mother of beasts or birds of the air, they are all alike. To them there is one all-important thing and that is a child that they carried in their womb."

Now he gestured with both hands at the stiffly noble Mrs. Fortescue.

"She acted as every mother acts, she felt as your mothers have felt. Everything else is forgotten in the emotion that carries her back to the time . . ." And now he motioned to Thalia. ". . . when this woman was a little baby in her arms whom she bore and she loved."

The sound of rustling handkerchiefs indicated tears were again flowing among the ladies of the gallery.

Darrow looked from face to face among the jurymen. "Life comes from the devotion of mothers, of husbands, loves of men and women, that's where life comes from. Without this love, this devotion, the world would be desolate and cold and take its lonely course around the sun alone!" He leaned against the rail again. "This mother took a trip of five thousand miles, over land and sea, to her child. And here she is now, in this courtroom, waiting to go to the penitentiary."

He rocked back on his heels and his voice rose to a near shout: "Gentlemen, if this husband and this mother and these faithful boys go to the penitentiary, it won't be the first time that such a structure has been sanctified by its inmates. When people come to your beautiful islands, one of the first places they will wish to see is the prison where the mother and the husband are confined, to marvel at the injustice and cruelty of men and pity the inmates and blame Fate for the persecution and sorrow that has followed this family."

Now his voice became gentle again as he began to pace before them. "Gentlemen, it was bad enough that the wife was raped. That vile stories circulated, causing great anxiety and agony in this young couple. All this is bad enough. But now you are asked to separate them, to send the husband for the rest of his life to prison."

His voice began to rise in timbre, gradually, and now he faced the gallery and the members of the press, saying, "There is, somewhere deep in the feelings and instincts of all men, a yearning for justice, an idea of what is right and what is wrong, of what is fair, and this came before the first law was written and will abide before the last law is dead."

Again he moved to the defense table; he stopped before Tommie. "Poor young man. He began to think of vindicating his wife from this slander. It was enough she'd been abused by these . . . men. Now she had been abused by talk." His eyes traveled back to the jury and his voice was reasonableness itself: "He wanted to get a confession. To get somebody imprisoned? For revenge? No—that did not concern him. He was concerned with the girl." And now Darrow looked affectionately at Thalia. "The girl he had taken in marriage when she was sixteen. Sweet sixteen. . . ."

He returned to Mrs. Fortescue, made a sweeping gesture,

saying, "The mother, too, believed it necessary to get a confession. The last thing they wanted to do was shoot or kill. They formed a plan to take Kahahawai to their house and have him confess. They never thought of it as illegal . . . it was the ends they thought of, not the means."

Now he positioned himself before Jones and Lord. "And these two common seamen, are they bad? There are some human virtues that are unfortunately *not* common: loyalty, devotion. They were loyal when a shipmate asked for help. Was that bad?"

He swiveled and pointed a finger at a random male face in the crowd. "If you needed a friend to help you out of a scrape, would you wait outside a prayer meeting Wednesday night . . . I guess that's the right night . . ."

There was a murmur of laughter at this wry uncertainty from the country's most famous agnostic.

"Or would you take one of these sailors? They did not want to kill, they made no plan to kill. And the house where they took Kahahawai was not a good place to kill—one family thirty feet away, another house twenty-five feet away. A lovely place to kill someone, isn't it?"

Solemnly he faced Mr. and Mrs. Kahahawai, in their usual spot in the front. "I would do nothing to add to the sorrow of the mother and father of the boy. They have human feelings. I have, too." Wheeling toward the jury, he pointed a finger that was not quite accusing. "I want you to have human feelings. Any man without human feelings is without life!"

Sighing, he began prowling before the bench. He seemed almost to be talking to himself. "I haven't always had the highest opinion of the average human being. Man is none too great at best. He is moved by everything that reaches him. Tommie has told you that there was no intention of killing."

His voice climbed again.

"But when Kahahawai said, 'Yeah, we done it!', everything was blotted out! Here was the man who had ruined his wife." Again he pointed at the jury. "If you can put yourself in his place, if you can think of his raped wife, of his months of mental anguish, if you can confront the unjust, cruel fate that unrolled before him, then *you* can judge . . . but only then."

His voice was barely audible as he said, "Tommie saw the picture of his wife, pleading, injured, raped—and he shot. Had any preparations been made to get this body out? What would you have done with a dead man on your hands? You would want to protect yourselves! What is the first instinct? Flight. To the mountains, to the sea, anywhere but where they were."

A humorless laugh rumbled in the sunken chest as he walked, hands in pockets again. "This isn't the conduct of someone who had thought out a definite plan. It is the hasty, half-coordinated instinct of one surprised in a situation. As for Tommie, gradually he came back to consciousness, realizing where he was. Where is the mystery in a man cracking after six or eight months of worry?"

Darrow returned to a position directly in front of the jury box. "This was a hard, cruel, fateful episode in the lives of these poor people. Is it possible that anyone could think of heaping more sorrows on their devoted heads, to increase their burden and add to their agony? Can anyone say that these are the type of people on whom prison gates should close? Have they ever stolen, forged, assaulted, raped?"

He slammed a fist into an open hand. "They are here because of what happened to them! Take these poor pursued, suffering people into your care, as you would have them take you if you were in their place. Take them not with anger, but with understanding. Aren't we all human beings? What we do is affected by things around us; we're more made than we make."

With a sigh, he strolled to where he could get a view of the green hills out a courtroom window. Almost wistfully, damn near prayerfully, he said, "I have looked at this Island, which is a new country to me. I've never had any prejudice against any race on earth. To me these questions of race must be solved by understanding—not by force."

One last time he positioned himself before the defendants, gesturing from Tommie to Mrs. Fortescue and finally to the quasi-defendant, Thalia herself. "I want you to help this family. You hold in your hands not only the fate but the life of these people. What is there for them if you pronounce a sentence of doom on them?"

And he plodded, clearly exhausted from his effort, to the rail of the jury box, where he leaned and said, softly, gently, "You are a people to heal, not destroy. I place this in your hands asking you to be kind and considerate, both to the living and the dead."

Eyes brimming with tears, Darrow walked slowly to his chair and sank into it. He was not the only one crying in the courtroom. I was a little teary-eyed myself—not for Massie or Mrs. Fortescue or those idiot gobs: but for the great attorney who may well have just delivered his last closing argument.

Kelley, however, was unimpressed.

"I stand before you for the law," he said, "opposed to those who have violated the law . . . and opposed to those—like defense counsel, who has distinguished himself during his long career by disparaging the law—who would ask *you* to violate the law."

Kelley paced before the jury, but more quickly than Darrow; his businesslike summation was quicker, too.

"You have heard an argument of passion, not reason," Kelley said, "a plea of sympathy, not insanity! Judge on the facts and the law, gentlemen."

Point by point, he took Darrow on: no evidence had been presented that Massie had fired the fatal shot ("He couldn't hide behind the skirts of his mother-in-law, and he couldn't put the blame on the enlisted men he inveigled into his scheme—so he took the blame"); he reminded the jury how Darrow had sought to remove Mrs. Kahahawai from the courtroom because of the unfair sympathy she might invoke, then himself put Thalia Massie on the stand in a "mawkish display"; he dismissed the insanity defense and the experts who supported it as a last refuge of rich guilty defendants; and he reminded the jury that had these four not formed a conspiracy to commit the felony of kidnapping, Joseph Kahahawai "would be alive today."

"Are you going to follow the law of Hawaii, or the argument of Darrow? The same presumption of innocence that clothes these defendants clothes Kahahawai and went down with him to his grave. He went to his grave, in the eyes of the law, an innocent man. These conspirators have removed by their violent act the possibility that he will ever be anything other than an innocent man, regardless of whether or not the other Ala Moana defendants are retried and found guilty."

Mrs. Fortescue's impassive mask tightened into a frown; it had not occurred to her that she had helped transform Joe Kahahawai into an eternally innocent man.

"You and I know something Darrow does not," Kelley said chummily, in one of the few instances when he leaned against the jury rail in the fashion Darrow had done, "and that is that no Hawaiian would say, 'We done it.' Kahahawai might have said, 'We do it,' or 'We been do it,' but never 'We done it.' There is no past tense in the Hawaiian language, and they don't use that vernacular so common on the mainland."

Now it was Kelley's turn to stand before Kahahawai's parents. "Mr. Darrow speaks of mother love. He singled out 'the mother' in this courtroom. Well, there's another mother in this courtroom. Has Mrs. Fortescue lost her daughter? Has Massie lost his wife? They're both here in the single person of Thalia Massie. *But where is Joseph Kahahawai?*"

Kelley wandered over to the defense table and panned a cold gaze across Lord, Jones, Massie.

"These men are military men, trained to kill . . . but they are also trained in the ways of first aid. When Kahahawai was shot, what attempt did they make to save his life? None! They let him bleed to death while they began trying to save their own skins. And where was the dying statement of a man about to meet his Maker with such a burden? I expected that in their defense by this high-powered attorney we would learn that as Kahahawai lay dying, he told what had happened."

Now Kelley fixed his gaze on Darrow, who sat with bowed head. "In the Loeb and Leopold case . . ."

Darrow looked sharply up.

". . . Darrow said he hated killing, regardless of how it was done, by men or by the state. But now he comes before you and says a killing is justified. That it is not murder."

Darrow bowed his head again.

"Well," Kelley continued, "if Lt. Massie had taken his gun and mowed these men down in the hospital the night his wife identified them, he'd at least have had the understanding of the community however unlawful that act might be. But instead he waited months, and dragged in these enlisted men . . . though they too are free and voluntary parties to the act, and are fully responsible. A killing is a killing, Mr. Darrow, and under these circumstances, it is clearly murder!"

Kelley moved quickly to the jury box and pounded a fist on the rail. "Hawaii is on trial, gentlemen! Is there to be one law for strangers and another for us? Are strangers to come here and take the law in their own hands? Are you going to give Lt. Massie leave to walk out and into the loving arms of the Navy? They'll give him a medal! They'll make him an admiral. Chief of Staff! He and Admiral Stirling are of the same mind—they *both* believe in lynch law."

Kelley pointed at the flag behind the bench.

"As long as the American flag flies on these shores—without an admiral's pennant over it—you must regard the constitution and the law. You have taken an oath to uphold it, gentlemen. Do your duty uninfluenced by either sympathy or the influence of admirals. As General Smedley Butler, the pride of the Marines, has said: 'To hell with the admirals!' "

I couldn't resist turning to get a glimpse at Stirling in the audience; his face was white with rage.

On this bold note, Kelley took his seat, and the judge began his instructions to the jury, pointing out the distinctions between the possible verdicts of murder in the second degree and manslaughter.

The defendants were to be held in the Young Hotel until the verdict came down; there was a palpable sense of relief among them as Chang Apana accompanied them out of court. Isabel, who hadn't spoken to me since our moonlight swim, smiled at me as she accompanied Thalia and Tommie out; what was that about? Ruby was waiting in the aisle as Darrow pulled me off to one side.

"That was a fine summation, C.D."

"Mine or Kelley's?"

"Both, actually."

"You need to get back to work."

"Why in hell? The case is over. It's time to go back to Chicago."

He shook his head, no, and the unruly hair bounced. "Not at all. We've just begun the battle." He smiled slyly. "Now, I'm going to howl indignantly when it happens and cry twenty kinds of injustice and bluster like a schoolyard bully, acting as surprised as hell my clients weren't found not guilty . . . but Nate, we're going to be lucky to pull manslaughter out of this."

"You think so? Your closing was brilliant—"

Looking around to make sure no one—not even Ruby— could hear, he laid a hand on my shoulder and whispered: "I'll be going after pardons from the governor, and the mainland press and politicians will put the pressure on, and that'll help me . . . but once and for all, I need to know the truth about that goddamn rape."

"C.D., how can you be sure your clients won't get off?"

He chuckled. "I knew they wouldn't the minute I saw those dark faces on that jury. I've been pleading this case to the press ever since. That's the only place this case can be won. Now, you come have some supper with us over at the Young—but then get your ass back on the job, son!"

Who was I to argue with Clarence Darrow?

SEVENTEEN

Chang Apana had offered to open doors, and he'd already done that for me with the local cops, in spades. Now I asked him to accompany me into the part of town where tourists seldom ventured, particularly white ones.

He was reluctant, but I pressed.

"This rumor about a second gang of boys," I said, "there must be somebody out there who can pin names on 'em. And I'm not going to find the answer on the beach in front of the Royal Hawaiian."

"Okay, but day only," he cautioned. "Chang not as young as he used to be. And dark night on waterfront not always friendly to white face."

"Fine. Lead on."

On River Street, facing the docks along the Nuanuu Stream, sat shabby storefronts—pawnshops, *saimin* cafes, and, predominantly, herb dens whose shelves overflowed with glass jars and reed baskets of such exotic commodities as dried seaweed, ginger root, shark fins, and seahorse skeletons.

The conversations between Chang and the shopkeepers were in Cantonese, and I understood nothing—except how feared and respected this wizened little man with the scarred skull face was in the toughest section of town.

"Fu Manchu in there was three times your size and a third

your age," I said, jerking a thumb back toward the musty-smelling hole we'd just exited.

"If strength were all," Chang said, "tiger would not fear scorpion."

"What stinger do you have in *your* tail?"

He walked quickly; I had much longer legs, but keeping up with him was a trick.

"They remember Chang from years ago. I make name running down gamblers, raiding opium dens. They not see me 'round here in long time, now I show up when they know police looking to remove black eye of Massie case."

"And they're not anxious to be the brunt of a new crackdown designed to restore the department's reputation."

"Correct. So I would think they would be anxious to help Chang Apana."

"Then why aren't we getting anything?"

He shrugged as he walked. "Nothing to get. Everyone hears rumor about second gang. Nobody hears name."

We spent the better part of two days prowling a maze of dark alleyways, crooked paths, and narrow lanes, street after unpaved street where if I were to outstretch my arms I could touch a wall on either side. I never quite got used to the sickly-sweet stench of the nearby pineapple canneries that merged here with the salty odor of the marshlands below the city. And the sagging balconies and rickety wooden stairs of tenements made the Maxwell Street ghetto of my childhood seem like Hyde Park.

Chang questioned various whores, pimps, and assorted hardcases, sometimes in Hawaiian, sometimes in Cantonese, occasionally in Japanese, in neighborhoods with names that were a little too vivid for comfort: Blood Town, Tin Can Alley, Hell's Half Acre. In Aala Park, Chang questioned rummies and hip-pocket bootleggers; but in Mosquito Flats, a disturbingly pretty, disturbingly young-looking prostitute in a red silk slit-up-the-sides dress told him something that made his eyes flash.

He grabbed her by the arm, tight, and spat Cantonese at her. Scared as hell, she squealed a stream of Cantonese back at him—but she seemed only to be repeating what she'd said before, louder.

And I thought I'd made out two English words: "Lie man!"

Now Chang was really walking fast. Something was bothering him.

"What did she say? What's going on, Chang?"

"Nothing. Crazy talk."

"What did she say? Did she give you a name?"

"Dead end."

"What? Chang, did I hear her call you a liar?"

But he wouldn't say any more about it, and the sun was going down, so it was time for the *haole* from Chicago to head to friendlier territory. We walked to our cars, parked on Beretania Street, and Chang paused at his Model T.

"So sorry I was of so small help," Chang said.

"We going to pick up tomorrow where we left off?"

"No. Nowhere else to ask."

"Hey, we haven't even tried the residential neighborhoods yet."

A rabbit warren of slum housing nearby included the home of the late Joe Kahahawai.

"With respect," Chang said, "I decline offer further assistance."

And the little man got in his car and rumbled off.

"What the hell," I said to nobody.

Before I drove all the way back to Waikiki, I used a pay phone and checked with Leisure at the Alexander Young.

"Any word?" I asked.

"Glad you called," he said. "We were just leaving for the courthouse. There's a verdict."

"Christ! How long did it take, anyway?"

"Fifty hours. Two hours ago, the judge asked the jury if they felt they could reach a verdict ... we all thought we were headed to a hung-jury mistrial, like the Ala Moana case ... but they said they could. And they did. See you over there?"

"See you over there."

* * *

Darrow was right: it was manslaughter.

When the court clerk read the verdict, Thalia stood up, next to her husband, as if she were one of the defendants upon whom judgment was being pronounced. All four were declared equally guilty, but with "leniency recommended."

The defendants took it stoically: a thin smile traced Mrs. Fortescue's lips, and Tommie stood erect, Lord too, though Jones was nibbling at his fingernails. Thalia, on the other hand, went completely out of control, weeping and wailing.

Over Thalia's sobs, the judge set sentencing for a week later, and prosecutor Kelley agreed to allow the prisoners to be kept in the Navy's custody, on the *Alton*, until that time. The judge thanked and dismissed the jurors.

Thalia's wailing continued, but Tommie said to her, surprisingly harshly, "Get ahold of yourself!" And she quieted down.

The public was filing out, but the reporters were swarming forward. Perhaps knowing he was under their watchful eye, Darrow went over to Kelley, shook the prosecutor's hand, and said, "Congratulations." Patient as a pallbearer, Chang Apana was waiting to escort the defendants to the Shore Patrol, and allowed Lord and Jones to shake hands with Kelley and proclaim no hard feelings.

Tommie held his hand out to Kelley. "If I ever had anything against you—"

Kelley, shaking Tommie's hand, interrupted, saying, "I've never had anything personally against you, or your wife."

Thalia snapped, "Oh really? Then you ought to look up the difference between 'prosecution' and 'persecution.' "

The reporters were grinning as they jotted down this juicy exchange.

Tommie was again quieting Thalia down, whispering to her. She folded her arms, looked away, poutily.

"Mrs. Fortescue!" a reporter called. "What's your reaction to the verdict?"

Her chin was, as usual, high; and there was a quaver in her voice, undercutting the casualness she affected: "I expected it. American womanhood means nothing in Honolulu, even to white people."

Another reporter asked Tommie the same question.

"I'm not afraid of punishment," he said, an arm around the sulky Thalia. "The Navy is behind us to a man."

"Go Navy!" Jones said.

Lord nodded and said the same thing, shaking a fist in the air. You know what? I think I *would* rather pick my backup out of the crowd at a Wednesday night prayer meeting.

Another reporter called out: "How about you, Mr. Darrow? What's your reaction?"

"Well," Darrow said, gathering his briefcase and other things off the defense table, "I'm not a Navy man, but this does bring to mind a certain phrase: 'We have not yet begun to fight.' "

"You beat the second-degree murder rap," the reporter reminded him.

"The verdict is a stunning travesty on justice and on human nature," he said, working up some steam. "I'm shocked and outraged. Now, if you'll excuse me . . ."

And as Chang Apana lead Darrow's clients into the waiting arms of the Shore Patrol, C.D. turned and winked at me, before trundling out, along the way filling the ears of the reporters with more expressions of his surprise and disappointment at this gross miscarriage of justice.

I caught up with Chang in front of the courthouse. Flashbulbs were lighting up the night as the defendants were piled into two Navy cars; Thalia was allowed to ride back to Pearl with Tommie.

"Chang!"

The little cop in the Panama hat turned and cast his pokerfaced gaze my way.

"What was that about this afternoon?" I asked him.

"I owe you apology, Nate."

"You owe me an explanation."

People were lingering in front of the courthouse. Kelley and Darrow had been buttonholed by reporters, and we were in the midst of a chattering crowd, mostly *haole*, mostly unhappy.

"This is no place to talk," Chang said. "At later time."

And he slipped away from me, into the crowd, stepping

into a patrol car that pulled away from the curb, leaving me just another unhappy *haole* in the crowd.

That evening, I kept an appointment at Lau Yee Ching's at Kuhio and Kalakaua Avenue, a sprawling, spotless pagoda palace that put any Chinese restaurant back home to shame. The beaming host, in black silk pajamas and slippers, asked if I had a reservation; I gave the name of the party I was joining and his face turned grave before he nodded and handed me over to a good-looking geisha.

The geisha, whose oval face was as lovely and expressionless as the white-painted women in the Chinese tapestries along the walls, was expecting me.

She was Horace Ida's sister.

"My brother is innocent," she whispered, and that was all either of us said as she led me through a fairly busy dining room that seemed more or less equally divided between tourists and locals, to a private dining alcove where her brother was waiting.

Then the geisha was gone, closing a door on us.

"Victory dinner, Shorty?" I asked, sitting across from him at a table that could have sat eight.

"We didn't win anything today," Ida said sourly. "That guy Kelley will prosecute us next."

"Sure this place is safe? It's hopping."

A steaming plate of almond chop suey was on the linen-covered table; a bowl of rice, too; and a little pot of tea. Ida had already served himself and was digging in. There was a place setting waiting for me—silverware, not chopsticks like Ida was using.

"Reporters don't bother tail me here," he said, shrugging. "They know my sis works at Lau Yee's, I eat here all the time, on the cuff."

"Your sister sleeping with the owner?"

He glared at me; pointed with a chopstick. "She not that kinda girl. I don't like that kinda talk. Her boss believes in us."

"Us?"

"Ala Moana boys. Lotta Chinese and Hawaiian merchants put up dough for our defense, you know."

"That's the rumor I heard. Of course, this is an island full of rumors."

This meeting was my idea; I had let him pick the place, as long as it wasn't the damn Pali. I'd wanted somewhere public, but not too public. Neither one of us wanted to be seen together, particularly by the press. Officially, we were in opposing camps.

"Rumors like the story that you fellas got blamed for what some other carload of boys did," I said. "It's all over the Island . . . but nobody seems to know who these invisible men are."

Ida, mouth full of almond chop suey, chuckled. "If I know who really do it, you think I wouldn't say?"

"Maybe. Of course, back where I come from, it isn't honorable to rat guys out."

He looked up from his food with spaniel eyes. "If I knew . . . if I hear anything, I'd say."

"I believe you. Of course, maybe they don't exist; maybe the second gang is nothing *but* a rumor."

"Somebody attack on that white woman, and it wasn't us."

I leaned forward. "Then, Shorty—you and your friends, you need to beat the bushes for me. I'm an outsider, I can only do so much."

He frowned. "Why do you want to help? Why don't you go home now? You and Clarence Darrow who is too big a shot to meet with us."

The chop suey was delicious; best I ever had. "I'm here on his behalf. I believe if Darrow is convinced of your innocence, he'll help you."

"Help how?"

"I don't know exactly. But I know he's dealing with the governor for his clients; he might do the same for you."

Ida snorted. "Why?"

"Maybe he agrees with you. Maybe he thinks he was on the wrong side of the courtroom in this one."

Ida thought about it. "What can I do? What can *we* do?"

"I know the Island's crawling with rumors, but I need leads, and I need leads with substance."

"There is one rumor," Ida said, frowning thoughtfully, "that does not go away. I hear it over and over."

"What's that?"

"That Thalia Massie have *kanaka* boyfriend."

"A beach boy."

He shrugged, ate some rice. "Maybe a beach boy."

"I don't suppose he has a name."

"No. Sometimes I hear he's a beach boy. More times I hear he's a music boy."

The doorman at the Ala Wai Inn said Thalia had talked to a music boy before she went out in the night.

And the music boy had a name—Sammy.

"Thanks for dinner, Shorty." I rose from the table, touched a napkin to my lips.

"That all you gonna eat?"

"I got enough," I said.

The dark, stocky doorman at the Ala Wai was wearing the orange shirt with flowers on it again. He didn't recognize me at first; maybe that's because I wasn't in my parrots-on-red silk number, though I did dress up my brown suit with a blue tie with yellow blossoms I'd bought in the Royal Hawaiian gift shop.

I held up a five-dollar bill, and that he recognized.

"We talked about Thalia Massie," I reminded him, working my voice up over the tremolo of the George Ku Trio's steel guitar. "This is the fin you were gonna get if that music boy, Sammy, showed up. . . ."

"But he hasn't, boss."

I put the five-spot away and fished out a ten. Held it up. "Has he been here for a sawbuck?"

A rueful half-smile formed on his moon face. He shook his head, saying, "Even a double sawbuck can't make him here when he never was."

"Tell ya what, Joe—that's what you will get . . . a double

sawbuck . . . if you call me when you see him. You still got my name and number?"

He nodded, patted his pocket. "Got it right here, boss. You at the Royal Hawaiian."

"Good. Good man."

"He may show, anytime."

I frowned. "Why's that?"

"I seen another guy here from Joe Crawford's band. So they must be takin' a break from that Maui gig."

His use of "gig"—a term I'd heard jazz players in Chicago use—reminded me how small the world was getting.

"Any of Crawford's music boys here tonight?"

He shook his head, no. "But one of those commanders you was here with last time is."

"Commanders?"

He grinned. "I call 'em all 'Commander.' They get a kick of that, those Navy officers."

"You know which 'commander' is here tonight?"

"Let me look." He had a clipboard hanging from a teakwood lattice. "Sure. Bradford. Lt. Jimmy Bradford."

I thought for a second. "Joe, are the private dining rooms in use upstairs?"

"No. Earlier tonight, not now."

"Where's 'Commander' Bradford sitting?"

Joe pointed, and I moved through a haze of smoke past the Chinese woodwork of booths and the press of couples on the dance floor, weaving through the mostly *kanaka* crowd until I found Bradford, casual in white mufti but no tie, seated in a booth off the dance floor. He was with a woman whose name I didn't recall but, from my previous visit to the Ala Wai, remembered as the wife of another officer. She was brunette and pleasantly plump and half in the bag.

"Good evening, Lieutenant," I said.

Hollowly handsome Bradford, a drink in one hand, a smoke in the other, looked up; his face went from blank to annoyed to falsely affable. "Heller. Uh, Judy, this is Nate Heller, he was Clarence Darrow's investigator."

Pretty, pretty drunk Judy smiled and bobbled her head at me.

"Actually," I said, "I still am."

"You're still what?" Bradford asked.

"Darrow's investigator. Sentencing isn't for a week; we're tying up some loose ends before going to the governor for clemency."

Bradford was nodding. "Slide in. Join us."

I stayed where I was. "Actually, I wondered if I could have a word with you, in private."

"Sure." He shrugged, grinned, nodded out toward the packed dance floor where couples were clinched, swaying to the soothing three-part harmonies and seductive rhythms of the George Ku Trio. "But where would we do that, exactly?"

"I need to get a look at the private dining room upstairs, where Thalia crashed the Stockdale party. Maybe you could point it out, and we could use that for a private chat."

He shrugged. "Okay. If you think it'd be helpful to the cause."

"I think it would."

He leaned forward and touched the brunette's hand, which was tight around her glass. "Can you take care of yourself for a couple minutes, hon?" he asked.

She smiled and said something unintelligible that passed for "yes," and then Bradford and I were wending our way through the crowd at the edge of the dance floor, heading for the front of the club. There were stairs to the mezzanine on either side; Bradford, carrying his drink in a water glass, was in the lead as we wandered toward the right.

"Don't get the wrong idea about Judy," Bradford said, looking back with a sickly grin. "Her husband Bob's out on sub duty and she's kinda lonely, needed some company."

"I won't."

He frowned in confusion. "Won't what?"

"Get the wrong idea."

Up the stairs, past a few booths where couples cuddled and kissed and laughed and smoked and sipped their spiked Cokes, we came to the first of several small dining alcoves, not unlike the one at Lau Yee Ching's where I'd spoken earlier with Horace Ida.

"Which one was the Stockdale party in?" I asked him.

Bradford nodded toward the middle one, and I gestured like a gracious usher toward the door; he stepped inside, and I followed, shutting the door behind us.

The walls were pink and bare but for, at left, a small plaque of a gold dragon on a black background; straight ahead, a window looked out on the parking lot; a cheap version of a Chinese chandelier was centered over a small banquet table.

"This is where Thalia was," I said, "when you came looking for her."

"I wasn't looking for her." He shrugged, sipped his drink. "She was just here already when I stuck my head in. I was, you know, socializing, goin' around the club, table-hoppin'."

"I think you'd noticed what a bad mood Thalia was in," I said. "And how drunk she was getting."

"I don't follow you."

"You were concerned about her behavior. You were aware, that ever since you dropped her . . . I assume *you* dropped *her,* as opposed to her dropping you, but that is just an assumption . . . that she'd gotten involved with a rougher breed of boyfriend."

He took a step toward me. "You're supposed to be helping Tommie Massie."

"You're the one supposed to be his friend. I'm not the one who was fucking Thalia."

He took a swing at me—in fairness, I should point out he might have been a little drunk—but I ducked it easily and threw a hard right hand into the pit of his stomach. He doubled over, reflexively tossing his water glass—it shattered against the left wall, splashing the dragon—and went down on all fours and crawled around like a dog, retching. What he puked up was mostly beer, but some kind of supper was in there, too, and it made an immediate awful stink.

I went over and opened the window; a breeze wafted in some fresh air. "What was it about, Jimmy? Did you want

Thalia to dump her native musician boyfriend, and come back to you? Or did you just want her to be more discreet?"

He was still on all fours. "You fucker. I'll kill you, you fucker . . ."

I walked over to him. "You know, Jimmy, I don't really care about your love life, or your sense of naval decorum. So whether you were dogging after Thalia's heels to get back in her pants, or just to settle her back down, I don't really give a rat's ass."

He glared up at me, clutching his stomach, breathing hard. "Fuh . . . fuck you."

I kicked him in the side and he howled; nobody out there heard it: too much booze and laughter and George Ku Trio.

"You trailed after her, Jimmy. It's time you told the truth. What did you see?"

Then he was up off the floor, tackling me, knocking me backward into the hard wood table, scattering chairs, and I had my back on the table, like I was something being served up and Bradford leapt on top of me, and his hands found my neck and he started to squeeze, fingernails digging into my flesh, and his reddening face looking down at me would make you think he was the one getting choked to death.

I tried to knee him in the nuts, but he'd anticipated that with the twist of his body, so I dug the nine-millimeter out from under my arm and shoved the nose into his neck and his eyes opened wide and the red drained out of his face and I didn't have to tell him to let go. He just did, getting off me, backing off, but I was getting up, too, and the snout of the automatic never left the place in his throat where it was making a painful dimple.

Now we were standing facing each other, only his head was raised, his eyes looking down at me and at the gun in his neck.

I eased up the pressure, took half a step back, and he gasped a sigh of relief right before I smacked him alongside the head with the barrel of the automatic. He went down on one knee, moaning, damn near sobbing. I'd torn a nasty gash on his cheek that would heal into a scar that would remind him of me every time he fucking shaved.

"Now, I'm not a trained killing machine like you, Lieutenant," I said. "I'm just a slum kid from Chicago who's paid to bring in pickpockets and other lowlife thieves, and I've had to learn my killing the hard way, in the street. Are you ready to tell me what happened that night, or would you prefer to retire on a disability pension after I shoot off your goddamn kneecap?"

He sat on the floor. Breathing hard. He looked like he was about an inch away from weeping. I pulled one of the chairs over that had got scattered, and sat and didn't train the gun on him, just held it casually in my hand.

"I . . . I wasn't interested in Thalia anymore. She's kind of a . . ." He swallowed and pointed to his temple. ". . . She's not all there, you know? After I broke off with her . . . you're right, it was me that broke off with her . . . she started to flaunt her loose behavior, runnin' around with this beach boy—they call him Sammy, he was here at the Ala Wai that night, did you know that?"

"Yes. Does Sammy have a last name?"

"Not that I know of. Anyway, people were talking about her sleeping around with colored trash, and when Ray Stockdale called her a slut and she slapped him, I knew things were *really* getting out of hand."

"So you followed her."

"Not right away. A couple people stopped me, to talk. So she was out the door by the time I got down there, but I saw her, tagged after her. She was moving quickly, not wanting to see me or talk to me, keeping out in front."

"You followed her down John Ena Road."

"Past Waikiki Park, yes. She was pissed off, wouldn't talk to me. . . . Frankly, I think this whole business with Sammy was her wanting to get back at me, to make me jealous."

He didn't look like much of a prize to me, not with blood on his face and puke on his white linen suit coat.

"She was almost running, and got herself so that she was up a good ways ahead of me, and some guys in a touring car pulled up . . ."

"A Ford Phaeton?"

He shook his head, no, shrugged. "I don't know. I didn't notice. Couldn't swear to it. To be honest with ya, I was a little
drunk myself. I did notice the ragtop being torn, flapping. Anyway, these guys, these niggers, how many I couldn't say, two or
more, cruise along by Thalia and one of 'em yells something to
her out the window. I don't know what exactly, you know how
those colored guys are—'Hey, baby, wanna go to a party.' I
think one of them said, 'Hey, Clara Bow, want some *oke*?' That
sort of thing."

"How did Thalia react?"

"Well . . . you gotta understand, I'd been lecturing her, as
we walked along, about how she was gonna get herself in
trouble, hangin' out with this rough crowd, I mean, she was
screwing this nigger Sammy, can you believe it? So I think,
maybe just to show me, she said, 'Sounds like fun' or some
such. I don't know what she said."

"But she sounded willing."

"Yeah. They probably thought she was a hooker. That's sort
of a red light district along there, y'know."

"I know. Go on, Jimmy."

"Anyway, she looked back at me and you know what she
did? Stuck her tongue out at me. Like a little girl. What an immature bratty cunt she is. So the car pulls along the curb, and
two or three niggers get out, and Thalia's kinda woozy from
drinkin' too much, and they're kinda guidin' her toward the
car, and I just threw up my arms, said to hell with her, and
turned back around."

I sat forward. "Was it the Ala Moana boys, Jimmy? Was it
Horace Ida, Joe Kahahawai . . . ?"

"Probably."

"Probably?"

He winced. "Maybe. Hell, I don't know, I didn't notice,
they're a bunch of fuckin' niggers! How the hell was I supposed
to tell 'em apart?"

"So you just walked off."

"Yeah. I . . . and, uh . . . yeah, just walked off."

"What?"

"Nothing."

"You were going to say something else, Jimmy. Finish your story."

"It's finished."

I stood up, looked down at him, the nine-millimeter in hand, not so casually now. "What else did you see? You saw a struggle, didn't you?"

"No! No, not . . . not exactly."

I kicked his shoe. "What, Jimmy?"

"I heard her kinda . . . I dunno, squeal or maybe scream."

"And you looked back, and what did you see?"

"They were kinda . . . draggin' her into the car. It was like, you know, she maybe changed her mind. Maybe she was just doin' it for show, saying yes to those boys, to get back at me, and once I turned around and walked off, she tried to brush the niggers off maybe . . . and they weren't takin' no for an answer."

"They dragged her in the car and drove off. And what did you do about it, Jimmy?"

We both knew the answer. We both knew he hadn't gone back and reported seeing an abduction, not to Tommie or the cops or anybody.

But I asked him again, anyway: "What did you do, Jimmy?"

He swallowed. "Nothing. Not a damn thing. I figured . . . she was an immature little bitch and a nasty little slut and the hell with her! Let her . . . let her get what she deserved."

"Is that what she got, Jimmy?"

He began to weep.

"Suppose ol' Joe Kahahawai got what he deserved, Jimmy?" I grunted a laugh. "You know what I think? Sooner or later we all do."

"Don't . . . don't . . . don't tell anybody."

"Do my best," I said, putting the nine-millimeter back in its holster, almost feeling sorry for the bastard. Almost.

That's where and how I left him—sitting on the floor, crying into his hands, sniffling, swallowing snot.

Getting back out into the smoky air of the noisy, boozy club felt damn near cleansing.

EIGHTEEN

The aftermath of the trial, in Honolulu, was surprisingly uneventful. The chief of police doubled the foot patrol and armed his squad cars with machine guns and tear gas, in case of unrest; who the chief expected to riot was never exactly clear, as the *kanaka* population was fairly content with the manslaughter verdict, and the *haoles* weren't likely to rise up against themselves. Admiral Stirling made noises about "henceforth viewing Hawaii as foreign soil," and a group of Navy wives announced a boycott of firms employing members of the jury. That was about it.

But back home, a tropical hurricane was pummeling the Capitol dome. Letters, wires, petitions, and long-distance calls bombarded Congress and President Hoover with outrage over the verdict, stirred by the Hearst papers running day-after-day front-page boxed editorials demanding that the Massie defendants be brought home and "given the protection American citizens should be properly entitled to."

"We have it on good authority," Leisure told me, "that Governor Judd received a bipartisan petition from both houses of Congress, pleading for the freeing of the defendants. One hundred thirty-some signatures."

We were seated at a small round table amid the indoor palms of the Coconut Grove Bar at the Royal Hawaiian; it was midafternoon and not very busy, more red-jacketed Oriental waiters than guests.

"If Capitol Hill wants a pardon for our clients," I said, sipping a Coke I'd spiked from my flask of rum, "why don't they get Hoover to do it?"

Leisure, casual in a blue open-neck silk shirt, sipped his iced tea and smiled lazily; either this case, or the balmy climate, seemed to have sapped his endless energy. "The President doesn't have the legal authority, Nate, to issue pardons in territories."

"So it's up to the governor."

Leisure nodded. "Meanwhile, back in the hallowed halls, senators and representatives are stumbling over each other in a rush to introduce bills proposing pardons . . . not to mention a revival of interest in the effort to place Hawaii under military rule."

"C.D.'s got the governor in a tight spot."

"Judd's not easily pushed around," Leisure said, raising an eyebrow. "In our first meeting, he spoke of not being blackmailed by the irresponsible, sensationalistic mainland newspapers."

"Hearst? Sensationalistic? Irresponsible? Perish the thought." I sipped my rum and Coke. "You said 'first' meeting."

"We meet again tomorrow evening. Darrow's hoping you'll have something for him on the Ala Moana case before then."

I hadn't told Darrow or Leisure about Bradford's story; I was still hoping to lay hands on Sammy, first.

"Tell C.D. I'll meet him for lunch tomorrow at the Young. I'll see what I can come up with."

I caught a glimpse of blond hair out of the corner of my eye, and glanced toward the entryway where Isabel, in a summery white dress with a navy belt and navy cloche cap, stood looking around for somebody. It must have been me, because when her eyes traveled my way, they stopped and her pretty face blossomed into a smile that made her prettier still, and she came quickly over.

"I thought you two weren't an item anymore," Leisure whispered.

"Me too," I admitted.

"I was just leaving," Leisure said, with a half-grin, standing, giving Isabel a courtly nod. "Miss Bell. You're looking alluring, as always."

"I hope I'm not chasing you off," she said.

"No, no. I have to meet Mr. Darrow in just a few minutes."

Her expression turned serious. "You're going to keep Tommie and Mrs. Fortescue out of jail, aren't you?"

"The effort's under way," he said. "We're even including the sailor boys in the bargain."

She clasped her hands in concern. "I meant them, too, of course."

"Of course," he said, nodded again, and was off.

I got up and pulled a chair out for her; her lovely heart-shaped face, perfectly framed by the short blond curls, beamed up at me. Her Chanel Number Five drifted up like an Island breeze and tickled my nostrils. The image of her face, eyes closed, mouth open, caught up in ecstasy on the beach, flashed through my mind.

We still hadn't spoken since that night.

"You've been avoiding me," she said, as I sat back down.

"No, I've been working."

"I wanted you to know something."

"Oh, really? What's that?"

Her smile was girlish, almost gleeful; she leaned in, touched my hand, whispered: "My friend is visiting."

"What friend?"

"You know—*my* friend. The one that comes every month."

"Oh. That friend."

So she wasn't pregnant by the Jewboy after all.

"I'm sure you're relieved," she said.

"I'm sure you are."

Her smile disappeared; her eyes drifted down. "I . . . I said some cruel things."

"Don't worry about it."

"Awfully cruel things."

"Yeah, well so did I."

She looked into my eyes and hers were tearful. "I forgive you. Do you forgive me?"

She was a stupid silly girl, and a bigot, to boot. But she was very pretty and under that summery white dress were two of the most perfect female breasts it had been my privilege in my imperfect male life to encounter.

"Of course you're forgiven," I said.

"Are you busy?"

"Not this minute."

"We could go upstairs to your room, or my room . . ."

"Won't that be awkward, with your 'friend' still visiting?"

She allowed her Kewpie lips to part a little wider than necessary for speaking purposes, then she licked them with the pinkest damn tongue and said, "There are all kinds of ways for a boy and girl to have fun."

"Yowsah," I said.

An Oriental waiter was drifting our way.

"You want something to drink, or eat, before we go up?" I asked her.

She shook her head, no, giving me a lovely lascivious look. "If we want something, there's always room service."

The waiter stopped next to me and I said, "Just the check, please."

"Uh, Mr. Heller . . . Chinese gentleman waiting to see you in lobby."

It was Chang Apana, standing with Panama in hand, looking mournful and very tiny next to a towering potted palm. I sent Isabel on up to her room, figuring this wouldn't take long.

"Have news," he said, bowing. "Shall we seek privacy?"

We found a table on the Coconut Grove *lanai*, which faced the manicured hotel grounds, flung with palms, bursting with blossoms; but most of the guests preferred the ocean view of the Surf Porch. Chang and I were alone but for a table of women playing bridge, well down from us.

"Detective Jardine asked me to report," Chang said, "that Joe Crawford's band on Maui no longer counts Sammy among its members."

I frowned. "What became of Sammy?"

"Maui police did us courtesy of making inquiry. Sammy, who seems to lack last name, is no longer in the Islands."

"Where *is* he?"

"Thought to be in California. Los Angeles. We have just contacted Los Angeles police. Too early for results."

"Damn. That was my only good lead on this possible second gang. . . ."

Chang sighed, lowered his gaze. "Not so. There is other lead."

"What?"

He was shaking his head slowly. "I feel shame for withholding information from brother officer."

"Come on, Chang—spill, already. That hooker in Mosquito Flats told you something! What *was* it?"

He sighed again. "Please understand, Nate. Rape of white woman in Hawaii, exception not rule. No matter what mainland papers say, no matter what Admiral Stirling says, rare thing in Hawaii."

"What's your point?"

"Point is, only other rape of white woman by colored man in recent memory is this prisoner Jardine been seeking."

"Yeah, the jailbird who was let out New Year's Eve to get *oke*, and never came back."

Chang was nodding. "White woman he raped, he grab her at lover's lane . . . off Ala Moana."

I sat up. "Not at the old Animal Quarantine Station?"

"No. But very nearby. Modus operandi all too familiar."

"Are you saying this guy might be a viable suspect in the Ala Moana case?" I shifted in my wicker chair, smirked. "Well, hell—surely you guys checked this out long ago! Where in God's name was the bastard the night Thalia was attacked?"

"We did check," Chang said, "and he was in prison. Serving murder sentence."

"Oh. Well, that's a pretty good alibi. . . ."

"Bad alibi like fish," Chang said distastefully. "Not stand test of time." He leaned forward, lifted a gently lecturing forefinger, squinted until his eyes completely disappeared. "If murdering rapist can walk out of jail on New Year's Eve, why not do same on twelfth of September?"

"Shit," I said. "Is Oahu Prison really as casual as all that?"

He was nodding again. "Yes. Warden Lane—recently re-placed—sent convicts out working on municipal projects 'round Honolulu. Is said any prisoner who not return from work assignments by six p.m. get locked out of jail, and lose dinner privilege."

"That's some strict warden."

Again he lowered his eyes. "Such laxity at prison well known by Honolulu police. I am ashamed for shoddy police work by my department, not following so obvious a lead. Of course, jailers at Oahu Prison, when questioned, lied to cover their own misdeeds."

"But they turned around and let the bastard out again on New Year's Eve! If they knew he most likely raped Thalia, why would they—"

Chang's eyes were knife-point sharp. "To allow him to *really* escape, and take his guilt with him. Remember—prisoners usu-ally returned when given temporary release. But Lyman did not."

"Lyman," I said. *"That's* what that hooker at Mosquito Flats said to you!"

He nodded gravely. "Please accept apology. Harlot's words hit this old man hard as brick."

"It's okay," I shrugged. "You think I haven't seen some pretty lousy things going on, in the Chicago PD? Lousy enough to make me ashamed to be part of it?"

In fact, I'd done a few.

So quietly it was barely audible over the rustle of fronds, he said, "Rumor say Lyman still in Islands."

"How do you know he hasn't gone to the mainland, like Sammy?"

Chang shook his head, no. "Is somewhere in these Islands, still. People help him hide, they protect him, because they fear him. He is one big mean bastard and they don't cross him."

"Where do we start? It's like looking for a needle in a haystack."

"Needle in haystack give away hiding place when fat man sit down." He dug in his pocket. "Meet Daniel Lyman."

Chang handed me a mug shot of Lyman—blank-eyed,

pockmarked, bulbous-nosed, shovel-jawed, a face designed for wanted circulars.

My laugh had no humor in it. "Well, we need to sit on the son of a bitch as soon as possible—and how likely is that, when Jardine and Major Ross and the entire goddamn Hawaiian National Guard haven't got the job done, in how long? Four months?"

The skull-faced little man smiled. "But you forget one thing, Nate—the main reason they not find him yet."

"What's that?"

"Chang Apana hasn't looked for him."

The Ala Wai Inn was its usual smoky self, and the music its usual syrupy mixture of steel guitar and tight harmonies. The George Ku Trio was finishing its engagement tonight, according to a poster tacked next to the door, outside. Inside, my doorman friend Joe Frietas said he was sorry, he hadn't seen Sammy yet.

"I know," I told him.

Chang Apana was at my side; he hadn't taken off his Panama or said a word since we'd entered the club. But for such a small man, Chang's presence seemed to loom large with Joe, who clearly recognized him, and was obviously nervous.

Now Chang spoke: "Sammy on mainland."

Joe grinned, nodded, and delivered a belated greeting: "You honor Ala Wai with presence, Detective Apana."

"Pleasure mine," Chang said, nodding back.

"Joe," I said, "you seen any of Joe Crawford's other music boys lately?"

He frowned at me, worried. "You're not gonna bust up *another* dinin' room, are ya, Mr. Heller?"

"I paid for the damage, didn't I?" I slipped a five-spot out of my pocket, held it up casually. "Have you seen anybody?"

He cocked his head. "Other night, you talkin' more than a *fin*, boss. . . ."

"Sammy was worth a sawbuck," I said. "This is what I figure a friend of Sammy's is worth."

Chang stepped forward and snatched the five-dollar bill from my hand; it startled me, and Joe, too. The frown on Chang's scarred-skull puss wasn't pretty. He shoved his face up into the doorman's. "No money. Just talk."

Joe backed away from the little Chinaman, holding his hands up, palms out, as if surrendering. Comical, seeing a burly guy who was at least in part the bouncer of the joint backing off from this lightweight bundle of bones.

"H-h-h-ey, boss, I'm happy to help out. There's a guy, friend of Sammy's, he's here right now . . ."

Chang and I exchanged glances.

". . . you should talk to him, half-French, half-Tahitian—I'll point ya there. I *like* helpin' police."

"Thank you," Chang said, handing the five-spot back to me. "Name?"

The guy's name, or anyway what they called him, was Tahiti. Frail, rail-thin, in a blue aloha shirt (yellow and white blossoms) and tan trousers his toothpick legs swam in, he was up next to the bandstand, by himself, swaying to the music, singing along, smiling, a glass in one hand, cigarette dangling from sensual, feminine lips. I made him twenty, twenty-two. His dark narrow face with its prominent cheekbones was almost pretty, his eyes dark, large, half-lidded, his eyebrows heavy and dark, his eyelashes long and dark and curling. When I approached he smiled at me, as if expecting me to ask him to dance.

"They call you Tahiti?"

"That's me," he said, sucked on the cigarette, and blew smoke to one side. "And what's your name, handsome?"

That's when he saw Chang. The lids of his eyes rolled up like windowshades, and he swallowed audibly.

"I didn't do anything," he said, backing away.

"Out on terrace," Chang said.

Tahiti swallowed again and nodded.

The dance floor opened directly onto grass that led to the rocky shore of the fetid canal. On really busy nights at the Ala Wai, couples spilled out onto this terrace. Tonight wasn't that busy, and only a few couples were out here holding hands, looking at the slice of moon reflecting on the shimmering surface of the smelly craphole of a canal.

The George Ku Trio went on break just as we were wandering out, so there was no music to talk over. Chang took Tahiti by the arm and led him to a wood-slat table near the thatched fence that separated the club from its residential neighbor. We were tucked beside a small palm and near where the grass stopped and the rocks began their fast slope to the lapping water.

"Nice night for swim," Chang said pleasantly.

"I don't know anything," the boy said.

"You don't know anything?" I asked. "Not anything at all? Not even your name?"

"Philip Kemp," he said.

"You know a guy named Sammy, Phil?"

He looked upward, shook his head, sucked on his cigarette again, looked down, shook his head some more. "I knew it, I knew it, I knew it. . . ."

"Knew what?" Chang asked.

"Trouble, Sammy was always trouble, too much booze, too many girls. . . ." Then wistfully he added: "But he plays steel guitar like a dream."

I put a hand on his shoulder. "He took off for the mainland, didn't he, Phil?"

"I don't like that name. Call me Tahiti, ya mind? That's what I like my friends to call me."

Hand still on his shoulder, I nodded toward his glass. "What you got there, Tahiti?"

"Little Coke. Little *oke*."

"Try this on." I removed my hand from his shoulder and took my flask from my pocket and filled his glass almost to the brim. "Take a sip."

He did. His eyes widened. He half-smiled. "Hey! Smooth stuff."

"Bacardi. Genuine article."

"Nice. Look—fellas . . . gentlemen . . . Detective Apana, we ain't met but I see you around. All I know about Sammy I told you already."

"No," Chang said, and he grabbed Tahiti's wrist, the one attached to the hand holding a cigarette. Chang tightened and Tahiti's fingers sprang open and the cigarette went tumbling, spitting orange ashes in the darkness.

"It got too hot for Sammy," I said, "didn't it? And he took a run-out powder to the City of Angels."

Chang let go of the wrist.

Tahiti, breathing hard, his eyes damp, nodded.

"So we agree on that much," I said. "But what I need to know is, *what* made the Islands too hot for Sammy?"

"He was afraid," Tahiti said. "We were . . . talking in a hotel room, back on Maui . . . this was in January . . . he had a gun, a revolver. He was afraid this friend of his would hurt him."

"Hurt him?" I asked.

"Kill him."

"What friend?"

"I can't say. *I'm* afraid, too."

"Lyman," Chang said.

Tahiti's eyes popped again. "You *know*?"

"What did Sammy tell you?" I asked. "What did Sammy know about Daniel Lyman?"

Tahiti covered his face with a hand. "Lyman's a nasty one. He'd kill me, too. I can't tell you."

"We can talk at headquarters," Chang said.

The dark eyes flashed. "Right, with billy clubs and black-snakes! Look, I'll tell you what Sammy told me . . . but don't ask me where Lyman is. I won't tell you. No matter what you do."

I glanced at Chang and Chang glanced back: interesting choice of words on Tahiti's part—he seemed to be saying he *knew* where Lyman was. . . .

"Fine," I said. "What did Sammy tell you?"

"It's something . . . big."

"We know."

The pretty eyes narrowed, lashes fluttering. "You *know* who was peeling Sammy's banana?"

I nodded. "Thalia Massie."

"You *do* know . . ."

"Yes. And Sammy was here at the Ala Wai the night Thalia Massie was supposedly attacked."

And the sensual mouth twitched. "No supposedly about it."

He seemed to want prompting, so I gave it to him: "Tell us, Tahiti."

"Sammy said she was a little drunk, tipsy. She came up to him, he was standing up by the door, and she said she was gonna get some air, you know, take a little walk in the moonlight. She told Sammy he could join her, but he should wait a little while, be discreet, you know. They were gonna go to one of those rent-by-the-hour rooms down by Fort De Russey that the soldiers use to bang their Island sweeties. Well, Sammy was waiting, being discreet, only first he saw this Navy officer that used to be Thalia's back-door man . . . I don't know whether she threw him over or he threw her over . . . but anyway, Sammy knew this officer had a history with her, and when the guy took off after her, Sammy got, well, jealous, I guess."

"Did Sammy have any words with the officer?" I asked. "Try to stop him or—"

"Naw. Sammy was too smart, or too cowardly or too something, to do that. He kinda followed along after the officer a good ways, till the officer caught up with Thalia, only he didn't exactly catch up. The officer sorta trailed behind her; they were arguing, lovers' quarrel kinda thing. So Sammy figures maybe he'll just say hell with it and butt out when he sees a ragtop cruise by with some guys in it, some guys Sammy knows, or *thinks* he knows."

"Did he know them or didn't he?"

"He knew 'em, but he thought it must be somebody else till he got a close look and, sure enough, it was his buddies, two wild guys who was supposed to be in prison."

Chang said, "Daniel Lyman and Lui Kaikapu."

Tahiti nodded. "Those two are *pilikia*, bad trouble. But Sammy used to go drinking with 'em, chasing women, they was his buddies, but they were supposed to be in Oahu Prison, Lyman for killing a guy in a robbery, and Kaikapu, he was a thief, too. Anyway, when Sammy realized it *was* them, he knew his *haole wahine* was in trouble. They was driving by whistling at her, saying things, like, you know, 'Wanna come for a ride, honey?' and 'Do you like bananas and cream, baby?' "

Sure were a lot of bananas ripening that September night.

He was getting his cigarettes, a pack of Camels, out of his front shirt pocket. "Anybody got a match?"

Chang found one for him, then took the opportunity to light up a cigarette himself. Tahiti drew smoke into his lungs in greedy gulps, like a guy on the desert getting his first drink in days. He blew the smoke out in a stream that dissipated in the gentle breeze. He was shaking a little. I let him calm down. Chang, eyes locked on our witness, sucked his smoke like a kid drinking a thick malt through a straw.

"How did Thalia react to this attention?" I asked.

"Like she liked it," Tahiti said. "She talked right back to them, 'Sure! Anytime, boys!,' stuff like that. She was acting like a whore and that wasn't smart 'cause that's a street where the chippies strut their stuff, y'know?"

"What did the officer do?"

"Nothing. Sammy thought the way she was acting musta made her officer boyfriend mad or jealous or something, 'cause he turned around and headed back the other way."

"Did he run smack into Sammy?"

Tahiti shook his head, no. "He didn't notice Sammy. Sammy musta been just another native on the sidewalk to him. This is along where there's a *saimin* shack and all sorts of shops, food and barber and all, and it's not like nobody was around."

"What did Sammy do?"

"He followed along and he came up and said, 'Hey, Bull, come on, leave her alone.' "

"Which one was named Bull? Lyman or Kaikapu?"

Tahiti shrugged. "Any of 'em. There was a third guy in the ragtop that Sammy didn't know, some Filipino. See, in the Islands, 'Bull' is a name like 'Mac' or 'Joe' or 'Bud' or 'Hey you.' Get me?"

I nodded.

"I don't know what Sammy did, but he went up and tried to help her, talk to her, talk his friends out of picking her up. And I think she started getting scared, changing her mind about getting in with these guys, if she ever meant to. Maybe she was just flirting to make her officer mad, that's what Sammy thought; or maybe she was just drunk. Hell, I don't know, *I* wasn't there. . . ."

"Keep going," I said, patting his shoulder. "You're doing fine."

Hand shaking, he drew in smoke in several gasps, exhaled it like a man breathing his last. "Anyway, Sammy said they shoved him away and grabbed her and pulled her into the car and drove off. And that's it."

"That's all Sammy saw? All Sammy did?"

"Yeah—except when Lyman and Kaikapu busted out, or anyway walked out, of prison on New Year's Eve, and their two-man crime wave started, Sammy got nervous, *real* nervous. He never came back to Oahu after that. Like I said, on Maui, he was packing a gun. He'd do his gigs with Joe Crawford's band, then he'd hole up in a hotel room. He was relieved when Kaikapu got picked up and put back inside, but it was Lyman he was really scared of. When the cops couldn't catch Lyman . . ." He gave Chang an apprehensive look. ". . . no offense, Detective . . ."

"None taken," Chang said.

". . . Anyway, Sammy finally caught a boat to the mainland, and that's it."

The George Ku Trio, back from their break, began playing again, the muffled strains of steel guitar and falsetto harmonies echoing off the water.

"That's everything I know," Tahiti said. "I hope I helped you fellas. You don't have to pay me or anything. I just wanna be a good citizen."

"Where's Lyman?" Chang said. His voice was quiet, but you could cut yourself on the edge in it.

"I don't know. Why would *I* know?"

"You know where Lyman is," Chang said. "You *said* you did."

"I didn't say . . ."

I put my hand on the boy's shoulder and squeezed; not hard—friendly, almost affectionate. "Detective Apana is right. You said you wouldn't tell us where he is, no matter what we did. That means you know where he is."

"No, no, you fellas misunderstood me . . ."

"Where is Lyman?" Chang asked again.

"I don't know, I swear on my mama's grave, I don't even *know* the bastard . . ."

I drew my hand away from his shoulder. "I can get you money, Tahiti. Maybe as much as five hundred bucks."

That caught his attention. His dark eyes glittered, but his full feminine lips were quivering.

"Money doesn't do you any good in the graveyard," he said.

That sounded like something Chang would say.

"Where is Lyman?" Chang asked.

"No," he said, and gulped at his cigarette. "No."

Faster than a blink, Chang slapped the cigarette out of Tahiti's hand; it sailed into the water and made a sizzling sound.

"Next time I ask," Chang said, "will be in back room at station house."

Tahiti covered his face with both hands; he was trembling, maybe weeping.

"If he finds out I told you," he said, "he'll kill me."

And then he told us.

NINETEEN

In the paltry moonlight, the squattersville along Ala Moana Boulevard looked like the shantytowns back home, with a few notable differences.

The squattersvilles in Chicago—like the one at Harrison and Canal—really were little cities within the city, miniature communities populated by down-on-their luck families, mom-pop-and-the-kids, raggedy but proud in shacks that were rather systematically arranged along "streets," pathways carved from the dirt, with bushes and trees planted around proud shabby dwellings, to dress up the flat barren landscape; fires burned in trash cans, day and night, fending off the cold part of the year and mosquitoes the rest.

The Ala Moana squattersville had bushes and trees, too, but wild palms and thickets of brush dictated the careless sprawl of the shacks assembled from tar paper, dried palm fronds, flattened tin cans, scraps of corrugated metal, scraps of lumber, packing crates, chicken wire, and what have you. No trash can fires, here—even the coolest night didn't require it, and the Island's meager mosquito population was down at the nearby city dump, or along the marshier patches along the Ala Wai.

Chang Apana and I sat in his Model T alongside the road; a number of other cars were parked ahead of us, which struck me as absurd. What kind of squattersville had residents who could afford a Ford?

Of course, I had it all wrong. . . .

"Native families build this village," Chang said. "But couple years back, city make us chase them out."

I could hear the surf rolling in, but couldn't see the ocean; it was obscured by a thicket across the way.

"Why didn't you tear it down, clean this area up?"

Chang shrugged. "Not job of police."

"Whose job is it, then?"

"Nobody ever decided."

"Who lives here now?"

"No one. But these shacks shelter bootleggers and pimps and whores, gives them place to do business."

I understood. This was one of those areas of the city where the cops cast a benignly neglectful eye, either for graft or out of just plain common sense. This was, after all, a town that lived on tourist trade and military money; and you had to let your patrons get drunk and get laid or they'd go somewhere else on vacation or liberty.

"Well, if Tahiti can be believed," I said, "*somebody* lives here."

Chang nodded.

Tahiti, who regularly bought his *oke* at the squattersville, told us he'd seen Lyman several times, on the fringes of the camp, over the last week or so. The boy, shocked to see Lyman there, had gingerly asked his bootlegger about the notorious escapee; he'd been told Lyman was pimping for some *hapa-haole* girls (half-white, half-whatever), building a bankroll to smuggle himself off the Island. Having spent the last several months staying one step ahead of Major Ross's territorial police, hiding all over Oahu, sheltered by criminal cronies, shifting between hideouts in the hills, in the small towns, and in Honolulu's slum neighborhoods (the very ones Chang and I had recently combed), Lyman was getting ready to make his move.

So was I.

We had discussed contacting Jardine and, through him, Major Ross, to launch a full-scale raid of the squattersville. But we decided first to determine if Lyman was really there; even then, if we could bring him down with just the two of us, so much the better. No chance of him slipping away in the hubbub.

Besides, people got hurt in raids; people even got killed. I needed him alive.

"I stay in shadows," Chang said. "Somebody might know me."

Hell, so far everybody had known him.

"Good idea," I said, getting out of the car. "I don't want to get made as a cop."

"When you need me," he said, "you will see me."

I went in alone—just me and the nine-millimeter under my arm. I was in the brown suit with my red aloha shirt—the one with the parrots—wandering down the twisting paths, around trees, past shacks, my shoes crunching bits of glass and candy wrappers and other refuse. The street lamps of this haphazard city were shafts of bamboo stuck in the ground, torches that glowed in the night like fat fireflies, painting the landscape— and the faces of those inhabiting it—a muted hellish orange.

I had no problem blending in—the squattersville clientele was a mixed group, the *haoles* including venturesome tourists and civvy-wearing soldiers (no sailors tonight, thanks to Admiral Stirling canceling liberty), plus working-class *kanakas* from the canneries and cane fields; and, of course, youths in their late teens and twenties—restless colored kids of the Horace Ida/Joe Kahahawai ilk, and collegians both white and colored, any male with a thirst or a hard-on that needed attention. A steady stream was coming and going—so to speak.

The hookers, leaning in the doorways of their hovels, were a melting pot of the Pacific: Japanese, Chinese, Hawaiian, and mixtures thereof, painfully young girls barefoot in silk tropical-print sarongs, shoulders bare, legs bare from the knee down, beads dangling from necks and arms, blood-red mouths dangling cigarettes in doll-like faces with eyes as dead as doll's eyes, too.

With Lyman's mug shot in mind, I furtively scrutinized the faces of the *kanaka* pimps and bootleggers, roughnecks in loose shirts and trousers, hands lost in pockets, hands that could emerge with money or reefers or guns or knives; men with dark eyes in dark faces, round faces, oval faces, square faces, every kind of face but a smiling one.

For a place where sin was for sale, there was a startling absence of joy here.

Up ahead was a central area, or as close to one as the randomly laid out village had; a gentle fog of smoke rose from a shallow stone barbecue pit where a coffeepot nestled among glowing orange coals. Nearby, cigarettes drooping from their lips, a pair of Polynesian pimps played cards at a small wooden table not designed for that purpose; they had to hunker over it, particularly the taller of the two, a broad-shouldered bearded brute in a dirty white shirt and dungarees. The other card-player, a wispy-mustached pig in a yellow and orange aloha shirt, had more chins than the Honolulu phone book.

I got out of the way of a couple *haole* college kids who were heading home (or somewhere) with two jugs of *oke*, and I almost bumped into somebody. I turned, and it was a Chinese girl with a cherubic face and a flicker of life in her eyes.

She asked, "Wan' trip 'round world, han'some?"

Second time tonight somebody called me that; unfortunately, the male who called me that had sounded more sincere.

I leaned in so close I could have kissed her. Instead, I whispered, "You want to make five bucks?"

The red-rouged mouth smiled; the teeth were yellow, or maybe it was just the bamboo-torch light. She was drenched in perfume and it wasn't Chanel Number Five, but it had its own cheap allure. She was maybe sixteen—sweet sixteen, as Darrow had said of Thalia. The angel face was framed by twin scythe blades of shiny black hair.

"Step inside, han'some," she said.

That time she sounded like she meant it.

As she was about to duck inside her hut, I stopped her with a hand on her arm, easily; her flesh was cool, smooth. "I don't want what you think."

She frowned. "No tie me up. Not even for five buck."

"No," I said, and laughed once. "I just want a little information."

"Jus' wan' talk?"

"Just want talk," I said softly. "I hear there's a *kanaka* who needs a boat to the mainland, no questions asked."

She shrugged. "Lot *kanaka* wan' go mainland. Don' you wan' go 'round world, han'some?"

Very softly, I said, "His name's Daniel Lyman."

She frowned again, thinking. Now she whispered: "Five buck, I tell you where Dan Ly Man is?"

I nodded.

"No tell 'im who tol' you?"

I nodded again.

"He got temper like *lolo* dog." She shook a finger in my face. *"No tell him."*

"No tell him," I said.

"I tell you where. I not point. You let me go inside, then you go see Dan Ly Man."

"Fine. Where the hell is he?"

"Where hell five buck?"

I gave her a fin.

She pulled the hem of her sarong up and slipped the five-spot into a garter that held a wad of greenbacks. She smiled as she saw me taking a gander at the white of her thigh.

"You like Anna Mae bank?" she asked.

"Sure do. Kinda wish I had time to make another deposit."

She laughed tinklingly and slipped her arms around my neck and whispered in my ear. "You got more dollar? We go inside, you talk Dan Ly Man later. Make you happy."

I pushed her away, gently. Kissed my forefinger and touched the tip of her nose. Her cute nose. "Save your money, honey. Go to the mainland and find one man to make happy."

The life in her eyes pulsed; her smile was a half-smile, but it was genuine. "Someday I do that, han'some." Then she whispered, barely audibly: "Beard man." And she nodded her head toward the two pimps playing gin.

Then she slipped inside the hovel.

The full-face beard had been enough, added to the dim, otherworldly torch lighting, to keep me from recognizing him. But as I wandered over to the barbecue pit, I could see it was him, clearly enough; the deep pockmarks even showed under the nubby beard.

And those were the blank eyes of Daniel Lyman, all right. And the many-times-broken lump of a nose.

I drifted over, stopping by the barbecue pit, very near where they were playing.

I spoke to the fat one: "What's in the pot? Tea or coffee?"

The fat one looked up from his hand of cards with the disdain of a Michelangelo interrupted at his sculpting. "Coffee," he grunted.

"Is it up for grabs?" I asked pleasantly.

Lyman, not looking up from his cards, said, "Take it."

"Thanks."

I reached for the pot, gripped it by its ebony handle. Casually, I said, "I hear somebody's looking for a boat to the mainland."

Neither Lyman nor the fat guy said anything. They didn't react at all.

Some tin cups were balanced along the stones; I selected one that seemed relatively clean—no floating cigarette butts or anything.

"I can provide that," I said, "no questions asked. Private boat. Rich man's yacht. Comfortable quarters, not down with the boiler room boys."

"Gin," the fat man chortled.

"Fuck you," Lyman said, and gathered in the cards and shuffled.

"You're Lyman, aren't you?" I said, slowly filling the tin cup with steaming coffee.

Lyman looked up at me; his face had an ugly nobility, a primitive strength, like the carved stone visage of some Hawaiian god. The kind villages sacrificed maidens to, to keep him from getting pissed off.

"No names," he said. He kept shuffling the cards.

I set the coffeepot on the stones that edged the pit. Tried to sip my cup, but it was too hot.

I said, "Tell me what you can afford. Maybe we can do some business."

"I don't know you," Lyman said. His dark eyes picked up the orangish glow of the torchlight and the coals in the pit, and seemed themselves to glow, like a goddamn demon's. "I don't do business with stranger."

That's when I threw the cup of coffee in his face.

He howled and got clumsily to his feet, overturning the table, cards scattering, and the fat man, quicker than he had any right to be, pulled a knife from somewhere, with a blade you could carve a canoe out of a tree with, and I grabbed the coffeepot and splashed the fat bastard in his face, too.

It wasn't scalding, but it got their attention, or rather it averted it, the knife fumbling from the fat man's grasp, while I drew my nine-millimeter. By the time Lyman had wiped the coffee from his face and eyes, I had the gun trained on him.

"I'm not interested in you, Fatso," I said. "Lyman, come with me."

"Fuck you, cop," Lyman said.

"Oh, did you want sugar with that? I'm sorry. We'll get you some downtown."

He was facing a gun, an automatic, the kind of weapon that can kill you right now, and he had every reason to be afraid, and I had every reason to feel smug, only feeling smug is always dangerous when you're facing down the likes of Daniel Lyman, who wasn't afraid at all and came barreling at me so fast, so suddenly, I didn't think to shoot till he was on top of me and then the shot only tore a place along his shirt, cutting through the cloth and a little of him, only, shit, it was *me* going backward into that barbecue pit, and I had the presence of mind to clutch him like a lover and squeeze and roll and we hit not the coals but the stones, which was good, but we hit them hard, or I did, my back did, which wasn't good, pain sending a white lightning bolt through my brain.

We rolled together, locked in an embrace, onto the ground and his shoulder dug into my forearm and I felt the fingers of my hand pop open and the gun jump out. Then I was pinned under him, and when I looked up into the contorted bearded orange-cast face hovering above me, the only thing I could hit it with was my forehead, and I did, hitting him in the mouth, and

I heard him grunt in pain as teeth snapped, and he let go of me and I was squirming out from under him when the same massive fist that had no doubt broken Thalia Massie's jaw slammed into mine.

This time there was no lightning bolt, but a flash of red followed by black, and consciousness left me, just momentarily, but long enough for Lyman to get up and off of me. Groggily, touching my jaw—unbroken jaw—I got to my feet and could see him cutting down a pathway between shacks, toward the road, I thought.

Meanwhile, the fat man was bending to pick up my nine-millimeter. He had it in his hand when I kicked him in the ass, hard enough to score a field goal, sending my gun flying again and him hurtling toward, and into, the barbecue pit, where he did a screeching scrambling dance, yow yow yow yow yow, sending orange sparks flying as he got himself out of there.

Where was my goddamn gun?

I didn't see it, and hell, it couldn't have gone far, only if I took the time to look for it, Lyman might get away. I had to go after him, *right now*, unarmed or not, and he didn't seem to have a weapon on him, so what the hell—this was why I *came* to the *luau*, wasn't it?

I trotted down the path Lyman had taken, stopping at a crossroads, not seeing my quarry anywhere. Had he ducked into a shack? The way the shacks were nestled in and around thickets and trees made for a maze of pathways. Squattersville seemed suddenly a ghost town—whether at the sound of a gunshot, its inhabitants had hidden inside the shacks, or had scattered into the woods or the street, I couldn't say.

Not daring to move too quickly, knowing Lyman could leap at me from any shadowy doorway, I moved cautiously if not slowly, and damned if I didn't find myself back at the central area, at the barbecue pit. No sign of Lyman here, of course. Or his fat friend, either.

I was about to set off down another path when from the convergent paths that joined here, one by one, figures emerged. None was Lyman, but they were just as menacing: three dark men, pimps, bootleggers, the city council among this rough-neck rabble perhaps, the men whose domain I had invaded.

Each had something in his hand—one a gleaming knife, another a blackjack, yet another a billy club. No unseemly repetition—variety . . .

A fourth man stepped into sight and it was Lyman. He had yet another weapon, a gun—not mine, his own, a revolver.

So he hadn't made a break for it—he'd got reinforcements, got himself armed.

And come back for me.

Lyman had an awful grin; it would have been awful even without the holes I'd put in it with my forehead.

"You make mistake, cop," Lyman said, "comin' alone."

The crack that split the air sounded like a gunshot, and the agonized cry that followed it might have been a bullet-wounded man's; but it was something else entirely.

It was a blacksnake whip in the deft hands of a little old Chinaman in a white suit. His knife-scarred face looked ghostly and ghastly in the hell-fire glow, his lips pulled back over his teeth in a grimacing smile as he moved nimbly among them, sending the leather tongue stingingly after each man, tearing clothing and flesh, moving in a circular fashion like a lion tamer in a cage full of beasts, with speed, with grace, and red slashes of blood appeared on the front of this one, on the back of that one, even down the face of another of these much-larger-than-he men he was flaying, their shrieks as long and jagged as their wounds and just as terrible.

Lyman had got his taste of lash across his shirt, shearing it angularly, and his revolver had flown from his hand reflexively. But unlike the other men, who had fallen to their knees in pain and tears, Lyman again took off down a path.

I took off after him.

This time he was headed for the road, for Ala Moana Boulevard where now only a few cars were parked, Chang's among them; none of them must've been Lyman's, because he headed straight across the road, into the thicket, and I was right behind him, as we both went into and through the undergrowth, snapping branches, shearing leaves, crunching twigs, and then we both burst through the brush, onto the beach, no white sand here, just a short rocky slope to an ocean that stretched in an endless ice blue shimmer, the tiny moon slice throwing silver highlights.

He probably figured he could follow the beach to nearby Kewalo Basin, where the sampans were docked, where he could find some kind of boat and elude capture once more.

Not tonight.

I tackled him and we both sailed toward the water, then plunged into its warm embrace, separating as we hit. We both got our footing on the sandy, rocky floor beneath us, water to our waists, but he was still in pain from that bloody gash on his chest and I slammed my fist into his bearded face with everything I had, hoping to hell I would break *his* jaw.

The blow sent him reeling back, and he fell backward into and under the water with a hell of a splash. I jumped after him, found him under there, breathing hard as I held the bastard under. When I felt him go limp, I hauled him by the arm and back of his shirt, up onto the shore, making no effort at all to protect him from the rocks I was dragging him over.

When I walked him through the thicket, he was like a man sleepwalking, guided largely by my steering him with my hand clutching a wad of the hair on the back of his head. We emerged, Lyman barely conscious as I guided him along, and I escorted him across the street, toward the handful of parked cars.

From the other side of them, where he'd been crouching, the fat man popped up like an unfriendly jack-in-the-box—with my gun in his hand. . . .

"*Haole pi'lau,*" the fat man snarled, raising the automatic toward me.

The crack of the blacksnake was followed by the howl of the fat man, who would have one hell of a scar down his back for the rest of his life. My gun went sailing out of his hand and I caught it perfectly, with one hand, as if it were an act we'd both long rehearsed.

I tossed Lyman against the running board of the nearest parked car. He collapsed there, breathing hard, head hanging, shoulders hunched.

The fat man was running down the road, toward Honolulu, and Chang was out in the street, cracking the whip after him, not landing a blow but lending the runner further motivation.

I was soaking wet, exhausted, breathing hard, throbbing with pain, and exhilarated as hell.

Chang was smiling as he approached me; with an agile flip of his wrist, he caused the long tail of the whip to curl up in a circle, which he grasped.

"Shall we take suspect in?" he asked pleasantly.

"I don't think that's the way Charlie Chan would do it," I said, nodding to the coiled-up whip.

"Hell with Charlie Chan," he said.

And, blacksnake tucked under his arm, he snapped the cuffs on the groggy Lyman.

TWENTY

The following afternoon, Prosecutor John Kelley joined Clarence Darrow, George Leisure, and me in the outer sitting room of the Darrow suite. Kelley, in the same white linen suit he'd worn so frequently in court, was pacing. His ruddy face was redder than usual, his blue eyes darting.

"I don't like it," he said. "I don't like it the least damn little bit."

"John, please sit," Darrow said gently, magnanimously gesturing to a place on the tropical-pattern sofa next to Leisure and me. Darrow, in shirtsleeves and suspenders, was sprawled in his easy chair, feet up on the settee, as casual and relaxed as Kelley was tightly coiled.

With a massive sigh, Kelley lowered himself to the sofa cushion, but didn't sink back in like Leisure and me, rather sitting forward, hands clasped tightly between his open legs. "These people killed a man, an *innocent* man, we now know, and you expect me to go along with some slap on the damn wrist?"

Wind was whispering through the open windows, rustling the filmy curtains, as if speaking secrets we could almost hear, nearly make out.

"There comes a time when every reasonable man has to cut his losses," Darrow said. "I prefer not to argue the point again, but my misguided clients truly believed they were dealing with one of the guilty parties. What pleasing choice do any of us have in this matter? Knowing what you now know, you can't in good conscience retry the Ala Moana defendants. But you can't exonerate them either, not without delivering a devastating blow to an already crippled police department and the local and territorial government it represents."

"Mr. Kelley," I said, "I'm as frustrated as you are. I risked my . . . life bringing Lyman in. But you've spoken to Inspector McIntosh, and the chief of police. You know the reality of this as well we do."

The reality was that even under all-night, back-room station house questioning, Lyman and Kaikapu had denied any involvement in the Thalia Massie abduction/attack. Further, prison records indicated they were present and accounted for on September 12 of last year; the prison officials and guards who could expose that lie would be setting themselves up for a stay on the wrong side of the bars in their own facility.

And even if these obstacles could be overcome, prosecuting two new defendants for the Thalia Massie abduction/attack—defendants who had walked out of Oahu Prison *twice* to commit rape and other crimes—would almost certainly result in a storm of embarrassment and ridicule that the beleaguered local government could scarcely afford.

"Of course," Darrow said, "both these individuals are serving life sentences . . . so, in a sense, justice has already been served."

Kelley's mouth was moving, as if he were muttering, but nothing was coming out.

"The only way you'll get them to talk," I said, "is to offer them immunity and a deal for shorter time."

"Promise them *parole*," Kelley said bitterly, shaking his head, "for confessing to the most notorious crime in the history of the Territory? It's scandalous."

"No," Darrow said, lifting a gently lecturing forefinger. "Going forward with a full *investigation* and a *prosecution* would be scandalous. No one would emerge a victor. My clients would be disgraced, Thalia Massie might as well sew a scarlet letter on her breast, and you would just about guarantee Hawaii losing self-government and see the reins handed over to the racist likes of Admiral Stirling."

Kelley had his head in his hands. "Christ Almighty." He looked up; now his face was very pale. "You're meeting with the governor tonight?"

"Yes."

"What does he know?"

Darrow raised his eyebrows, set them back down. "To my knowledge, nothing about Lyman and Kaikapu. That's up to your office and the police department, should you think this is information Governor Judd need be privy to." He shrugged elaborately. "Though, you know . . . I would assume the governor has enough on his mind, at present, knowing that if he doesn't release my clients, he'll be remembered as the governor who brought martial law to Hawaii, by provoking the United States Congress, and financial ruin to local businesses, by alienating the United States Navy."

Kelley snorted, sneered. "You'd prefer that he be remembered as the governor who ignored law and order, and arbitrarily freed four people convicted of killing an innocent man."

Weariness passed over Darrow's face in a wave; then he blinked a few times slowly, and a smile came to his lips at about the speed it takes for a glacier to form.

"I prefer to put this suffering behind us. Two of the three men who assaulted Thalia Massie are in prison on life sentences; a possible unidentified third party has fled to parts unknown. Those innocent Ala Moana boys have seen their number diminished by one, and their lives turned inside out and upside down. My clients have been held in custody for months, and have lost their dignity and their privacy and have, goddamnit sir, suffered enough. So, I would dare say, have these fair islands." He slammed a fist on the arm of the easy chair, and a frown turned the kindly face into a mass of angry wrinkles. "Enough, sir! I say enough."

Kelley swallowed, nodded, let go another sigh, said, "What precisely do you propose?"

"George," Darrow said to Leisure, "would you show Mr. Kelley that document you prepared?"

Leisure sat forward and removed a sheet of paper from the briefcase at his feet. Handed the document to Kelley, who read it.

"You're not asking the governor for a pardon," Kelley said. He looked up at Darrow. "You're asking him to commute the sentence. . . ."

Darrow nodded slowly. "A pardon can be viewed as a reversal of the jury's decision . . . while commuting the sentence is a fine way for the Territory of Hawaii to save face. After all, the felony stays on the record, the crime is not officially condoned in any way. Prison time, in this instance, would serve no rehabilitative purpose. . . . Does anyone really believe Tommie Massie and Grace Fortescue are dangers to society? And, remember, the jury did recommend leniency."

Kelley seemed somewhat overwhelmed by all this. He sounded almost confused as he said, "Sentence hasn't even been handed down yet. . . ."

"We'd like it to be, tomorrow."

The prosecutor frowned in surprise. "It's not scheduled till Friday. . . ."

Darrow cocked his head, raised one eyebrow. "If we move it up, we get less press attention."

Kelley shrugged facially, then gestured with the document. "Commuted to what? Time served?"

Darrow shrugged. "Whatever. As long they're allowed to leave Honolulu."

"I'm going to be expected to prosecute the Ala Moana boys, you know. I certainly have no desire to, particularly knowing what I do about Lyman and Kaikapu."

Darrow's smile turned sly. "You won't be able to prosecute without your complaining witness."

Sitting so far forward, he seemed about to tumble off the sofa, Kelley said, "So you'll advise Thalia to leave the Islands?"

Darrow looked at his pocket watch. "I will. In fact, I'm expecting her in just a very few minutes. . . . Would you care to stay to pay your respects?"

Kelley, twitching a smile, rose. "I think I'll pass on that mor-

bid pleasure, gentlemen. . . . Don't get up, I can see myself out."
He went to Darrow and extended his hand; the two men shook
hands as Kelley said, "I won't stand in your way on this. You
can expect my cooperation . . . as long as you make sure Thalia
Massie is off this island as soon as possible."

Darrow nodded gravely, then lifted a gesturing hand.
"Understand, I'll be making some public statements at odds
with our private agreement. I'll be outraged that my clients
have been denied the full pardon they so rightfully deserve . . .
that sort of malarkey."

Kelley chuckled. "Well, you can expect me to bray like a
mule about taking the Ala Moana boys to trial. . . . Of course
some people will suggest that, having prosecuted Joseph Kahahawai's killers, I in good conscience should step down. You
know what I may do? I might suggest to the press that the man
to prosecute that case is the man who so eloquently defended
the wronged family: Clarence Darrow."

A smile tickled Darrow's lips. "You wouldn't . . ."

Kelley was at the door. "I may be seized by an uncontrollable impulse."

And he was gone.

Darrow was chuckling. "I like that Irishman. Hell of a
prosecutor."

Leisure folded his arms and leaned back. "He wasn't happy,
but I believe he will cooperate."

Darrow began to make a cigarette. "He's a man of his word.
He'll cooperate. And I don't believe any of us are happy." He
looked up. "Nate, do you feel gypped out of the glory of nab-
bing the man who raped Thalia Massie?"

"No," I said. "I had the pleasure of knocking some of his
teeth out, even if I didn't quite manage to break his goddamn
jaw."

Leisure was laughing softly, shaking his head. "Where'd
you find this roughneck, C.D.?"

"On the West Side of Chicago," Darrow said as his slightly
shaking hands did a nice job of dropping tobacco into the curve
of cigarette paper. "That's where America turns out some of its
best roughnecks."

A knock at the door brought Ruby Darrow out of the bedroom; she was straightening her hair, smoothing her matronly gray dress, saying, "Let me get that, dear."

It was Thalia, of course, and she was accompanied by Isabel. Thalia wore a navy blue frock with white trim, Isabel the blue-and-white-striped crepe de chine from the Ala Wai, both in cloche hats, carrying clutch purses, two stylish, attractive, modern young women; but they also wore a cloak of unhappiness. Thalia seemed jittery, Isabel weary. They stepped inside, Thalia first, digging in her purse.

Darrow, lighting his cigarette, got to his feet, and so did Leisure and I. Thalia was moving toward us, handing a stack of telegrams toward Darrow.

"You simply must see these, Mr. Darrow," she said. "Such wonderful support from people all over the United States . . ."

"Thank you, dear." He took them and said to his wife, "Would you put these with the others, Ruby? Thank you."

Ruby took the telegrams and Darrow turned to Leisure and said, "George, would you mind accompanying Mrs. Darrow and Miss Bell for some refreshments in the lobby? I recommend the pineapple parfait."

Leisure frowned. "You don't want me here when you speak to—"

"Mr. Heller and I have a few details to discuss with Mrs. Massie that I think would be best served by . . . a limited audience."

Leisure seemed vaguely hurt, but he knew his place, and his job, and took Ruby by the arm and led her to the door. Isabel looked at me with an expression that mingled curiosity and concern; we never had connected last night.

I threw her a smile and that seemed to console her, and then Leisure and his two charges were gone, and Darrow was gesturing to the sofa for Thalia to sit.

"My dear, there are several things we need to . . . chat about. Please make yourself comfortable."

She sat on the sofa, her slightly bulging eyes darting from Darrow to me, as I sat next to her, but not right next to her, giving her plenty of space.

"Is something wrong?" she asked. "Please don't tell me you think Tommie and Mother are actually going to have to serve any . . . prison time."

"I think we can avoid that," Darrow said, "with your help."

Relief softened her expression and she sighed and said, "I'll do anything. Anything."

"Good. Does my cigarette bother you, dear?"

She shook her head, no.

"Fine, then. Here's what I need to ask of you . . ."

"Anything."

". . . I need you to leave Hawaii, with the rest of us, once I've worked things out with the governor."

Her eyes tightened. "What do you mean?"

"There will be public pressure, here in Honolulu, and from back home, to retry those boys you accused. I need you to spare yourself the pain of going through this yet again, testifying for a third time; I need you to go back to the mainland and never return to these shores."

She smiled, but it was a smile of astonishment. "You can't be saying this. You can't be saying that I should turn my back on what was done to me. That I let those terrible black creatures *get away* with what was done to me!"

He was shaking his head somberly, no. "There must not be a second Ala Moana trial, dear."

"Oh, but you're wrong . . . there *must* be. Otherwise, you're sentencing me to a lifetime of gossip and humiliation, putting my word, my reputation, in doubt forever."

Darrow's expression turned sorrowful. He drew in on his cigarette, and when he exhaled smoke, it was a sigh of smoke, and he nodded, reluctantly, toward me.

I nodded back, and took a manila envelope off the coffee table before us and removed the Oahu Prison mug shots of Daniel Lyman and Lui Kaikapu. I handed her the photos.

Puzzled, she looked at them, shrugged, tossed them back on the table, and said, "Is this supposed to mean something to me? Who are they?"

I glanced at Darrow and he sighed again, nodded again.

I said, "These are two of the three men who abducted you."

Her puzzlement turned to perplexity, with irritation work-ing at the edges of her mouth and eyes. "Why are you saying this? Kahahawai and Ida and the others, they're the ones, you *know* they're the ones—"

"The ones you accused," I said. "But those two . . ." And I indicated the mug shots on the table. ". . . are the ones who re-ally grabbed you."

"You're insane. Insane! Mr. Darrow, must I listen to this insanity?"

Darrow only nodded, poker-faced.

I said, "I'm going to give you the benefit of the doubt and figure you were confused as to how many of them there were in the car . . . which is only natural, considering that your pre-eclampsia impairs your eyesight in low-light conditions."

Her eyes bugged with alarm; the blood drained from her face, turning her Kabuki white.

"Yes, dear," Darrow said softly, compassionately, "we know about your condition. Did you think our mutual friend Dr. Porter would keep that from me?"

"Oh, how *could* he?" she asked. Desperation mingled with despair in her voice. "That was privileged communication, be-tween doctor and patient. . . ."

"Sorry, Thalia—this time there's nothing for you to tear up," I said. "These are facts you can't discard."

She covered her mouth. "I think . . . I think I'm going to be ill."

Darrow glared at me; he'd warned me not to be too rough on the girl.

"If you need the bathroom, dear . . ." he began.

"No." She removed her hand from her mouth; folded her hands in her lap. Her features drew tight, became a blank mask. "No."

"We also know there was no pregnancy," Darrow said. "But that doesn't make your *fear* of pregnancy any less real. . . ."

She said nothing. She was almost frozen—almost: her eyes moved from Darrow to me, as we talked.

"Mrs. Massie—Thalia," I said, "what I'm about to tell you, only Mr. Darrow and myself are privy to."

She nodded toward Darrow, but said to me: "He's not my lawyer, he's Tommie's lawyer. I don't want to go any further with this unless this conversation *is* privileged."

"Fair enough, dear," Darrow said. "As my client's spouse, the privilege of privacy due to him extends to you. This discussion is entirely an extension of Tommie's case."

Now she looked at Darrow and nodded toward me. "What about him?"

"He's my investigator. He's bound by the same pledge of privacy."

She thought about that, nodded, said, "Then we can continue."

"Fine, dear. Let's allow Mr. Heller to tell us what he's discovered in his investigating these past several weeks."

Her cow-eyed gaze fell coldly, contemptuously my way.

I said, "You'd been having an affair with Lt. Bradford, while your husband was away on duty. For whatever reason, it went bust, and, on the rebound, you began having a fling with a music boy named Sammy."

Her lips were trembling; she had her chin up, though, the way her mother had in court.

"You didn't want to go to the Ala Wai that night," I continued, "because you knew Bradford would be there and also knew the place was one of Sammy's favorite hangouts. And being with your husband in the proximity of two lovers, past and present, could be . . . awkward."

, She made a throaty sound that was almost a laugh. "You're guessing. These are just more stupid rumors, more silly scurrilous stories . . ."

"No. You were seen talking with Sammy right before you walked out of the Ala Wai into the night—right after you slapped Lt. Stockdale for calling you a . . . well, for insulting you. You see, Sammy wasn't discreet, Thalia. He told friends in his crowd about his affair with you . . . and he told them what he saw."

"Nobody saw anything," she snapped, but her eyes weren't sure.

"Sammy saw Bradford follow you, and he followed along

behind Bradford while you two were arguing. Sammy also saw the carload of cruising *kanakas* pull along the curb and give you the wolf whistle . . . saw and heard you egg 'em on, too, probably to make Bradford jealous. Well, Bradford took off, and when Sammy saw who these boys were . . ." I tapped the photos of Lyman and Kaikapu. ". . . he knew you were in a jam. These were mean, nasty, lowdown criminal boys. Sammy rushed up, tried to help you, got shoved away. That's part of the story you never mentioned, isn't it, Thalia? Sammy's presence. You couldn't include *him*, could you? Not without your fling with a colored boy getting out. Couldn't mention Bradford, either—that very night, when the police had arrested him, you assured him that you wouldn't involve him, told him not to worry."

Her mouth and chin trembled; her eyes were shining wetly. "I was abducted. I was beaten. I was raped."

I shrugged. "Maybe you *were* raped . . ."

"Maybe!" She lurched toward me, on the couch, flew at me with her fists raised, ready to pummel me, but I clutched her wrists and her face was inches from mine, emotions passing across her face in waves: rage, shame, despair. . . .

I felt the fight go out of her and released her.

She backed away, and said, almost gasped, "I . . . I . . . *am* going to be sick."

And she ran to the bathroom and slammed the door. The sound of her retching made Darrow shiver. I was having trouble feeling sorry for her.

"You're too harsh with her," he whispered, raising a hand. "Try to remember she's in hell."

"Joe Kahahawai's in the ground," I reminded him. "And you don't believe in hell, remember?"

"Oh, I believe in hell, Nate. It's right here on Earth . . . and she's in it. *Go easy.*"

"There's a good chance the reason she got her jaw broken," I said, "was she wouldn't come across for those guys. Because of things Sammy said to 'em when he tried to intervene, Lyman and Kaikapu probably realized they had hold of a Navy wife, not a hooker or some loose lady. So they roughed her up, snatched her purse, and dumped her ass out."

"Or they may have raped her."

"They may have," I granted.

The sound of the toilet flushing announced Thalia's imminent return.

"We need her as an ally," Darrow reminded me.

I nodded and drew in a breath as the bathroom door opened and she walked slowly toward us, head down, shoulders stooped, as if shame were weighing her down.

She took her place on the sofa but sat as far away from me as she could.

"I *was* raped," she said quietly, both pride and a tremor in her voice. "By Joe Kahahawai and Horace Ida and those others . . ." She pointed to the pictures on the table. ". . . *not* by *them*."

"According to Sammy," I said, "it was Lyman and Kaikapu who dragged you in the ragtop. There was another boy along, but nobody has a name for him; a Filipino kid."

"Where . . . where *is* Sammy?"

"In Los Angeles."

"But you talked to him?"

"How I got this information isn't important."

"What is," Darrow interjected, "is that if Nate here could dig it out, so could somebody else. There's been a reorganization among the police, and a second Ala Moana trial would mean a new, full-scale investigation. The governor is talking about bringing in the FBI."

She frowned, swallowed.

"Thalia," I said, "it's not your fault some incompetent cops put the wrong boys on a platter and served 'em up to you. They practically forced you to ID Ida and the rest."

Her eyes were narrowed; she was thinking. Darrow was smiling at me—I was finally going easier. But I didn't want to. I knew there was another strong possible reason for Thalia identifying the wrong boys: Sammy may have told her *not* to ID Lyman and Kaikapu, because it would put both their lives in danger.

But she had to finger *somebody* to protect her good name, her honor as the wife of a naval officer, her stature as a member of a prominent family. Maybe she figured the Ala Moana boys would never be convicted; but as rumors began to fly, she desperately needed to sacrifice these innocent boys (just "niggers," after all) at the altar of her reputation and her marriage.

That's what I wanted to throw in her face.

Instead, I said, "Protect yourself. Leave the Island. The Navy'll give Tommie stateside duty, you can bet on that. Put this ugly nonsense behind you."

Darrow leaned forward and patted her folded hands. "He's right, dear. It's time . . . time to go home."

She began to nod. Then she let out a huge sigh, stood, smoothed out her dress, and said, "All right. If it's best for Tommie and Mother."

He stood, nodding sagely, pressing her hands in his. "It is, dear. Why subject yourself to a needless ordeal? Now, I must warn you, there will no doubt be a summons issued for you to appear as complaining witness in a new Ala Moana trial. Prosecutor Kelley needs to do that to save face. . . ."

"He's an awful man."

"He's cooperating with me, dear, and that's all that matters. I'll be saying things for appearance sake, too, but it'll be bluster and show. Understand? What the public hears, and what's really going on, are two different affairs."

I'd have to pass that one on to Chang Apana; anyway, it was a concept Thalia Massie, of all people, ought to grasp.

I was on my feet, too. Forcing a smile for her.

She fixed those bulgy eyes on me. "No one knows what you've discovered, Mr. Heller? Just you and Mr. Darrow? Not even Mr. Leisure?"

"No one," I said.

"You won't tell Isabel . . ."

"No."

"I don't want Tommie to hear these lies."

"They aren't . . ."

Out of her sight, Darrow was waving at me not to finish.

". . . anything anybody's going to hear but you."

She smiled, drew in a breath, and said, "Well, then—I think

I'll go down and join Isabel and Mrs. Darrow and Mr. Leisure. I could use some tea to settle my stomach."

Darrow took her arm, showed her to the door, small-talking with her along the way, soothing her, smoothing a wrinkled feather or two, and then she was gone.

Slowly, Darrow turned to me and said, "Thank you, Nate. Now we can do what's right for our clients."

"What about doing something for the poor bastards that bitch wrongly accused?"

He came over and settled a hand on my shoulder. "Now, now—don't judge Thalia too harshly. She was the first victim in this affair, and she's suffering still."

"What about the Ala Moana boys?"

He shuffled back to his easy chair, settled back in, putting his feet back up, folding his hands across his ample belly. "We're going to see to it, with Thalia's help, that those boys aren't put through a second trial."

I sat across from him, where Thalia had been sitting. "Their supporters are demanding complete exoneration. You've seen the papers—the colored population here, egged on by Princess What's-Her-Name, thinks the Ala Moana boys deserve to be freed of this stigma." I gestured to the pictures of Lyman and Kaikapu. "Sure, the real bad guys are already doing long, hard time, and that's peachy; but to the public, Horace Ida and his pals've been branded rapists."

"In due time, the case will be officially dropped, over insufficient evidence." He shrugged. "There's no way you can undo something like this, not entirely. In the eyes of the white population, both here and at home, yes, the Ala Moana boys will remain forever rapists. To the various ethnic groups on this island, these boys are heroes, tragic heroes perhaps, but heroes nonetheless—and Joseph Kahahawai a martyred hero."

"I suppose."

He grunted a humorless laugh. "What do you think, Nate?" He nodded toward the photos of Lyman and Kaikapu. "Your informed opinion—did they rape her? Or just rob her and thrash and throttle her?"

"I don't know," I said, "and I don't care."

Darrow shook his head, smiled sadly. "Don't get hardened so soon in life, son. That poor girl went for a moonlight walk and came back damaged for life. . . ."

"Joe Kahahawai went for a morning ride and never came back at all."

Darrow nodded, slowly; his eyes were moist. "You must learn to reserve the lion's share of your pity for the living, Nate—the dead have ceased their suffering."

"What about Horace Ida and his buddies? They're alive— with that one little exception. Are you going to meet with them, now, finally?"

A pained frown creased his brow. "You know I can't do that. You know I can't *ever* do that."

It was time for his afternoon nap, and I left him there, and that was the last time I suggested he meet with Ida and the others.

There is a rumor, however—unsubstantiated but persistent to this day—that the old boy and the Ala Moana defendants sat together for dinner in a private alcove at Lau Yee Ching's; and that the only word spoken of the case, at this unique and singular meeting, was C.D. raising his teacup of *oke* in a toast to an empty chair at the table.

TWENTY-ONE

Even in Hawaii, mornings in May came no more beautiful. Sunlight glanced through the fronds of palms and a sublimely sultry breeze riffled lesser leaves as reporters—who the night before had been given the news that the sentencing had been moved up two days—milled about the sidewalk. The only hitch in this perfect day was some grumbling from a surprisingly modest crowd of gawkers, annoyed over Governor Judd's order banning the public from the courtroom; only those involved in, or reporting, the case would be allowed inside.

It was nearly ten, and I'd been here since nine, accompanying Darrow and Leisure; the old boy had met Kelley here and together they had disappeared into Judge Davis's chambers, and hadn't been seen since. Leisure was already at the defense table inside. I was leaning against the base of the King Kamehameha statue, just enjoying the day. Soon enough I'd be back in Chicago, watching spring get bullied aside by a sweltering summer.

Four Navy cars drew up to the sidewalk, armed Marine guards in the first and last, Tommie and Thalia and Mrs. Fortescue in the second, Jones and Lord in the third. Chang Apana met them, and escorted them through the swarming reporters, who were hurling questions that went unanswered.

For defendants in a murder case, they seemed curiously

calm, even cheery. The Massie contingent was smiling, not bravely, just smiling; Thalia had traded in her dark colors for a stylish baby blue outfit with matching turban, while Mrs. Fortescue wore dignified black, though trimmed with a gay striped scarf. Tommie looked dapper in a new suit with a gray tie, and Lord and Jones also wore suits and ties; the sailors were laughing, smoking cigarettes.

The fix, after all, was in.

I wandered in and joined Leisure at the defense table. The ceiling-fan whir seemed louder than usual, probably because what had seemed a tiny courtroom when packed with people now felt cavernous, with the spectators limited to that one table of press.

Soon a beaming Darrow and glum Kelley emerged from a door near the bench, their session in the judge's chambers complete; the lawyers took their positions at their respective tables. Judge Davis entered and took the bench. The clerk called the court to order, and the bailiff called out, "Albert Orrin Jones, stand up."

Jones did.

Judge Davis said, "In accordance with the verdict of manslaughter returned against you in this case, I hereby sentence you to the term prescribed by law, not more than ten years' imprisonment at hard labor in Oahu Prison. Is there anything you wish to say?"

"No, Your Honor."

Jones was grinning. Not the usual response to such a sentence. Darrow seemed suddenly uncomfortable: it would have been nice if this seagoing dolt had had the decency to put on a poker face.

The same sentence was passed on the other defendants, who at least didn't smile through it, even if they did seem unnaturally calm in the face of ten years' hard labor.

Kelley rose, smoothed out his white linen suit and said, "Prosecution moves for a writ of *mittimus*."

Judge Davis said, "Motion granted, Mr. Kelley, but before turning these defendants over to their warden, I want the bailiffs to clear the courtroom of all except counsel and defendants."

Now it was the press who were grumbling as the bailiffs herded them out, where they joined other gawkers in the corridor.

As the reporters were leaving, a tall, rather commanding figure moved down the aisle; though he wore a brown suit with a cheerful yellow tie, there was something immediately military about his bearing, this hawkishly handsome man with hard, amused eyes.

"That's Major Ross," Leisure said.

I had to smile as I watched the judge issue the writ turning the defendants over to the man whose name Mrs. Fortescue had forged on the summons that had lured Joe Kahahawai into "custody."

Ross led the defendants out of the courtroom, with Darrow, Leisure, and me close behind. Kelley didn't come along—my last glimpse had him half-seated on the edge of the prosecution table, arms folded, a sardonic half-smile eloquently expressing his opinion of the proceedings.

In the corridor, the press and a few friends and relatives of the defendants (Isabel among them) joined the parade as we streamed into the streaming sunshine. Passing the statue of King Kamehameha, the group paused for traffic at the curb where Joe Kahahawai had been abducted.

Then Major Ross led the way, across King Street, through an open gate and up the wide walk past manicured grounds, like the Pied Piper leading his rats, on up the steps of the grandly, ridiculously rococo Iolani Palace. The major led the group past the massive throne room with its hanging tapestries, gilt chairs, and framed pompous portraits of Polynesians in European royal drag, and soon the press and other camp followers were deposited in a waiting room, while the rest of us headed up a wide staircase to a large hall, off of which were governmental offices—including the governor's.

I was walking alongside Jones, who was grinning like a goon (he'd had the decency to discard his cigarette, at least), glancing up at the high ceiling and elaborate woodworking.

"This is a swell jail," the sailor said. "A lot better than your pal Al Capone's. Wonder how he's doin'? I hear they took him to the Atlanta pen the other day by special train."

"He should've had your lawyer," I said.

The major showed us into the spacious, red-carpeted office where Governor Judd—a pleasant-looking fellow with an oval face and black-rimmed round-lensed glasses—rose politely behind his formidable mahogany desk. He gestured to chairs that had been arranged. We were expected.

"Please sit," the governor said, and we did. When everyone was settled, Judd sat back down, folding his hands; he seemed more like a justice of the peace than a governor. He said, respectfully, "Mr. Darrow, I understand you have a petition you would like me to hear."

"I do, sir," Darrow said. He held out a hand and Leisure, beside him, filled it with a scroll. To me this formality was a little ridiculous, but it fit the surroundings.

"The undersigned defendants," Darrow read, "in the matter of the Territory of Hawaii versus Grace Fortescue et. al., and their attorneys, do hereby respectfully pray that your Excellency, in the exercise of the power of executive clemency in you vested, and further in view of the recommendation of the jury in said matter, do commute the sentences heretofore pronounced in said matter."

Darrow rose, stepped forward, and handed the scroll to the governor. The old boy sat down while the governor—who damn well knew every word of the document—held it and read it and pretended to ponder it awhile. Who was he trying to kid?

Finally, Judd said, "Acting upon this petition, and upon the recommendation by the jury of leniency, the sentence of ten years at hard labor is hereby commuted to one hour, to be served in custody of Major Ross."

Mrs. Fortescue bolted to her feet and clasped her hands like a maiden in a melodrama. "This is the happiest day of my life, Your Excellency. I thank you from the bottom of my heart."

Then Judd was subjected to a round of pump-handle handshakes, including Lord and Jones, who said, "Thanks, Guv! You're okay!"

Eyes tight behind the round lenses, Judd was clearly un-

comfortable, if not ashamed of himself, and after some mind-
less chitchat (Tommie: "I only wish I could be in Kentucky to
see the smile on my mother's face when she hears this!"), Judd
checked his watch.

"We'll, uh, have that hour begin with the approximate time
you left Pearl Harbor this morning, which means . . . well, your
time is up. Good luck to you all."

Before long, our little group (minus the governor) was
posing for the press photogs on a balcony of the palace. When
the press found out I wasn't one of the attorneys, just a lowly
investigator, I was asked to step outside of the already crowded
grouping. That was fine with me, and I stood smiling to myself at the absurdity of these group portraits; it was as if
the class honor students had been gathered in all their self-
congratulatory glory, not some convicted murderers and their
lawyers and the woman who had inspired the crime.

Darrow was smiling, but there was something weary and
forced about it. Major Ross seemed frankly amused. Only
George Leisure, arms folded, staring into the distance, seemed
to have second thoughts. Playing second chair to the great
Clarence Darrow had been an education for him, but maybe he
hadn't got quite the schooling he expected.

Grace Fortescue was flittering and fluttering around, social
butterfly that she was, making one silly comment after another.
"I will be ever so glad to get back to the United States," she told a
reporter from the Honolulu *Advertiser*, who did her the courtesy
of not reminding her she was already standing on American soil.

But her silliness stopped when a reporter asked her if she
would ever come back, under more normal, pleasant circumstances, to enjoy the beauty of the Islands.

The repressed bitterness and anger poured out, as she almost snarled, "When I leave here I will *never* come back, not as
long as I live!"

Then she launched into a trembling-voiced speech of her
hope that the "trouble" she'd suffered would result in making
Honolulu "a safer place for women."

Isabel had found her way into this madness, and she
grasped my arm and bubbled, "Isn't it *wonderful*?"

"I can hardly keep from jumping up and down."

She pretended to frown. "You're a grump. I know something that will improve your attitude."

"What's that?"

"My friend is gone."

"What friend?"

"You know—*my* friend, *that* friend."

"Oh? Oh! Well. Want to go back to the hotel and, uh, go swimming or something?"

"Or something," she said, and hugged my arm.

If she wanted to celebrate this wonderful victory, I was her guy. After all, the job was done, we weren't sailing for a couple of days, and I didn't even have a suntan yet.

Not that I planned to get much of a tan pursuing the "or something" Isabel had in mind.

First to leave, with the Navy's blessing, were the sailors. Deacon Jones and Eddie Lord retained their ranks (Admiral Stirling publicly stated, "We refuse to consider legal either the trial or the conviction") and were taken by destroyer to San Francisco for routing to the Atlantic Coast via the Panama Canal, where they were transferred to the submarine *Bass*.

The Navy also smuggled Thalia (and Tommie and Mrs. Fortescue and Isabel) aboard the *Malolo* via a minesweeper that pulled up along the cargo hold. The summons Kelley had issued for Thalia to appear as complaining witness may have been only for show, but the coppers didn't know that, and several made a determined effort to serve her.

When Darrow, Leisure, their wives, and I arrived at the dock for a noon sailing, we were pleasantly accosted by Island girls who draped us with *leis*; and the Royal Hawaiian Band played its traditional "Aloha Oe" as we walked up the gangplank to head for our respective staterooms.

In the corridor, on my way to my cabin, I came upon a shouting match between a plainclothes Hawaiian copper with a round dark face and a shovel-jawed Navy captain in full uniform.

The cop was waving his summons at the captain, who blocked a stateroom door that was apparently the Massies'.

"You can't give me orders!" the cop was saying.

"Say 'sir' when you speak to me," the naval captain snapped.

The Hawaiian tried to shove the captain aside, and the captain shoved him back, saying, "Don't lay your hands on me!"

"Don't lay your hands on *me*!"

I was wondering if it was my responsibility to try to break up this childish nonsense, when a familiar voice behind me called out: "Detective Mookini! Noble effort goes past reason. Treat captain with respect!"

Then Chang Apana, Panama in hand, was at my side.

"You could always use that blacksnake," I said, "if they won't listen."

Chang smiled gently. "They listen."

Miraculously, the two men were sheepishly shaking hands, acknowledging that each was only trying to do his job.

"Mookini!" Chang called, and the round-faced cop, two heads taller than Chang, almost ran to him, stood with head bowed. "Too late to dig well when house is on fire. Go back to headquarters."

"Yes, Detective Apana."

And the copper and his summons went away.

The captain said, "Thank you, sir."

Chang nodded.

The stateroom door opened and Tommie poked his head out. "Is everything all right, Captain Wortman?"

"Shipshape, Lieutenant."

Tommie thanked him, nodded to me, and ducked back inside.

Chang walked me to my cabin.

I said, "Did you come aboard just to make sure that summons didn't get served?"

"Perhaps. Or perhaps I come to say *aloha* to a friend."

We shook hands, then we chatted for a while about that big family of his on Punchbowl Hill, and how he had no intention of ever retiring, and finally the "all ashore" call came and he bowed and started back down the corridor, snugging his Panama back on.

"No parting words of wisdom, Chang?"

The little man looked back at me; his eyes damn near twinkled, even the one surrounded by discolored knife-scarred tissue.

"Advice at end of case like medicine at dead man's funeral," he said, tipped his Panama, and was gone.

On the second night of the voyage home, leaning against the rail of the *Malolo* in my white dinner jacket, gazing at the silver shimmer of ocean, my arm around Isabel Bell, her blond wind-stirred hair whispering against my cheek as she snuggled to me, I tried to imagine myself back chasing pickpockets at LaSalle Street Station. I couldn't quite picture it; but reality would catch up with me, soon enough. It always did.

"I heard you and Mr. Darrow talking," Isabel said, "about you going to work for him."

Our entire party—Tommie and Thalia, Mrs. Fortescue, Ruby and C.D., the Leisures, Isabel, and I—took meals together at one table in the ship's dining room. One big happy family, even though Thalia hadn't yet spoken to me. Or I to her, for that matter.

I said, "I'm hoping to work for C.D. full-time."

"You'd leave the police department?"

"Yes."

She snuggled closer. "That would be nice."

"You approve of that?"

"Sure. I mean . . . that's romantic. Important."

"What is?"

"Being Clarence Darrow's chief investigator."

I didn't pursue it, but I think she was trying to talk herself into thinking I might be somebody she could consider seeing, back home, at journey's end, on solid ground. She was kidding herself, of course. I was still a working-class joe, and a working-class Jew, and only under the special circumstances of a shipboard romance could I ever measure up to social standards.

"Why is Thalo mad at you?" she asked.

"Is she?"

"Can't you tell?"

"I don't pay much attention to her. I got my eyes on a certain cousin of hers."

She squeezed my arm. "Silly. Did something happen back there I don't know about?"

"Back where?"

"Hawaii! I shouldn't say this, but . . . I think she and Tommie are squabbling."

I shrugged. "After what they been through, bound to be a little tension."

"They're in the cabin next to me."

"And?"

"And I thought I heard things breaking. Like things were being thrown?"

"Ah. Wedded bliss."

"Don't you think two people could be happy? Forever, together?"

"Sure. Look out at the ocean. That's forever, isn't it?"

"Is it?"

"Forever enough."

We made love in my cabin morning, noon, and night. I can picture her right now, the smooth contours of her flesh, the supple curves of her body, the small firm breasts, eyes closed, mouth open, lost in ecstasy, washed ivory in moonlight, from a porthole, on a beach.

But I never kidded myself. It was, quite literally, a shipboard romance, and I was telling her what she wanted to hear. Back home, I wasn't good enough for her. But on this steamer, I was the suave detective on his way home from a distant tropical isle, where I'd been engaged successfully to solve a dastardly crime perpetrated against a lovely innocent white woman by evil dark men.

And a guy like that deserves to get laid.

On February 13, 1933, Prosecutor John Kelley appeared in Judge Davis's court and moved for no prosecution in the case of the Territory vs. Horace Ida, Ben Ahakuelo, Henry Chang, and David Takai. The judge passed the motion. Sufficient time had passed for the public, both in Hawaii and on the mainland, to greet the shelving of the case with indifference.

This was as close to vindication as the Ala Moana boys ever got, but they did receive the blessing of fading into the obscurity of Island life. Ida became a storekeeper; Ben Ahakuelo a member of a rural fire department on the windward side of Oahu; the others, I understand, drifted into various routine pursuits.

Of course, exoneration of a sort came to them, by way of Thalia Massie, who did enter the limelight from time to time, now and then—most prominently when, two years to the day of Joseph Kahahawai's murder, she traveled to Reno to divorce Tommie. The evening her divorce became final, Thalia swallowed poison in a nightclub.

This suicide attempt proved unsuccessful, and a month later, on the liner *Roma* bound for Italy, she slashed her wrists in the tub in her cabin. Her screams while doing so, however, alerted help and this attempt also failed.

I felt bad, when I read the accounts in the Chicago papers; Darrow had been right: Thalia Massie lived in a personally crafted hell, and she was having no luck getting out of it.

Now and then, from time to time, the twentieth century's most famous rape victim turned up in the press: in 1951, she attacked a pregnant woman, her landlady, who sued her for ten thousand dollars; in 1953, she enrolled as a forty-three-year-old student at the University of Arizona; the same year, she eloped to Mexico to marry a twenty-one-year-old student; two years later she again divorced.

Finally, in July of 1963, in West Palm Beach, Florida, where she had moved to be closer to her mother (they lived separately, however), Thalia escaped her personal hell. Her mother found her dead on the bathroom floor of her apartment, bottles of barbiturates scattered about her.

Tommie Massie, like the Ala Moana boys, enjoyed the blessing of a notoriety-free private life. He married Florence Storms in Seattle in 1937; in 1940, he left the Navy. He and his wife moved to San Diego, where they lived quietly and happily as Tommie pursued a successful civilian career.

Mrs. Fortescue outlived her daughter, but she is gone now,

as so many of them are: Clarence "Buster" Crabbe, who never returned to law school after Olympic fame led to Hollywood B-movie stardom; New York Mayor Jimmy Walker, who resigned in disgrace (Darrow did not defend him); Detective John Jardine, whose reputation as a tough, honest cop eventually rivaled Chang Apana's; Duke Kahanamoku, whose Hollywood ventures were not as successful as fellow Olympian Buster Crabbe's, but who wound up a successful nightclub owner; Major Ross, who took over Oahu Prison and brought discipline to the institution, starting with placing Daniel Lyman and Lui Kaikapu in well-deserved solitary confinement.

Admiral Stirling, John Kelley, and George Leisure also long ago said aloha to this life.

What became of the officers and sailors—Bradford, Stockdale, Olds, Dr. Porter, and the rest—I have no idea. Last I heard, Eddie Lord was still alive; had a well-paying, respectable job but was something of a loner, living in an apartment over a suburban bar and grill, spending his time glued to a television set.

Other than Darrow, Jones was the only principal player in the farce I ever ran into again. Completely by chance, we wound up side by side at the bar in the Palmer House in the summer of '64. I didn't recognize him—not that he'd changed that much, a little grayer, a little heavier, but who wasn't?

What I guess I didn't expect was to find Deacon Jones wearing a tailored suit and a conservative striped tie—even if the double Scotch he was collecting from the bartender did make sense.

"Don't I know you?" he asked, gruffly affable.

I still hadn't made him. "Do you?" To the bartender I said, "Rum and Coke."

"Aren't you Heller? Nat? Nate!"

I smiled and sipped my drink. "Guess you do know me. I'm sorry, but I can't seem to place—"

He thrust out a hand. "Albert Jones—Machinist's Mate. Last time I saw you was in the Iolani Palace, when I was gettin' sprung."

"I'll be damned," I said, and shook hands with him, and laughed, once. "Deacon Jones. You look damn respectable."

"Executive at a bank back in Massachusetts, if you can believe it."

"Barely."

"Come on! Let's find a booth and catch each other the hell up. Shit! Imagine, runnin' into Clarence Darrow's detective, after all these years."

We found a booth, and we talked; he was in town for a bankers' convention. I, of course, was still living and working in Chicago, my A-1 Detective Agency flourishing. These days, sometimes I felt more like an executive than a detective, myself.

We both got a little drunk. He said the last time he'd seen his friend Eddie Lord was in '43 on the submarine *Scorpion*; thought about him often, though. We discussed Thalia Massie, who was recently dead, and Jones admitted he didn't have a very high opinion of her.

"Her personality was zero," he said. "She didn't have the personality of your big toe. She didn't have a good-lookin' leg, ankle, or calf."

"Well, you must've liked Tommie."

"Massie was all man, all officer. He was a little scared, you know, when we snatched that boy, but put yourself in the lieutenant's place—really high-class academic training, that upper-class background. *Of course*, he'd feel nervous—we were breakin' the law!"

"How about ol' Joe Kahahawai? Was *he* nervous?"

Jones chugged some Scotch, chortled. "He was damn near scared white. Look at it this way—suppose you and me are sitting here and we got a nigger sitting right there and I got a gun. Sure as shit he's gonna be scared, right? Unless he's a goddamn fool, and this guy was no fool."

"Did he really confess?"

"Hell no. Tell you the truth, pal . . . he wasn't all *that* goddamn scared. After while he started gettin' his nerve back—you could almost see the fear kinda changin' into this overbearing attitude. Maybe he was thinkin' about what he could do if he ever got one of us *alone*."

"You didn't hate the guy, did you? Kahahawai, I mean?"

"Hell no! I don't hate anybody. Besides, hate's an expression of fear and I didn't fear that black bastard. I had no use for him—but I wasn't afraid of him."

"So Tommie was questioning him, but he didn't confess. Deacon . . . *what the hell really happened* in that house?"

Jones shrugged. It was strange, seeing this well-dressed banker drink himself back into a salty seaman spouting racist bile. "Massie asked him somethin', and the nigger lunged at him."

"What happened then?"

He shrugged again. "I shot the bastard."

"*You* shot him?"

"Goddamn right I did. Right under the left nipple. He went over backwards and that's all she wrote."

"Did you even know what you were doing?"

"Hell yes I knew what I was doing. Of course, I knew right away this thing had got completely away from us. We were in a pack of trouble and we knew it."

"Where were Mrs. Fortescue and Lord when the bullet was fired?"

"They were outside. They came in when they heard the shot."

"How did the old girl react?"

"She was scared shitless. She went over and hugged Tommie. She was fond of him."

He told me about how it was his "stupid idea" to put the body in the bathtub; and how Thalia's sister Helene had tossed the murder weapon into some quicksand by the beach. I asked him if he still had his scrapbook and he said, yeah, he dragged it out once in a while to prove to people he was "famous, once."

"Funny," he said. Shook his head. "First man I ever killed."

"How do you feel about it?"

"Now, you mean? Same as then."

"And how's that?"

He shrugged. "I never shed a tear."

And he took a slug of Scotch.

A few years later I heard Jones had died; I didn't shed a tear, either.

Chang Apana was injured in an automobile accident later in 1932—a hit-and-run—and this finally forced him to retire from the Honolulu police, though he continued working in private security till shortly before his death in November 1934. Scores of dignitaries and the Royal Hawaiian Band gathered to send off the Island's greatest detective; obituaries appeared all over the world, paying tribute to the "real Charlie Chan."

In 1980, when my wife and I went to Oahu to attend the U.S.S. *Arizona* memorial dedication at Pearl Harbor, I went looking for Chang's gravestone in the Manoa Cemetery, and found it overgrown with vines and weeds, which I cleared away from the simple marker, draping a *lei* over the stone.

Isabel died in Oahu, too, only she is buried on Long Island. She married a lawyer in 1937 who became an officer in the Navy who, ironically, was stationed at Pearl, meaning Isabel wound back up in Honolulu. She and I had stayed in touch, casually, and she wrote me a very warm, funny letter about ending up back in Honolulu, and confided that she'd taken her husband to "our beach," but didn't tell him its history. The letter was dated Dec. 3, 1941. I received it about a week after the Jap attack on Pearl Harbor; she was one of the civilian casualties, though her three-year-old son, whose middle name was Nathan, survived.

Now her son and I keep in touch.

Clarence Darrow never took another major case. I helped him out on a minor matter, later in '32, but he was not able to realize his dream of returning to full-time practice. The strain of the Massie case on his health made Ruby put her foot down, though he did go, with Ruby, to Washington, D.C., to chair a review board into the NRA at FDR's behest, a mistake on the part of the President, who had wrongly assumed the old radical would rubber-stamp any New Deal programs.

We spent time together at his apartment in Hyde Park, and Darrow continued to encourage me to leave the Chicago Police Department, and in December 1932, prompted by outside events, I took his advice and opened the A-1 Detective Agency.

C.D. wrote an additional chapter that was added to his autobiography, a chapter on the Massie case, and when he showed it to me for comment, I told him, frankly, that it didn't seem to have much to do with what really had happened.

Gentle as ever, he reminded me that he still had a responsibility to his clients, not to betray confidences or make them look bad.

"Besides," he said, looking over his gold-rimmed reading glasses at me, "autobiography is never entirely true. No one can get the right perspective on himself. Every fact is colored by imagination and dream."

And I told C.D. that if I ever wrote my story down, it would be exactly as it happened—only I was not a writer, and couldn't imagine doing that.

He laughed. "With this wonderful, terrible life you're leading, son, you'll turn, like so many elderly men before you, to writing your memoirs, because yours is the only story you'll have to tell, and you won't be able to sit idly in silence and just wait for the night to come."

He died March 13, 1938. I was with his son Paul when C.D.'s ashes were scattered to the winds over Jackson Park lagoon.

When we went to the dedication of the *Arizona* memorial, and we stood on the deck of that oddly modern white sagging structure, contemplating the lost lives of the boys below, my wife said, "It must be emotional for you, coming back here."

"It is."

"I mean, you serving in the Pacific, and all."

A natural assumption, on her part: I'd been a Marine. Guadalcanal.

I said, "It's other memories."

"What other memories?"

"I was here before the war."

"Really?"

"Didn't I ever mention it? The case with Clarence Darrow?"

She smiled skeptically. "You knew Clarence Darrow?"

"Sure. Didn't you ever wonder why it took so long for Hawaii to become a state?"

So I took her around, in our rental car, and gave her a tour no tour guide could have given her. The Pali was still there, of course, and the Blowhole; and the beach nearby, which my wife was excited to see.

"It's the *From Here to Eternity* beach!" she said. "Burt

Lancaster and Deborah Kerr! That's where they made passionate love . . ."

And it was, too.

But so much was gone. Waikiki was ugly high-rise hotels, cheap souvenir shops, and hordes of Japanese tourists. The Royal Hawaiian (where we stayed) seemed largely unchanged, but dwarfed by its colorless skyscraper neighbors, and a shopping center squatted on the original entrance off Kalakaua Avenue.

The *mauka* (mountain) side of Ala Moana Boulevard was now littered with office buildings, shopping centers, and pastel apartment houses. On the seaward side, a public park with coral pathways and bathhouses lined the beach shore. Hard as I tried, I couldn't turn any of this into the Ala Moana of the old Animal Quarantine Station and squattersville and thickets leading to the ocean.

In Manoa Valley, the bungalow where Thalia and Tommie had lived was in fine shape; it looked cozier than ever. I wondered if the current residents knew its history. The house where Joe Kahahawai had died was there, too—the shabbiest house on an otherwise gentrified block, the only structure gone to seed, the only overgrown yard with a dead car in it. . . .

"Jesus," I said, sitting across the way in the rental car. "It's like the rotting tooth in the neighborhood's smile."

"That's not a bad line," my wife said. "You want me to write it down?"

"Why?"

"For when you write the Massie story."

"Who says I'm going to write it?"

But she'd seen the stacks of handwritten pages in the study in our condo in Boca Raton; she knew, one by one, I was recording my cases.

"Well," she said, getting out her checkbook, using a deposit slip to jot down the line, "you'll thank me for doing this, later."

Thank you, sweetheart.

Because I did use it, didn't I? And I did write the Massie story, colored by imagination and dream.

It was either that or sit idly in silence and just wait for the night to come.

I OWE THEM ONE

Despite its extensive basis in history, this is a work of fiction, and a few liberties have been taken with the facts, though as few as possible—and any blame for historical inaccuracies is my own, reflecting, I hope, the limitations of conflicting source material.

Most of the characters in this novel are real and appear with their true names. Jimmy Bradford and Ray Stockdale are fictional characters with real-life counterparts. Dr. Joseph Bowers is a composite of two prosecution psychiatric witnesses. Isabel Bell is a fictional character, whose moral support for her cousin is suggested by that of the various real members of the Bell family and of Thalia's teenage sister, Helene. Nate Heller's "date" with Beatrice Nakamura is fanciful; most of the damning information Thalia Massie's maid gives Heller is based on interviews she gave to the Pinkerton operatives who in June 1932 undertook a confidential investigation into the case at Governor Judd's behest. A good deal of what Heller uncovers in this novel parallels this actual investigation.

The Pinkerton investigators and Nate Heller came to similar conclusions, although the notion that Daniel Lyman and Lui Kaikapu may have been among Thalia Massie's actual attackers is my own and, to my knowledge, new to this book.

The only major shifting of time in this novel pertains to the

capture of Daniel Lyman, which took place earlier than its cli-
mactic placement, here (although Lyman did elude authorities
for an embarrassingly long time). The participation in that capture by my fictional detective Nathan Heller (and real-life detective Chang Apana) is fanciful.

Devotees of the Massie case will note that I have omitted or
greatly downplayed some individuals with significant secondary roles in the case. To deal substantially with every police officer, lawyer, and judge involved with both the Ala Moana case
and the Massie murder trial would have been a burden to both
author and readers. Clarence Darrow and George Leisure, for
example, were backed up by local Honolulu lawyers (already
attached to the Fortescue/Massie defense and mentioned
in passing, here) and by a Navy attorney (who does make a
brief appearance in the novel). While other members of the
Honolulu Police Department are mentioned in passing, John
Jardine—who did play a major role in the Ala Moana investigation—represents the plainclothes cops who worked the case,
just as Inspector McIntosh (also a key player) represents the hi-
erarchy of the department. While I stand behind my depiction
of Admiral Stirling Yates, I must admit that others in the Navy
Department—notably, Rear Admiral William V. Pratt and Admiral George T. Pettengill—shared similar racist, uninformed,
antidemocratic views of Hawaii; in fact, Stirling often seemed
the voice of reason compared to Pratt, then Acting Secretary of
the Navy.

My longtime research associate George Hagenauer—a val-
ued collaborator on the Heller "memoirs"—again dug out
newspaper and magazine material, and spent many hours with
me trying to figure out what really might have happened to
Thalia Massie on September 12, 1931. In particular, George's
enthusiasm and feel for Clarence Darrow led the way not only
to key research information about the twentieth century's fore-
most criminal lawyer, but provided me with a basis for my
characterization of Nate Heller's surrogate father.

Among the books consulted in regard to Darrow were Irv-
ing Stone's seminal *Clarence Darrow for the Defense* (1941) and
Darrow's autobiography, *The Story of My Life* (1932). Stone's

glowing portrayal would seem the source of such romanticized versions of Darrow as those found in Meyer Levin's *Compulsion* (and the play and film that followed) and Jerome Lawrence and Robert E. Lee's play *Inherit the Wind* (and its film version). For the purposes of this novel, Stone's account of the Massie case proved overly brief and surprisingly inaccurate. Darrow's is one of the most enjoyable autobiographies I've ever read, though it is almost absurdly sketchy about the facts of his life (and his famous cases), with an emphasis on his philosophy.

Two later Darrow biographies—*Clarence Darrow: A Sentimental Rebel* (1980), Arthur and Lila Weinberg, and *Darrow: A Biography* (1979), Kevin Tierney—are both worthwhile. *Rebel* suffers from hero worship of its subject and is, again, brief and inaccurate where the Massie case is concerned (Arthur Weinberg also edited an excellent annotated collection of Darrow's closing arguments, *Attorney for the Damned*, 1957, which provided a basis for Darrow's summation here). The Tierney book is a more objective study, the closest thing to a "warts-and-all" treatment of Darrow, with a solid Massie chapter. Perhaps the frankest, most illuminating Darrow book to date is Geoffrey Cowan's *The People vs. Clarence Darrow* (1993), which raises fascinating questions about the great attorney's ethics and beliefs in focusing on his 1912 bribery/jury tampering trial.

Having ascertained that Chang Apana had not yet retired from the Honolulu Police at the time of the Massie case, I was determined to have Nate Heller meet the "real" Charlie Chan. The indefatigable Lynn Myers took on the key assignment of searching out background material on Apana, who is frequently mentioned in discussions of the Chan movies and/or novels, but about whom I hadn't found anything substantial. Lynn did: an extremely good, in-depth 1982 article in the *Honolulu Star-Bulletin* by Susan Yim, "In Search of Chan," detailing the successful efforts of a Chan fan, Gilbert Martines, to learn the truth about the real detective who provided inspiration to author Earl Derr Biggers for his famous Honolulu-based Chinese sleuth. Lynn also found, among other Apana materials, an obituary that filled in gaps the Yim article did not.

The only liberty I took with Chang was to ignore the

suggestion in Yim's article that the detective, while fluent in several languages, spoke a badly broken pidgin English; I felt this would get in the way of the characterization. Chang Apana's aphorisms are largely drawn from Derr Biggers's novels (some are of my own invention) and reflect the real Apana's pride in having been Chan's prototype. Incidentally, the black-snake whip was indeed Chang Apana's tool of choice. In addition to rereading several of Derr Biggers's novels, I drew upon Otto Penzler's Chan article in his entertaining *The Private Lives of Private Eyes, Spies, Crime Fighters and Other Good Guys* (1977), as well as *Charlie Chan at the Movies* (1989), Ken Hanke. Very helpful was the only Chan movie shot on location in Honolulu—*The Black Camel* (1931)—which includes scenes shot at the Royal Hawaiian Hotel. Material on Chang Apana (and John Jardine) was also culled from *Detective Jardine: Crimes in Honolulu* (1984), John Jardine with Edward Rohrbough and Bob Krauss, which has an excellent chapter on the Massie case from the police point of view.

In addition to searching out Chang Apana material, Lynn Myers located a crucial multipart 1932 *Liberty* magazine article by Grace Fortescue, entitled "The Honolulu Martyrdom." Also, unrepentant B-movie fan Lynn lobbied for the inclusion in this narrative of Buster Crabbe, which I resisted (my policy is no celebrity cameos for the sake of a celebrity cameo) until I came upon Crabbe's connection to the Waikiki beach boys, which did seem pertinent to the narrative. An interview of Crabbe by Don Shay provided much of the basis for the characterization, and information about Crabbe and the beach boys in general was drawn from *Waikiki Beachboy* (1989), Grady Timmons.

Three book-length nonfiction studies of the Massie case have been published to date, all of them in 1966: *The Massie Case*, Peter Packer and Bob Thomas; *Rape in Paradise*, Theon Wright; and *Something Terrible Has Happened*, Peter Van Slingerland. The coincidence of the only factual books on the case being published more or less simultaneously results in three very different views of the case (including numerous conflicting "facts" for me to sort out). Significantly, none of these authors accept the Ala Moana boys as the guilty parties. Each book has its merits: Thomas and Packer present a tight, novelistic, highly readable narrative; Wright, a reporter who covered the trial, is more in-depth and pursues various theories and tangential events; and Van Slingerland is at least as in-depth as Wright, with perceptive social commentary and follow-up interviews with some of the participants. Nate Heller's latter-day barroom conversation with Albert Jones mirrors an interview Van Slingerland reports having with Jones, who indeed did freely admit pulling the trigger on Joseph Kahahawai. If pressed, I would give Van Slingerland the nod, but any of these three books would provide an interested reader with a worthwhile true crime version of this tale; a paperback edition of Wright's volume, with a good introduction by Glen Grant, is at this writing in print (Mutual Publishing, Honolulu).

Several books devote chapters or entire sections to the Massie case: *Crimes of Passion* (1975), published anonymously by Verdict Press (useful pictures but a wildly inaccurate account); *Lawrence M. Judd & Hawaii* (1971), Lawrence M. Judd as told to Hugh W. Lytle; *Sea Duty: The Memoirs of a Fighting Admiral* (1939), Yates Stirling; and *Shoal of Time: A History of the Hawaiian Islands* (1968), Gavan Daws.

Two famous novels inspired by the Massie case may be of interest to readers who enjoyed *Damned in Paradise*. Norman Katkov's *Blood and Orchids* was a bestseller a decade ago; I avoided reading it so as not to be unduly influenced here, but am told that while Mr. Katkov intentionally took great liberties with the facts (including changing dates, names, and events), he presents a vivid, large landscape picture of the political and social turmoil of this fascinating time in Hawaii's history. Many years ago I read and enjoyed another book very loosely based on the Massie case (so loosely the Hawaii setting is jettisoned), *Anatomy of a Murder* by Robert Traver; I particularly admire the Otto Preminger film based on that novel.

Many books on Hawaii were consulted, but none was more valuable than *When You Go to Hawaii* (1930), Townsend Griffiss; this 350-page travel guide, which I rooted out in a Honolulu used bookstore, was to *Damned in Paradise* what the WPA guides have been to previous Heller novels. Also helpful were

Aloha Waikiki (1985), DeSoto Brown; *Around the World Confidential* (1956), Lee Mortimer; *Hawaii and Its Race Problem* (1932), William Atherton Du Puy; *Hawaii Recalls* (1982), DeSoto Brown, Anne Ellett, and Gary Giemza; *Hawaii: Restless Rampart* (1941), Joseph Barber Jr.; *Hawaiian Tapestry* (1937), Antoinette Withington; *Hawaii! ". . . Wish You Were Here"* (1994), Ray and Jo Miller; *Hawaiian Yesterdays* (1982), Ray Jerome Baker; *The Japanese in Hawaii: A Century of Struggle* (1985), Roland Kotani; *The Pink Palace* (1986), Stan Cohen; *Remembering Pearl Harbor* (1984), Michael Slackman; *Roaming Hawaii* (1937), Harry A. Franck; and *The View from Diamond Head* (1986), Don Hibbard and David Franzen.

Coverage by Russell Owens in the *New York Times* was also of great help.

Of use in researching the non–Hawaii aspects of this novel were *The Great Luxury Liners 1927–1954* (1981), William H. Miller Jr.; *New York: The Glamour Years (1919–1945)* (1987), Thomas and Virginia Aylesworth; and *Off the Wall at Sardi's* (1991), Vincent Sardi, Jr., and Thomas Edward West.

I would again like to thank my editor, Michaela Hamilton, and her associate, Joe Pittman, for their support and belief in Nate Heller and me; and my agent, Dominick Abel, for his continued professional and personal support.

My talented wife, writer Barbara Collins, accompanied me on a research trip to Oahu in May 1995. Like Nate Heller and his wife, we tracked down the houses where the Massies and Mrs. Fortescue had lived. After accompanying me on the previous two Nate Heller research trips (to the Bahamas and Louisiana), Barb understandably said, "Could we just once go to a vacation wonderland and *not* be looking for the murder house?" Thank you, sweetheart.

ABOUT THE AUTHOR

Max Allan Collins has earned an unprecedented seven Private Eye Writers of America "Shamus" nominations for his Nathan Heller historical thrillers, winning twice *(True Detective*, 1983, and *Stolen Away*, 1991).

A Mystery Writers of America Edgar nominee in both fiction and nonfiction categories, Collins has been hailed as "the Renaissance man of mystery fiction." His credits include five suspense novel series, film criticism, short fiction, songwriting, trading card sets, graphic novels, and occasional movie tie-in novels, including such bestsellers as *In the Line of Fire*, *Maverick*, and *Waterworld*.

He scripted the internationally syndicated comic strip *Dick Tracy* from 1977 to 1993, is co-creator (with artist Terry Beatty) of the comic book feature *Ms. Tree*, and has written both the *Batman* comic book and newspaper strip. His most recent comics project is *Mike Danger* for Tekno-Comix, co-created with bestselling mystery writer Mickey Spillane.

Collins directed, wrote, and executive-produced *Mommy*, a made-for-television suspense film starring Patty McCormack and Jason Miller, which had its world broadcast premiere on Lifetime in 1996, and was screenwriter of *The Expert*, a 1995 HBO World Premiere film. Several Collins–scripted films are now in preproduction by the author's midwestern company, M.A.C. Film Productions.

Collins lives in Muscatine, Iowa, with his wife, writer Barbara Collins, and their son, Nathan.

• A NOTE ON THE TYPE •

The typeface used in this book is a version of Palatino, originally designed in 1950 by Hermann Zapf (b. 1918), one of the most prolific contemporary type designers, who has also created Melior and Optima. Palatino was first used to set the introduction of a book of Zapf's hand lettering, in an edition of eighty copies on Japan paper handbound by his wife, Gudrun von Hesse; the book sold out quickly and Zapf's name was made. (Remarkably, the lettering had actually been done when the self-taught calligrapher was only twenty-one.) Intended mainly for "display" (title pages, headings), Palatino owes its appearance both to calligraphy and the requirements of the cheap German paper at the time—perhaps why it is also one of the best-looking fonts on low-end computer printers. It was soon used to set text, however, causing Zapf to redraw its more elaborate letters.